FATAL IMAGE

FATAL IMAGE

FATAL IMAGE

DC Mel Cotton Thrillers
Book 5

BRIAN PRICE

This edition produced in Great Britain in 2024

by Hobeck Books Limited, 24 Brookside Business Park, Stone, Staffordshire
ST15 0RZ

www.hobeck.net

ISBN 978-1-913-817-66-2 (pbk)

ISBN 978-1-913-793-65-5 (ebook)

Cover design by Jayne Mapp Design

Printed and bound in Great Britain

Are you a thriller seeker?

To Simon – keep on fighting...!

Note from the Author

This novel is set some months after the events described in *Fatal Blow* and before the 2024 general election. A new police station has replaced the old building that was destroyed in the explosion, but there are still some traumatic memories of the attacks by the Organised Crime Group. It can be read as a standalone story.

I have attempted to represent police procedures accurately but have omitted much tedious detail which would have made the book unreadable. Similarly, for reasons of pace, I have telescoped timescales somewhat, such as the time taken for a post-mortem, the return of toxicology and forensic results and the collection of telephone surveillance data. I hope the experts will bear with me on this.

As with all my books, there are 'Easter Eggs' hidden in the text, notably musical references to Beatles and Fairport Convention songs. A full list can be found on the Hobeck website, and in my newsletter. Also, as you read, you might like to consider why a firm producing honey should call itself Two-

Fifty Honeys and why the name of an oil exploration financing firm reflects its attitude to the Greens (or Les Verts)!

I hope you will subscribe to my newsletter – please go to my website at www.brianpriceauthor.co.uk.

Prologue

IT WAS ACTUALLY GOING to happen. The nods from the
Whips' Office. The whisper from Number Ten. The knowing
glances in the Commons tea room – they all meant that the
ministerial post would be his. He'd worked hard for it, after all.
He'd voted how he was told to, given the right interviews to the
Daily Mail, backed the right candidate for party leader and
kept quiet about his colleagues' numerous indiscretions. The
job was his by right, and then what next? One of the Great
Offices of State? He quite fancied being Chancellor – a post
which sometimes held more power than the Prime Minister.
And he would be able to repay the chaps who had supported
him financially all this time, ensuring the contracts and tax cuts
went where they should. But there were obstacles: six to be
precise.

The image was clear in his mind: a mental snapshot of
what some people called depravity and he called fun – one of
Marnie Draycott's special parties. Seven guests in a plush room
in Mayfair, redolent with the smells of champagne, cannabis
and sex. Little clothing in evidence and no orifice left unex-

BRIAN PRICE

plored. Everything was consensual but, should anything about his participation reach the press or the internet, he knew his journey towards high office would be irrevocably derailed. Their phones had all been taken away at the door but, nevertheless, people could talk. And he couldn't trust them not to, especially with the lure of money from the tabloid press once he became well-known. He couldn't afford to pay for their silence and there were no bonds of friendship.

There was only one option. For him to realise his ultimate ambitions, at least six people had to die.

PART I
Preparations

Chapter One

METICULOUS PREPARATION WAS the key to success, Hugh Ventham realised. You couldn't just murder someone without planning every detail and hope to get away with it. Murdering six or more people multiplied the risks. He had always been a planner, and he was confident he could cover every eventuality, but something was still bothering him. That night, years ago, had been rather a blur, with only enticing fragments of pleasure coming back to him. He was reasonably clear about who was there, and what they'd done. But did he remember correctly? Were there only six other people there? Or was there someone else? A nondescript man whose face was hard to remember? He would have to make do with the names he could recall and hope that the other's came back to him. He felt safe in dismissing the women who worked there. They weren't the sort of people who would keep up with current affairs or read the *Daily Telegraph*.

BRIAN PRICE

Something else unsettled him. Had he really seen the flash of a Polaroid camera and heard the whirr as it ejected a potentially damning photograph? If so, who was in it and who the hell had the photo now? Could it have been Marnie Draycott who took it? The word was that she was a blackmailer, but she had never approached him and now she was dead. But was that photo sitting somewhere, waiting to be discovered, like an unexploded bomb or a silent tumour in his lungs? He would have to find out.

It took him nearly a month to formulate a plan. He bought a cheap laptop, loaded up a project management software package and disconnected the machine from the internet. He was ready to go. It was easy to trace his victims; they all had social media presences and had achieved a degree of fame. A senior police officer, a lawyer, a banker, a TV presenter, the owner of a profitable recycling firm and the CEO of a charity. On the surface, there was nothing to connect them, so even if the deaths were identified as murder by the police, no-one would link them together, or to him. Unless, of course, they found the Polaroid.

Over the course of the month, he purchased various items of kit that he knew would be useful – anonymous dark clothing, some industrial workwear and a selection of knives, bought in different shops in distant towns. He also acquired some illicit pharmaceuticals that would make some of his tasks easier.

Could he deal with them all by himself? That could take time and expose him to increased risks. Perhaps there was someone who could do some of the work for him? Obviously, he couldn't put a post on social media asking if anyone knew a reliable hitman. But how about the dark web? He loaded up the Tor software on another laptop and began browsing. Ignoring the obvious traps and con artists, he settled on three possibilities. Two seemed to have ceased operations, but a third, using the handle #Rebalance456, which offered to 'right wrongs', appeared to be live.

It took him half an hour to compose a suitable text; one which would convince the site operator that he was genuine and had a real grievance. He decided to pose as an anguished parent and picked the charity CEO as his first target.

'Hello,' his message began. 'I need justice for my daughters. The man who raped them is untouchable. He's too well known and the police won't do anything. He kidnapped my fourteen-year-old twin girls, abused them and beat them. One now needs a wheelchair and the other is in a psychiatric unit. He said if they talked to anyone about what he did, he would have them killed, and their younger brother too. His name is Dale Moncrieff. He is not fit to live. Can you help?' He re-read the message several times, mentally crossed his fingers and then pressed send.

The Technician pursed her lips, thought for a moment, then closed her laptop. *There's something odd about this,* she sensed. *A public figure like this surely can't be that evil? Mind you, they said that about Jimmy Savile, didn't they?* Since she'd been set up by a gangster to kill his rival, by a series of fake emails purporting to come from the victim's wife which described unspeakable cruelty, she'd been wary of taking on contracts unless she was absolutely sure they were genuine. She'd developed an instinct, and her instinct told her that this one was dubious. Reaching a decision, she picked up one of many burner phones and sent a message.

'I'm sorry, but I can't help you.'

Then she removed the battery, shredded the sim card and shattered the body of the phone with a hammer. The bits would go out with the rubbish the following morning. In the meantime, she would consider the press reports of a young woman who had tried to commit suicide after her so-called boyfriend had persuaded her to send him naked pictures of her, and then posted them on the internet. *Some non-lethal retribution was needed there*, she thought, *and this one would be a pro bono job.*

Chapter Two

VENTHAM SIGHED and ran his hands through his expensively-styled hair. 'I suppose I'll have to do it all by myself,' he grumbled. But who to start with? Which of the targets was most likely to leak damaging information, deliberately or accidentally? Could any of them be the prey of an investigative journalist or the subject of scandalous allegations by a partner? He produced a rough list, based on a reliability index which he devised, and identified the weakest links. They should be the priorities; he would also have to take whichever opportunities presented themselves.

First, he needed an untraceable car. He couldn't afford to be picked up on ANPR cameras. It needed to be disposable too. He couldn't risk leaving forensic traces in it, and he couldn't torch his precious BMW, could he? But how could he find an alternative without leaving an electronic trail? A reputable dealer wouldn't take cash, for money-laundering reasons. And he couldn't take the chance of buying an unreliable old banger for cash from a dodgy garage. He didn't have the skills to create a false identity either. Perhaps he could borrow someone else's? But whose?

———

'Look at this Vic. She's just what we need. For the meth.'

'Whassat?' slurred Vic, juggling a spliff, a phone and a can of industrial-strength cider.

'This thing in the paper. Found it in the laundrette. "Chemistry teacher gets award". And she's in town.'

Vic peered at the crumpled copy of the *Mexton Messenger* that Gaz brandished under his nose. It showed a woman proudly holding a certificate under the headline 'Mexton woman gets chemistry teacher of the year award'. The article went on to describe how Rachel Willstone, Head of Chemistry at Mexton Premier Academy, had been rated the best chemistry teacher in the country by the UK Science Education Council. It gave a brief summary of her career and included a quote from the Chief Executive of the academy trust, saying how pleased he was that Rebecca Millstone had won the award.

'So what, Gaz?'

'It's what we talked about. Remember? Making our own meth.'

'Oh. Yeah. But we don't know nothin' about this science shit.'

'No, you dickhead. But she does. Chemistry teachers know all this stuff. Like Walter White.'

'So, we're just gonna go up to her and say please will you make meth for us?'

'No. 'Course not. We'll grab her and make her. We got knives. We can give her the fear. Piece of piss.'

'Well, I think you're fucking mad.'

'You're too limited, Vic. We make our own, it's all profit. No paying the big dealers. You gotta think big. So, we know where she works. We're gonna follow her. Find out where she lives and where we can snatch her. We can give a coupla kids some weed to help us watch her. Then we'll have her.'

'So, we've gotta get a fucking great caravan to make the stuff in, have we? Someone will notice if we nick one.'

'No. My cousin's doing eight months in Channings Wood. We can use his flat until he comes out. It's got leccy and water.'

'But someone will miss her. She's got family.'

'We're on the Eastside, for fuck's sake. No-one will grass us up, and the cops won't find her. Fucking chill, will you?'

Vic sucked on his spliff and tried to think. He sort of trusted Gaz. He had brains, of sorts. Maybe it would work. 'Yeah. Why not?'

———

For three weeks Gaz and Vic, aided by a couple of local kids, shadowed Rachel Willstone. They built up a detailed picture of her daily routine and also checked for likely places to stage a kidnap, looking for sites where CCTV coverage was poor or non-existent. After much discussion, they decided on the multi-storey car park attached to the supermarket where Rachel shopped every Thursday evening. The place was usually quiet by the time their target returned to her car, so the chances of being seen by other shoppers were slight, but there was CCTV covering most of the parking bays. They would have to take their chances, or wait for Rachel to park in a less well-monitored spot.

The first Thursday they tried was hopeless. A liquidation sale at one of the major retailers meant that the car park was busy, and an abduction was impossible. The next time was more promising. Fewer shoppers were using the car park, and Rachel had parked next to a large SUV that blocked the sight-line of the nearest camera. To make sure that no car park staff, if there were any on duty, would be likely to spot them, Gaz sent Vic off to set fire to a rubbish bin, two storeys up from their level, as soon as Gaz saw Rachel approaching the check-out. Hooded and masked, with knives in their pockets and a grubby cloth bag for Rachel's head, they were ready to strike.

PART II
Execution

Chapter Three

Day 1

IT WASN'T the most appropriate club for a senior police officer to attend. The entertainments provided were not exactly illegal but would have raised more than a few eyebrows had they been featured in the tabloid press. Discretion was the club's watchword, however, so Detective Superintendent James Raven felt reasonably safe from prying eyes and those who could make his position untenable. As he slipped out of the anonymous door in the Mayfair side street, turning up his collar against the misty rain and ruminating on a pleasant evening, he didn't register the revving of a car twenty metres away. But he did notice the car when it struck him from the side, just above the knees, and catapulted him across the road.

Dazed and terrified, in excruciating pain, he watched as the car reversed, revved again, and headed back towards him. He closed his eyes, expecting his life to end in seconds. *So, this was it, was it?* Then he heard the car turning and retreating into the distance. He opened them again to see blue lights flickering and a paramedic running towards him. Then the pain overwhelmed him and he lost consciousness.

Much later, he woke in St. Thomas's Hospital, attached to various tubes and monitors, with morphine-induced muzziness clouding his brain and nausea flooding his stomach. He remembered something bad happening, but he couldn't quite work out what. Something involving a car, possibly. But why couldn't he move? Everything hurt and he thought he might sleep again, but a nurse, poking her head around the door of the private room, smiled when she saw he was conscious and approached the bed.

'Hello. How are you feeling? You've had some serious surgery and we've given you pain relief, but please say if you need more.'

'I... I don't really know. What happened?'

'It seems as if you were the victim of a hit and run. The police will want to talk to you later but you suffered some serious injuries. The doctor will be along soon and will explain what we've done. You were lucky.'

Even in his muddled state, Raven couldn't see anything lucky about being run over.

'What do you mean?' he croaked, through parched lips.

'An ambulance crew, on another call, saw you flying across the road and stopped. They were on their way here, so they brought you with them. They saw a car heading towards you but it turned back as they arrived and shot off. They think the blue lights scared the driver away. Now, would you like some water? It will be a while before you can eat, I'm afraid.'

Raven nodded and the nurse held a glass with a straw to his lips. He sipped slowly, fighting the nausea, and smiled his thanks. When she had left, two thoughts penetrated his opiate haze. *Who did this to me? And why?* Then he relapsed into an uneasy sleep.

Day 2

It was the following day before he was coherent enough to understand what the doctors were saying to him. His pelvis was fractured as well as the femur and fibula of his right leg. Two ribs broke when he hit the pavement, but he had escaped serious internal injuries. He had extensive bruising, and, despite temporary concussion, his brain appeared undamaged. Whether he would walk properly again, or be fit to return to duty, was, as yet, unclear. Although he wasn't injured at work, and, fortunately, nobody had pressed him over what he was doing at that location in the first place, the Met arranged for him to recuperate at a specialist clinic in the rural south of England, near the town of Mexton. He didn't fancy the prospect. He hated the countryside and would miss visits from colleagues.

Little in the way of memories came back, but the sound of revving car engines on the TV petrified him. He'd been unable to help the officers investigating the incident, and there were no reliable witnesses. ANPR and CCTV had yielded nothing of use, and there were no witnesses. Yet another unsolved crime on the overworked Met's books.

Chapter Four

Day 3

SHIT! *Killing someone with a car is not as easy as I imagined. If only that fucking ambulance hadn't come along, I'd have been able to finish the job. The sooner the NHS is privatised the better. It's vital that this one die, and quickly. If his proclivities come to light, which they may well do, then everything could be fodder for the tabloids. Including me.*

I'll never be able to get at him in a hospital to finish the job. But surely, they won't keep him there until he recovers? They're bound to send him to some half-way house or recovery place. Perhaps I'll get a second chance there?

Posing as Raven's brother, Ventham managed to find out the location of the clinic where his victim was destined to recuperate. He would be transferred there in a few days.

That's convenient. A bit close to home, perhaps, but easier to do the job without anyone asking where I was. I'll have to think about this. But not for too long.

That was a bloody waste of time, thought Rachel, as she dumped her bag of shopping behind her Volvo and reached into her handbag for the keys. Half the things she wanted were out of stock and the prices of many other items had gone through the roof. Preoccupied by her thoughts and the search for her keys, she was unaware of the two young men in hoodies and balaclavas who stepped quietly up behind her. A hard shove in her back sent her reeling.

She grabbed ineffectually at the back of her car for support. Her legs turned to marshmallow as the point of a knife pricked the skin below her ear. She felt a cable tie binding her wrists behind her back. Darkness fell as a hood was shoved over her head, and her handbag was snatched from her. She resisted as she was dragged away from her car, but her assailants were too strong. A gust of evil-smelling breath penetrated the hood.

'Do as you're fucking told and you won't get hurt. Piss about and you're dead.'

Another prick from the knife, this time in her back, reinforced the threat.

Fear and fury competed for pole position, as she was dragged and thrown into a vehicle. A van, she guessed, as the doors were slammed behind her. It moved off with a screech of tyres throwing her against the metal sides as it cornered. Her cable-tied hands could do little to protect her from the constant impacts with the vehicle's walls, but she managed to wedge herself between the wheel arches. Some stability at least, but the pain of bracing was excruciating.

Rachel tried to quell her rising panic by objectively assessing the situation. She worked out that two men were involved, probably fairly young, given what little speech she could overhear, but what the hell could they possibly want with her? Did they think she was a rival drug dealer or something? Ridiculous! Had they mistaken her for someone rich who could provide them with a substantial ransom? No chance. She was a teacher, not a stockbroker. Whatever they wanted, she was sure of one thing. She was in deep shit.

The van came to a sudden stop and Rachel was dragged out of the vehicle, stumbling as her feet hit the ground and her burning muscles adjusted to moving again.

'Don't try to take the hood off or run away,' a voice hissed. 'Me blade's at the back of yer neck and no-one around here would give a shit if I used it. Now fucking move.'

The smell of decaying rubbish was dominant, with an undertone of weed smoke. Monotonous music came from several directions and she could hear a small motorbike racing up and down a road. The noise diminished once she was inside the building and the outdoor smells gave way to rotting food, cigarette smoke and mould. She gagged. She was shoved into a chair and any momentary relief as her wrist bindings were cut ended, as they tied her wrists and ankles to its arms and legs. She bucked in protest, but the bindings held fast, cutting into her skin.

The hood was ripped off her head. Rachel screwed her eyes up against the sudden light, but the room was gloomy, and she adjusted in a few seconds. She was in a shabby lounge, with takeaway food containers piled on every surface, some acting as ashtrays, and piles of beer and cider cans strewn over the floor. Dirt and damp covered much of the walls and any clear spaces within reach had been decorated with improbable drawings of genitalia. A sofa looked as if it had been attacked by a werewolf, and the only undamaged item in the room was a 55-inch television, hanging lopsidedly on the wall, with a games console attached. Suppressing her mounting anxiety, she sat up as straight as she could and took a deep breath, half choking on the stench.

'What the hell's going on?' she demanded, glaring at the two balaclava-clad young men who stood in front of her, brandishing gleaming combat knives. 'If you think you can ransom me, you're wasting your time. I'm a teacher not a millionaire. So let me go before the shit really hits you.' She kept her voice steady despite the hypnotic pull of the wicked blades.

'You're gonna help us,' one of them sneered. 'You're a chemist and you're going to make us meth. When you've made enough, we'll let you go. If you don't help us, or try to escape, they'll find your body in the fucking canal. Understand?'

Chapter Five

THE NONDESCRIPT MAN in the corner of the Morpeth Arms finished his pint and stood up to leave. Buttoning his coat, he glanced at the free newspaper, discarded on the table next to him. He froze. He knew that name, although James Raven wasn't a superintendent when they met. Bittersweet memories came flooding back and he recalled the change of direction he had taken in the aftermath of that night.

It seemed as though Raven had just had a lucky escape. Lucky for him, too. If evidence of that event was found in Raven's belongings when they were sorted out after his death, a diaspora of shit would engulf him, and several other people, too. He would keep an eye on Raven's progress. If there was a second, successful, attempt on the police officer's life he would have to take action. Swiftly.

'Have you any idea what you're asking, you idiots?' Rachel glared furiously at the two youths. 'You can't just knock up a batch of methamphetamine in a bucket, using household chemicals.'

'They did it on the telly,' snarled Gaz. 'And my mate said you can make it from cough mixture. You're a clever fucking chemist, it says so in the paper, so you'd better work it out.'

He waved his knife in front of her face and pricked her throat, raising a tiny bead of blood.

Despairing at the prospect of explaining the difference between fact and fiction to these two morons, Rachel sighed.

'All right. I'll have to think. Give me an hour and some paper and a pen. But first you'd better untie me and take me to a toilet, or you'll have to buy me some clean pants.'

The young men looked embarrassed and Gaz untied her.

'This way. And if you try anything clever, I'll fucking stick you.'

He led Rachel to a filthy bathroom that featured a spectacular display of mould on the walls. The shower unit hung loose over a grimy bath and the stench of sewer gas, from a dried-out U-bend, made her gag. Half the toilet seat was missing and there was no loo paper – a faded copy of *The Sun* would have to do. At least there was running water.

When she'd finished, she rinsed her hands and shook them dry. She looked around for something she could use as a weapon – some bleach or acidic toilet cleaner, perhaps. But the state of the bowl had already told her that cleaning was an alien concept to the flat's occupants and she looked in vain. There wasn't even a toothbrush she could sharpen, but, given the plethora of micro-organisms in the room, if there had been one, it would have been classified as a biological weapon.

Gaz, still waving his knife, led her to a grimy kitchen piled high with mouldering takeaway food containers. He pushed a pile of pizza boxes off a dirty table, handed her a chewed biro and several metres of the brown paper used as packing by online retailers, and pointed to a rickety chair.

'There you are. Use that. And don't piss about. My mate will keep an eye on you. I'm going out for a bit and you'd better sort this by the time I get back.'

He waved the knife menacingly again and slammed the door as he left.

Rachel sat down gingerly while Vic slumped on the floor in the corner, smoking weed and playing a game on his phone. She sat thinking for a moment and started to write, covering the sheet with chemical formulae. This was just for show. She had only a vague idea about how methamphetamine was made but she realised that Vic wouldn't know the formula for meth from the Latin name of the walrus. Eventually, she came up with a list of materials and some apparatus. As soon as they arrived, she would start mixing chemicals and looking busy while she worked out how she was going to escape. When Gaz came back, she was ready.

'Right. I need this glassware, an electric heater, and these chemicals.' She indicated two lists, neatly written on the brown paper. 'I'll need to get this lot online, so you'd better steal me a laptop. I also need a bottle of bleach and this brand of toilet cleaner.'

'What? Are you gonna clean the bog?' asked Vic.

'No, you moron, though it desperately needs it. I need an acid for the reaction and the toilet cleaner's the easiest one to get hold of. Oh, and you'd better get me one of these masks from a builders' merchant.'

Vic bridled at the insult but said nothing, and Gaz sent him out to acquire a laptop. When Vic returned, Gaz watched carefully as Rachel ordered items online using a stolen credit card, ensuring she didn't email anyone for help. Once she'd finished, he steered her to a seedy bedroom, handed her half a cold pizza and a bottle of cola, and locked her in.

Rachel lay on the unsavoury mattress, fully clothed, and counted the cobwebs on the ceiling. *How the hell am I going to get out of this?* She cursed herself for not being more alert, but Mexton shopping centre was hardly downtown Baghdad. Her TA training should have helped, but running around with an SA80 rifle on exercise in the Welsh countryside was miles different from dealing with knife-wielding thugs in a car park. Still, at least the TA kept her fit, and she could use that to her advantage.

Her captors were obviously deeply stupid, but that didn't mean they were any less dangerous. She knew they would hurt her if she didn't play along. What they planned to do when she had met their demands, she couldn't bear to think about, so she parked that thought and concentrated on an escape plan. Brute force probably wouldn't work, despite her training. They were strong and ruthless; she was sure of that. So, she would have to think of something more elaborate. Something which drew on her chemical knowledge, perhaps?

Was there any way of alerting the authorities? she wondered. They'd taken her phone and they wouldn't let her email. She was being watched all the time and was locked in this bedroom with boards nailed over the window. Calling for help on the Eastside would be about as effective as politely asking a charging rhino to stop.

That useless twat Nigel might get around to reporting her missing, but she couldn't rely on him. He'd become increasingly distant since he joined the Scrabble club and she suspected he knew about her affair with the school's head of physics. He was clearly playing away as well, although he didn't know she knew. Sod him. She would have to find a way out by herself. In the meantime, she would need all her psychological resources to keep herself from panicking.

Chapter Six

Day 4

'CAN I HELP YOU, SIR?' asked the civilian receptionist at Mexton police station.

'Yes. Well. I don't know. My wife didn't come home last night, and I'm worried about her.'

'OK. If you give me a few details, I'll get someone to come and talk to you.'

'Thank you. My name's Nigel Willstone. My wife's Rachel. She's a teacher at Mexton Premier Academy. She went shopping and didn't come back.' *Probably shagging that physics teacher. Bastard.*

The receptionist typed a few notes into her computer, picked up the phone and, shortly after, DC Sally Erskine appeared.

'Please come with me, Mr Willstone,' she said, leading him through the card-controlled door to the comfortable interview room. 'I've got the basic facts, so can we go through them in more detail? When did you last see your wife?'

'About half six last night. We'd had an early dinner; I was getting ready for Scrabble club and she went off to the shopping centre. It's our usual Thursday night routine. She's normally back home by the time I get in but she wasn't there, and her phone was switched off.' *Too busy playing away. Bitch.*

'Could she have stayed with a friend?'

Nigel looked uncomfortable. *Friend? Shag more like.*

'No. I phoned a few people and no one had seen her.'

'Has this sort of thing happened before?'

More discomfort. *For bloody months since you ask.*

'Well, once she didn't come back after a parents' evening. She said they went for drinks afterwards and she stayed with a friend because she wasn't safe to drive. She did let me know, though.' *Lying cow. She was with him. I should have gone over to Tania's for a shag.*

'I have to ask, Mr Willstone, but are things all right between you and your wife?'

'Er... yes.' Nigel flushed. 'If you're suggesting she's left me, you're wrong. Her clothes and things are all there. It was only a bloody shopping trip, for goodness' sake. We didn't row or anything.' *Wait 'til I see that bitch. It'll be more than a row I can tell you. Wish I could give her a slap like Gerry does when his missus steps out of line.*

'OK. I was just checking. Can you let me have her phone number, car registration and a photo? We'll ask our patrols to keep an eye open for her and we'll get someone to check the shopping centre car park. Have you phoned the hospital?'

'Yes, of course. They've had no-one answering her description admitted. I'm beginning to get really worried.'

'It's OK, Mr Willstone. I understand. But most missing adults turn up within a day or so. Try not to worry. We'll keep you informed, and, please, let us know if she comes home before we find her.'

Sally shook Nigel's hand and led him out to reception.

Something's a bit off, there, she thought, as she returned to the CID office. *I'm sure he's hiding something. But what?*

Following a night during which sleep had eluded her, Rachel banged on the door and demanded to use the bathroom and toilet. A splash of cold water on her face, wiped off on her sleeve, was all she could manage for a wash. There was no soap. Gaz put an out-of-date box of cereal, a bottle of milk and a bowl on the kitchen table and she ostentatiously polished the spoon he gave her on her sleeve before eating her breakfast.

'Right,' she said, 'I'll need to use the kitchen as a laboratory, so you won't be able to come in once I start. The fumes will be dangerous, hence the mask. I'll need food from time to time. And coffee.'

'Are you takin' the piss?'

'No, you cretin. You can't handle dangerous chemicals when you're falling asleep or starving hungry. Mistakes can be lethal. You do know what lethal means?'

'Course I fuckin' do, you stuck-up bitch,' snarled Gaz. 'If we didn't need you, I'd fuckin' do you. All right, we'll get you food and coffee. And we'll let you use the toilet. But if you piss us about, you'll bleed. Got it?'

'Yes, dear,' replied Rachel, smiling sweetly. 'And there's a few more things I'll need. She pointed to a list. 'Buy these from a pharmacy – twelve bottles of acetone, two bottles of hydrogen peroxide, and as many bottles of this decongestant as you can find. You'll have to go to several shops. There's a few more bits of equipment you can get online. And, as your company is far from delightful, you can get me a couple of books of cryptic crosswords, an A4 notebook and a copy of *New Scientist* magazine, otherwise I'll die of boredom.'

Gaz left the flat to acquire the items Rachel had demanded, with the uncomfortable feeling that the captive had somehow got the upper hand. Surely, she should be trembling with fear, asking for privileges and begging for mercy, not ordering him about. *Just like a fucking teacher*, he thought, not that he'd had a great deal of experience of school. Still, if she did the job, that was what mattered. He'd deal with her attitude afterwards. Come to think of it, what were they going to do afterwards? They couldn't keep her there, making meth, for ever. He shrugged, his attention caught by a BMW someone had left outside a newsagents, with the keys still in the ignition. Another time, perhaps.

A pharmacist phoned another pharmacist, then a second and a third. He thought for a moment, pulled a leaflet from his desk drawer and logged into his email account. An official in the Home Office read the email, consulted colleagues and telephoned the pharmacist. More phone calls were made, emails were sent, plans were laid and surveillance was put in place. Two days later, firearms were drawn from the armoury and two armed response vehicles slid out of the police station car park and headed towards their target. Pulling up out of sight of any suspects, the armed officers waited for the order to strike.

'What's happening with your missing person, Sally?' asked DC Mel Cotton, as they queued at the till in the canteen. 'Rachel Millstone, wasn't it?'

'Almost. It's Willstone. No-one's seen her since she left the shopping centre. She was picked up on CCTV as she left, and uniform found her Volvo in the car park with a bag of shopping underneath it. Her phone was switched off at 19.42 and hasn't been on since, so we can't track it.'

'What about car park CCTV?'

'Nothing. Her vehicle was in a blind spot. One of the civilian investigators is going through footage of cars leaving around the time her phone was switched off, but there are hundreds. There was a small fire on one of the other levels shortly before, which kept the security staff busy.'

'Well, if she was kidnapped, which seems quite likely, that could have been a diversion. But who would want to kidnap a chemistry teacher?'

'Someone desperate to pass their GCSE Science?' joked Sally.

'Yeah, right. No, it must be more sinister than that. You're looking into friends and relatives, I presume?'

'Yes, and I'm also learning to suck eggs. Give us a chance, we only got the report a few hours ago.'

'Sorry.' Mel smiled apologetically. 'I know you know what you're doing. Just thinking aloud. Come on. Find us a table and I'll fill you in on Tom's latest DIY disaster.'

31

Chapter Seven

Day 5

THE CHEMICALS and equipment began to arrive, and Rachel unpacked them in front of Gaz and Vic.

'What do you need all that for?' asked Gaz. 'And why the fuck do you need a soda syphon?'

Rachel fixed him with a penetrating gaze, as if she was addressing a student who claimed their homework had been eaten by the dog.

'Do I tell you how to sell drugs or steal cars?'

'N... no.'

'Then don't try to tell me how to do chemistry.'

She turned her back on him and continued unpacking.

'Who are you anyway?' she asked, looking back over her shoulder.

'Don't tell, her Ga...' Vic's reply was cut short as Gaz slapped him across the mouth.

'You don't need to know. You can call me er... Mr White and my mate's Mr Pink. OK?'

'More like Mr Thick and Mr Thicker,' muttered Rachel under her breath, uncomfortably aware that the chances of her getting out of this mess alive had substantially diminished.

'Good morning,' said the bespectacled man in the expensive suit, addressing the receptionist at the Mexton Recuperative Clinic. 'My name is Dr Robert Raven. I understand my brother, James, is being transferred to you following a serious accident in London. I wonder if you could fill me in on what you have to offer here?'

'Certainly, sir. Here's our brochure. I'll just get hold of the clinical director. I'm sure he'll be glad to show you around. We're expecting James in a day or so. We've got a room on the ground floor reserved for him.'

As the woman was dialling, the visitor looked quickly around the reception area, checked for CCTV and watched a member of staff as he pushed a patient, clutching a pack of cigarettes, into the fresh air. He pulled a pager out of his pocket and frowned.

'Look, I'm terribly sorry. I'm on call and I've just been paged. I have to go. I'll take the brochure but perhaps I could make an appointment in the next few days? Then I'll be able to see my brother as well.'

'I do understand,' the receptionist smiled. 'It's no problem at all. We'll look forward to hearing from you, Dr Raven.'

Hugh Ventham walked briskly to his car, parked out of sight of the clinic's CCTV camera, and glanced around. Yes, he thought. It's doable. *And I know just how to go about it.*

Bored out of her mind waiting for the last few bits of equipment to arrive, Rachel decided to have some fun at her captors' expense. She knew how she was going to escape, or at least try to, but couldn't put her plan into operation until everything was in place.

'I need some more bits and bobs, gentlemen,' she said. 'Can one of you get me four of those plastic lemons full of juice, a large bag of ice cubes – I assume the freezer compartment in that cesspit of a fridge works – and three packets of sodium bicarbonate, otherwise known as baking soda. Would you like me to write that down for you?'

Gaz glowered at her but said nothing.

'Oh, I also need a bottle of vodka – not the cheap under-proof stuff – and some non-chemical bits: a large ball of string, a one litre saucepan with a lid, a set of kitchen scales, and a plastic spatula no more than nine centimetres wide at the end. You can get them at Maxwell's Tools and Hardware in the shopping centre. While you're in the shop, ask for a long weight for the scales.'

Gaz scribbled the list on the back of a final demand for Council Tax payment and handed it to Vic.

'Anything else?' asked Vic. 'Cos we're gettin' pissed off running fuckin' errands.'

Rachel turned to Gaz.

'Mr White. If you've got a brain cell to spare, which I doubt, can you share it with Mr Pink and explain that I need the right tools to do the job?'

Gaz drew his knife and moved as if to cut her, but restrained himself just in time, confining himself to a stream of repetitive and unimaginative swear words.

'I don't want to be in these charming premises any longer than I have to,' Rachel continued, 'and I'm sure you want your merchandise as soon as possible. So, get me what I need while I do some calculations. That's sums, to you.'

She turned her back on the two lads, but not before she'd seen a look in Gaz's eyes which convinced her that she wouldn't be going anywhere, while still breathing, once the job was completed. This was confirmed later when she heard Vic moaning to Gaz that the woman in the hardware store had laughed when he had asked for the long weight and then wandered off for half an hour, returning to report that it was out of stock. By that time, the ice had melted, the bag had leaked in his rucksack and the back of his trousers looked as though he'd had an embarrassing accident.

As she lay on the rancid mattress, with sleep a fugitive, Rachel's amusement at Vic's discomfort was crowded out by trepidation, verging on fear. Her two captors had clearly not thought things through when they embarked on their batshit-crazy enterprise. Apart from a fundamental misunderstanding about the process of making methamphetamine, they hadn't thought about how and when they would release her. That was obvious. They couldn't keep her here indefinitely, even if she made the drug for them, and, although they might be as foren-sically aware as a hibernating hamster, they must realise that she had accumulated enough information to lead the police to them if she was released. But she had taken measures and she had a plan, which she would put into practice in the morning. If nothing worked, she would just have to fight them with whatever weapons came to hand, a prospect which hardly filled her with confidence. Fighting back the fear, she lulled herself to sleep by working her way through the Periodic Table,

recalling, as far as possible, the atomic masses of each element.
Halfway through the second iteration, she fell asleep.

Chapter Eight

Day 6

FOR THE PAST HOUR, Rachel had been bubbling chlorine through a flask of acetone and passing the waste toxic gas out through a crack in the window via a plastic tube. Now it was ready, and she stopped the process which made the chlorine. She slipped the mask over her face, poured the contents of the flask into the soda syphon and fitted the gas cartridge. Then she called to her captors.

'All right, you little shits. I've got something for you.'

Gaz and Vic bounded into the kitchen like puppies at feeding time, Gaz first. The stream of homemade tear gas hit him full in the face, soaking his balaclava, as Rachel pulled the trigger of the syphon. As Gaz screamed and tried to uncover his face she switched the jet to Vic, who stood there open-mouthed until it hit him. They coughed, spluttered and clawed at their eyes, which only made the symptoms worse. Gaz stumbled blindly towards where he thought Rachel was standing, swinging his fists wildly, knocking over a flask of bleach which

37

smashed, making the toxic atmosphere in the kitchen even more unpleasant.

Rachel took her opportunity, kicking the incapacitated Gaz in the groin and hitting Vic over the head with the empty syphon, before bursting out of the kitchen. Coughs and swearing followed her as she ran down the passageway and yanked open the front door. She pulled off the face mask, breathed the fresh air with pleasure and stared in shock at the two carbines aimed at her chest.

'Get down on the floor. Now. Keep your hands where I can see them.' shouted the Tactical Firearms Commander through a megaphone. 'Do exactly as I say, and you won't get hurt.'

Rachel complied and started to laugh, as PC Adeyemo lowered his weapon, and another PC cuffed her hands behind her back.

'I must apologise for the smell,' said Rachel, as Mel handed her a coffee in the interview room. 'I haven't had a decent wash for days.'

Mel grinned.

'That's all right. I've smelt far worse in this job. Sorry about the firearms – we thought we had a bunch of terrorists.'

'So, it worked then?'

'Pardon?'

'I sent the kids out to buy a large quantity of acetone and some hydrogen peroxide. I knew it would attract suspicion and a pharmacist would notify the Suspicious Chemical Reporting Service at the Home Office. I was gambling that you would be able to trace them back to the flat.'

'That was fairly easy. CCTV picked up Gary – the brighter one – at the pharmacies and he wasn't at his usual address. His cousin is in prison, so it was reasonable to suppose that his flat was being used by Gary for something illegal. A surveillance team confirmed that he was using it, so we planned a raid. We thought explosives, but you told the officers you were making controlled drugs. An offence, of course, but you were coerced.'

'Actually, I wasn't. Making drugs. You can make methamphetamine from a decongestant, pseudoephedrine, but I don't exactly know how. I sent them to buy lots of a completely different medicine. I pretended to make the drug while I was working out how to escape.'

'How did you manage that? The firearms officers said the air in the flat made their eyes water and their dog wouldn't go in.'

'I made something called chloroacetone, a type of tear gas. I loaded it into a soda syphon and sprayed them with it. A kick in the balls and a blow to the head did the rest and I fled, only to find myself staring down the barrels of a couple of guns. I couldn't help but laugh. Perhaps it was the stress of the past few days.'

'Well, I think you're really brave,' smiled Mel. 'I suppose, technically, a soda syphon full of tear gas counts as a prohibited weapon under the Firearms Act, but I doubt that the CPS would be interested in prosecuting.'

'I should bloody well hope not,' said Rachel, slightly indignantly. 'I didn't know when, or if, I would get out of that squalid little flat. I was pretty sure they were going to kill me when they'd finished with me. Reasonable force, I call it.'

'I quite agree. Now, I'd like to run over the details of how you were captured, what they did to you, and how you escaped. Then I'll type up your statement and you can sign it. We'll take you home, as Forensics still have your car. Your husband's waiting and we've assured him you're OK, though we haven't told him what's happened. Let me know if you want some more coffee. I must say,' Mel added, 'you seem to have coped with your ordeal extremely well.'

'I've handled whole classes of people like that who resented being in school, being expected to learn GCSE science and, in some cases, being taught by a woman. Those two were easy. It was just a question of working out how to overpower them without getting stabbed. But I'll be more careful in multi-storey car parks in future. What will happen to them? The kids, I mean.'

'They were checked over at A&E and are now in the cells. They'll be charged with kidnapping, assault and, possibly, conspiracy to manufacture controlled drugs. They also stole the van you were put in, and there are various driving offences which the CPS may consider as well. They'll be out of circulation for a while, that's for sure. Now, let's get you home.'

Chapter Nine

THE WELCOME RACHEL received when the police car dropped her off at home was not what might have been expected. Instead of a hug and a cup of tea, she was greeted by a raving Nigel, much the worse for drink, who gave her no chance to explain what had happened.

'You've been away shagging that physics bastard, haven't you? What's his name? Lewis? You've gone too bloody far this time. I won't have it, do you understand? You're my bloody wife and you'll behave like it.'

'What the hell are you talking about? Shit, Nigel, I was kidnapped by drug dealers who wanted me to make them meth.'

'Bollocks. You think I'm stupid? You were shacked up in some seedy love nest with that streak of nothing. And you've been at it for months.'

'You can talk. You've been screwing Little Miss Lexicon, or whatever her name is, after your Scrabble club. I know why you come home late.'

'That's... that's... none of your fucking business. I wasn't

41

getting anything from you so what was I supposed to do? I have needs, you know.'

'Well so do I, and you were no bloody good anyway.'

Nigel's eyes took on a murderous gleam and he reached for a kitchen knife, which he waved at Rachel's face. *Not more sodding knives*, she thought, determining to resolve the situation, one way or another.

'Nigel, stop,' she shouted. 'You're drunk and I'm tired, so put the knife down and go and sleep it off. If I have to take it off you, it'll hurt. So don't be silly.'

Nigel only grew angrier.

'Fuck you, you and your so-called training. Think you're a tough soldier, do you? Well come and take it if you're so hard.'

Rachel had never seen this side of Nigel's character before but, then, she'd never seen him this drunk. He was clearly losing control and she had to act. She stepped forward, reaching for the knife. He slashed clumsily for her face, missing the end of her nose by a few centimetres. She moved away, wincing as her back hit the corner of the kitchen island, and nearly falling over backwards. Nigel advanced, yelling. There was only one thing for it. She kicked him in the balls as hard as she could. As Nigel doubled over, his head struck the granite worktop and he fell to the floor, unconscious.

Rachel caught her breath, relieved at the silence. Then she froze. A bright red pool oozed from under Nigel's thigh. He had fallen onto the knife. She turned him over and watched in horror as his femoral artery pumped blood in vivid spurts from the top of his leg.

She remembered a video she'd seen, on wilderness survival first aid, at a TA meeting. If the femoral artery is hit, there's little chance of survival unless the bleeding is stopped quickly. Desperate measures are called for. She grabbed the knife and cut away Nigel's trousers. She pressed the spurting with all her strength, compressing the upper end of the artery against bone. The bleeding stopped, only a small amount oozing past her hand. *So, what the hell do I do now?* she asked herself.

Looking around the kitchen, she spotted Nigel's phone on the worktop, much too far away for her to reach it. She couldn't stay holding the artery closed for ever, and he needed urgent medical attention. Her eyes fell on a loaf of sliced bread. It had already been opened and the bag was held shut with a plastic clip to keep it fresh. Could that work?

Still compressing Nigel's artery, she raised herself up on one leg, straightening it and swinging her other leg over the worktop, as if in some particularly uncomfortable yoga position. She kicked the loaf and it fell to the floor beyond Nigel's head. Too far away to reach with her spare hand.

By now, Nigel was beginning to stir, and she knew she wouldn't be able to hold on when he started thrashing about. She twisted her body and reached out with her leg, just managing to hook the loaf with her foot. She drew it towards her, pain stabbing in her hip. Finally, she managed to reach it with her hand. She yanked open the plastic clip, cut away some of the muscle and shoved it in Nigel's wound, fastening it tight over the end. The blood flow stopped, but she had her doubts that the clip would stay in position on the slippery walls of the blood vessel. But it did give her time to grab Nigel's phone, call 999 and unlock the door.

Nigel groaned as she sat on his leg, holding the clip in place with her dripping fingers. How would she explain this to the police, and to Nigel, if he survived? She also wondered whether she wanted him to.

Chapter Ten

'...MAY BE GIVEN IN EVIDENCE.'

Rachel nodded her understanding as Mel finished reciting the caution, sitting in a police car.

'It was an accident, you know. I was defending myself and he fell.'

'I hear you,' replied Mel, 'but given the circumstances I had no alternative but to arrest you. I strongly advise you to talk to a solicitor before you say anything else. We'll go back to the station now, and wait until you've got legal representation before questioning you formally.'

'OK. I'll call someone. Can I go back into the house and get some clean clothes? These are rancid.'

'I'm afraid not. The house is now a crime scene. We'll need the clothes you're wearing, but we'll find you something to wear at the station. And some food.'

Mel smiled encouragingly but all Rachel could do was stare blankly out of the car window. Nothing was said on the journey and, once Rachel was booked in by the custody sergeant, she was led to a cell. Sparse as it was, it was more comfortable than the grotty conditions in the flat where she had spent the last three days. With her solicitor not due to arrive for another hour, Rachel declined food and drink, changed into the clothes provided, collapsed on the thin mattress and slept.

When her solicitor arrived, Rachel was woken by a custody officer and led to a private room where the two of them could talk. While wolfing down a sandwich and drinking a cup of alleged coffee, she outlined what had happened, from the time she was kidnapped to the arrival of the ambulance.

'It was an accident, Clive,' she said, emphatically. 'He went for me with the knife and fell on it when I tried to take it away from him. I kicked him in the balls, and he banged his head on the worktop. Surely the police will believe me?'

'Not necessarily. You've described to me the row between you and Nigel, and how you both admitted to having affairs. Either of you could be said to have a motive to kill the other. Furthermore, you're in the TA, trained to kill. That could go against you.'

'That's nonsense. We don't do knife-fighting in the TA. In fact, a video they showed us during training enabled me to stop the bleeding.'

'Well, the police are considering asking the CPS to charge you with attempted murder, or murder if Nigel dies. A jury may take a different view. Is there any word on his condition?'

'They haven't said. I'll ask when they interview me.'

'Is there anything else before I tell them we're ready? I must emphasise that "No comment" is a perfectly acceptable answer to their questions.'

'No, nothing more. Let's get on with it.'

'Before we start, Rachel,' began Mel, 'Nigel is out of surgery. He's still unconscious and can't receive visitors at the moment.'

'Thank you.' Rachel nodded, visibly relieved.

Mel started the recording equipment, repeated the caution and asked those present to identify themselves.

'For the recording, Rachel, please will you tell us what happened after the police took you home.'

'I went in and found Nigel drunk and raving. He didn't believe me when I said I'd been kidnapped and accused me of spending the last three days with a lover. We exchanged insults and he grabbed a knife. I told him to put it down, but he went for me with it. Using reasonable force, I kicked him in the testicles. He doubled over, still holding the knife, and, unexpectedly, hit his head on the worktop and fell to the floor. I quickly realised he had fallen onto the knife and was bleeding badly. I performed emergency first aid and was able to summon help. The rest you know.'

'What would you say to the suggestion that you took the knife from him and, using your army training, deliberately stabbed him, because he had found out about your affair?'

'I would say it was nonsense. Apart from anything else, the TA doesn't train us to fight with knives. And before you ask anything else, I admit to an affair and know that Nigel was having one. If I'd wanted to kill him, I wouldn't have saved his life.'

'How would Nigel describe the events, do you think?' asked Sally.

'I've no idea. He was drunk and crazy. I'd never seen him that bad. He'd probably claim I attacked him as soon as I came in the door.'

'Can you prove that things happened as you say?' Mel asked.

Rachel's solicitor intervened.

'As you know, DC Cotton, it is not up to my client to prove her innocence. It's for the police to prove her guilt.'

'It's all right, Clive,' said Rachel, before Mel could ask another question. 'I believe I can. Much of the exchange was recorded on our smart speaker. The phrase which starts it recording is "shit Nigel" and I used that as soon as I realised he was losing it. You should be able to reconstruct things from the recording. I don't think I have anything more to say.'

Mel looked at Sally and nodded.

'OK. Interview terminated at 18.27.'

'It's a pity you didn't mention this earlier,' said Sally.

'I didn't think I'd need to and, anyway, I didn't really want our row aired in public. I'd set up the record words a couple of months ago, as Nigel was getting a bit flaky, and I was thinking about a divorce. I didn't expect him to become violent. I'll give you my cloud details and you can play back the audio file. So, what happens now?'

'We'll keep you in custody for the time being, until we've checked the recording. I'm afraid you'll be here overnight. After that it's up to the Superintendent whether we ask the Crown Prosecution Service to charge you, in which case you'll be remanded. Otherwise, you could be released under investigation or simply released without charge. We'll get you some food and drink in the meantime. You must be starving. All you've had is a sandwich.'

Chapter Eleven

Day 7

'Do you believe her?' asked DSup Gorman, after the recording had been played for the third time.

'Yes, sir,' said the two DCs in unison.

'It ties in with what she said when I arrived at the scene,' said Mel, 'and it fits with the interview.'

'It's obvious Nigel was out of control,' added Sally, 'and picking up a knife in that situation is never going to end well. He was lucky Rachel had the knowledge to save his life. Will he be charged with assault or attempted murder?'

'I'll have a word with the CPS,' said the DSup, 'but I suspect they'll say it's not in the public interest to charge him.'

'I'm sure Rachel won't want him charged, either,' said Mel. 'I think all she wants is a quick divorce. I guess being attacked with a kitchen knife counts as irretrievable breakdown of a marriage.'

'Right then,' said Gorman. 'Let her go, and make sure she

gets home safely. The SOCOs have finished, but we'll probably not need the results of their work.'

'I will, sir. And I'll give her the details of that firm that cleans up crime scenes. I'm sure she won't want to scrape up Nigel's blood herself.'

'What will you do now?' asked Sally as she helped Rachel out of the police car.

'Firstly, I'm going to have a long, hot shower and put on some clean clothes. Then I'm going to check in to a decent hotel and have a massive lunch, accompanied by a bottle of wine. Then I'll sleep for the rest of the day.'

'What about Nigel? Will you visit him?'

'I'll let my solicitor do that, with divorce papers. To use the vernacular of my recent captors, the arsehole can go fuck himself.'

Sally smiled as Rachel walked wearily up her front path. What a remarkable woman!

Chapter Twelve

THE TRICK WAS to look as if you had every right to be there. He assumed that most of the night staff would be from an agency and wouldn't always know who was on shift with them. So, walking purposefully down the corridor to Raven's room, wearing a nurse's uniform which matched those he'd seen on his previous visit, and a lanyard which could have had a picture of Mickey Mouse on it, for all the attention anyone paid to it, he was confident that he would not be challenged. This didn't stop his heart from going into overdrive. It was much riskier than the attempt with the car. More personal and messier, too. But it was absolutely necessary.

Easing open Raven's door, Ventham noted a collection of crutches and walking aids ranged along one wall. He hadn't expected Raven to be fully mobile and was unsurprised by the various braces and casts that enveloped his target. *Perhaps this won't be as hard as I feared*, he thought.

He approached the gently snoring figure on the bed, his shoes squeaking faintly on the vinyl flooring. He slipped the small, razor-sharp knife from his trouser pocket and jammed his hand over Raven's mouth to prevent him from making any noise. Before he could make the cut, his victim jerked awake, one hand groping for the call button beside the bed and the other jabbing at his face. Ignoring the scratches, he pressed the blade into Raven's neck, worked it through muscles and tendons and sliced the carotid artery. Within seconds Raven ceased struggling, and two and a half minutes later he was dead.

He wiped the blood from his eyes with a gloved hand and paused for a moment. *Those scratches. There'll be DNA.* Calmly, he used the knife to remove the fingers from the hand that had scratched him, pocketed his grisly trophies, and stepped towards the window, avoiding walking back through the building looking like an abattoir worker. The window only opened part way, but he used one of the crutches to lever off the thin metal stays which restricted it. He eased himself out and ran, crouching, through the clinic's extensive grounds and back towards the road.

By the time he reached his car, half a kilometre from the clinic, he had stripped off the uniform and stuffed it in a plastic bag, using a clump of bushes as cover. He hoped that the over-alls which the uniform had concealed, together with a cap and face mask, would prevent any of Raven's blood transferring to the vehicle. A pair of thick-rimmed glasses further obscured his face. He may have to get rid of the car, he mused, but that would be a small price to pay for peace of mind. He drove back into Mexton, avoiding the ANPR cameras he'd located online, his mind at rest, and the horror of the murder scene leaving no emotional traces whatsoever.

Chapter Thirteen

Day 8

'WELL, THIS IS A BLOODY MESS,' said DI Emma Thorpe as she peered over the face mask that formed part of her protective clothing.

Dr Durbridge stepped back from Raven's corpse.

'Welcome back, DI Thorpe,' he said. 'All I can tell you at the moment is that death appears to be the result of exsanguination, consequent upon the severing of a carotid artery, and that he died at some time during the night. I may have more later.'

'Thank you. I can't say I'm surprised.'

She managed a half-smile.

'How's the baby, by the way?' continued the pathologist. 'You've got bags under your eyes which suggest to me that you're not exactly rested.'

Emma grimaced.

'She's lovely, doctor, but you're right. Sleep has been a stranger for months. I'm only back part time and, much as I adore her, it will be good to get back to normality for a bit. It's really hard to leave her, though, as she's developing so quickly.'

'The normality of cut throats, you mean?' The pathologist grinned wryly. 'Not the nicest way to start back. Still, at least no-one's trying to blow you up.'

Emma nodded her agreement. The Albanian OCG bomb attack on the police station was never far from her thoughts, and she still mourned her lost colleagues.

'I'll leave you and the SOCOs to carry on. I just thought I'd look in while the scene was fresh. I'll brief DCI Farlowe and we'll look forward to your report.'

Emma turned, nodded to a SOCO who was meticulously photographing the room's plethora of bloodstains, and walked back to her car, stripping off the forensic suit as she went and dropping it in the bin provided. She wondered, for at least the tenth time since she left the house, how baby Genevieve was getting on without her. Would she miss her mother? Even worse, what if she didn't? And what about Mike? How was he coping? She trusted him completely, but it was the first time he had looked after her on his own for a prolonged period. Once she was sat in her car, she switched into professional mode and banished these thoughts, although she knew she was bound to return to them throughout the day. Frequently.

DCI Colin Farlowe tapped his fountain pen on the side of his china teacup to call the team to order.

'Good afternoon, everyone. Firstly, can I welcome DI Thorpe back to active duty following her maternity leave. Her baby is doing well, I understand. She's working part-time, and we'll be working together to ensure that investigations proceed effectively and efficiently.'

There were welcoming murmurs from the assembled detectives and civilian support staff.

'I would also like to formally note our thanks to DI Chidgey who so ably stepped in while Emma was away. I see that some of you are still recovering from his farewell do in the Cat and Cushion last night. I trust it will not impair your ability to work. We have a murder to solve.'

Three officers looked sheepish while another two studied the floor intently.

'Finally, I'd like to introduce Detective Constable Kamal Chabra, who has transferred to us from the Met. I trust you will all make him welcome.'

Smiles and a few waves acknowledged the newcomer.

'Now, to business. Last night, Detective Superintendent James Raven was murdered. He was a patient at the Mexton Recuperative Clinic, a specialist physical rehabilitation establishment, four miles out of town. He was found with his throat cut early this morning. We expect the pathologist's report later today. The victim was a serving police officer from the Met. He was in the clinic because he was involved in a hit-and-run incident, in London, a week ago, so a reasonable hypothesis is that someone finished off the job they started.'

An angry rumbling rolled around the room and several officers swore under their breath.

'Now, I realise you all do your best, irrespective of the identity of the victim, but we can't let a murder of a fellow officer go unsolved. I knew Mr Raven in the Met and, although we were not close, I'm horrified at his death. Because of my personal involvement, I'm asking DI Thorpe to act as SIO, with DS Vaughan as her deputy. I will, of course, follow developments in the case, but I cannot be directly involved. So, I'll hand over to you, Emma. Please keep me informed.'

As Farlowe left the room a grim atmosphere settled around

its occupants. All murders were deplorable, but the killing of a fellow police officer was particularly horrific. This was not the first time that an officer had been killed in Mexton in the line of duty and memories were still raw.

'OK, everyone,' began Emma, 'Let's get on with catching this bastard. Mr Raven was last seen alive by a nurse who gave him his medication at ten o'clock. That's all we know at the moment, so I want all staff interviewed, whether they were on duty last night or not. Has anyone unusual visited or asked after him? Have they noticed anyone hanging around the premises in the past few days? Are there CCTV cameras in or around the clinic? What about ANPR cameras nearby? How did the killer get in and out? He would have been covered in blood so he must have left traces somewhere. Jack – can you deploy the troops, please? I'll be in my office starting the policy book.'

'Righto,' replied the DS. 'And welcome back.'

Emma smiled and headed for her office that was tucked into the corner of the open-plan area set aside for major crimes. She had seen it for the first time earlier that morning and hadn't yet made it her own. The new police station, rapidly constructed following the bombing of the old one, was a distinct improvement but took some getting used to. Modern LED lighting was better than flickering fluorescent tubes, but was slightly cold, while air conditioning, efficient as it was, left the air dry. Hopefully, the heating would work better than the antediluvian system at the old station. Resisting the urge to phone Mike to check on Genevieve, she switched on her computer.

Chapter Fourteen

'I CAN'T UNDERSTAND how it happened,' said Dr Robert Cartwright, the clinic director, wringing his hands. 'No visitors are allowed after nine pm and staff are scrupulous at enforcing the rule.'

'How about the staff, doctor?' asked Mel. 'Is there anyone new to the clinic?'

'All our regular people have been with us for a long time, well before Mr Raven came here. And, of course, they are all DBS checked.'

That doesn't stop someone going crazy, thought Mel.

'How about the night staff?'

'They generally come from an agency. We have a nurse sleeping in at all times, as well as waking staff, but it's easier to hire outside staff for night shifts. Again, they are all checked.'

'OK. I'll need the names of the agency and all the people they've supplied. We'll need to talk to them and check references and so on.'

'Just a thought,' interjected Sally, 'could someone have

impersonated a member of staff, or just slipped in wearing an appropriate uniform?'

'I suppose it's possible,' replied the doctor. 'I think there's quite a high turnover of agency staff so a new face wouldn't necessarily raise an alarm. But no-one should be on the premises without a pass on a lanyard.'

'Well, we'll be talking to everyone who was on duty. I believe the nurse who found Mr Raven isn't here?'

'Yes. She was badly traumatised, so I sent her home. I was called in at the same time as the police were notified, but she'd gone by the time your colleagues arrived.'

'OK,' said Sally. 'We'll need her home address. It's important we speak to her as soon as possible. Can you find us a room to use for interviews?'

'Yes, of course. I'll ask the head of nursing to arrange it. I told the rest of the night shift to remain behind as I knew you would want to take statements from them.'

Dr Cartwright made a phone call to the nurse and turned back to Sally.

'How about our patients and their treatment?' he asked.

'I'm afraid the corridor leading to Mr Raven's room must remain closed for the time being, as well as the area outside the building. SOCOs have found blood on the windowsill, and the safety stays have been forced, so it looks like the killer escaped that way. We'll be bringing in a dog unit later to try and track his route. I say his, as it's most likely it was a man, although women can kill as well.'

'But not like this, surely,' said the doctor, appalled.

'You'd be surprised,' said Mel. 'Anyway, we'd better get on with the interviews. We'll take a formal statement from you in due course, but we'll concentrate on the staff who were on duty first. Thank you for your co-operation.'

The two detectives left the doctor looking pale and scared, as they headed for the room provided, each with their own list of people to interview.

'So how did you get on at the clinic?' Emma asked Mel and Sally, when they returned to the station. 'Any leads?'

'Not a lot, guv,' replied Mel. 'We've still got a few people who were on leave, or work for the agency, to interview, but we've spoken to most of the staff. The nurse who found him is still pretty upset, and all she could tell us was, she opened his door to wake him up for his medication at 8am and found him in the same state as we did. She didn't touch anything in the room.

'No-one saw anything unusual, either on the day of the killing or in the days beforehand. Mr Raven had been there a day and a half, and his only visitors were colleagues from the Met who came once. His brother called in a couple of days ago, to find out what the clinic provided, but he didn't get the tour as he was called away at reception. He's a doctor, apparently, and was paged. He said he would return on another occasion but hasn't so far.'

'OK. Get onto the Met and find out who visited him. Find out if he said anything to them of use. Also, see if they have contact details for the brother. It could be useful to talk to him as well, and he should be notified. How about CCTV?'

Sally spoke up. 'There's a camera outside the building covering the main entrance but there was nothing useful on it. Just staff coming and going. There's nothing inside – it's not the sort of place where patients are likely to wander around at night and get into difficulties.'

'Hmm. Anything from forensics, Jack?'

'A bit. The Crime Scene Manager was pretty sure the killer left by the window. Dogs traced him to a point some way along the road. They were particularly interested in some bushes in the grounds. There was blood on a few leaves, which suggests that he may have changed his clothes there. SOCOs found no tyre tracks or footwear marks where the trail ended, as the ground was hard and dry. There was a smudged shoeprint in the blood by the window where he trod in it, but it had no useful detail. Blood spatter suggested he was standing over Mr Raven when he killed him, pressing the back of his head down on the bed as he cut the carotid. There may have been some struggle.'

'Thanks, Jack. The pathologist confirmed that he was killed with a sharp knife and death was caused by loss of blood. He thinks the killer removed some fingers possibly with the same knife, after death. There was bruising to Mr Raven's face that came out later, which supports the view of the blood spatter analyst.'

'So, what do we make of it, guv?' asked DC Trevor Blake.

'Well, I don't think we need a profiler to tell us this was a carefully planned killing by a methodical and ruthless individual,' replied Emma. 'I suspect it's personal, probably the same individual who knocked Mr Raven down in London. I've asked for some details from the team investigating the hit-and-run, but we may need to talk to someone personally. I might need a volunteer for a trip to London, if we can justify the expense. Mr Raven probably made enemies during his career, so perhaps the Met could help us with that. It could be that the answer lies in London, so this might end up being a joint investigation. I'm sure the Met will want to work with us. The cutting-off of the fingers suggests to me that he may have scratched his assailant, who was sufficiently forensically aware to remove the evidence. OK. You've all got things to do so we'll convene again tomorrow, unless anything major comes up in the meantime. Jack – you wanted a word?'

A gaunt Jack followed Emma into her office and closed the door behind them.

Chapter Fifteen

LATE IN THE AFTERNOON, Sally sat at her desk leafing through a pile of witness statements with a steaming mug of coffee beside her and a puzzled look on her face.

'Mel?' she called. 'How many people were on duty during that night?'

'Three.' Mel replied, checking her notes. 'Maureen O'Toole, Prudence Harris and Marek Reid. They've all been checked out and couldn't have killed Mr Raven.'

'Look. Both Maureen and Prudence said they remembered seeing Marek moving about the place, just after midnight. But he told us he was in the toilet for nearly half an hour around that time, as he had a stomach upset. God knows why he was working, but I suppose the agency doesn't do much in the way of sick pay. So, if he was in the loo with the shits, the man the others saw must have been the killer. The lights were on low, they only saw him briefly, from behind, and they didn't speak. If he was wearing the right uniform, they could easily have mistaken him for Marek.'

'He was taking a chance, wasn't he? What if they'd challenged him?' wondered Mel.

'He could have claimed he was on the permanent staff, picking up an extra shift, then buggered off. He'd have had to have found another way of getting to his target but, by the time he managed to make the kill, days later, no-one at the clinic would have remembered him. Mr Raven was obviously going to be there for some time.'

'So, we're looking for someone roughly the same height and build as Marek. That's progress. It might be worth having another chat with him. What do we know about him – he was one of yours, wasn't he?'

'Yes. A nice bloke. He's a registered nurse with a wife and two kids. He works nights and she works days in order to pay the mortgage.'

'An unusual name, though.'

'His mother's Polish and his father's English, so they compromised on the name. It's Marek Philip Reid in full.'

'OK. I'll call him this evening and confirm his account. Anything else?'

'No. That's about it. Something for the morning briefing, anyway. Changing the subject, how's Tom getting on?'

'Fine, all things considered. He's getting used to the prosthetic hand, although he can't use a keyboard as quickly as he used to. It's really brilliant. It's controlled by signals from his brain, via muscles in his arm, and is pretty flexible. It seems to be made of a mixture of metal and plastic. When these were first designed, the NHS restricted them to forces personnel injured in combat, but now they're more generally available. Amazing, really. It's been three months since it was fitted and he's still improving his skills. It sounds a bit sci-fi, so it's unsurprising that his techie colleagues are calling him The Tominator.'

Sally grinned.

'Sounds great, but how is he in himself?'

Mel grimaced.

'He's still haunted by the bomb blast. When he's with me, he's supportive and kind, but I think he's making an effort. On his own, he gets depressed. He won't go to the doctor about it, even if he could get an appointment, and I think he might be drinking too much. The prosthesis hurts at times, although that should improve.'

'Oh shit. Have you said anything?'

'No, I wouldn't dream of it. His Tae Kwon Do has suffered,' continued Mel. 'He can't use the prosthesis, and sparring and chucking people about with one hand isn't easy. His skill at the sport meant a lot to him. It helped him rebut the suggestion that he was just a weedy computer geek. Being back at work has done his morale no end of good, though. He's beginning to feel happier now. At least, he says so.'

'Well, he certainly looked pleased at your wedding.'

'He knew he was on to a good thing, didn't he?' joked Mel. 'Seriously, we wondered whether it would ever happen, what with Covid and the bombing. But we're happy and the garden's looking great, since the SOCOs dug it over looking for Alan Fearon's remains and Tom got some shrubs in. We've had netting installed to make an outside aviary so Bruce and Sheila can fly around and play with parrot toys. How about you and Helen?'

'We're planning a wedding in a few months' time, if we can still stand each other.'

'What do you mean?'

'Helen's rented flat is cramped, and we keep getting in each other's way. Different shift patterns don't help either.'

'But you've been together for, what, two years? Surely, you've ironed out the creases by now?'

'Yeah. But we desperately need a place of our own with more space. No garden for us though. We can barely afford to buy a two-bed flat. A nurse's and a DC's salaries don't go far in this economic climate.'

'I know what you mean. Our mortgage is fixed but bugger knows what we'll do if it goes up a lot in a couple of years. And we can hardly afford to heat the place as it is. At least part of it has to be kept warm for the parrots, and Ernie the tortoise doesn't like it too cold, either.'

'You and your exotic pets,' grinned Sally. 'Should have just got a cat like we did.'

Mel pretended to scowl, but before she could say anything DC Trevor Blake came over, brushing biscuit crumbs from his jumper.

'You know the clinic was visited by Mr Raven's brother a couple of days ago?'

'Yes,' replied Mel. 'So what?'

'Well, I've been on to the Met and he didn't have a brother. His parents died some years ago and a sister was listed as his next of kin. She lives in Lancashire and hadn't spoken to him in months.'

'So that's how the killer knew about the uniforms, the layout and security at the clinic. He checked it out before he pretended to be called away. The devious bastard. We'd better let Jack know.'

'He left early,' said Trevor. 'An urgent personal matter, he said. And the guv's gone home. We'll save it for tomorrow's briefing.'

So that was it. Raven was dead. He stared again at the reports on the Internet, both public and official. Someone had cut his throat, and the police had no idea who was responsible or why. The material, if Raven had it, would most likely be at his home. It was too sensitive to keep in his office at the Yard. He would need to act fast, before the place was searched. Looking up Raven's address, he logged off and left work early, mentioning, in vague terms, a meeting. Hurrying along the Embankment to the tube station, his heart was pounding. He had hoped it wouldn't come to this. But he had the skills to do what was necessary, and do it he would. His liberty depended on it.

Chapter Sixteen

Day 9

Now for the charity CEO. He'd never liked people like that, going around begging money from people to give to causes he thought were pointless and people he thought were a waste of space. *This one helped those bloody illegal immigrants. He'll be no loss to society, that's for sure.* He opened his laptop, set up another project file and considered how he could get access to Dale Moncrieff.

As an MP, he could arrange to bump into him at some charity event or another, but perhaps meeting in public was not the best of ideas. An invitation could leave a trace, either electronically or in his target's diary, so he would have to think of another way. Would it be too risky to lure him to Mexton on some pretext, concealing his own identity and not actually meeting him? He would know the terrain better than Moncrieff's London district, and, if his own name wasn't directly associated with him, the chances of discovery would be minimised.

He clicked on Moncrieff's folder and perused it closely, working his way through the online information on his target he'd downloaded via Tor. *That's a possibility,* he thought. Moncrieff was a keen narrowboat sailor and kept his boat at a marina a dozen miles north of Highchester, where the canal joined the River Mex. Near enough for a midnight excursion, but not so close that a link with Mexton would automatically occur to the police. He was on the boat most weekends and at various other times during the week, presumably working there. It wasn't difficult to find out, via an anonymous phone call, that Moncrieff was already on the boat and would not return to London for several days.

He studied Google Maps and Street View, working out a plan of approach, and decided on a quick drive-by. He considered how he could make Moncrieff's death look like an accident and thought back to a dismal week he had spent on a narrowboat on the Norfolk Broads with his ex-wife, when they were trying to get away from the bustle of the city – a big mistake that started the process of their break-up. He remembered her yelling at him for something or other he'd done with the bottled gas cooker. He couldn't quite remember what. But then it came back to him. He had an idea. *Yes!* he thought. *That should work, and it wouldn't even look like murder.*

Ventham was pleased to find that security at the marina was minimal and that the lighting was sparse. He managed to squeeze through a gap in the fence, unseen by the single CCTV camera, and made his way to Moncrieff's boat while its owner was in Highchester, dining at L'Andouillette, the town's only Michelin-starred restaurant. No-one else seemed to be about; the craft in the marina were either unoccupied or closed up against the evening chill. His clothing was dark. He wore a baseball cap pulled low over his eyes, and thin leather gloves. Emboldened by his slaying of Raven, he moved quietly and confidently across the deck, his pulse barely raised.

The door to the cabin was padlocked, but pale moonlight showed that the screws holding the hasp were exposed. Big mistake. It only took him a couple of minutes to undo the screws, the screwdriver slipping slightly on the rusty heads, and remove the hasp. He flipped the tongue of the rim latch back with a credit card and slipped down the ladder into the cabin unseen.

The narrowboat was comfortably furnished, with cush-ioned benches, velvet curtains and a small flat screen TV, connected to a DVD player and fixed to the top of a bulkhead. Beyond the bulkhead was a small galley fitted with a gas cooker, a sink and a microwave. A drinks cupboard held a couple of cans of beer, some soft drinks and a bottle of twelve-year-old malt whisky. Reasoning that Moncrieff would be more likely to take a malt, rather than beer, after a heavy meal, Ventham tipped the contents of a small packet of ketamine, obtained from an obliging waiter at the House of Commons, into the spirit and swirled the bottle gently to dissolve the drug. Checking he hadn't disturbed anything else, he slipped out of the boat, replacing the hasp and screws as he left. He found a corner of the marina away from the feeble lighting and settled down to wait.

An hour later, cramped and cold, Ventham snapped to attention as a taxi dropped his target off outside the marina. Moncrieff fumbled with his keys and left the gate unlocked as he stumbled towards his boat. His progress onto the vessel and into the cabin was similarly uncoordinated and he left the door half open, with the padlock hanging loose, as he slid down the ladder. *Perfect!* Ventham waited for an hour and, almost silently, approached the boat. He crept in, making very little noise, and navigated his way through the cabin from memory.

Moncrieff's snores resonated through the vessel, and it was clear that nothing short of a sonic boom would wake him. Ventham unwrapped a scented candle, placed it on a small table beside his victim's bed, and lit it. He pocketed the wrapper, turned one of the cooker's gas taps full on, and loosened the connection with the propane cylinder. Gas hissed out and he moved quickly away. Closing the cabin door and snapping the padlock shut, he made his escape. He moved swiftly along the canalside path to the place where he had left his car. As he drove slowly away, the sky lit up behind him.

Chapter Seventeen

Day 10

'WHERE ARE we on Mr Raven's murder?' asked DCI Farlowe.

'We think we know how the killer got in,' replied Emma. 'He posed as a nurse, after pretending to be his brother and scoping the place out beforehand. There's nothing new from forensics. Trevor's been looking at ANPR cameras in the area, although there are only two which would have been useful.'

'Would have been?'

'Afraid so. One has been out of order for weeks, and several days ago a drunk driver crashed into the other and bent the post. All it can record is the occasional bird or bat, if they're big enough. Anyway, we've put out an appeal for dashcam footage from anyone driving in the area that night, but no one's come forward yet. I think I should postpone holding a briefing until we've got something concrete to discuss.'

'I'm inclined to agree, Emma. I've got to get some figures together for a budget meeting, so I'll get on with that. Keep me informed, please. Thanks.'

'Mel – can you and Sally take a look at an explosion on a boat?' Jack rubbed his eyes wearily as he addressed his colleague. 'At Babbacott Marina. It went up in the early hours. The fire service put the flames out, but there was a fatality.'

'Why us? Something suspicious?'

'The fire investigator thinks it was probably a drunken accident, but the boat was owned by a Dale Moncrieff and he was killed in the blast. He's well known for his charity work, apparently, so there could be a lot of publicity. The coroner's officer has been notified.'

Fire investigator Peter Dalgliesh greeted Mel and Sally as they picked their way past a pile of wreckage heaped on the canal bank. A smell of half-burnt diesel and charred wood hung in the morning air, and a mother duck hastily shepherded her seven charges past floating pieces of wood, avoiding the oil slick that oozed from the burnt-out narrowboat.

'Mind how you go,' he called. 'The bank's slippery from the foam our guys used and I don't recommend a swim in this mucky water.'

Mel grinned an acknowledgement.

'What do you reckon happened?' she asked.

'The gas cooker was turned on,' replied Dalgliesh, 'and the remains of a candle were plastered against the wall of the sleeping quarters. A possible scenario is that the deceased turned on the cooker to make a late-night snack, went away and lit the candle and either forgot the gas was on or fell asleep. When the drifting gas cloud met the candle, it all went up. Not supposed to happen, but I suppose it could. I found

71

the remains of a whisky bottle which implies he could have been drinking. The boat has a steel hull so it didn't sink, but the fire destroyed most of its contents. A couple of boat owners collected some of the wreckage from the water and put it on the bank. The Environment Agency will be along later to assess the damage to the waterway.'

'Anything suspicious?'

'Not that I've found, but that's for you to decide.'

'OK. Thank you, Mr Dalgliesh. I don't think we need to look any further. I'll notify my boss. The coroner will order a post-mortem anyway.'

Sally waved at the undertakers waiting in a private ambulance parked a dozen metres away, indicating that they could collect their grisly burden.

As the two detectives headed back along the canal bank, Mel tripped over a half-hidden piece of wood and steadied herself on a pile of wreckage. She frowned as her eyes drifted over the remains of the cabin door.

'Stop!' she shouted, halting the undertakers in their tracks. 'I think we have a crime scene.'

'Why do you think it's suspicious?' asked DI Thorpe, when Mel phoned her.

'The fire investigator described a perfectly credible accident scenario, guv, and we were just leaving when I noticed from the wreckage that the cabin door had been padlocked on the outside. I nearly fell over it, in fact. I don't see how that could have happened by accident. Somebody must have locked the padlock in place after Mr Moncrieff boarded the boat.'

'Hmm. Good spot, Mel. I'll send a forensic team and get

some uniforms down there to secure the scene. I'll come along myself later on. Don't let them remove the body yet.'

'Will do, guv, but I should warn you it's a forensic nightmare. Apart from fire and blast damage there's water and foam all over the place. Firefighters have trampled over the scene and other boat owners have handled the wreckage in an attempt to tidy up. It's a total bloody mess.'

'I suspected as much. OK. Keep everyone away and get the details of anyone who's been on site in case we need prints or samples for elimination. From what you're saying, we won't get anything useful, but we have to try. I'll tell Dr Durbridge that he's got another customer for his dissection table.'

Within an hour, officers had taped off the narrowboat and set up an outer cordon along the canal bank and approaching paths. A forensic team was busy photographing, sampling and collecting material from the boat, while uniformed officers searched the banks for physical evidence. The marina was closed for the day, and anyone already present was asked to stay on their craft until further notice. Once the SOCOs had finished inside the boat they moved on to the wreckage on the bank, Emma signalled to the undertaker and the burned and blasted body of Dale Moncrieff was zipped into a body bag and stretchered to the private ambulance.

Hugh Ventham slept late. Very late, aided by the copious quantity of whisky he had taken when he returned from his murderous mission. He woke during the afternoon from a half-dream, in which he re-enacted the previous night's activities. A jolt of terror speared him in the guts. The padlock. The bloody padlock. *Why the fuck did I put it back?* A stupid, automatic reaction, a leftover from securing the locker at the gym. *What if they found it? But surely the sodding boat will have been destroyed?* Yes, the chances of the police finding it and working out the significance were minimal. But, nevertheless, he couldn't shake the feeling that he had screwed up. Badly.

Chapter Eighteen

Day 11

'QUIET PLEASE,' called Emma, as the team took their seats for the morning briefing.

'We have a suspicious death on a narrowboat moored at Babbacott Marina. The deceased is Dale Moncrieff, CEO of the charity Welcome Relief UK which provides help to refugees. It looks as though a gas tap on his cooker was turned on deliberately and a candle was left burning in the sleeping accommodation. When the gas cloud reached the flame it exploded, killing the victim and setting fire to the boat.'

'Why didn't he notice?' asked Trevor. 'Surely the gas smells, so you can tell when there's a leak.'

'There's evidence suggesting he'd been drinking, and a nearby boat owner was disturbed by Moncrieff returning to the site by taxi, late in the evening. He was stumbling onto his boat, making a noise and fumbling with his keys. The witness thought he was drunk. The coroner would probably have gone for accidental death, but Mel spotted that the cabin was

75

padlocked on the outside. So, we think someone broke into the boat while Moncrieff was asleep, lit the candle and turned on the gas, hoping that the explosion and subsequent fire would not only kill his victim but destroy any evidence.'

'Why padlock the cabin?' asked Kamal. 'Surely he must have realised it would look suspicious?'

'Perhaps he thought Moncrieff might wake up,' suggested Jack. 'He probably thought the destruction from the fire and explosion would conceal what he'd done. Maybe he just did it automatically. Big mistake.'

'OK, folks,' said Emma. 'The PM is this afternoon and Dr Durbridge has promised a preliminary verbal report once he's finished. Samples and bits of wreckage have gone to labs, but the Crime Scene Manager is not hopeful that there will be any DNA or prints.

'We need to canvass boat owners who were at the marina for anything suspicious they might have seen, either on the night in question or during the previous few days. ANPR and speed cameras on roads around the marina need to be checked, and someone must trace the taxi driver. Find out how drunk Moncrieff was when he was dropped off, and was there anyone with him when he was picked up by the taxi? Did he eat at a restaurant? If so, talk to the staff. Trevor's started building up a profile of the man, but we need to talk to colleagues, friends and relatives to see if he had any enemies. So far, there appears no motive for his murder. Jack, can you sort out the jobs?'

'Yes, guv.'

'One thing, boss,' said Trevor. 'His charity helps refugees. Maybe it's some of those right-wing racists we dealt with a while back? There's been some nasty stuff on social media recently.'

'Could be, I suppose,' replied Emma. 'Their activities died down a bit for a while but built up again when the press started bigging up the asylum seekers issue. This sounds a bit sophisticated for those Neanderthals but it's worth considering, though. Perhaps Tom Ferris has come across something in his computer crime job, Mel? At least the current MP doesn't seem to share his predecessor's views. Thank you, everyone. I've a meeting to attend. Keep me posted, please, Jack.'

Chapter Nineteen

'HOW CAN I HELP YOU?'

Martin Rowse ushered Mexton Investigations' latest client into his office and invited him to sit down. The lanky young man, wearing casual clothes which gave off a sweetish aroma, brushed a lock of hair from his forehead and looked at Martin with a worried expression.

'I'm not sure you can, but I had to go somewhere for help. The police said they were too busy but they'd look into it if I had proof.'

'OK,' said Martin, opening an A4 notepad and clicking a pen bearing the company's logo. 'Let's start at the beginning. Your name's Steven Calthrop, and you have a problem, but that's all I know.'

'That's right. I'm the owner of Two-Fifty Honeys.' He indicated his T-shirt which bore the company name and the image of a large bee. 'And someone is trying to put me out of business.'

'How so? I know business is very competitive these days, but that sounds a bit extreme.'

'I started my company eight years ago, with a couple of hives on my allotment. Demand really took off, and I've expanded in recent years. I now have a small factory and employ several staff. You can't control where bees fly, obviously, but all the plants on my land are organically grown. I supply health food shops and cafés throughout the county, and also run a mail order service which delivers my honey to customers and businesses throughout the UK. I was doing very well until a couple of months ago when people started returning honey, claiming it had given them stomach aches or made them feel sick. I've lost several important contracts and I'm not sure how much longer I can keep going.'

'I'm not an expert,' said Martin, 'but could it be just a case of food poisoning? Bugs getting into the honey?'

Steven bridled.

'Everything in the factory is kept scrupulously clean. Bacteria don't grow in honey, but I've had samples tested by a microbiology lab and there were no harmful organisms present. It's true that honey sometimes contains spores which can cause botulism, which is why you shouldn't give it to babies, but my honey was clean – and it cost me a lot of money to prove this.'

'All right. Just checking,' apologised Martin. 'So, it's possible someone tampered with the products in the factory or the distribution system. Is there any kind of pattern to the illnesses? Were the returned jars all from the same batch or delivery?'

'I haven't had time to look in detail. I had a quick look and nothing obvious leapt out at me. But isn't that the sort of thing you do?'

Martin smiled encouragingly.

'Yes, of course. One more thing; is there anyone who might bear you a grudge?'

'Not really. There is competition in this market but it's not serious. People can't seem to get enough local honey instead of the stuff which you get in the supermarket, some of which is diluted with sugar solution anyway, so there's no major rivalry.'

Steven thought for a moment.

'Come to think of it, I did have a run-in with another firm. I made a comment in the local paper that much of the Manuka honey on sale is fake – if you look at the tonnage on sale world-wide and compare it with the tonnage actually made in New Zealand, there's a massive discrepancy. There's a lot of money in Manuka honey, which people are deluded into thinking is almost magical. Shortly afterwards, the managing director of Mexton Sweeteners, who sell a lot of it, turned up at the factory, effing and blinding and threatening to sue. As I didn't mention his firm by name, he had no grounds for a libel action, so I told him to get lost.'

'All right, Mr Calthrop. I'll certainly try to help. Here's a list of our terms and conditions, as well as a standard contract. If you're happy with them, and the charges, we can proceed, and I'll visit the factory in a day or so. Would you like some coffee while you read the documents?'

Steven nodded and grabbed the papers eagerly.

Chapter Twenty

Day 12

'So, what have we got?' asked Emma, when the team settled down. 'I've had the pathologist's report, and he found ketamine in Moncrieff's urine. Much of his viscera was squashed by the blast or burned, but Dr Durbridge managed to get enough from what was left of his bladder to carry out a screening test. It seems likely he was drugged as well as drunk.'

'Could he have taken it recreationally?' asked Sally.

'Possibly,' replied Emma, 'but he doesn't look like the partying sort, and he has no drug convictions.'

'Forensics have got back to us,' said Jack. 'No DNA or prints, anywhere. It looks like the suspect got into the marina through the fence. There's a smeared footwear mark in some mud next to a gap big enough to squeeze through. There's not enough detail to match with the footwear in the database, but it looked like a size ten to twelve.'

'Did they find anything else?'

'A few dark fibres caught on the fence. Synthetic and

extremely common,' Jack replied wearily. 'Not much use to us unless we can match them to a tear in a suspect's clothing. Also, there were fresh scratches on the padlock hasp and the screws fixing it.'

'Could that suggest that the killer visited the boat twice?' asked Trevor, sitting up eagerly. 'Perhaps he took the padlock and hasp off, put the ketamine in something Moncrieff was likely to eat or drink, replaced them and then returned later to set the explosion?'

'Quite possibly,' replied Jack. 'SOCOs said there was the remains of a bottle of whisky on the boat, but the lab said it was shattered in the blast and whatever was in it was destroyed in the fire. One thing, though. Cookers on boats are supposed to have a safety cut out so gas doesn't flow when there's no flame. The lab reckons the gas cylinder was tampered with, to let the gas out.'

'Thanks, Jack. Anything on CCTV, Trevor?' asked Emma.

'Nothing on the site, guv. ANPR on the main road picked up something odd, though. A VW SUV with plates that belonged to a Range Rover, owned by the landlord of a pub in Hereford called The Double Tap. It was driving south at one-thirty but wasn't picked up after that, so I'm assuming the driver changed the false plates and stuck to the back roads.'

Emma frowned and drummed her fingers in frustration.

'I talked to the taxi driver,' volunteered Sally, hoping to improve her boss's mood. 'He confirmed Moncrieff was drunk and stumbling a bit. He dropped him off just before midnight and there was no-one else with him. He'd been eating at L'Andouillette.'

'That bears out what the waiter at the restaurant told me,' said Mel. 'He arrived, dined and left without speaking to anyone apart from the staff, to whom he was perfectly friendly. He drank a bottle of wine with his meal and several brandies.'

'So, basically, we've got bugger all,' grumbled Emma. 'Anyone got any thoughts about a motive?'

'Still working on it, guv,' replied Kamal. 'So far, on social media everyone seems to have liked him, apart from racist internet trolls.' He grimaced. 'Tom Ferris is looking into them.'

'How about the profile, Trevor?'

'He seems pretty much to have been a model citizen. He's not on the PNC and there don't seem to have been any major scandals involving him. He worked for various charities, environmental and human rights, since leaving university and founded Welcome Relief UK when his wife, a human rights lawyer, was killed in an RTC. I spoke to his PA at the charity, and she said he was great to work for, had no enemies that she knew of, and everyone would miss him desperately. He had a full social life up in London, but also liked to spend some time alone, to relax and think. Hence the narrowboat.'

'Thanks, Trevor. He looks clean, but there must be a secret, somewhere. Keep digging, please.'

'Yes, boss.'

'OK, folks, it looks like we've nothing so far. Please, please find me something for tomorrow's briefing. Now go and get your coffee.'

Chapter Twenty-One

IT WAS chilly at the top of Paradise Tower, one of the newest monuments to Mammon in the redeveloped Docklands. Since the ban on vaping in the office, there were few places where Justin Kite could get his nicotine hit and, when the fancy took him, the odd toot of marching powder.

He also liked to come up here to think and, holding tightly to the steel rail enclosing the roof to quell his vertigo, to look down at his Lamborghini in the car park below. The sight of the car, bought with a couple of serious bonuses and the proceeds from a bit of insider trading, always reminded him that he was a success. But clouds were gathering. If there was a change of government, the oil and gas bonanza could dry up. Then what would he do?

Usually, he was alone with his thoughts and stimulants, but this time some maintenance guy, in a hi-vis jacket and a baseball cap, was aimlessly pushing a broom around. Why the roof needed sweeping he couldn't imagine. He was completely uninterested in how the building functioned, as long as the systems worked and he could make money.

Looking westwards, he smiled to himself at the modern skyscrapers which housed the new financial heart of the city. The Shard, the Cheesegrater, the Walkie Talkie – all symbols of wealth and progress. That was what it was all about. He had no time for the preservationists who tried to block the demolition of old buildings and stand in the way of the future. Fuck the Wren Society. They should have flattened the Square Mile and rebuilt years ago. And as for King Charles' famous remark about a carbuncle being built next to St Pauls...

His ruminations were interrupted when the workman in the hi-vis jacket approached him.

'You don't remember me, do you?' he said, his cultured accent contrasting with his menial appearance.

'Why on earth should I?' Justin replied. 'I hardly think we move in the same circles.'

Nevertheless, there was a slight flicker of recognition. He couldn't place the face but maybe...?

The massive blow in his solar plexus doubled him over and made him vomit. He heard his attacker mention two words: Marnie's party. Powerless to resist, he felt his legs scooped up from under him and the scraping of the rail across his back. Terror gripped him as he started to fall. He wet himself and barely noticed the wind whistling through his Paul Smith suit as he tumbled thirty floors onto the unforgiving roof of his precious Lamborghini.

Unhurriedly, Ventham replaced the broom in the window-cleaners' cradle and descended the service stairs, keeping the cap pulled low over his eyes, until he reached the ground floor. Pausing on a deserted landing, he slipped the jacket and cap into a jute bag, from an upmarket department store, replaced his hat and glasses, and sauntered out through reception. He handed the visitor's badge and lanyard in at the reception desk and smiled.

'Waste of bloody time. The lad couldn't help me after all.'

The receptionist nodded sympathetically and, within five minutes, had completely forgotten the bespectacled, tweed-clad gentleman with a Yorkshire accent, the howling sirens of the ambulance and police cars arriving outside drawing his attention.

A small crowd of horrified office workers had gathered at the side of the building where Justin had landed, gawping at the mess which remained of the financier. Several of them had vomited. Ventham walked swiftly in the opposite direction and, ducking into a side alley, pulled a light-coloured rain jacket over his suit. He dispensed with the glasses, removed his moustache and replaced his trilby with the baseball cap. Ten minutes later, he was on a Docklands Light Railway train, heading back towards town and the security of his flat.

Chapter Twenty-Two

A SWEET, almost sickly, aroma hung over the Two-Fifty Honeys plant and permeated the small office that overlooked the packing area. Martin watched as honey was filled into labelled jars, the lids were screwed on, and the final products were packed into cardboard boxes bearing the company's name and a picture of a church tower.

'Why Two-Fifty?' asked Martin, as he sat down at a spare desk and picked up a pile of complaints forms.

'It's that poem by Rupert Brooke,' replied Steven. 'The Old Vicarage, Grantchester. "Stands the clock at ten to three / And is there honey still for tea?"' he recited.

'My wife's an English graduate and she suggested the name.'

'Oh, right. I think I remember it from school, but I never really got into poetry. Now, I'll go through these complaints and see if there's a pattern. I'll need a list of employees, including those who've left recently. I take it there've been no problems with staff?'

'None at all. They're a happy crew and I trust them

completely. It sounds like a cliché, but we are a bit like a family. We've got a couple of temps in, one covering for a woman on maternity leave and one for a driver who broke his leg in a rugby match. I'd hoped to be able to give them permanent jobs, but then this trouble came along, so I may even have to lay off staff.'

Martin smiled sympathetically.

'OK. Well get me the list and I'll get to work. Perhaps you would show me round the place when everyone's gone home?'

'Glad to, and I'll bring you some coffee.'

———

Two hours later, Martin called to Steven.

'I've been through these forms and checked for patterns. I'm afraid I can't find any. The only thing these complaints have in common is that they refer to set honey rather than clear. The batch numbers, which you helpfully noted, are all different and the problem jars were sold in several different shops. So, if we're looking for some kind of contamination, which seems most likely, it must have happened after the honey was filled into the jars, but before it was received by the retailers.'

'So, you're thinking an employee added something to random jars in the storage room and they ended up in different places?'

Steven paced agitatedly around the room.

'That seems a distinct possibility. Also, if someone opened the jars, they would need to replace the paper safety strips that run across the lids, which also suggests someone who works here is doing it. Do you have any CCTV?'

Steven shook his head.

'I don't like the idea of snooping on staff. They're allowed regular free jars, so I don't think anyone would pilfer stock.'

Martin sat back in his chair.

'OK, but it's something to consider. The big question, though, is what could someone be adding to the honey that would give people stomach aches and not be detected? You could get the affected jars analysed but you'd need to tell the lab what to look for. When I was in the police, we had a serial poisoning case in Mexton. I'll chat to a former colleague and see if anything like this came up. Don't worry,' he said, when Steven's eyes widened in alarm. 'The poisoner's safely locked up.'

'Thanks. I appreciate it. If you'd like that tour now, I'll show you around. You'll need hair covering, an overall and booties. Ready?'

The tour of the factory took barely more than half an hour, which left Martin some time to look through the staff lists before he left for home. None of the names rang alarm bells with him, not that he could have said anything to Steven if they had committed offences, but it helped him to know that there weren't any out-and-out villains on the staff.

'Where did you get your temps from?' he asked Steven, as he prepared to leave.

'An agency, Mextemps. I checked their references and they seemed fine. As I said, I would have liked to have kept them on.'

'Hmm. I'll do some digging myself tomorrow. In the meantime, can you rack your brains for anyone who might have a personal grudge against you or your family? Someone you've upset outside work?'

'I'll talk it over with Ginny, my wife, tonight. But I don't think there is anyone.'

I don't think so, either, thought Martin, as he climbed into his sports car. *Steven's too mild-mannered and friendly to put people's backs up. Still, appearances can be deceptive.*

Nine weeks previously

Money for old rope, this, he thought. *Get a few jars off the shelf, stir in some of these shiny white crystals, and swap them over in the deliveries. Make sure they go to different places and don't leave fingerprints on the jars. A bit of mischief, the bloke said, and one he was prepared to pay for. Mind you, it wasn't a fortune. Nothing like enough to clear his debt with the bookies. But, like the supermarket said, every little helps. And the next bet is bound to be a winner.*

Chapter Twenty-Three

Day 13

BEING CALLED out to the solvent recovery plant on a hot day when he was supposed to be on holiday was not Mark Sutton's idea of a good time. He had intended to spend the afternoon in the garden, drinking beer while his wife worked on the flower beds. But, as the owner, and the only senior person in the country at that moment, he had little option but to abandon his shorts and T-shirt for more formal dress and head down the motorway to Mexton.

The Mexton Solvent Services plant had been closed for the past few weeks, following enforcement action by the Environment Agency. *Meddling bureaucrats,* he fumed. The solvent escapes from the site into the River Mex were nothing compared to the sewage discharges from the local water treatment works. It was costing thousands to re-route the drainage to a treatment pond and replace the soil contaminated by leakage from the crack in the ancient iron pipe. *Water companies seemed to have carte blanche to pollute, while entrepre-*

neurs like himself had to watch their step, he grumbled to himself. *And he'd always tried to be one of the good guys, doing something useful for the environment.*

It was pure bad luck that some meddling angler reported the company to the Agency, which hadn't had the staff to inspect the plant in years. Now, someone from the EA was insisting that a person in authority should meet an inspector at the site immediately, to deal with complaints of a strong solvent odour emanating from the premises, and he had drawn the short straw. Most of his employees were away on a stag do in Prague, without their wives and partners, and he thought wistfully back to the hedonism of his younger years. Still, he was happily married now. If he needed an engineer to sort out the problem, he would know who to call. Hopefully, he would be able to return to his beer before the afternoon was over.

Arriving at the site, his first thought was: *what's all the fuss about?* Certainly, there was a smell of solvents, but it was far from strong. When the plant was in operation, the odour was much more pronounced, but that, at least, complied with the environmental permit conditions and no-one on the small industrial estate complained.

Sloppy, he thought, as he noticed the padlock hanging, unfastened, on the main gate. *I'll give someone a bollocking for that.* He pushed the gate open, pulled a hi-vis jacket from the BMW's boot and, leaving his car outside, entered the site to await the arrival of the official who'd called him. A clattering sound to the rear of the thin-film evaporator plant caught his ear and he advanced towards it, purposefully.

'Who's there?' he called. 'This is a hazardous industrial site. No-one's allowed here without permission.'

There was no reply. *This is wrong,* he thought to himself, feeling chilly despite the warm sun. He walked slowly towards the source of the noise, wondering whether he should contact the police about a possible break-in. *Nonsense. He was being paranoid. They wouldn't be interested, anyway.*

As he rounded the corner of the structure, he heard a slight chuckle and something hard and heavy struck him on the back of the neck. Pain flared and he fell to his knees, unable to resist when a powerful arm slipped across his throat from behind. He flapped his arms feebly and tried to reach behind him, hitting only air. Terrified he tried to kick backwards with one leg, but only succeeded in falling sideways, taking his assailant with him. The arm began to crush his windpipe. His chest hurt as he struggled to breathe. His vision darkened and consciousness slipped away.

He didn't feel himself being dragged over to a stack of solvent drums, or hear the lid of one vessel being levered off. He was oblivious to the tide of liquid poured over him and didn't hear a match striking. But the searing pain as the solvent ignited briefly roused him until, screaming, he lapsed into a sleep from which he would never wake.

The fire burned well into the evening as solvent containers burst and caught fire. Explosions threw burning drums over the rooftops of adjacent premises and several secondary fires developed. Clouds of foul-smelling smoke rose into the sky and, on cooling, descended to ground level and drifted over Mexton. The usual evening starlings found somewhere else to murmurate. The emergency services were deluged with calls and residents were advised by Environmental Health to keep windows closed and remain indoors until the fumes dispersed. It wasn't until the following morning that the fire service pronounced it safe for the police and the Health and Safety

Executive inspector to enter the site. The remains of Mark Sutton were not discovered until the early afternoon.

Another job well done, he thought. The massive conflagration at the plant was unintended – he had just wanted to make sure Sutton was dead and forensic traces were obscured. But the total destruction of the site meant that any clues as to how his victim had died would have been completely obliterated. Accidents happen at industrial sites all the time, he thought, so the chances of his efforts being identified as murder were minimal. With every death he felt more secure, but there was still more to do. But haunting him, always at the back of his mind, were the questions of the Polaroid and the possible seventh guest.

Chapter Twenty-Four

'So what's this bloke doing, face-planting on a Lambo from thirty floors up? I gather it was his own car.'

Carl Plover, a detective constable in the Metropolitan Police, scratched at a patch of stubble his shaver had missed and waited for his sergeant to reply.

'Looks like suicide, but we won't know until the inquest. Pathologist had a rummage through the bits, but all he would say officially was that he died from massive trauma consequent upon a fall from a great height. Off the record, he said that he could have been knocked off the roof by a charging elephant and he wouldn't have been able to tell.'

'That's bleedin' helpful. So why are we interested?'

'There's no obvious reason for him to top himself. His name's Justin Kite. He worked for Vatten-Cooley, a Norwegian-Irish finance firm which specialises in putting up the money for oil and gas developments. With this new free-for-all in the North Sea, the firm is on the up and big bonuses are expected. He was flush and, according to his husband, had no problems at home. The doc found traces of charlie in his blood but nothing else. There was a pool of sick near where he took off, but he couldn't give an explanation for it.'

'So, what do you want me to do?'

'Have another chat with his husband. Poor sod not only lost his mate, but their flat was also turned over while he was at work. Total mess. Talk to his colleagues as well. See if there's anyone who had a grudge against him – apart from the eco-mob of course, who hate the whole firm. It's possible that someone lifted him over the fence on the roof and dropped him, but there's no forensics or CCTV up there. Get a list of visitors in the hours before he took flight – you've a nose for oddities, so see what you can find. Don't spend more than a couple of days on it, though.'

'OK, sarge. I'll start with his colleagues and check who the visitors came to see. Could be something there. There must be some CCTV in the building.'

'Right. Get on with it and let me know what you find. I'll tell the DI what's happening.'

DC Plover chucked his paper coffee cup in the rubbish bin, brushed biscuit crumbs off his suit and thought, morosely, that the suits Kite and his colleagues wore probably cost more than two months of his salary.

Chapter Twenty-Five

Day 14

'JACK, there's a Moira Brook on the phone. From the Health and Safety Executive. She wants to talk to someone about the fire at the solvent plant.'

'OK. Put her through.'

Jack reached for a notepad.

'Good morning, Ms Brook. DS Jack Vaughan here. How can I help you?'

'Hello. I've just had a meeting with Peter Dalgliesh, the fire investigator. We have grave suspicions about the fire at Mexton Solvent Services. We can't see how it could have started accidentally.'

'Why's that? Surely there's loads of flammable stuff there.'

'That's true, but the plant had been shut down for some time because of pollution issues. The power was off, and no processing was taking place, so there should have been nothing going on that could cause a fire in the event of a malfunction. I've talked to Gavin Ward, the inspector from the Environment Agency, and there was nothing on the site which could have combusted spontaneously. So, it looks like the fire was started deliberately. I understand there was a fatality?'

'Yes,' replied Jack. 'The owner. Mark Sutton. His wife said he had been called to the plant by someone from the Environment Agency because of an odour problem.'

'That's odd. Gavin didn't mention anything about an odour. He was concerned about solvents contaminating the river. Anyway, as I said, the plant wasn't operating and there shouldn't have been much of a smell. We will be conducting a thorough investigation, but you might like to send some of your forensic people along as well.'

'Thank you, Ms Brook. I'll talk to my DI and we'll be in touch. I think we should work together on this one, pool expertise, as it were.'

'Absolutely, DS Vaughan. And it's Moira.'

'OK. And it's Jack.'

'Why would anyone want to kill the owner of a recycling plant?' asked Emma, when Jack told her of his phone call with Moira Brook.

'No idea. But he was definitely lured there. No-one from the EA phoned him, I checked.'

Emma sighed.

'OK. I'll notify Mr Farlowe. He'll open an investigation. It would be useful to have some background information on the victim and the firm before the first briefing. Can you organise it?'

'Will do.' Jack hesitated. 'Emma,' he asked, 'how are you doing? I hope you don't mind me mentioning it, but you look incredibly tired.'

'No, that's OK, Jack. Genevieve is wonderful but she's keeping us up at night. I'm bloody exhausted but I'm not giving up the job. I'm sure things will settle down eventually. It is difficult, though, switching from murders and mayhem to nurturing a young baby, but she does lighten the darkness.'

'It's easier once they get over the six months mark. At least, it was with ours.'

Jack tried to smile reassuringly.

'Anyway, you and Sarah have got your own problems. Any news?'

'No, nothing yet. But thanks.' He stood up. 'Right, things to do, enquiries to be made.'

Emma smiled as Jack left and picked up her phone to call DCI Farlowe.

'So, what did you find, Birdy?'

'Not a lot, sarge,' Plover replied. 'As you said, there was no reason for Kite to jump off the roof. Home, work, and social relationships were all cushti. I spoke to a whole wunch of bankers and they all said he was hard-working and happy in the job. The only odd thing I found is a visitor to the building who can't be accounted for. He signed in at the desk as a Mr George Arkwright and gave an address in Bradford. West Yorkshire police checked it and no-one there had heard of him. The receptionist remembered the bloke – they don't get many people with Yorkshire accents there – and said he claimed to have an appointment with a financial advisor on the thirteenth floor. The receptionist gave him a pass and let him through the barrier without checking, as he said he was desperate for the toilet and would find his own way up afterwards. The financier in question had never heard of him.'

'That's promising. Anything else?'

'We've got images from the CCTV in reception and the lift banks. He did go up to the thirteenth floor but, a few minutes later, took another lift to the top. There's no recording of him going up to the roof and I think he must have used the service stairs to get back to reception. The guy on the desk remembers him saying something about wasting his time.'

'Did the cameras get his face?'

'Yeah. A few blurry images, but he had a hat pulled down fairly low and a 'tache, which was probably false, and glasses. I'll get the facial recognition guys to run the pics through their system, but I don't hold out much hope. It's all over social media and the tabloids, though. Cracks about "flying kites" or "bouncing kites".'

'Bouncing? No-one calls cheques kites any more, do they?'

'Well, *The Star* does. Heartless bastards all of them. Still, bankers are almost as unpopular as estate agents to some people. There was nothing of any use to us on the socials, though.'

'Nice work, Birdy. I'll tell the DI. He'll notify the coroner's office and declare it a suspicious death. Looks like we'll be getting some overtime out of this,' chuckled DS Fenton, reaching for his phone.

Chapter Twenty-Six

Day 15

'YOUR ATTENTION, PLEASE, LADIES AND GENTLEMEN,' called DCI Farlowe, at the start of the morning briefing. 'This is the first briefing of Operation Flashpoint, the inquiry into the suspicious death of Mark Sutton in an arson attack at Mexton Solvent Services. Can you summarise what we've got please, Jack?'

'Yes, guv. At 4.05 in the afternoon, two days ago, the fire service was called to a blaze at the recycling plant. By the time they arrived, the fire was well underway and it took them six hours to extinguish it. They also had to deal with fires at other nearby industrial premises, where burning drums of solvent, ejected from the main fire, had spread the flames. Fortunately, none of them was serious. The only fatality was the owner of the plant, Mark Sutton, whose remains were found near what the fire investigator estimated was the point of origin of the blaze.'

'What exactly do they do there?' interrupted Sally.

Jack frowned and consulted his notes.

'Various chemical processes which take used solvents and clean them up so they can be reused. Very green. That's all I know. The site is registered with the Health and Safety Executive and has a permit from the Environment Agency.'

'Why is the death suspicious?' asked Kamal.

'Firstly, my contact at the HSE said it was unlikely that the fire would have started accidentally, particularly as the plant wasn't operating at the time. Secondly, the fire investigator placed the point of origin at a storage bay for drums of solvent. There's no credible reason for them catching fire spontaneously.'

'So, arson, then,' said Mel, 'but what was Mark Sutton doing there?'

'We think he was lured there. Trevor, you were looking at the phone call that summoned him to the site?'

'Yes, Jack. His wife picked up Mark's phone and answered the call, which came from an unidentified number. The voice was male, polite and seemed educated. No discernible regional accent. We haven't been able to trace the call. Probably a burner.'

'What do we know about Mr Sutton?' asked Farlowe.

Kamal replied.

'He did a degree in chemical engineering at Imperial College and worked for various waste management companies in different parts of the country. During this time, he did an MBA with the Open University and, with the aid of a small legacy and some input from venture capitalists, bought the old waste treatment site which he upgraded to a state-of-the-art recycling plant. It was closed down a few weeks ago for repairs, as chemicals were leaking into the river, but, otherwise, it has a good environmental record. He employed eight staff, and had a wife but no children. That's all we've got, so far.'

'Thank you, Kamal,' said the DCI. 'I've had a preliminary report from Dr Durbridge. He couldn't carry out much of a postmortem because the fire was so intense. He was unable to say whether the fire started before or after Sutton died – there was nothing left of his respiratory tract to test for smoke inhalation. He could have been strangled, stabbed, bludgeoned or poisoned beforehand – there was no way of telling, so no cause of death could be determined. However, given that Sutton was lured to the site under false pretences, and the fire was non-accidental, we are treating this as murder. The inquest will be opened and then adjourned.

'So, we need to look more into Mr Sutton's background to see if he had any enemies or business rivals. Talk to family and friends. Interview the employees. Try again to locate that call. Check for ANPR around the site. Look at financials. I'll leave it to you to allocate actions, Jack. Thank you everyone.'

Chapter Twenty-Seven

'Hı, MATE. HOW ARE YOU DOING?' said Mel, answering Martin's call. 'What's it like in the private sector?'

'Safer,' he replied, 'but more boring. I miss the excitement of taking down serious villains, but at least no-one's trying to stab me or cut my brakes. How about you?'

'Not too bad. There are still aftershocks from that Albanian business but people are generally coping. You must come and join us in the pub one evening.'

'I'd like that. But I'm ringing to ask a favour.'

'Oh, I thought you just wanted to hear my dulcet tones?' teased Mel.

'Of course. But I'm looking at a possible food contamination case and I was thinking about that poisoner we had a while back. Do you remember if any of the stuff that was used caused stomach upsets and headaches?'

'Not offhand. I think Jenny Pike had headaches from the mercury she breathed in, but I can't be sure. Why don't you ask Dr Durbridge?'

'Yeah, I could, but I know he's always busy. I just wondered if anyone on the team knew.'

'Well, I'll ask around and I'll try to have a word with our friendly pathologist. And I'll let you know about a pub visit. I think a few of us are going to watch Jack do one of his pub quizzes next month, sometime.'

'Sounds good. Thanks Mel. Great to talk to you.'

'You too. Stay safe.'

Mel smiled as she ended the call. She had always liked Martin and was sorry to see him leave the force, although she understood his reasons. Getting stabbed and blown up was bound to traumatise anyone, and for someone with a young family it was much worse. She hoped he was happy in civvy street.

Three hours later an email pinged into Martin's inbox.

Dr Durbridge said it could be a number of things, possibly a metallic poison. There's a link at the bottom to a lab which can carry out chemical analyses but he said they're not cheap. Cheers, Mel.

Martin quickly typed his thanks and reported his findings to Steven.

'So where do we go from here?' his client asked.

'Knowing what it is, if, in fact, we can find out, is only part of the solution. If tampering is going on we need to find out who's doing it, otherwise it will keep on happening.'

'It bloody is. We had two more jars returned, with complaints, this morning, along with threats to report us to Trading Standards and the press. That would ruin us.'

'All right. I've looked through your staff list and checked references. So far, they're all fine. My next step is to talk to everyone and see how they react to the suggestion that some-one's poisoning the honey. Did you have any thoughts about people with a personal grudge?'

'Yes. The only one I could come up with, apart from the Mexton Sweeteners guy, was a farmer adjacent to one of the fields I rent, where my bees forage. I have some hives there. He was using a neonicotinoid insecticide on his crops during the time it was banned. I argued with him and eventually reported him to Defra, but nothing happened. He was furious, though, and threatened to spray the bees directly. That stuff is lethal to them. I put up a CCTV camera to deter him and that seems to have done the trick, although I still sometimes find rubbish dumped on my land. Of course, now the government has legalised neonicotinoids the bastard can spray them as much as he likes.'

Steven sounded uncharacteristically bitter.

'I'll have a chat to him, but he's under no obligation to speak to me,' said Martin. 'In the meantime, I'll get on with interviewing your staff.'

'Are you still listening to those history podcasts?' Martin asked his wife as they sat down to their evening meal.

'Of course,' replied Alice. 'I'm really hooked. I may even do a history degree with the Open University. When Rosie's off to school, I'll have the time, even if I go back to work for half the week.'

'What's today's topic?'

'The Roman Empire. Here's a question for you. Why do you think it declined?'

'I dunno. History was never my strong point. Foreign wars? Inbred emperors? Syphilis? You're gonna have to tell me.'

'Lead poisoning.'

'Really? Oh, hang on, didn't they have lots of lead pipes? My mum said she had hers replaced in the eighties. But surely that wouldn't cause the collapse of an empire?'

'It wasn't the pipes. It was the wine. They used to add something called sugar of lead to wine to sweeten it. It affected the brains of the ruling class and sent them mad. Or so the theory goes.'

'Interesting. Hey, this pork is really good. I think we've got a nice Chianti to go with it.'

Alice smiled and fetched a couple of glasses.

Chapter Twenty-Eight

'Do I know you?'

Madeleine Hollis looked up from the legal document on the bar table in front of her, clearly irritated at being interrupted.

'Well, you used to. Hugh Ventham. Mayfair 2007.'

'Oh Christ.' She flushed a deep pink. 'I've tried to forget that party. I've moved on from all that.'

Ventham smiled. 'Yes, but it was fun, wasn't it?'

She bit her lip and smiled slightly. 'I suppose so. I've never told anyone else about it and I read somewhere that the hostess was murdered not so long ago. I've been terrified of blackmail ever since I was called to the Bar.'

'I know what you mean. I was relieved when she died. Just down the road, in fact, in a side alley. Look, can I get you another drink? You can tell me what brings you to a wine bar in Mexton.'

'OK. Malbec, please. A large one. I'm defending a fellow lawyer accused of murder. I was at uni with him and he contacted me out of the blue. I have a bit of a reputation for winning difficult cases, so he wanted me to help.'

Ventham stood up to get the drinks. He handed the barman a twenty-pound note and, as the young man turned away to the till, swiftly moved his hand over Madeleine's wine, dropping a pinch of white powder into the dark liquid.

'So, what have you been doing with yourself?' Madeleine asked, as he put the drinks on the table. 'An MP, aren't you?'

'Yes. The local one, in fact. I got the seat in a by-election after the other chap committed suicide. Got caught doing something nasty and couldn't face the music, apparently. His brother, the Home Sec, was murdered by a madwoman. Horrible business.'

'Yes, I read about that.' Madeleine took a large gulp of her wine. 'No-one's safe these days. The police are too busy arresting people for insulting gays and hanging up gollies in pubs to chase murderers. Mind you,' she grinned, 'I shouldn't complain. I make much of my living from murderers. There's still plenty out there.'

Ventham laughed and sipped his own drink. 'So where are you based? Still in London?'

'No. My chambers are in Bristol. It's a great city and there's plenty of crime to keep me busy. What about you?'

'I'm in London much of the time. I've got a few directorships which keep me busy. I pop down here for the occasional surgery when I have to, but I've got a girl who sends out standard letters and fobs off the more irritating constituents. There's the odd opening or gala dinner to attend, and the infrequent constituency party meetings, but I really don't have to be here much.'

'Married?'

Madeleine drained her glass and looked at him curiously.

'Divorced. Nearly didn't get the seat because the party

likes its MPs to be family men. But, following the scandal which caused the by-election, there wasn't much interest. They were glad to have me. Anyway, I've been tipped for a ministerial post, so they're obviously happy. How about you? Anyone special?'

'Not at the moment. Divorced, like you, but no kids. It's a high-pressure job and, even in the twenty-first century, women are held to higher standards than men. I've no time for a serious relationship.'

For another dozen minutes the two people chatted, Ventham watching Madeleine carefully.

'Where are you planning to eat?' he asked.

'Sorry. What did you say?'

Madeleine looked confused and her speech slurred slightly.

'Are you OK?' asked Ventham, his voice radiating concern.

'Feel a bit odd. Should have had some food before the wine. I'll get room service when I get back to the hotel.'

'Let me get you a taxi. Here, I'll help you with your things.'

He gathered up the documents on the table and slid them into the lawyer's briefcase which he tucked under his arm. The glass he had been drinking from went into his pocket, unseen by the bar staff. He helped Madeleine to her feet and guided her out of the bar, taking care to turn his face away from the CCTV camera over the door.

'Look, taxis are hard to come by at this time of night. My car's just along the road. Let me give you a lift.'

Madeleine nodded slowly.

'Er. Thanks. Yes. I'm at the Excellent, um Escalator, I mean Excelsior.'

'That's fine. I'll have you there in ten minutes.'

Madeleine leaned on Ventham's shoulder as she stumbled along, looking as though she'd had far too much to drink. The

MP helped her into the back of his car, checked that the child locks were on, and drove quickly but unobtrusively through a series of back streets, free of CCTV and ANPR cameras.

A confused slurring came from the back seats.

'Where are we? Don't recognise way to hotel.'

'It's OK. Roadworks. Just a bit of local knowledge. Relax.'

Ventham looked in his mirror and noted, with satisfaction, that Madeleine was slipping into unconsciousness. Two minutes later, he pulled into a disused yard, adjacent to the canal towpath. He put on a pair of vinyl gloves, climbed into the back seat and fastened his hands around Madeleine's neck. She didn't stir as he compressed her carotid arteries, cutting off the blood supply to her brain. Within four minutes she was dead.

On his previous visit, he had noticed various pieces of rusting scrap iron in a corner of the yard. It was a matter of moments to tie a few kilos of metal to Madeleine's body with some discarded pieces of rope. Checking that there were no joggers or dog walkers on the towpath, he dragged the corpse to the canal and heaved it in, stepping back as the mucky water splashed over his expensive suit trousers. Satisfied that nothing was visible at the surface, he got back into his car and drove home, again avoiding cameras where possible. He would get the vehicle thoroughly cleaned and valeted in the morning, and his suit. But tonight, he could sleep easy, knowing that another witness to his misbehaviour would be unable to talk.

Chapter Twenty-Nine

Day 16

'HOW WAS THE DECEASED FOUND?' asked Trevor, gazing at the body bag which lay on a trolley, en route to a private ambulance.

'The Scouts were doing a sponsored canal clean, fishing for supermarket trolleys and so on,' replied Jack. 'One of them snagged some clothing and he and his mate hauled the body out. It had lumps of iron tied to it, so it took two of them. They were pretty shocked, as you can imagine, and the Scoutmaster is trying to calm them down.'

'Obviously foul play then,'

'Well, there wouldn't be sodding cordons and a crime scene log if it wasn't,' snapped Jack. 'And we wouldn't be wearing these bloody suits.' He paused. 'Sorry. Didn't mean to be short with you. I doubt that there'll be much forensic evidence. Half a troop of Scouts marched through here, as well as a couple of vehicles churning up the dirt, but the SOCOs have been looking for tyre tracks and footwear marks anyway. Nothing doing, so far.'

'Do we know who the victim is?'

'SOCOs found a driving licence in the name of Madeleine Hollis and a key card from the Excelsior Hotel. You're not needed here, so get over there, talk to the staff and take a look at her room. When you get back to the station, start building up a profile. You're good at this internet stuff. Off you go.'

'Will do, Jack,' replied Trevor, puzzled by Jack's uncharacteristic abruptness.

Stuck behind a clapped-out lorry that was pumping out Stygian clouds of partly-burned diesel, Martin reflected on how much it had cost him to modify his classic sports car to run on unleaded petrol. Lead again, he thought. Obviously bad for the brain. A thought began to crystallise but vanished when he saw the opportunity to overtake, so he put his foot down and shot past the filthy lorry which bore the slogan 'Mexton Waste Services – working for a cleaner environment'. Ten minutes later he was at Two-Fifty Honeys, with no recollection of what he had been thinking about.

'First off," reported Martin as he addressed a worried Steven, early that afternoon, 'the farmer refused to talk to me. When I mentioned the insecticides, he accused me of being a green terrorist, whatever that means.'

Steven grinned ruefully.

'Yes, he's a bit of a dinosaur.'

'I've talked to all the staff,' continued Martin. 'Nearly all seemed horrified at the idea that someone could be adding something noxious to the honey and couldn't see how it would happen. They obviously take pride in the product.'

'So no-one unhelpful, then?'

'Not really. The temporary driver seemed a bit indifferent and said he had nothing to do with making the honey, and the other temp said she didn't see why she should answer my questions as I wasn't a police officer. She did eventually. One of the women went off at me, claiming I was accusing her of betraying you and poisoning people. All I did was ask her if she knew how something noxious could have found its way into the jars. I didn't imply she was responsible.'

'Ah. That would be Janet. She doesn't so much take offence from a situation as extract it with an industrial juicing machine. I'll go and have a word with her. Put her mind at rest.'

When Steven left, Martin opened his laptop and started making notes. He glanced again at Mel's email, and the thought he had lost on the way in came back to him. *A metallic poison. Lead. Sugar of lead. Could that be the substance someone was putting in the honey? Lead's a metal, after all, and a sweet taste could easily be hidden in honey.* He looked up the lab's website on Mel's email, noted down the phone number, and made a call. Then he Googled the early symptoms of lead poisoning. Stomach pains, headaches – that fitted with the complaints.

'Steven,' he called, as his client passed the office door. 'I think I'm on to something. It could be lead acetate, otherwise known as sugar of lead. I've spoken to this lab and they can analyse the honey for it. This is how much it'll cost.'

Steven winced at the price but agreed they should go ahead with the tests, so Martin packed up three returned jars of suspect product and, at the end of the day, took them to the post office. *That's the means*, he thought, *but we still need motive and opportunity*.

Returning to collect his car, and lost in thought, Martin didn't notice the figure following him. As he turned into the deserted narrow road that led to the factory, he heard footsteps behind him. He tried to turn. Too late. There was a brief whooshing sound. His head exploded with pain and he fell to the floor, unconscious.

This is bloody odd, he thought. *Raven, Kite, Moncrieff, and Sutton, suddenly dead in suspicious circumstances, if not outright murder. Something's going on. Another player, perhaps?* Not believing in coincidence had kept him ahead of the game throughout his career and he wasn't about to start now. First, he would need to do some search and recovery. Failing that, destruction. Then he would check on the others. Maybe take some direct action himself. Regrettably, that would make him show his hand, but it might be necessary. He had the feeling that things were unravelling and that made him very uneasy indeed.

Chapter Thirty

'YOU'VE BEEN in the wars, mate. What happened?'

Mel Cotton greeted Martin in the A&E department as he waited to be seen by a doctor.

'Someone hit me from behind. No idea who. I was walking back to Two-Fifty Honeys and bang! And I thought being a private detective would be safer than being on the force.'

'But how are you feeling? What have the doctors said?'

'I've got a sore patch on my scalp and a bloody awful headache. The nurse took a look, said I'm not concussed, and now I'm waiting for a doctor to check the results of a CT scan and clear me to go home. Alice will collect me when I'm ready.'

'Nonsense. I'll take you back myself. You'll need to give a formal statement, obviously, but you can do that at home. Anyway, you think this was something to do with the job you're on?'

'That or another one, but most of my work has been on divorces and minor fiddles. This food tampering case has been a bit more interesting. I really miss the Job. It wasn't a mugging

– my phone and wallet weren't taken – so I assume someone was trying to warn me off. Or worse.'

'But you're looking at contaminated honey, not stolen diamonds or heroin. It's hardly high stakes, is it? More Midsomer than mafia.'

Martin grinned, despite his discomfort.

'That's what I thought. But there is money in fake Manuka honey and Steven, the firm's owner, seriously pissed off a competitor when he raised the issue in the press. I'm thinking that someone there could be behind the tampering. I've no proof yet, but there is someone I need to look at more closely.'

'Do you want us to get involved? I mean, we're stretched, as usual, but if this is really happening, and isn't just some kind of mistake, it's a serious offence. As well as the attack on you.'

'I'll let you know how I get on. When I've got something concrete, I'll bring it to you. Now, it looks like the doctor's calling me so, if you don't mind waiting, I'll take you up on your offer of a lift.'

One floor above, Nigel Willstone gathered up his personal belongings and prepared to discharge himself from the hospital. His leg still hurt but the fire in his healing wound was nothing compared with the burning hatred he felt for Rachel.

'So, what are you going to do, babes?' asked Tania, as she helped him along the corridor to the lift. 'You'd better come and stay with me for a bit.'

Nigel winced at the endearment but nodded his thanks.

'I'm not sure, Tania. But, one way or another, I'll get that bitch. And you're going to help me.'

Chapter Thirty-One

Day 17

'I REALISE we're all incredibly stretched,' said Emma, at the start of the briefing, 'and I appreciate all your hard work as well as the extra hours you've been putting in. Superintendent Gorman has authorised additional overtime, and we may be getting a few bodies from Highchester to help, but, for the moment, it's down to us. Please let me know if things are getting too much and I'll do whatever I can to support you.'

The team's expressions varied from resignation to delight, presumably at the prospect of paid overtime.

'Now, before we get on to the latest case, is there anything new on the other murders? I'm holding the fort as the DCI's off on a course.'

'Nothing much on Mr Raven, I'm afraid,' replied Jack, 'but Trevor found something on ANPR near the solvent plant.'

'Yes, guv,' said Trevor. 'There wasn't much traffic in the area at the time, and we've been able to eliminate all but one of the vehicles picked up by the camera on the main road. A dark-coloured VW SUV was seen coming from town an hour before the fire was reported, returning fifty minutes later. The plates were false, belonging to a van owned by a company, Reeve and Miller, in Canterbury. I couldn't make out the driver, and it wasn't recorded by any other cameras. He could have changed the plates again. Reasonable to think that's the killer, I suppose.'

'Nice job, lad,' said Emma. 'Now, to Madeleine Hollis. The cause of death was manual strangulation, according to Dr Durbridge. She was dead before she entered the canal as there was no water in her lungs. She had consumed a couple of glasses of wine before she died, but there was no food in her stomach. Significantly, there was ketamine in her system which, it's reasonable to assume, was in the wine. So, we need to know where she went for a drink and who she was with.'

'Anything on time of death, guv?' asked Kamal.

'Nothing reliable, according to the good doctor. It's difficult enough if the body's left on land under known conditions, but dumping it in the water messed up all the usual calculations. All he would commit himself to was between the last time someone saw her alive and the discovery of the body. Another reason to find out where she was drinking.'

'Could we trace her through the wine? Find out which bars serve it?' suggested Sally, her expression animated.

'Nice try,' said Emma, 'but all he could say was it was red. It could have been Chateauneuf du Pape or Chateau Pis du Chat – you can't tell after it's been sloshing around in someone's stomach with everything else.'

Sally looked disappointed but Mel smiled at her.

'Right,' continued Emma. 'We know, from Trevor's efforts, that Ms Hollis was a barrister and that she was due to appear for the defence in a trial in Mexton. She's based in Bristol so why is she in court here? We need to look into what this trial's all about – could her appearance have alarmed someone enough to kill her? There was nothing of interest in her room, the staff reported nothing suspicious, and nobody visited her. She would have had a briefcase or something with court documents in it, but nothing's been found, only box files in the hotel. We need to canvass wine bars, starting with the upmarket ones near the court building. She wouldn't be drinking in the Fife and Drum.'

This reference to Mexton's roughest pub brought a chuckle from several officers.

'Her car is still in the hotel car park, so someone needs to take a look at it. Check if she used a taxi that evening. Is there anything on street CCTV or ANPR which could help? There should be something outside the court so check that first. Jack will allocate actions.'

Jack nodded and scribbled on a notepad.

'Anything on Dale Moncrieff?' Emma continued.

'Tom's been looking at anti-immigration groups online,' replied Mel, 'but there's no suggestion that they're behind it. There's plenty of hate speech, and they've organised the odd protest outside hostels, but no suggestion that they were going after him. He had his trolls, as we know, but none of them look like potential murderers.'

'Thanks, Mel. Right, everyone. Back to work, and please keep me informed.'

'Jack, can I have a word? In private,' asked Mel, as they queued for the coffee machine.

'Of course. Give me a minute to get a drink.'

The two officers found a quiet corner of the breakout area

and sat on the squashy easy chairs that were already stained with spilt coffee.

'What's worrying you, Mel? Is the PTSD getting to you again?'

Jack's words were supportive, but his tone was remote, as if he was reading a script.

'Actually, Jack, it's you.'

He started, and a frown embedded itself in his brow.

'What the hell do you mean?'

'I hope I'm not speaking out of turn, and I wouldn't say anything if I hadn't known you for a good few years, but you've been pretty off for a while now. You look bloody exhausted, you're snappy and abrupt, and you seem to drift off at times. Sometimes you look as though you've won a lifetime's supply of beer and been handed just a single bottle. I know we're busy, but things have been much worse in the past. What's wrong?'

Jack scowled and opened his mouth as if to snap back, but then his shoulders slumped, and he suddenly looked extremely vulnerable. He took several deep breaths before responding.

'It's Sarah. She's got cancer.'

'Oh shit, Jack. I'm so sorry.'

Mel paused and continued, tentatively.

'What sort, if I can ask?'

'Melanoma. I guess it's a legacy of too much time spent in the sun without protection. She never bothered with sunscreen. She developed this growth on the back of her neck. It didn't hurt, so we never worried about it until a doctor, standing behind her in the queue at Waterstones, noticed it. He advised her to get it checked, the GP referred her to an oncologist. And then the sky fell in.'

'What's the prognosis?'

'She's had surgery. They've removed the growth, but we're waiting on the results of tests on her lymph nodes and elsewhere to see if, and how far, it's spread. Then they'll talk about treatment options. She may need radiotherapy or chemotherapy if things are bad. We're both shit scared and cursing ourselves for not taking it seriously before.'

'God, I'm really sorry. Look, I know there's nothing practical I can do, but if you want to chat, or go for a beer or something, I'm always up for it. We could all go out for a meal, if that would help. And do give my love to Sarah.'

'Yeah, thanks Mel. I will do. I know I should leave it all at home, but it's been a hell of a shock. You could let the troops know, discreetly, that there are health problems at home, without giving details. I don't want to make a public announcement.'

'Sure. I will. And keep me informed, won't you?'

'Of course. And thanks again.'

Chapter Thirty-Two

'I'VE FOUND out who Madeleine Hollis is defending,' Mel said, knocking on Emma's open door.

Emma turned her attention from a photo of Genevieve and blinked at the DC.

'Oh? Who?'

'Another lawyer. The one who was charged with the murder of a sex worker in Highchester.'

'Oh. Him. But she's a high-flyer in Bristol. Why is she down here doing it?'

'I spoke to the clerk at her chambers. Apparently, she and the defendant were old friends from university and she was asked for specifically. She's very good at getting people off murder charges, it seems.'

'Well, she'd have had a bloody hard job with this one. They've got confessions and plenty of circumstantial evidence. If her client thought she could magic a not guilty verdict he would have been seriously disappointed.'

'So there's a vacancy for a legal magician,' grinned Mel.

'Aye. Is there anything else new?'

'We've found the wine bar where she was drinking. The Magnum and Flute. A man met her and they had a drink together. A Nancy McGill, who was collecting glasses, remembered she looked unsteady when she got up, and the man had to support her. Nancy assumed she'd had a few too many.'

'Any CCTV?'

'The bar's gear was broken. There's a camera outside, but her companion had a hat pulled down over his eyes, and was obviously avoiding it, so all we could get was he seemed to be about medium height, not thin not fat. The staff didn't know him and could only give a vague description.'

'We need to eliminate this person from enquiries. Can you let Jack know I want him to find a few bodies to talk to regulars in the wine bar?'

'Yes, guv. Will do.'

'Anything else?'

'Yes. Trevor's been through ANPR on roads near the canal for that night. He's still processing it but he did find something. A dark SUV with plates that belong to a motorbike registered to Julia Bluejay, a writer of erotic paperbacks who lives in Tamworth. I suspect the name's as fake as the plates. Not the first vehicle with phoney plates near a scene, is it? He'll keep you informed.'

'Right. Any useful documents turned up?'

'We couldn't go through her legal papers, obviously. Someone from her chambers is coming to collect them. But we did find a printout of an online news story in the glove compartment of her car. Some financier fell from the top of an office block in London. The Met initially thought it was suicide, but then decided it was suspicious.'

'OK,' said Emma, wearily. 'See if you can find a link between the dead bloke and Ms Hollis. There must be a reason for her having the report. Find out who's dealing with the case up there and give them a ring.'

Mel left Emma's office, concerned that her boss seemed so tired. Perhaps the quiet joys of motherhood were taking their toll.

Chapter Thirty-Three

Chapter Thirty-Three

MARTIN RETURNED to Two-Fifty Honeys late in the morning, still with a headache but determined to find out who was behind the assault. He rang up Mextemps and, eventually, was put through to a manager.

'Good morning,' he began. 'I'm Martin Rowse from Mexton Investigations. I've been engaged by Two-Fifty Honeys to investigate suspected food tampering and I'd like to find out more about two of the temporary staff you've placed with the company. Kylie Mason, a factory floor worker, and Barry Mangan, a driver. Can you help me?'

'I'm sure you realise, Mr Rowse,' the manager replied, 'that we are bound by the GDP regulations, so there's not a lot I can tell you. What sort of information are you after?'

'I'd like to see their references, for a start. And I'd also like to know where they've worked before. Their application forms would also be useful.'

'I'm sure they would, but I'm afraid the application forms are confidential. The first items I can help you with, however, as our staff accept that any references can be passed on to the employers we place them with. I've already sent them to Mr Calthrop. I'm not sure I can tell you anything about their work histories, as that's personal information.'

Martin thought for a moment.

'Look, this is really important. Several people have been made ill by something in the honey, and the company is suffering badly. It's vital that whatever is going on is stopped, quickly, otherwise someone could get seriously hurt. Possibly fatally.'

'I do sympathise, Mr Rowse, and, obviously, it would reflect badly on Mextemps if one of the people we supplied turned out to have killed someone. But I'm afraid my hands are tied.'

'OK. How about this? Without naming names or gender, so nothing can be linked directly to a specific employee, can you tell me whether either or both of the two people have worked for a company in the food manufacturing industry in the past year? I mean making food products, not working in shops or restaurants.'

There was silence at the end of the call, punctuated only by the click of a pen.

'OK. I'll see what I can do. Give me your email. And good luck with your investigation.'

Martin thanked him and ended the call. Half an hour later, a one-word email appeared in his inbox.

'One.'

As Martin was explaining to Steven that one of the temps could be a viable suspect, his phone rang. He answered the unfamiliar number.

'Mr Rowse? It's Dr Thorndike, Mexlab Analytics. That

honey you sent us – I've had a look at it. I've found something interesting.'

'Oh, yes? What?'

'First off, I looked at samples under a microscope. I could see some shiny crystals which looked different from the sugar crystals in the honey. I managed to collect a fair few of them, which I prepared and analysed on one of our machines. They were lead acetate crystals. Pretty poisonous, and nothing that could appear in honey naturally. So, you were right. It is a case of food tampering.'

'Thank you very much, Dr Thorndike. You've confirmed my suspicions. Where do you get lead acetate?'

'You don't, unless you have a legitimate use for it, and you need a licence. I suppose you could make it, if you were determined, but you'd have to know how to.'

'Right. How much of this stuff would kill you?'

'I'm not a toxicologist but I've had a quick look at the literature. It would take quite a lot to kill someone, but much smaller doses can cause serious problems, especially if ingested over a long period. There are tight limits for lead in food and the levels in the samples you sent were way over the top. I'll put the figures in my report.'

'Thank you again, Dr Thorndike. I'll be handing this over to the police shortly and your report will be invaluable.'

Martin ended the call and turned to Steven.

'I was right. It was sugar of lead – lead acetate, officially – and it couldn't have been accidental. We know what, we have a couple of suspects and, if my suspicions are correct, we have a why. All we need now is a how – and, of course, the who. But we're getting there. There are two more things we need to do. We must talk to the two temps again and we need to search the premises for this lead acetate. I gather it's white crystals.'

'What will you do if you find any?'

'Leave it in place for the police. If you or I handle it, a defence lawyer could claim we planted it. We'll film any search on a phone. It's not a perfect procedure but it will have to do. Do you have keys to the staff lockers?'

'There's a master key somewhere. I'll dig it out.'

'OK. We'll interview the temps tomorrow, the two of us, if you don't mind.'

'Sure. But what about the rest of the honey? Am I supposed to destroy it? A product recall would be devastating to our reputation. We really can't take that kind of a loss and we're not insured against that sort of thing.'

'Try not to worry, Steven. It looks like it's only a small number of jars. I hope we can persuade the culprit to tell us how many. Then we can match them with the number returned.'

If not, Martin thought, Two-Fifty Honeys was well and truly screwed.

Chapter Thirty-Four

Day 18

'MEXTON? Mexton? Where the bloody hell's Mexton?' asked DS Fenton.

'Down south somewhere, I think,' replied DC Plover. 'Why?'

'I've had a message to call a DC Mel Cotton at Mexton nick. Wants to talk about the flying financier. Can you take it, Birdy? You know as much about it as anyone.'

'Sure, sarge. Wasn't Mexton where that DSup from the Met was murdered? The hit-and-run victim?'

'Yeah – it's coming back to me. DSup Raven. He had his throat cut in a physiotherapy place near Mexton. The local DI contacted his guv'nor for details of the attack in Mayfair. Seems to think the driver was the killer and went down there to finish the job. One of the civvies sent her some info. Give this DC a bell, tell him or her what they want to know and find out how they're getting on with the murder.'

Birdy nodded and reached for his phone.

Mel frowned when her phone rang, just as she was heading for the canteen. An unknown number, probably junk. She answered it anyway, preparing to give a robust opinion about people who rang you up to tell you you've been in a non-existent accident.

'Yes?' she said, coldly.

'Err... am I speaking to DC Mel Cotton?'

Mel's manner switched to a more professional one.

'Yes, you are.'

'Great. I'm DC Plover, Met CID. We had a message to ring you about Justin Kite. How can I help?'

'Oh, great, thanks. Sorry I sounded rude. I thought you were a junk call. What can you tell me about this fatality? Why is it suspicious?'

'Well, for a start, he had no motive for topping himself. His life was fine and he was due a big bonus. He wasn't off his face and there was no strong wind up there on the day he fell, so an accident is unlikely. More to the point, there was a bloke lurking around the building who no-one seemed to know. He claimed to have an appointment, to get through the security gate, but it was phoney. We've never been able to trace him so we suspect he chucked Kite off the roof and then vanished.'

'No CCTV or anything?'

'Nope. Nothing of use. Something from reception and the lifts, but it's not helpful. We're still interviewing people who knew him, but I reckon we'll never get to the bottom of it. We've got plenty of other murders to investigate, cases where we're more likely to get a result. We'll probably just have to keep this one on file. What's your interest, anyway?'

'We've had a murder down here, a barrister. She had a printout of a report on your case in her possession when she died. We've no idea why, as Justin Kite wasn't on her contacts list.'

Birdy suddenly sounded more interested.

'Give me her name. I'll see if it's come up in the investigation or is in Kite's contacts. In fact, why don't you come up here? You could look at what we've got and we could go for a drink or a meal. I'll show you the sights. Have some fun.'

Mel laughed thinly.

'Thanks, but I don't think I'd get the expenses for a trip to London. But I'd be grateful for any help you can give me.'

'Yeah, OK.' Plover sounded slightly disappointed. 'While you're on, what's happening about the dead DSup? He wasn't from my division but he was still Met.'

'A bit like your financier. We've got no real leads. We've asked for details of anyone who could have hated him enough to want him dead, but we've had nothing back yet.'

'Well, I could try and chase that up for you if you like? Another reason for a visit to the smoke. I can put you up, if you like.'

'Chasing it up would be great, thanks,' replied Mel, again ignoring his invitation.

'Did he just try to pull me, over the phone?' she asked herself when the call ended. 'I think I need some lunch.'

Chapter Thirty-Five

KYLIE MASON TWISTED a tissue nervously as she sat in Steven's office, facing her inquisitors.

'What's this about? I've done nothing wrong. Why are you picking on me? Is it 'cos I'm not part of your "family" Mr Calthrop?'

'We're not picking on you, Kylie,' said Martin, gently. 'It's just that someone's been putting a dangerous substance in the honey and we need to find out who. We're talking to everyone.'

'Yeah, but I've already told you I don't know anything about it. Is there something wrong with my work?'

'No, not at all,' said Steven. 'In fact, until this happened, we were hoping to keep you on permanently. If you wanted to stay, that is.'

At this Kylie brightened up.

'Yes, I would, I mean, I do. It's great here. But I don't like being accused wrongly.'

She frowned again.

'We're not accusing you,' said Martin. 'We just have a few questions. So, have you worked in the food industry before?'

'Yes. I've worked in Burger King, McDonalds and KFC but I got fed up of smelling of fat at the end of each shift. I then worked in a couple of large stores but, when the local Wilko's closed down, I started temping. I can give you a list of jobs if you like.'

'So, nothing involving actually manufacturing food, as opposed to serving it?'

'No. Nothing.'

'OK. Thanks. One other thing. Have you seen anyone behaving oddly around the factory?'

Kylie thought for a moment.

'No. No, I don't think so. I mean, us two temps tend to stick out a bit. We don't always get the in-jokes and that, but everyone's been friendly.'

'How do you get on with Barry, the driver?'

'He's OK. A bit reserved but he did try to get me to go for a drink with him. Flashed a bit of cash, you know. I told him I wasn't interested 'cos I already had someone and he didn't take it hard.'

Martin looked at Steven and nodded, then turned back to Kylie.

'That's all, Kylie, thank you. You can go now. And don't worry, you're not in trouble.'

Kylie left the room, looking considerably more cheerful than when she entered it. As soon as the door closed, Martin spoke.

'It looks like we've got a viable suspect. Barry Mangan. If only one of the temps has worked in food manufacturing, and it's not Kylie, it must be Barry.'

'So, what do we do now?' asked Steven. 'Shall we search his locker?'

'I'm not sure. I'd prefer to leave it to the police, but there's not enough evidence for them to get a search warrant.

We don't need one, especially as it's company property, but there could be questions about planted evidence. If there is any.'

'Could we make him open it and film the process?'

'We could, but he could always claim that we used the master key to plant stuff beforehand. Shit!'

'Are we going to talk to him, then? He's due back from his delivery about five o'clock.'

'Yes, we must. It's a pity I can't interview him under caution, but those days are gone, I'm afraid.'

'You used to be in the police, then?' asked Steven. 'I think you mentioned it before.'

'Yes. I left a little while ago. Long story. Anyway, I think I'll give an old colleague of mine a ring while we're waiting for Mangan. See what she advises.'

'Right. I'll get on with some paperwork. I need to write letters of apology to the latest complainants.'

Martin finished up writing his account of the day's events and looked at his watch. He had an idea. It's nearly going home time, so I might get away with it, he thought. He looked up the phone number for Mexton Sweeteners, dialled and, when the call was picked up, asked for human resources. An irritated voice answered.

'Oh, good evening,' said Martin. 'Sorry to bother you so late in the day, and I do realise you need to get off, but I've just a quick query. It's George Martin here, from HMRC. I'm trying to find when one of your employees left so I can correct his tax code. We don't seem to have the details. It's Mr Barry Mangan.'

Martin recited Mangan's national insurance number.

'Well can't it wait until tomorrow? And aren't you supposed to send an email or something?'

'No and yes. It's a bit urgent, and we would normally email, but our system's down at the moment. They think we've been hacked. Russians, probably. I'm really sorry to be such a nuisance. I do need the information now and I can send a formal email request when things are working again, if that would help.'

'Well, all right,' the voice said, and the conversation gave way to a clatter of computer keys being pressed with obvious annoyance.

'I've checked and Mr Mangan wasn't directly employed by us. He came from an agency, Mextemps. He was here for three months and left ten weeks ago. But all his tax details are with them.'

'Of course! That explains it. Our records are obviously in error. Thank you so much for your help. Again, I'm sorry to bother you. I'll send you that email as soon as I can. Enjoy the rest of your day.'

Martin cut the call with a grin on his face. Result!

Martin called Mel Cotton and explained what they'd found.

'We're going to talk to Mangan when he gets back to the factory,' he told her. 'Then we'll be able to involve you, I hope.'

'Well, be careful. If he's the one, he's already hurt you. Do you want some back-up? I could come along unofficially, as it were.'

'It would be nice to see you, but there are two of us.'

'Hmm. Well, you know what number to call if things get nasty.'

'Yep. Thanks, Mel.'

Now where's Steven got to? he wondered, and went in search of him. He wasn't in his office or on the factory floor and nor did he answer when Martin shouted his name. Increasingly apprehensive, Martin pulled open the door to the loading area. Steven lay on the floor, blood covering his face and his arm at an awkward angle. A groan escaped his lips and he slowly raised the other arm, pointing in the direction of the exit.

'Bastard,' he croaked, and lapsed into unconsciousness.

Chapter Thirty-Six

Mel steered the unmarked police car through the narrow gap between two buses and headed for Two-Fifty Honeys. She was worried about Martin – not that he would do anything stupid, but the honey tamperer, if that's who it was, could easily have killed him in the previous attack. Despite his reassurances, she decided to call in on him anyway.

There must be a lot of money involved, she thought. Or some kind of psychosis. Her musings were interrupted when a white van with a bee logo erupted from the lane leading to the factory, just in front of her. Shit, she thought, something's happened, and it's probably bad.

She called Martin's mobile, hands free, and simultaneously swung round to follow the van. She was neither trained nor authorised for a high-speed pursuit so she could only follow at a distance. Fortunately, the van slowed down once it reached the main road, presumably to avoid being stopped for speeding.

'What the fuck's going on, Martin?' she asked, when her

call was answered. 'I'm following a honey van which nearly crashed into me leaving the lane. Are you hurt?'

'No, Mel. I'm not but Steven's injured. Barry Mangan smashed him in the face and broke his arm. An ambulance is on its way and I've spoken to the police call handler. They've got the van's reg.'

'OK. I'll keep him in sight and liaise with Control. Glad you're OK.'

Mel cut the call, rang the control centre and concentrated on following the van. She debated whether to switch on the siren and hidden blue lights, in an attempt to make the driver stop, but rejected the idea, thinking that it might make him speed up and take risks. But something spooked him once they were on a clear stretch of road leading out of town.

Fuck! He's seen me, thought Mel. Mangan speeded up and Mel put her foot down, keeping within the speed limit and watching the van pulling away from her. She had just followed him round a bend when, horrified, she saw him swerve to avoid a camper van parked beside the road and hit the offside wing of a supermarket delivery van coming in the opposite direction. The supermarket van slewed towards the side of the road while Mangan's vehicle spun around and ended up half in a shallow ditch. The back doors burst open and jars of honey spilled out onto the ground. The front doors remained shut.

Mel pulled her car in behind the crashed vehicle, switched on the blue lights and phoned Control as she ran to the van. Just as she reached it, the driver's door was pushed open and Barry Mangan jumped out, and towards her, holding a wheelbrace.

'Police!' shouted Mel. 'Put that down and stay where you are.'

'Fuck off, bitch,' Mangan screamed. 'Come near me and I'll fucking do you.'

'Don't be silly, Barry,' said Mel, switching her phone to record and slipping it into her pocket as she ran after him. 'Don't make things worse. Come on, give me that wrench.'

As she approached, Mangan stopped and then lunged towards her, swinging the tool at her head. She stepped back and it swished past. Before she could curse herself for leaving her baton in the car, he swung again, catching her on the shoulder and sending a flare of agony along the length of her arm. She kicked at his groin, but he was too quick and her foot merely bounced off the front of his thigh. Mangan sneered and she jumped back as he tried, once more, to smash her head in. He overbalanced and Mel moved in, but he swung back and his elbow caught her in the face. Blood poured from her nose and she stumbled, falling backwards onto the ground. Mangan stood over her and raised the tool, preparing to bring it down on her skull. But the fury in his eyes gave way to blankness when something flew through the air and hit him on the side of the head. The tool fell from his grasp and he collapsed, dazed, beside her. A jar of Two-Fifty honey rolled along the ground, leaving a sticky trail behind it.

Chapter Thirty-Seven

As MEL CRAWLED AWAY and reached for her handcuffs, she heard feet running along the road and a voice called out.

'Are you OK? Can I help?'

She looked up to see a white-moustached man, in his late sixties, heading towards her, somewhat out of breath. She cuffed Mangan, who was cursing volubly, clamped a tissue to her nose and rose unsteadily to her feet.

'Yes, Thank you. Just a bloody nose. Um... was it you threw that jar of honey?'

'Yes, I did. I used to bowl for the Mexton First Eleven. I saw the jars on the ground and what that scoundrel was trying to do, so I thought I'd better have a go. I haven't played cricket for years, but it all came back to me. I won't get into trouble, will I? I heard you say you were police.'

'No, no you won't. You saved me from serious injury, if not worse. Thank you, Mr...'

'Spence. Patrick Spence. I'm afraid our camper van broke down, which is why we were in such an awkward position. The mechanic's taking bloody ages.'

'Well, thank you again. We'll need you to drop into the police station at some point to make a statement, but you don't have to do it this evening. My name's DC Mel Cotton, by the way.'

As Mel talked to Patrick, the sound of sirens grew louder and two police cars appeared, coming from opposite directions, and pulled in at either side of the crash site.

'This is a crime scene, guys,' called Mel to the first crew reaching her. I'll caution this suspect but he'll need to go to hospital for a check-up. He's had a blow to the head but didn't seem to have been knocked out.'

'OK, Mel,' said the driver. 'I'll call for an ambulance.'

He turned to Mangan and hauled him to his feet.

'Come along with me, please. We can't have you lying around here. It makes the place look untidy.'

His mate walked over to the driver of the supermarket van while Mangan was led, cursing, to the police car.

'Are you all right sir?' he asked. 'Do you need an ambulance?'

'No. No. I'm fine. Or at least I will be when my nerves calm down. I've got a flask of coffee in the cab. I'll drink it in a minute. I don't think the van's fit to drive. There's some metal jammed against the wheel. I've phoned the breakdown service.'

'Well, it looks like a few people won't be getting their supper tonight,' said the police officer.

'You're not wrong,' replied the driver, attempting a smile. 'I can give you a statement while I'm waiting if you like. There's not much to say. The van came round the bend, bounced off my wing and ended up in the ditch. I didn't see much of the fight.'

'OK, sir. I'll record what you say on a statement form and

you can sign it. There's one in the car. It'll save you coming into the station.'

Mel sat beside the road, holding a tissue to her nose to try to halt the bleeding. *I'm not yet thirty but I'm too old for this shit*, she thought. *I could have been killed over some dodgy honey. What the fuck's that all about? At least it wasn't a bloody knife.* She pulled herself to her feet and trudged back to the car, aware that her colleagues would find something to rib her about.

Half an hour later, diversion signs had been set up and SOCOs were photographing vehicles and the scene of the fight. An ambulance took Mangan, handcuffed to a police officer, to the hospital and Mel returned to the station. Word had got round about the incident, and someone had mocked up a photo of Superman, with an elderly man's face, below a caption which read 'Heroic OAP saves police officer.'

'Very funny,' grinned Mel. 'I feel enough of a tit without you lot rubbing it in. But he was a very nice gentleman.'

'It's your turn for the Grateful Dead T-shirt,' called Trevor. 'Look at you.'

Mel glanced down at her blood-soaked top and ruefully walked over to the cupboard where the traditional garment for the use of blood-stained detectives was kept.

'All right,' she said, 'but no photos. It really isn't my colour.'

As soon as she had changed and washed her face, Mel wrote up her statement, switched off her computer and headed for home where, she knew, she would get a more sympathetic response from Tom.

'I'm not happy with this, babes,' said Tania. 'Why can't you just let it go?'

'Let it go? Let it go? How the fuck can I do that?' Nigel shouted. 'The bitch nearly killed me and the divorce will ruin me.'

He took another swig of lager and calmed down slightly.

'I needed her income and the house. You know I earn fuck all. I'm gonna get her. I've made plans. And you're gonna help me. Just a few phone calls, alright?'

'I dunno. It's sort of illegal, isn't it? I mean, what if the cops come round?'

'They won't. Use this burner phone. I can't do it. It has to be a woman. And try and sound a bit posh. I've got other things to do. You're just the warm-up act.'

'You're not gonna do anything stupid, are you? You were lucky they didn't charge you with attacking her.'

'Don't you worry about that. Just do what I ask, and I'll move out for a bit in case they come looking for me. Then we'll be together when things settle down.'

'OK then, I suppose,' Tania replied, although her enthusiasm at the prospect of spending her life with Nigel seemed slightly muted.

'This is what I want you to do,' said Nigel, handing her a sheet of paper. 'Destroy the phone when you've finished and chuck it in the bin. I'll do my bits and we'll meet up in a few days, OK?'

'I won't get into trouble? Are you sure?'

'Course. You can trust me. I wouldn't let anyone hurt you. Come on,' he said, leading her to the bedroom. 'I'll show you what a solid bloke I am.'

Chapter Thirty-Eight

Day 19

'I CAN ASSURE YOU,' said an exasperated Rachel Willstone, 'there is nothing wrong with my roof and I don't need any inspection or repairs.'

'But you called the office,' replied the irritated roofer. 'You said you needed someone to come round urgently and give you a quote for mending a couple of leaks. You are Mrs Willstone, aren't you?'

'For the moment. But I didn't phone you.'

'Well, some woman did and gave your name. Said they needed someone immediately. Sounded desperate, the girl in the office said. I had to delay starting another job to get here.'

'I'm really sorry you've had a wasted journey. It was obviously a prank call, targeting either you or me. It could be a student from the school where I teach, I suppose, unless someone's got a grudge against your firm. An unhappy customer, perhaps?'

The roofer bridled.

'All my customers are satisfied with my work. I've been doing this for twenty years and I'm not a bleeding cowboy. You can see the reviews online.'

'OK, OK, I'm sorry. It must be aimed at me. Come to think of it, I've had a few late night, anonymous phone calls lately which could be related. Anyway, that's my problem, not yours. Again, I'm sorry for your wasted time.'

She was just closing the door on the aggrieved builder when a shiny black saloon pulled up across the road. A smartly-dressed young woman climbed out, consulted a clipboard and walked purposefully towards Rachel's house.

'Mrs Willstone?' she said, in quiet, respectful tones, as Rachel held the door open. 'I'm Stacey Fletcher, from Chalker and Johnstone. I'm very sorry for your loss.'

'What on earth are you talking about?'

'Your dear mother. You asked us to arrange her funeral.'

'But my mother is fine. She's currently walking the Ridgeway long-distance path with her second husband. Look,' Rachel picked up her phone. 'I had a WhatsApp from her last night, showing the two of them on Ivinghoe Beacon. No way is she dead.'

'Oh. Oh dear. I'm so terribly sorry. There must have been a mix-up. We had a Voicemail last night from a woman, asking us to call this morning.'

'Don't worry, it's not your fault,' replied Rachel, seething inside. 'The builder who just left was summoned here under false pretences. Someone's clearly pestering me. I'm sorry your time's been wasted.'

'No, no. That's quite alright. I apologise for causing you such distress.'

As Stacey walked back down the path, she turned back.

'Is that Volvo yours? What's happened to it?'

Rachel's heart sank as she rushed past Stacey and stared at

her car, parked outside the house. The erstwhile gleaming paintwork was a mess of blisters, slimy trails and exposed metal.

'The bastard!' she hissed. 'No, not you, Ms Fletcher. 'I've a bloody good idea who's doing this and it's not someone from school.'

She left the puzzled funeral director by the gate and stalked into the house, stabbing angrily at her phone's keypad.

'CID, please,' she said, when the call was answered. 'Put me through to DC Cotton.'

———————————

'It's that shit. Nigel,' spat Rachel as Mel guided her to the comfortable interview room. 'He's going for me.'

'OK, Rachel. Step back a bit. What's been happening? You said you were under attack, so let me have the details.'

The two women sat down and Mel opened her notebook.

'For the past two nights,' began Rachel, 'I've been getting calls in the early hours from an unknown number. There was no-one there and I assumed they were prank calls, possibly from a student at school. It's the holidays and some of them get up to mischief out of boredom. This morning, I had a roofer turn up at the house, followed by a funeral director, neither of whom I had asked for. They both said I'd phoned them, requesting their services. And, sometime last night, paint stripper was poured over my car. I'll need to get the whole bloody thing resprayed.'

'Why do you suspect Nigel?'

'The sheer malice of it. Our divorce proceedings are not exactly going through amicably. He's lost his job at the Council and is shacked up with Tania, the woman he was cheating on me with. He'll not get much in the settlement and he's consumed with resentment. I think he's becoming quite deranged.'

Mel looked thoughtful.

'That seems perfectly credible but we do need proof before we can take action. Are there any recordings of the phone calls which sent people round?'

'I don't know about the roofer but the funeral director said they had a Voicemail. They may have kept it. It was Chalker and Johnstone. In both cases it was a woman who called.'

'Then how do you know Nigel's behind it?'

'He must have persuaded Tania to make them.'

'Hmm. How about your car? Do you have a doorbell camera which could have picked up whoever did the damage?'

'No. He kept saying he would get one but never did. Always putting things off.'

'Perhaps you could ask your neighbours. Look, the problem is, Nigel is a likely suspect but we do need evidence. Clearly, offences have been committed but we can't arrest him without some kind of proof. Do you think he would attempt to harm you physically?'

'Probably not. Last time he tried, it didn't end well for him. Is there anything you can do?'

Mel thought for a couple of seconds.

'We're incredibly busy now but, if I have the time, I'll try to have a word with him. You'd better give me Tania's address before you go. In the meantime, I suggest you keep a detailed log of any suspicious incidents, switch your phone off at night and keep alert. I would advise you not to confront Nigel. It may weaken your case for a restraining order if there's a row, and it could be dangerous.'

'Is that all?' Rachel looked dumbfounded.

'Yes, I'm afraid so. I really wish I could do more. Perhaps

we should have charged Nigel over the knife incident, but you didn't want us to. It's not too late to change your mind.'

'I'll think about it.'

'Again, I'm sorry. Here's my card with a direct number on it. Please call me if you think you're in danger.'

'Don't you worry, I will.'

Mel showed a disappointed Rachel out of the station and resolved to talk to Nigel as soon as she got the chance. *How many more women are unprotected from stalkers because of the lack of police resources,* she wondered? *And how many of them end up getting killed? Now for another little shit,* she told herself, as she prepared for the interview with Barry Mangan.

Chapter Thirty-Nine

MANGAN SAT SLUMPED in the interview room, a cold cup of tea in front of him.

'Are you sure you don't want a solicitor?' repeated Mel.

'No,' he replied, sullenly. 'Let's get this over, can we? But if I give you everything, what can you do for me?'

'It's not like on the TV, Mr Mangan,' said Sally. 'We don't do deals. We'll be recommending to the Crown Prosecution Service that you be charged with two counts of common assault occasioning actual bodily harm, assaulting an emergency worker, and maliciously administering poison or a noxious substance with intent to injure, aggrieve, or annoy any other person. How they decide to proceed is up to them. We make no promises, but, if you co-operate with us, the judge may take it into account when deciding what sentence to impose.'

Mangan looked uncertain but then spoke.

'OK. You see, I've got a gambling problem and they found out about it when I worked for Mexton Sweeteners as a driving temp. I got caught putting petrol in my own car and charging it to their account. Instead of sacking me, the guv'nor took me aside. He said he would forget about the petrol and pay me a decent wedge if I could get into Two-Fifty Honeys and fuck them up. I couldn't refuse. When a driving vacancy came up there, I persuaded Mextemps to put me with them.

'I was given this stuff and, every so often, I'd pinch a couple of jars of honey, take some honey out and stir in these white crystals. I'd put new paper strips across the lids and put them back into random deliveries. He promised me it wouldn't kill anyone, just make them a bit sick.'

'Where's this stuff now?' asked Sally.

'In the van, in an old coffee sweetener jar.'

'Right. We'll retrieve it and get it analysed. So, what we need from you is the details of who gave you the stuff, all meetings with them, and every time you poisoned the honey, with dates. Can you give us that?'

'Yes, yes, I think so. And you will tell the court I co-operated?'

'Yes, we'll make it known.'

It took the rest of the morning for Barry to complete his statement. As he was led to the cells, Mel and Sally shared a moment of quiet triumph.

'Of course,' said Mel, 'most of this is down to Martin. We must get him to the pub and he can tell us what put him on to Mangan. Pity he couldn't have been there when we nicked him.'

'Yeah, but he'll be glad we did.'

'I do miss him,' Mel said, wistfully.

'Well call him now,' smiled Sally, 'and tell him the drinks are on us in the Cat and Cushion tonight. Will Jack come, do you think? He's been like a wet week for days and he was really arsey with me over some paperwork the other day.'

'There's a reason for that,' said Mel. 'Family illness. I can't say any more, but he's going through it.'

'Yeah OK. Perhaps a pint or two will cheer him up.'

Chapter Forty

PANDORA BLYTHE's scream echoed along the corridor in Carter Hall, as she stumbled out of her dressing room, blood dripping from her face.

'Look at me! My face! I nearly fucking died. I'll kill someone for this.'

Cassie Morgan, the producer of the Wellness Roadshow, rushed up to the wounded presenter and wiped ineffectually at the blood with a tissue. Pandora howled as Cassie tried to comfort her.

'What happened, lovey? Who did this to you?'

'There was this box, addressed to me. A treasury of wellness delights, it said.' She gulped back her tears. 'When I opened it, something shot out and cut my face. Oh God, it hurts. I'm maimed for life.' She resumed her sobbing as blood dripped onto her expensive blouse.

'OK. Let's go and look at it shall we?'

The producer's calming manner had little effect on Pandora's crying, which increased in volume as the two women entered the presenter's dressing room. On a table by the window lay an opened, sturdy cardboard box, with some sort of mechanical contrivance inside it. Torn floral wrapping paper was strewn across the table, together with a gift tag bearing Pandora's name. Looking up, Cassie spotted a small arrow-like object, embedded in the ornate plaster ceiling. A few drops of blood were visible on the carpet, marking Pandora's path from the table to the corridor.

'Two things,' said Cassie, briskly. 'This was no joke. You could have been badly hurt, so we need to call the police. Also, you need to go to hospital to get that cut seen to. I'll get one of the camera crew to drive you – it could take hours for an ambulance to turn up. They've got a first aid kit too. There should be some gauze or something in it to put over the wound for the time being. Obviously, we'll have to cancel today's recording but, don't worry, we'll reschedule. Now come and sit down over here. I'll get you some water.'

Pandora nodded and winced as Cassie pressed a fresh pad of tissues against her bleeding cheek. She accepted an open bottle of water and drank with one hand while holding the tissues with the other. Cassie busied herself on her phone and, ten minutes later, a camera operator led Pandora to his car and drove her to Mexton General Hospital. Cassie closed the dressing room door, locked it, and waited for the police to arrive.

Chapter Forty-One

MEL PULLED the unmarked police car up outside the gates to Carter Hall, leaving space for other vehicles to come and go. She walked up the drive towards the eighteenth-century stately home, now used to host conferences and events such as weddings, garden parties and, currently, the Wellness Roadshow TV programme. Once inside, she showed her warrant card to a receptionist and gazed around at the restored opulence which made her feel slightly uncomfortable.

'Oh, you've come about Pandora,' said the young man. 'She's just down that corridor, third door on the left. She's very upset, as you can imagine.'

Mel smiled and followed the directions.

'Ms Blythe? I'm Detective Constable Mel Cotton. You've obviously had a nasty shock, but can you tell me what happened?'

The two women sat in a small lounge sipping coffee.

Pandora's cheek was partly covered by a taped piece of gauze and her eyes were red with crying.

'I found this parcel in my dressing room. It was in a pretty box and looked like a gift or free samples, so I opened it. There was a sort of twang and something flew out. It cut my face and got stuck in the ceiling.'

'What did they say in A and E?'

'That I was lucky not to have lost an eye or been hit in the throat. It should heal OK, as it wasn't as deep as I thought.'

'That's some good news then. I saw the thing in the ceiling. It looks like a small crossbow bolt. We'll get a SOCO to remove it so we can take a closer look. Where is the box now?'

Pandora gestured to a table in the corner of the room.

'I didn't want it in my dressing room, so I asked a technician to put it somewhere safe. I thought you'd want to see it. Should I have left it there?'

'We do indeed. And I don't think it matters that you moved it, as long as no-one else handled it. We'll need the technician's fingerprints and DNA.'

Mel wrestled on some nitrile gloves and peered cautiously into the box.

'It looks like some kind of mini crossbow. There are strings and pulleys attached. It was obviously meant to fire when the box was opened. You were lucky you weren't seriously injured.'

'You mean this wasn't just a prank? Someone really wanted to hurt me? Cassie thought so, too.'

Pandora looked as though she was about to be sick.

'It looks that way, I'm afraid. Can you think of anyone who dislikes you enough to do this?'

'N... no. I mean, there's always rivalry in show business, and I'm a bit older than some of the girls presenting this type of show, which has attracted comment, but no-one I know could be this vicious.'

'All right. We can talk about this again. Right now, I need to know the names of everyone who handled the box, so we can take their fingerprints and DNA for elimination purposes. Yours too. Did anyone see who delivered the package?'

'I don't know. You'll have to ask the others.'

'OK. We will take statements from everyone who was present in due course. It's getting late so that will have to wait until tomorrow. In the meantime, is there anything I can do for you?'

'No. It's all right. My producer has been really supportive, and I think the best thing to do is to record the programme as planned. If someone's trying to stop it, the best thing to do is to show the bastard he's failed.'

'I admire your spirit,' smiled Mel. 'Here's my card. Call me if you find out anything or need to talk. And be careful with unexpected packages.'

'I will, DC Cotton. Believe me, I will.'

That's an odd one, thought Mel as she drove away from Carter Hall. *A prank or something more sinister? Whoever was behind it clearly has some mechanical aptitude and a thoroughly devious mind. Let's hope he or she hadn't been as skilled at avoiding leaving forensics.*

Chapter Forty-Two

'CAN I get you an orange juice or something, Kamal?' asked Mel, as the detectives piled into the Cat and Cushion.

'No, I'll have a pint of Theakstons, please. I'm Hindu, not Muslim.'

Mel blushed.

'Shit. I'm sorry, Kamal. I shouldn't make assumptions. Please forgive me.'

'Don't worry about it. I know a few Muslims who also don't mind the odd pint. Besides, it's not the worst assumption I've had aimed my way. There are plenty of people who see someone who looks like me and think terrorist or illegal immigrant. But I have to say that you guys have made me feel welcome.'

'So why did you leave the Met?' asked Sally. 'London must have been much more exciting than a small town like Mexton.'

He frowned.

'I don't want to go into too many details, but I couldn't stand the everyday racism. Snide remarks just loud enough for me to hear. Sneering glances. Minced beef poured into my boots. Always getting the shit shifts. I know that the top brass are trying to change things, but they really need to get the sergeants on board. And some of them are fucking dinosaurs, with Tommy Robinson's approach to diversity.'

He smiled.

'I'm a lot happier here. And the beer's good.'

Mel ordered a round, still feeling uncomfortable, and Kamal helped her to carry the drinks over to the corner of the pub where the detectives were gathered.

'What made you suspect Mangan, Martin?' asked Jack, taking a hearty gulp of his pint.

'Well, it wasn't rocket science. The firm was a happy place to work and nobody on the regular staff bore any grudges. It more or less had to be one of the temps and the agency confirmed that one of them had previously worked for a food manufacturing company, but wouldn't say which. Steven Calthrop, the owner, had a run-in with the managing director of Mexton Sweeteners, who make a lot of money from Manuka honey, much of which is probably fake. He pointed this out in the local paper, although he didn't name names. I phoned their HR department, on a pretext which I won't go into, and the woman confirmed that Mangan had worked for them. His behaviour, when he hit Steven and did a runner, simply confirmed his guilt.'

'Blimey, mate. You should be a detective,' teased Mel.

'Yeah, yeah. But it was a bit more interesting than the usual stuff. How about you? Sounds like he could have killed you. I didn't realise he was so psychotic.'

'Yeah, he totally lost it. Heat of the moment, I suppose.

Tom reckons he's got poor impulse control, which fits with his gambling habit. I don't think he realised what he was doing.'

'So, what's going to happen to him?'

'He co-operated. It seems the managing director of Mexton Sweeteners bribed-stroke-coerced him into doing the sabotage. We've got enough to arrest the MD on suspicion of conspiracy, and he'll be picked up shortly. Apparently, Mangan sabotaged twenty-two jars and all of them were returned to the company. Steven Calthrop will be sending out some free honey, with letters of explanation, to the customers affected. Mangan will go down for quite a while, though. Nice job Martin. Have you ever thought about coming back to us?'

'I don't think Alice would approve. She said the Job was too dangerous. Mind you, this turned out a bit rough, too.'

'True. Mangan thought a bang on the head might scare you off. He really didn't know you. Right. Whose round is it?'

Trevor stood up and brushed off Martin's attempt to buy the drinks.

'Who's for another pint?' he asked. Nobody declined.

Chapter Forty-Three

Day 20

'So, what's happening with this assault on the TV presenter, Mel?' asked Jack, as they queued for coffee.

'Not a lot. The receptionist at Carter Hall vaguely remembered someone in motorcycle gear leaving the parcel, but he had his visor pulled partly down. There was a CCTV camera in reception, but all the image tells us is that the man was of medium height and build.'

'How about the bike?'

'He would have had to park it on the road outside the grounds. The car park inside was closed for the TV shoot, so he would have walked from the gate. The drive from the gate to the house was still open for pedestrians.'

'Any tyre marks on the approach road?'

'There were plenty from the film crew's vehicles, visitors, staff etcetera, but nothing of any use. SOCOs couldn't find any from a motorbike, which is a bit odd. You'd expect to find them beside the road, where a bike would be parked, but there was nothing.'

'How about ANPR cameras in the area?' Jack stirred sugar into his coffee and blew across the cup to cool it.

'Nothing, and that's odd, too. Carter Hall is at the end of a side road and there's a pub, the Miles Cross Inn, at the corner where it joins the main road. They have CCTV in the car park and it picks up traffic in the road, though the angle doesn't give us number plates. There were plenty of cars and vans going past but no motorbikes. I think our suspect travelled by car and used the biker gear as a disguise.'

'OK – nip out there and see if you can find a likely parking place. We'll get SOCOs out if you find anything. I'll ask Mr Farlowe if we can put out an appeal for dashcam footage. You never know, we might get something.'

Mel drove slowly down the road leading to Carter Hall, scanning the right-hand side while Sally covered the left.

'Stop, Mel,' Sally called. 'Over here. There's a clear space. Could be big enough for a car.'

Mel pulled the car in and the two detectives got out, slipping booties on their feet before approaching a gap in the trees.

'Something's bashed against these bushes' said Sally, excitedly. 'There's broken branches and it looks like paint on this thick bit.'

'Good spot. And there's some tyre tracks here as well. Mind where you tread. I'll call Jack and ask for SOCO support. We'll wait in the car in case anyone else feels like parking here. I don't suppose you brought a flask of coffee?'

'In your dreams. But you can share my bar of chocolate if you like.

Chapter Forty-Four

'So, what have you found out about Pandora Blythe?' asked Emma, once everyone had settled down. 'I presume that's not her real name.'

'Half right, boss,' replied Kamal. 'Her birth name was Pauline Blythe, but she changed it to something more distinctive when she went into TV. She's originally from Reading and did her degree there. She worked as an apprentice-stroke-dogsbody for the BBC in London for three years, did a stint in local radio and was a regional TV news presenter in Bristol for a while. During this time, she became interested in alternative health theories and did some kind of online qualification, not recognised by the medical profession. When the independent production company TrimTV announced it was planning a wellness roadshow, she lobbied hard for the job of presenter and got it. She's been doing it for a couple of years now.'

'Any enemies?'

'I've looked at social media and online news stories,' said Trevor, putting down a biscuit. 'She's attracted a fair few trolls and sniping comments. When she got the presenter's job there was some surprise. Many people thought it should have gone to another candidate, Tamsin Riley, and a few more complained that she wasn't medically qualified, or was too old. Several said she must have bribed or slept her way into the job, but her colleagues denied that could have happened.'

'Relationships?'

'She's been married – it lasted four years – and there was an acrimonious split when her husband, a PR expert, got a job with a large pharmaceutical company,' said Sally. 'She called him a traitor and threw a plate of pasta over him in a restaurant when he announced it to her.' She grinned at the image. 'The tabloids had a field day. She's been single for a year, although she's been papped a few times with different men.'

'Guv?' said Mel, 'suppose the attacker didn't intend to kill her but just wanted to damage her face. It could be someone jealous of her position and fame. A would-be rival or perhaps someone whose partner she's dated.'

'Worth looking into, Mel,' said Emma, 'but I had a quick word with Dr Durbridge who said the crossbow bolt could have been lethal, if it had hit her in the throat, for instance. I still think it's attempted murder. But see what you can find out.'

'OK, guv. She's still down here, staying at Carter Hall to finish recording her show. I'll nip over there now.'

'Ms Blythe,' began Mel, as the presenter sat hugging a cup of coffee in her dressing room at Carter Hall. 'Have you thought again about anyone who would wish to harm you? A rival, or a jealous partner perhaps?'

Pandora straightened up, her eyes flashing.

'You can forget what you read in the gutter press,' she

snapped. 'I've been out with a few men, it's true, but none of them was in a relationship at the time. As to a rival, Tamsin Riley was really pissed off that I got the job instead of her. She's spread some malicious rumours about me but she wouldn't have the brains to build that crossbow trap. Though, come to think of it, I heard her brother works in the props department of the BBC, so perhaps she's batshit crazy enough to get him to make it.'

'I'll have a word with her. Is there anyone else?'

'Not that I can think of. I'm not on good terms with my ex, but he's in California now, sucking on the tit of Big Pharma. The bastard.'

'Well please let me know if anything else occurs to you. You've got my card. And do be careful. Whoever did this could try again.'

'Thank you, DC Cotton. I will. Now, if you'll excuse me, I have to get ready for a recording.'

'That's OK. I'll see myself out.'

Mel walked down the corridor reflecting on the brief interview. *Pandora seems to have been targeted unfairly, on social media and in the press,* she thought. *But why is she so bitter about her husband's job after all this time?* A chat with Tamsin Riley would certainly be worthwhile, and she needed to interview her brother. She was coming round to the DI's view that this was attempted murder. But why?

Chapter Forty-Five

'DC COTTON! DC Cotton! Nigel's put dogshit through my letterbox and smashed half my windows.'

'OK, hold on Rachel. I'm on my way.' She Bluetoothed her phone to the car's infotainment system and pulled out of the police station car park. 'Tell me what's happened.'

'I got home ten minutes ago and noticed the stink as soon as I opened the door. It's worse than the hovel those kids kept me in. I shovelled the dog mess into the dustbin and went to open a window in the front room. Then I saw that four of the panes were broken. I think they were shot at.'

'Whoa. Hold on. What makes you think that?'

Rachel looked irritated.

'Because the holes are small, there's no stones on the floor and there's an airgun pellet stuck in one of the frames. I'll look for the other pellets in the room when I've cleaned up the mess.'

'Don't do that. We'll get some SOCOs round to collect them. Is there any sign of a shooter?'

'No, but, if he was using a rifle, he could be some distance away, even if it's only an airgun.'

'How do you know it was Nigel? I mean it seems most likely, but I have to ask.'

'Who else could it be? Did you talk to him?'

'He wasn't at Tania's address and she said she didn't know where he was. I asked her about the phone calls. She denied making them but seemed a bit evasive, so we'll talk to her again, when we've spoken to Nigel. For now, can you go to the back of the house, away from the windows. I'll be there in ten minutes.

An hour earlier

Delivering the dogshit was easy. Hire a white van, put on a hi-vis jacket, walk up the path purposefully holding a parcel, and no-one notices you. The rubber gloves might have been a give-away, but who looks at a delivery driver's hands? He would have to be more careful over the next bit, though. The gun wouldn't make much noise, but someone might see him or notice the van parked oddly. A small chance, but he'd rubbed mud on the number plates, just in case anybody tried to record it.

He parked up on a patch of waste land at the top of a slight hill. The front windows of the house were in plain view, through the van's partially-open back doors, and, although the distance was further than ideal, the telescopic sight and the little trick he'd picked up on the internet would ensure the weapon did its job. He stretched out in the back of the van, supported the barrel on a block of wood, and sighted on his target. He squeezed the trigger. A dull crack, a tiny flash and, through the telescopic sight, he could just make out a hole appearing in the window glass. He reloaded, fumbling slightly, and fired again. He managed five shots in all, four hitting the target and one missing, before an approaching car forced him to stop firing. Once the road was clear, he closed the van doors, climbed into the driving seat and drove sedately away, congratulating himself on the afternoon's work. 'If the bitch wants to take the house away from me,' he muttered to himself, 'she'll fucking pay for it.'

'Can you match the pellets to the gun which fired them?' asked Rachel, as the SOCO dropped the last of the projectiles into an evidence bag.

'In ideal conditions, yes,' she replied, 'although it's not so easy as with a normal bullet. Unfortunately, these are so distorted by the impacts that I shouldn't think it's possible. Contrary to what you see on the television, the labs can't perform miracles.'

'Pity. I know who's doing this and I'm desperate to find some proof.'

'One thing, though. I noticed some dark residue on the backs of the pellets and smears of oil on the front. I think he's dieseling.'

'What do you mean?'

'It's possible to increase the power of an air rifle using a drop of linseed oil. It explodes as the weapon is fired, like the fuel in a diesel engine, and this increases the speed of the pellet. It can cause more damage, from further away, which will make it even more difficult to pin down where it was fired from. The lab will check it, but that's my guess about what's happening. If the police find the weapon, the guys can look for residues in the barrel, so that may help link it to the damage.'

'Thank you. That's interesting. Right, I'd better put some tape over these holes and tidy up. I'll call a glazier in the morning. I appreciate your coming out.'

As Rachel closed the door on the SOCO, an image flashed into her mind. She turned excitedly to Mel who was preparing to leave.

'I think I know where he's hiding.'

Chapter Forty-Six

'WHERE THE HELL'S ARMED RESPONSE?' Mel muttered to Sally as they waited in an unmarked car, a hundred metres from Nigel's parents' home. 'I'm not going anywhere near him if he's got a bloody rifle, even if it's only an airgun. I saw what it did to Rachel's windows.'

'I don't blame you. Wait! Isn't that him? Coming down the path?'

'Yes, it is. And he's not carrying anything. Brilliant! Pull the car up in front and I'll grab him.'

Sally switched on the blue lights, accelerated after Nigel and swung the car onto the pavement, cutting him off. He kicked at the door panel, turned and ran back as Mel leapt out of the vehicle and Sally called, again, for backup.

'Stop, Nigel!' she shouted, reaching for her baton. 'It's over.'

'Fuck off,' he slurred, running past Mel at a surprising speed. She turned to follow, almost tripping over an uneven paving stone. She had just caught up with him when he pulled a knife from his pocket. He turned to confront her and she froze. Another blade. Echoes of her PTSD returned. Taking a deep breath, she forced herself to confront her fear and lashed at his arm with her weapon. She missed. Nigel stepped forward and slashed at her chest, the knife sliding across her stab vest. She punched him in the side, below his knife arm, as his momentum unbalanced him slightly, but he merely grunted.

'Drop it, Nigel,' she yelled, as he glared at her and readied himself for another attack. 'Armed officers are on their way and they will shoot you if they believe I'm in danger.'

'Sod off. I've lost everything thanks to that bitch. I don't fucking care.'

He launched another blow, this time at Mel's stomach. She twisted sideways. The knife missed by millimetres. She jerked her elbow up into his throat. Willstone fell to the ground, spluttering and gurgling, as the knife dropped from his hand. Mel kicked the weapon into the gutter and Sally helped her to turn Willstone over and cuff him. Then she checked his airways. He appeared to be breathing with some difficulty.

'Ambulance?' queried Sally.

'Better had. Just in case.'

As Sally was calling 999 a dark armed response vehicle pulled up and PC Adeyemo jumped out, weapon at the ready.

'Missed all the fun, have I?' he said, when he saw the secured suspect.

'I'm afraid you have,' grinned Mel. 'But there's an air rifle somewhere about which you need to seize. Try the shed at the back of number sixty-four. It's the suspect's parents' place, and his wife said he used to store stuff there.'

'OK, Mel. Good to see you again.'

'You too, Addy.'

As the ambulance pulled away, with Sally accompanying Nigel Willstone to the hospital, Mel reflected on the fight. Ever since someone tried to decapitate her with a sword, she had tended to freeze at the sight of a blade heading towards her. Yes, she had paused, momentarily, but she had managed to overcome her fear and disarm her attacker. Surely that meant she was getting better? Still some way to go, obviously, but perhaps the treatment was working. She would make another appointment with the force's counsellor. Buoyed up, she climbed into the police car and headed back to the station to write up her statement.

Chapter Forty-Seven

Day 21

'Firstly,' said DI Farlowe, opening the briefing, 'congratulations are due to Mel and Sally who apprehended Nigel Willstone yesterday. He has been harassing his wife, Rachel, for some days now and this culminated in shots fired at her home from an air rifle. He was found carrying a knife and Mel managed to disarm him without either DC getting hurt. Willstone was checked over at the hospital and is now in custody.'

There was a brief round of applause.

'AFOs found the weapon, which had been modified to take its power above the limit at which a firearms certificate is required, in Willstone's parents' shed. He will be charged with the illegal possession of a firearm, as well as possessing a bladed article, the assault on Mel and other offences relating to his harassment of Rachel.'

He paused as the team murmured their satisfaction.

'Now to Operation Apple, which we are definitely treating

as attempted murder. The forensic reports have come back on the crossbow package. No fingerprints on the bolt, the weapon or the box. There was, however, a short length of hair caught up in the wrapping. There was no root, so only mitochondrial DNA is available, which means we can't run it against the database. It would be too expensive to take and process hair samples from everyone at the scene so the lab will hold onto it until we get a suspect. We do know it wasn't from Pandora Blythe – it's brown and she's a redhead.'

'Where did the crossbow come from?' asked Trevor.

'That's a good question. Any identifying marks have been removed so it's impossible to trace. It could have come from a shop, a dodgy online site, or even a car boot sale. You don't need a licence as things stand, but there is talk of changing the law.'

'How about the secondary scene, boss?' asked Mel. 'Surely they found something?'

'Yes, they did. The SOCOs recovered some tyre tracks and paint scrapings. Both point to a Volkswagen SUV of fairly recent make, although this still needs to be confirmed. The tyres didn't appear to have any distinctive damage, so the tracks would be hard to match with a particular vehicle, but there should be scratch marks on the vehicle's paintwork, if the driver hasn't had them repaired. The pub CCTV picked up what looked like a large VW heading into town along the main road. ANPR cameras picked up such a vehicle on a main road, but the plates were false, belonging to a Fiat owned by a Michelle Harding of Milton Keynes. No genuine plates matching a VW were seen by any ANPR cameras.'

'Bollocks,' muttered Mel, under her breath.

'We don't know whether the vehicle in the bushes had anything to do with the offence, though, do we?' asked Trevor.

'It could have been people dogging the night before, for all we know.'

Several officers sniggered.

'Unlikely, Trevor,' said Farlowe. 'The damage to the shrubs was recent. Anyway, the clearing was only big enough for one vehicle and I understood that dogging involves several at a time. Not that I have any personal experience,' he smiled slightly.

'Wow. That's the closest he's come to a joke in a long time,' whispered Mel to Sally, who giggled.

Farlowe glared at them.

'So what we have,' he continued, 'is a probable attempt on the life of a well-liked TV presenter by someone with a degree of mechanical ingenuity and forensic awareness. We have no witnesses or CCTV, and forensic evidence that will only be of use if we find a suspect and his vehicle. There appears to be no motive for the crime. Just to check that you've all been paying attention,' he looked again at Mel, 'there is something possibly significant which stands out. Any takers?'

'The plates,' volunteered Kamal. 'A VW SUV with false plates. We've seen one in the vicinity of Babbacott Marina, the canal and the solvent recycling plant. Also, the forensics you mentioned at Carter Hall probably belonged to a VW SUV. Possibly the same person?'

'Exactly,' said Farlowe. 'But what we don't know is how these cases are linked, if, indeed, they are. The victims are completely different and appear to have no connection with each other. So our job now is to find a connection. Please put your heads together and, if it helps, do so in the Cat and Cushion, provided that you're not overheard. That's all for now. Thank you.'

Shit! The bloody bitch was lucky. And she was an important target. If anything came out about her misdemeanours, the tabloids would be all over it. They revel in ripping TV personalities to shreds, and the link to him would be bound to emerge. He would have to try again. He had hoped that the crossbow incident would be treated just as a prank by someone jealous of Blythe's success, but his next attempt would obviously be murder.

His attempts to pass off some of his efforts as accidents had clearly failed. The blunder over the barge padlock was stupid, and the police had obviously seen through it. He vowed not to make the same sort of mistake again. After all, he wasn't to know that the solvent recycling plant couldn't catch fire accidentally and that the police would treat it as arson and murder. He was confident that no-one suspected him so far, but how long could it last? There was no obvious link between his targets and himself. As long as nobody made the connection between Marnie's party and the deaths, and it came out that he was also there, he would be in the clear. He was determined to continue his campaign until the risks to his career were eliminated completely, whatever it took.

Chapter Forty-Eight

'You KNOW,' said Mel, 'there's something these murders all have in common.'

'What's that?' asked Emma, sipping a pint of Theakstons in a rare visit to the Cat and Cushion.

'There's no obvious motive, at least as far as we've been able to find.'

'Hardly a reason to link them together, though,' said Jack.

'True. But perhaps there's some underlying reason why these people were killed. And I reckon the attack on Pandora Blythe is part of it.'

Jack looked unimpressed.

'Don't forget the vehicles,' said Kamal. 'A dark SUV, probably a VW, was seen in the vicinity of the crimes, with false plates. And we now know it was a vehicle like that which tried to run down Mr Raven in London. I mentioned this at the briefing.'

'But there are thousands of dark SUVs about,' said Sally. 'You'd think there wasn't a climate crisis.'

'Yes,' persisted Kamal, 'but they don't all have dodgy

plates. It looks like too much of a coincidence. If there is a link between them, a common motive if you like, then the same person is cleverly targeting the victims. It's not some random serial killer or a whole bunch of individual murderers. And Pandora's attack was definitely attempted murder.'

'Well the only other link we've found so far,' said Jack, 'is the details of the financier's death in Madeleine Hollis's possession. And as far as we, and the Met, can tell, they didn't know each other.'

'There's something else,' said Sally, slowly. 'They all spent some time in London. Madeleine studied and was called to the Bar there, and Mark Sutton did his degree at Imperial College. DSup Raven worked there, obviously, and Dale Moncrieff lived in London, except when he was down here on his boat at weekends. Pandora Blythe, who I'm including as she could have been killed, works and lives there. If there is a link with the financier, that's a sixth.'

'Yes, but if you picked a dozen people at random in this part of the world, I bet that at least half of them would have a connection with London. It's not Cornwall or the Scottish Highlands,' said Jack, sceptically.

'Hold on, Jack,' said Emma. 'There could be something in what Sally says. It might be worth seeing if the timings overlap.'

'Can't do any harm, I suppose,' he replied. 'Anyway, I must be off.' He paused and cleared his throat. 'I think some of you know that Sarah was recently diagnosed with skin cancer. She's had the melanoma removed and the tests have come back clear, so we're going out to dinner to celebrate. And, er... I'm sorry if I've been a bit of an arse lately. See you tomorrow.'

The rest of the team smiled.

As Jack left, Mel was thinking about her meeting with DC

Plover. He had offered to help so perhaps he could look into what the victims did in London.

'I've a contact in the Met,' she announced. 'I'll talk to him in the morning. Now, whose round is it?'

Looks like I dodged a bullet, there, thought The Technician as she perused an online account of Dale Moncrieff's murder. *I knew there was something off about that request. Whatever the motive the client had for wanting him dead, I'm damn sure it was nothing to do with the abuse of his daughters. Nothing has come up, on the dark web or anywhere else, about Moncrieff having an interest in children, although he did seem to like frolicking with more than one partner at a time. Pure fabrication. Maybe I should have a sign pinned to the wall. When in doubt, trust your instinct. But should I do anything about this? Perhaps a post on social media or a comment on a podcast? Once I've dealt with this wife-beater I'll work something out. I do not like people trying to take me for a mug.*

Chapter Forty-Nine

Day 22

'BIRDY — it's Mel. Mel Cotton. Thanks again for your help the other day. I wonder if I can ask you a favour?'

'Anything for Mexton's answer to Jane Tennison,' he replied.

Mel winced and continued.

'We have four murders, including Mr Raven's, and an attempted murder down here, and we're looking for links between them. They all spent time in London, in the mid-to-late two-thousands. Would you be able to find out what they were doing and whether they could have met each other?'

'Christ, that's a big job. And we're not exactly sitting around twiddling our thumbs up here.' He thought for a moment. 'OK. I'll run it past my DS and see if he's happy for me to spend a bit of time on it. But you have to promise me something.'

'What's that?'

'You'll have dinner with me next time you're in London.'

You cheeky sod, Mel thought, but replied diplomatically.

'OK. If you find anything useful, I'll try to get permission to travel. But don't be disappointed – I'm married and I don't look anything like Helen Mirren.'

'Do you really think it's worth trekking up to London?' asked DCI Farlowe.

'I do, boss,' replied Mel. 'DC Plover sounds a bit creepy over the phone, but I think he could be helpful. Perhaps I could talk to someone dealing with Mr Raven's case while I'm up there.'

'Good idea. I'll make a call and clear the way for you. Please make it a day trip, though. We can't afford an overnight stay, and there's plenty to be getting on with down here.'

Mel thanked the DCI and went to look up train times, with slightly mixed feelings. She didn't want to go for a meal with DC Plover but, at the same time, she didn't want to appear ungrateful for his help. She decided to plead a prior evening engagement and promise to buy him a curry the next time she was in London.

Chapter Fifty

Day 23

MEL SIGNED in at the front desk of Charing Cross police station and was issued with a visitor's pass on a lanyard. Five minutes later, a PC led her into the depths of the building and showed her into a CID office.

'Good morning, DC Cotton,' said a tall, heavily-built detective inspector. 'I'm DI Pleshey. Did you have a good journey?'

'Not too bad, thank you. A few minor delays, that's all. Thank you for agreeing to see me.'

'You're on the team investigating Detective Superintendent Raven's tragic murder, I understand?'

'That's correct. I've been asked to find out more about the hit and run incident that put him in the clinic in Mexton.'

'There's not much more to tell,' said Pleshey, chucking a folder on the desk in front of Mel. 'We've already sent your DI something. DSup Raven said he was planning to meet an old friend in a wine bar when this car came out of nowhere and knocked him flying. It was coming back for another try, when an ambulance appeared and it drove off. He only saw the headlights but thought it was a fairly large vehicle, possibly an SUV. The only witnesses were some distance away and had been drinking, but they said the car was large and dark. The paramedics saw a vehicle but didn't notice any details. They were focused on the victim.'

'Was there any CCTV?'

'Not at the scene and an ANPR trawl proved fruitless. Have you any idea how many large, SUV-type vehicles there are on London's roads, especially in a wealthy area like Mayfair?'

'Quite a few, I should imagine,' replied Mel. 'What sort of man was DSup Raven?'

'I worked with him for a while. He was a well-respected detective. He got on with colleagues of all ranks and had a good clear-up rate. After his wife died, about ten years ago, he threw himself completely into the job, not that he was less than fully committed before that. He didn't have any children but always helped to provide meals and presents for homeless kids at Christmas. He spent his spare time restoring classic cars.'

'How about enemies?'

'He'd put away a few wrong 'uns in his time, and had the usual threats from the dock, but there's no-one we could think of who would do this sort of thing. We made some enquiries but came up with nothing. Unfortunately, his house burnt down while he was down your way. An electrical fault, the fire investigator thought, so we couldn't find anything in his papers or on his personal laptop suggesting a motive. We thought the fire was suspicious at first, but there was no evidence of arson. There was nothing of relevance in his office, here.'

'But you don't think it was some random, motiveless attack?'

'No. The second attempt strongly suggested it was targeted and his murder confirmed it. How's your investigation going?' the DI asked.

'Not very well. It looks like the killer gained entry to the care home at night by posing as a member of staff, sent by an agency. He cut Mr Raven's throat and removed some of his fingers, presumably because his victim fought back and scratched him. He forced open a window and made his way to the road where his car was parked, some distance away. There's no CCTV of any use, and ANPR gave us nothing. Presumably he used back roads to avoid the cameras.'

'Local knowledge, then.'

'It looks likely. But why someone with local knowledge of Mexton would be running down a Met officer in Mayfair is a real puzzle,' said Mel.

'Agreed. And nobody on his contact list has any connection with your part of the world.'

'We haven't come across anybody locally with criminal connections to London, either. Not still living, anyway. May I keep this?' She indicated the folder of documents.

'Yes, do. These are copies I had prepared for you.'

'Well thank you very much for your help, sir,' Mel smiled. 'We'll keep you informed of progress.'

'Likewise. We're extremely keen to co-operate when it's one of our own. Are you going straight back to Mexton?'

'No, I've got to talk to a DC Plover, in Specialist Crime at Barking, about a financier who was pushed off an office block. A murder victim on our patch had details of the death in her pocket and we wondered why.'

'Interesting. Well, good luck and a safe journey.'

Chapter Fifty-One

MEL DECIDED to walk from the police station in Agar Street to the Embankment tube, where she could take a District Line train to Barking. As she ate her sandwiches in Victoria Embankment Gardens, she wondered about DC Carl Plover. He had sounded a bit dodgy over the phone and was obviously delighted when she said she was coming to London to meet him. She was well aware of the reputation some Met officers had, so she was a little wary. At least they would be meeting in a coffee shop, rather than his office, so he would be unlikely to try anything in a public space.

Mel's apprehensions about DC Plover proved unfounded at first, although his gaze did seem to linger on her chest. He had a friendly smile and wasn't bad looking, in a lean and slightly wolfish way, but his appearance was let down by a rather shabby suit and a careless shave. He greeted her politely, shook her hand firmly, and bought her a coffee and a pastry.

'So how can I help?' he asked, when the waiter had brought their order.

'I need background information on Justin Kite for a start, please.' She kept her manner friendly but professional. 'Anything that could link him with Madeleine Hollis, our murdered barrister.'

'He seems to have been a typical modern financier. He'd lived in London all his life, apart from when he did his degree at Exeter University, and had a generally clean record, although he was cautioned for possession of a small amount of cocaine last year. He had been married to a bloke for eighteen months, apparently happily.'

Plover's lips twitched at the last sentence.

'He had plenty of money, a Lamborghini and took expensive foreign holidays. There were no problems at home, apparently, and, although there's always rivalry in firms like Vatten-Cooley, no-one appears to have hated him. Since your call, I've asked his friends and colleagues if he could have known Ms Hollis, but none of them recalled him ever mentioning the name. She doesn't appear on any contacts list or email correspondence. What can you tell me about her?'

'She was a well-respected barrister and had a reputation for getting people off murder cases. She was in Mexton for the trial of someone she was at university with, here in London. Her chambers are in Bristol, where she moved after being called to the Bar. She was divorced, well-off and had no criminal record.'

'Do you have any leads?'

'Not really. She met someone in a wine bar and left with him, looking a bit wobbly. We're pretty sure she was drugged. We've only got a rough description of him from the bar staff, but they did say they seemed to know each other. Her car was left at her hotel and she was fished out of the canal the following morning by some Scouts.'

'Do you reckon the same person killed both of them?' asked Birdy.

'If there was a strong link between them, I'd be inclined to think so, but all we've got is the printout in Ms Hollis's car.'

'And the fact that both lived in London at some point.'

'But that applies to millions of people,' argued Mel.

'I know. Look, I'll send you the CCTV footage of our suspect. If you've got anything, send it to me. We'll compare them and maybe show them to witnesses. Perhaps get some gait analysis done.'

'Good idea. We've got nothing to lose, although gait analysis isn't that reliable. Anyone can fake a limp.'

'True. Look, we must keep in touch in case any links emerge,' He stood up and Mel followed. 'I've got to get back to the office now, but please feel free to call me. Are you staying around for that meal? We could make a night of it. A club, maybe, then who knows?'

A hint of a leer flickered over his face at the last phrase.

'Sorry.' She shuddered inside. 'I have to get back. Parrots to feed.'

'Parrots? Big blue and yellow things?'

'No. Those are macaws. Ours are eclectus parrots. Tom, my husband, rescued one from a warehouse full of illegally traded wildlife products and he found a companion from an adoption site. He's away on a course, so I have to get back to feed them. They need a lot of company. Anyway, thanks for your help, DC Plover.'

'No trouble. And it's Carl – or Birdy.'

'Mel.'

'Before you go, can I take a photo of us? Demonstrating inter-force co-operation?'

Fatal Image

Mel agreed reluctantly and flinched as Birdy's thigh pressed into hers while he held his phone in front of them. She smiled coolly and shook his hand as briefly as courtesy permitted, then wished him good day.

Birdy gazed disappointedly at Mel's retreating rear as she headed for the Tube station. A pleasant interlude, but had it been a complete waste of time? Why on earth wasn't she interested?

Chapter Fifty-Two

Day 24

'So what more have we got on Mark Sutton?' asked DCI Farlowe, at the start of the briefing.

'Not a lot, guv,' replied Sally. 'We applied to his provider for his call history. The phone call he received luring him to the site was made from the Mexton area, but we don't have a name to match with the number. Financially, his company was in a good position, despite setbacks during the pandemic. A couple of the big waste management companies had tried to buy him out but he wasn't interested. He had a clean record and hadn't been involved in any legal disputes. His wife said their marriage was pretty stable – they'd been together for six years and neither of them wanted children. They didn't like the look of the world any child would grow up in. She couldn't think of anyone who would want to harm Mark. They had no major debts, and he paid off the credit cards in full every month. She has her own income as a sculptor and teacher.'

'Anything on his laptop or phone?'

'His phone was missing,' replied Amira Khan. 'It was either taken by the killer or destroyed in the fire. There was so much debris on the site, the SOCO's couldn't find any traces of it. The laptop was more interesting, if you like this sort of thing. He'd downloaded a load of group sex videos from porn sites. He seemed to like to mix and match, at least in his imagination.'

Several officers sniggered. Farlowe gave them a cold stare.

'I suppose there could be some motivation there,' he said. 'If he was doing this in real life and his wife found out. But we know she remained in the garden when he went to the plant. A neighbour confirmed it.'

'Perhaps she was into swinging, too,' suggested Mel. 'Has anyone mentioned the videos to her?'

'No,' replied Amira. 'I've only just cracked his password and seen them.'

'Mrs Sutton seemed genuinely upset by her husband's death,' said Jack. 'Also, their place was burgled a couple of nights ago, while she was visiting friends, and we didn't have anyone to investigate. Uniform gave her a crime number for the insurance and left it at that. She's not overly fond of us at the moment, so I don't think we need bother her unless we have to.'

'Agreed,' said the DCI. 'But if we need to, we will. It might be worth taking a look at the burglary, just in case there's a link with the murder. Is there anything more on the Blythe assault?'

'I'm off to interview Tamsin Riley this afternoon,' replied Mel. 'She could have had a motive, since Pandora got the presenting job she wanted. I don't think there's anything else.'

'Anything on the Hollis case?'

'My contact in the Met has sent me some CCTV footage of the suspect. I'm still looking through it and I'll compare it with the material from outside the wine bar. I'm not hopeful.

We still haven't found a link between her and Justin Kite, apart from the printout of his death report. Her briefcase turned up in the canal, caught by an angler who thought he'd got a big one. The documents inside are being dried out in the lab but much of the print has gone. Some of them appear to be legally privileged, so we'll send them down to her chambers without examining them.'

Farlowe nodded his approval.

'I had a video call with her clerk, who was devastated by the murder,' continued Mel. 'She said that Madeleine was highly successful and extremely hard-working. Her standards were very high and, provided you met them, she was good to work for – almost inspirational. She had no time for slackers, though. She didn't seem to have much of a personal life.'

'OK. Thanks, Mel. It looks like the Raven case has gone cold but we need to redouble our efforts,' said Farlowe, the anger in his voice undisguised. 'We will not let this one go.'

Chapter Fifty-Three

TAMSIN RILEY SHOWED Mel into a cramped home office, dominated by recording equipment and computers. She moved a pile of papers from an office chair and invited her to sit. When Mel explained the reason for her visit, she snorted at the suggestion that she had anything to do with the attack on Pandora Blythe.

'Look, DC Cotton, I haven't been anywhere near that bitch since she got the Wellness Roadshow job. Of course I resented it at the time, but I've done much better since. I present a true crime programme on a streaming channel and my podcast on supernatural sightings is consistently in the top ten. I've also ghost-written a celebrity's attempt at a murder mystery, set in a "get me out of here" type of programme. I wouldn't have had the time to do these if I'd been traipsing around the country appealing to those dreary-looking people who frequent health food shops and never look very well. And I wouldn't have earned as much, either.'

'So you really don't bear a grudge?' said Mel.

'Nope. I'm quite indifferent to her. I found out about the

incident on social media and I didn't even feel any schaden-freude. I was out of the country at the time, filming. You can check with my agent if you like.'

'I may well do that. Can I ask about your brother? Is he still in the BBC props department?'

'He is, but he's been off work for the past three weeks. A Dalek fell on him and broke his leg. Why on earth do you want to know about him?'

'We're looking for people who might have the skills to make the device which hurt Ms Blythe. A small crossbow, in a box, that fired when she opened it.'

Tamsin burst out laughing.

'Even if he was motivated to do so, which he isn't, he wouldn't have the skill to make anything more complicated than a milk shake. He's always been totally cack-handed. He doesn't make props for the BBC, he catalogues them and manages their storage. I'll tell him what you've just suggested. It might cheer him up. Now, if there's nothing more, I need to get on with my podcast.'

'All right. Thank you, Ms Riley. If you can email me the contact details for your agent, I'd appreciate it. Here's my card.'

Tamsin turned her back on Mel, started fiddling with recording equipment and waved vaguely in her direction when she said goodbye.

Well, that was a bloody waste of time, thought Mel as she returned to her car. *At least I didn't have to go further than Maidenhead to talk to her. I'll check with the BBC about her brother's role, but it doesn't sound promising.*

Chapter Fifty-Four

PANDORA BLYTHE DROVE SLOWLY through the gates of Carter Hall, just before midnight, and headed for home, not enjoying the prospect of a two-hour drive, but glad that the final Wellness Roadshow episode was in the can. They had even made something of the cut on her face. A last-minute call to the makers of a vitamin-enhanced seaweed preparation, marketed, just the right side of legality, for promoting healing, had produced an extra wedge of sponsorship. Whether or not it worked, she wasn't worried. Product placement was the name of the game, and the bean counters at the production company would be pleased.

Realising that the offerings on the radio at that time of night would probably be soporific, she slipped her phone out of the bag on the seat beside her, intending to connect it to the car's infotainment system via Bluetooth. A peppy playlist, to which she could sing along, should keep her awake on the tedious journey. She slowed down as she approached the junction with the main road and cursed as a badly-repaired pothole jolted the car. The phone slipped out of her hand and, as she reached down to pick it up in the still-moving vehicle, a shotgun blast ripped through the darkness, blowing out both windows.

Exactly what happened next, she could never remember. Fortunately, most of the shot had passed over her head and neck while she was bent forward. A few pellets must have grazed her because her hair was full of blood and she felt a warm sticky liquid coursing down her neck a few seconds later. Then it started to sting. She didn't consciously accelerate, but, somehow, she ended up speeding towards the junction and hurtling out onto the main road, causing an oncoming HGV to brake suddenly, the howl of its horn scaring her almost as much as the gunshot. She swerved, clipped a milepost and rocketed onto a grass verge. Fifty metres further on she managed an emergency stop, a few centimetres before she would have smashed into a bus shelter.

She threw up, put her head on the steering wheel and burst into tears.

'What the fuck do you think you were doing, you stupid... oh shit.'

The HGV driver's tirade was truncated when he saw the fragments of broken glass, twinkling in the glare from his headlights, and the blood in Pandora's hair.

'What happened, love?' he asked. 'Are you badly hurt?'

Pandora kept on sobbing, unable to speak.

'It's OK. Hold on. I'll phone for an ambulance. Are you in the AA or anything?'

Pandora managed to gulp out a couple of words before she fainted.

'Police. Gunshot.'

'Boss,' said the call handler, 'there's a lorry driver on the line. Says a woman he nearly ran into claims she was shot at by the police.'

'Put him through,' said the duty inspector. 'I'll talk to him. I'm sure there are no firearms operations running tonight, but I'll get someone to check.'

'How can I help you sir?' he asked, when the driver was connected.

'This woman shot out of the side road that leads to Carter Hall, and I nearly hit her. Her car ended up on the verge and she collapsed at the wheel. All she said was: "police gunshot". She had blood on her head and the windows were smashed in. She's breathing and she's got a pulse. I've called an ambulance and they're on the way. What should I do?'

'What advice did ambulance control give you?'

'They said to keep an eye on her and try to stop the bleeding. I wrapped a clean cloth round her head and it seems to have helped.'

'Can you see her from the cab of your vehicle?'

'Only if I pull up next to her and open the door.'

'OK. Could you do that? If she wakes up, take note of what she says. Please stay in your cab unless you absolutely have to get out, in case there is still someone with a firearm in the vicinity. An armed response unit will be with you shortly. Thank you for calling this in. We really appreciate it.'

Within ten minutes, an armed response vehicle was heading towards the scene, followed by a patrol car. The force helicopter arrived shortly afterwards, bathing the area in bright white light, just as the ambulance drove away with its blue lights flashing. The ARV blocked the entrance to the side road while the patrol car pulled up alongside the lorry.

'Did the victim wake up and say anything?' PC Halligan asked the driver.

'A bit,' he replied. 'She said she was driving towards the junction when she heard a gunshot and her side window blew in. Something hit her and she drove away on instinct. She was asking me to call the police. I thought she meant they'd shot her.'

'Well, we don't normally shoot unarmed people,' said Halligan, stiffly. 'Did you see anyone else in the vicinity?'

'I was focusing on the woman. I'm sure I've seen her face somewhere. I saw no-one on foot, but a vehicle came past while I was helping her. Dark, large-ish. I can't be more specific, sorry.'

'That's OK. You've been very helpful. Can you call into the station tomorrow – and give a formal statement? We may need a DNA sample as well.'

'I've got to get this load to Brum by the morning, but I'll be back in Mexton by the afternoon. Will that do?'

'That's fine sir. I won't keep you any longer.'

Chapter Fifty-Five

WHILE HALLIGAN WAS TALKING to the witness, and deploying blue and white tape around Pandora's car, the Tactical Firearms Commander was considering the options. A building or vehicle with an armed suspect inside was relatively easy to contain, but open countryside, with plenty of vegetation to act as cover for a shooter, was a nightmare. Officers in the helicopter had failed to spot anyone in the area but that didn't mean there wasn't someone lurking. Rather than risk harm coming to an officer, he sent a firearms dog down the lane while PC Adeyemo and his colleagues took cover behind their vehicle. For five minutes nothing could be heard apart from leaves rustling in the wind. Then the dog returned, wagging its tail.

The TFC considered the options. Perhaps the suspect had already left the scene. The absence of a reaction from the dog certainly seemed to suggest so, but he didn't want to send officers down the lane on foot in case there was still a risk to life.

'Addy,' he called. 'Take the van down the lane, slowly, with Jim on board. Stay alert and don't take any risks.'

'OK,' replied Addy, a hint of nervousness in his voice.

The van pulled up beside a pile of glass fragments, obviously blown out by the shotgun blast. On the opposite side of the road a small tree bordered the lane. Addy got out of the ARV, his heart in his mouth and his carbine at the ready. When he got close to the tree and shone his torch on it, he relaxed and picked up his Airwave.

'No-one here, guv, but I think I've found where the shooter fired from.' He had to shout to be heard over the clatter from the helicopter. 'There's what looks like a scorch mark on a branch and some leaves seem to have been blown away. There's glass on the other side of the road, from the car windows, I guess.'

'OK. Addy. Wait there and I'll send for someone to secure the scene. And keep your eyes and ears open.'

The helicopter continued to illuminate the scene until daylight, switching to infra-red imaging from time to time and stopping only to return to base to refuel. Come morning, a search team combed the area around the firing point, finding no-one and nothing of use. SOCOs examined the tree, sampling the bark and branches, as well as photographing the scene. A tracker dog picked up a trail which led up the lane and onto the main road, stopping in a lay-by sixty metres from the junction.

Chapter Fifty-Six

Day 25

'PANDORA BLYTHE'S BEEN SHOT!'

Mel burst into the incident room just as Emma was about to start the morning briefing.

'Fatally?' queried the DI.

'No, but she's in hospital. A couple of shotgun pellets winged her, apparently, and she got a bit of broken glass in her eye. There's no permanent damage but she's virtually mute with shock. It happened as she was leaving Carter Hall for home, late last night.'

'That ties in with something on the overnight reports,' said Jack. 'A shooting and a traffic incident out that way. An ARU attended but there was no suspect at the scene. Pandora's name wasn't mentioned.'

'Right, we'd better bring the incident into Operation Apple. I'll ask Mr Farlowe to make the arrangements when he gets back from his strategy meeting. It looks like someone is really determined to kill her.'

'What have forensics got to say?' Jack asked Emma.

'Not a lot. The weapon, a shotgun, was fired beside a tree and if Pandora had been sitting upright it would have shattered her skull. Fortunately, she was bending down to pick up a dropped phone. SOCOs found a couple of fibres, on a thorn, which will be compared with those found on the fence around the marina, just in case there's a link with that murder, although they're pretty generic. There were some tyre marks in the layby which match those they found where the vehicle was parked when the booby trap was delivered, so we're pretty certain this was a second attempt by the same attacker. Basically, not much to go on.'

'This is becoming a pattern. It's the same for all these bloody murders. Nothing to go on, and it's making us look bloody stupid,' said Jack. 'Before we do anything else, we need to set up a safety plan for Pandora. She'll need advice, alarms and her details flagged on force computers in case she makes contact in an emergency. We can do some things here but it's down to the Met to protect her where she lives and works. I'll liaise with them.'

'OK,' Emma sighed. 'Thanks, Jack. We'd better get a list of all holders of shotgun certificates in the area. I suppose there's an outside chance the attacker used a legally held weapon. We can't match anything ballistically, but it might throw up a suspect. Keep looking for dark SUVs registered to addresses in the south of England and get some noticeboards up along the main road asking for witnesses and dashcam footage. Not that there will be any, I'm sure. Jack'll divvy up the actions, so get some coffee and have a bloody good think.

'This is fucking ridiculous,' said Trevor, standing behind Mel in the coffee queue. 'How many dark SUVs can there be registered in that area? Bloody hundreds? Thousands? And the countryside's not short of shotguns, either. It'll take a month of Sundays to get through this lot. Half the civilian investigators are off with the trots, after celebrating someone's birthday at a dodgy restaurant, and there's still a few cases of Covid going around.'

'Come on Trevor. This is what the job's all about. And you're good at this sort of thing. I'll buy you some biscuits.'

Mel smiled encouragingly.

'OK.' Trevor looked chastened. 'But it's still a ridiculous amount of work.'

'We should get some overtime, if that's any consolation.'

'Yeah. Susie's gonna be thrilled about that. Still, I suppose the money will be useful. Better get to it, I suppose. Bagsy the shotguns.'

Chapter Fifty-Seven

'HOW ARE YOU FEELING, PANDORA?' asked Mel, pulling a chair up beside the hospital bed.

'Crap,' to be honest,' the patient replied. 'They say I can go home shortly, but I'm terrified. The shot didn't do me any real harm, but every time I hear a bang it all comes back to me. Have you caught him yet? I won't sleep until you do.'

Pandora's voice was rising as panic took over.

'We're following some leads,' said Mel, 'but, to be honest, there's not a lot to go on. We've talked to Tamsin and she and her brother seem to be in the clear. I can't give you any more details, I'm afraid. We really need to know who could want to harm you.'

Pandora's hands trembled as she reached for a glass of water.

'I've been through my old emails and so has the production company. There've been no threats or anything remotely like hate mail. I've had a few nutters saying that some of the products and treatments featured in the show don't have the right sort of cosmic energy, or something. A few medical people have criticised things, saying that they don't have any scientific foundation, but my viewers don't particularly care about that. I really don't know.'

Mel frowned and thought for a moment.

'Just as a matter of interest, do any of the names Madeleine Hollis, Mark Sutton, Dale Moncrieff or James Raven mean anything to you?'

Pandora looked thoughtful then started to speak.

'I think I've seen some of them in the papers or on social media. I don't know...'

Her eyes widened and she looked away, pausing for a second before continuing.

'I mean I don't know any of them.'

'How about Justin Kite?'

'No, no. I don't think I've ever heard of him. Why do you ask?'

'It's public knowledge, so I'm not disclosing anything I shouldn't. They have all been murdered recently, most of them in this area. We're trying to find a link between them.'

'Well I can't help you. Sorry,' said Pandora, her voice strained.

'That's OK. It was just a long shot. I'll leave you to rest. There's a police guard outside. When you're discharged, have you anyone you could stay with? It may not be a good idea to go back to your flat.'

'My cousin in High Wycombe. She's picking me up from the hospital. I'm staying with her while her husband's away. I need to get some stuff from home and then we'll go back to her place. No one else in my circle knows where she lives.'

'Good idea. Please be careful and don't hesitate to call 999 if anything worries you. Explain what's happened and give my name and phone number. You still have my card?'

Pandora nodded.

'Thank you. I will. And DC Cotton?'

'Yes?'

'Please let me know when you catch the bastard.'

'Of course, and if anything occurs to you, call me. Whatever time of day. Good luck and stay safe.'

As soon as Mel left, Pandora shuddered. The names had come back to her in a rush, evoking a memory long since buried. A memory which, although largely pleasant, caused her no little embarrassment. But why were people at that particular event being killed? She tried to remember who else had been there. She'd seen a half-recognised face somewhere recently, but couldn't place it. Perhaps she nearly remembered him from that party. And someone else? Someone pretty taciturn? One thing was certain; she couldn't tell the police about the connection. If it came out, her career would be ruined. All she could do was lie low and hope the police caught the murderer before he tried to kill her again.

———————————

Four miles away, Hugh Ventham was still raging. *Does that fucking cow lead a charmed life? The shotgun blast should have dealt with her once and for all. Christ, I can hit a four-inch-wide clay pigeon travelling at fifty miles per hour but missed a human head moving at barely more than walking pace. So, what happens next?* He didn't think he would be linked to either attempted murder. He'd been so careful. If he tried again, it would increase the chances of him getting caught. But could he afford not to? Perhaps he should leave it for a while and let things cool down. Or try a different approach. Now, he would clean his shotgun and lock it away, but not before he'd found something to shoot at. He really wanted to kill something, and woe betide any stray cat that wandered into his grounds.

Chapter Fifty-Eight

'NO LUCK WITH PANDORA, GUV,' said Mel, knocking on Emma's open door. 'She still can't think of anyone who would want to harm her. She's going to stay with a cousin in Buckinghamshire for a while – she's shit scared. Mind you, when I told her the names of the other victims, she reacted a bit oddly.'

'What do you mean, lass?'

'I got the impression there was something she wasn't telling me. She denied knowing them, but I'm not so sure.'

'But what would she have in common with a chemist, a barrister, a charity CEO and a police officer? Or a banker, if he's connected as well.'

'No idea, apart from the fact that they were all in London at the same time, around 2007. Mark Sutton was at Imperial College, as was Dale Moncrieff. Justin Kite and Mr Raven were working there and Madeleine Hollis was training for the Bar. Perhaps something happened which affected them all, but I can't think what.'

'Did you get anything from your mate in the Met?'

'Nothing of any use. He's pretty busy with a teenage

shooting at the moment so I don't think he's had much time. He did check whether any of them had been arrested or cautioned together but he drew a blank. Mr Raven didn't arrest any of them either. In fact, apart from Justin Kite and his charlie, none of them had come to the Met's attention.

'If we had addresses, someone could check the electoral rolls and see if any of them lived together, but we don't. It would be pretty laborious, anyway. Social media was still fairly new so there's nothing there.'

Emma nodded and Mel went off in search of coffee.

'My flat's been trashed, DC Cotton. Fucking trashed.' A near-hysterical Pandora Blythe howled down the phone at Mel. 'I called in to collect some stuff and found everything chucked all over the floor. Cupboards broken, furniture wrecked and mattresses ripped open. I can't take any more of this shit.'

'I'm really sorry to hear that. Was anything taken?'

'Not really. I don't understand it. The TV and my sound system weren't touched and my jewellery was left on the floor where they'd thrown it. They'd taken the base unit for my old desktop computer, which I don't use any more, but left the monitor. Some cash in a bedside cupboard was left behind, as well.'

'Clearly this wasn't an ordinary burglary, or all the valuables would have gone. If it was just another attempt to get at you, they would have smashed the TV and other tech. It does sound as though they were looking for something. Have you any idea what? Do you hold any share certificates, valuable papers or anything like that?'

'No. Anything important is in a safety deposit at the bank.'

Mel thought for a moment.

'Where do you live? I don't have your details in front of me.'

'East London. A small flat in a refurbished house. Do you need the address?'

'No. Not at the moment. Look, the Met police wouldn't normally bother with a crime like this. They're too busy and no-one was hurt. They would give you a crime number, a leaflet on home security and leave it to the insurance company to sort out. But I've a contact, a Detective Constable Plover, who works in your area. Give him a ring and explain that I gave you his number and that the break-in could be connected to the attacks on you in Mexton. He may be able to help you. In the meantime, I would urge you to get an emergency carpenter to fix your door, if it needs it, and get off to your cousin's as soon as you can.'

'Thank you, DC Cotton,' said Pandora, now slightly calmer. 'I can't bear to stay here a moment longer than necessary. The door's OK and I'll phone your contact. If he or she needs me to come back to London I will. But not just yet.'

After reciting Birdy's number and urging Pandora to be careful and keep in touch, Mel ended the call. *This is weird,* she thought. *Someone tries to kill Pandora, twice, but, when that fails, ransacks her flat to look for something. But what could she have that was so important? And did they find it? If she had some vital secret in her possession, wouldn't it make more sense to find it first and then kill her to prevent her blabbing? You're moving into thriller territory here, Mel,* she reproved herself. *But, nevertheless, it was weird.*

———

Pandora and her cousin didn't notice the anonymous dark car which pulled in behind them as they drew away from the flat.

209

It remained several vehicles back on the tedious stop-start journey past Kings Cross, Euston, Marylebone and out to the Westway. On the M40 it was just another vehicle in the rush-hour traffic and, by the time they reached High Wycombe, they were so preoccupied with getting home that they wouldn't have spotted an elephant on skis following them. The driver cruised slowly past as they unloaded their luggage, noted the number of the house and pulled in to a side road, miraculously free of 'residents parking only' signs. Then he waited and formulated a plan.

Chapter Fifty-Nine

'WHAT's this Blythe woman all about, Mel?' asked a slightly annoyed Birdy when Mel answered her phone. 'D'you think we're just sitting here playing with ourselves and waiting for something to do?'

Mel pushed the image from her mind and tried to mollify the Met detective.

'Sorry to lumber you, Birdy, but the victim has been attacked twice, both murder attempts, and we think it's linked to our murders. The break-in wasn't for theft — someone was looking for something, but Pandora has no idea what. Could you at least have a look at it and maybe get some SOCOs to dust for prints?'

'Blimey. You don't ask much, do you? I'll see what I can do, seeing as it's you. I'd love to keep you abreast of things.' He paused slightly. 'I'll have to run it past my guv'nor though.'

Birdy's annoyance had gone, replaced by something which could almost be construed as a verbal leer.

'But next time you're in London, you owe me a curry and a drink. A big one. Deal?'

'Deal,' replied Mel. 'And thanks again, Birdy.'

She ended the call feeling uneasy. Was the Londoner just being friendly or did he want something other than inter-force co-operation from her? OK, he wasn't bad looking but there was something about his manner which set her on edge, and his behaviour in London was distinctly iffy. Perhaps she should let slip that her husband was a red belt at Tae Kwan Do... omitting the bit about the prosthetic hand, that is.

Pandora and her cousin, Lorna, had just finished their evening meal when a ring on the doorbell dripped ice down Pandora's spine.

'Don't answer it Lorn! It could be him.'

'Don't worry, love. I've got a doorbell camera. I'll check who it is on my laptop.'

The image on the screen was of a man in an expensive-looking overcoat, his face impossible to make out owing to the trilby hat that cast a shadow from the overhead security light and the Covid mask which covered his mouth and nose.

'He seems harmless enough,' said Lorna. 'He looks a bit like one of Doug's colleagues from work, but I can't be sure. I'll open the door, on the chain, and see.'

'For fuck's sake be careful. Don't let him in, whoever he is.'

Lorna smiled, went to the door and slid the chain into its socket. She opened the door slightly and had barely got the word 'Hello' out of her mouth when the door was rammed open, the screws holding the chain ripping clean out of the flimsy woodwork. She stumbled backwards, tripped over a rug and banged her head on the newel post at the bottom of the stairs.

'Where is she?' yelled the intruder, kicking the door shut behind him. 'Pandora Blythe. I saw her come in.'

He pulled his hand out of his coat pocket and produced a pistol which he brandished in Lorna's face.

'Get her out here or I'll blow your head off.'

He worked the slide of the semi-automatic to emphasise the point.

'Help me, Pan!' called Lorna, dizzy in the head and sick to her stomach. 'Help me, please!'

The man turned at a sound behind him and saw Pandora rushing out of the kitchen, a carving knife in her hand.

'Drop it or she dies. Go on. Drop it.'

Pandora faltered, stopped and threw the knife away, tears streaming down her cheeks.

'I'm sorry, Lorn. I'm so sorry.' She turned to the intruder. 'What the fuck do you want? You've tried to kill me twice. Have you come to finish me off, you bastard?'

'There's no need for anyone to die,' he replied, his voice slightly muffled by the Covid mask which covered most of his face. 'I just want the photograph.'

'What the fuck are you talking about? Is that why you trashed my flat? Looking for a photograph? You'd better fucking explain.'

'All right. I'll spell it out for you. Some years ago, you were at a party. A rather special one. Somebody took a photo. A Polaroid. I want it.'

'What party? I've been to loads? What so special about this one?'

'You should remember. You were naked much of the time. London, 2007. A woman called Marnie. Ring any bells?'

'Oh shit. Yes, I know which party you mean.'

Pandora blushed crimson and Lorna, now recovering from the bump on her head, looked puzzled.

'But you're out of luck. I don't remember a bloody photo and I certainly don't have one. I've tried to forget that party and I'd hoped everyone else had too. Were you there?'

'Never you mind. I need that photo. I know it's not in your flat so you must have it somewhere else. I could tie you both up and search this place but that would take time. So, here's the deal. You find the photo, put it in a plastic bag and drop it in the dog waste bin at the end of the road by midnight tomorrow. Then I won't shoot you and this woman – your sister? – in the head. And don't even think of making a copy or contacting the police, because I will find you. Wherever you go. Understand?'

'But I keep telling you. I don't have a photo,' Pandora wailed. 'And why are you picking on me?'

'Because most of the others are dead, and if the police had found the photo, I would have known about it. Remember, midnight tomorrow.'

The intruder let himself out, waving the pistol at the terrified women once more and closing the door behind him.

Chapter Sixty

Day 26

DCI Farlowe intercepted Emma as she passed his office.

'Can I have a word, please, Emma?'

'Of course, Colin. Is anything wrong?'

'No, not at all. Come in and sit down.'

Emma sat nervously in a comfortable chair facing the DCI's desk. *Was there something wrong with her performance? She was doing her best, but perhaps that wasn't good enough?* She declined his offer of tea.

'Firstly,' he began, 'DSup Gorman and I are both extremely impressed by how quickly you got up to speed since your return. You do seem pretty tired at times, and I wanted to ask you how you're coping with juggling the job and the baby.'

Emma looked warily at her boss. *Something's up,* she thought.

'Good days and bad days, I suppose. We're not getting enough sleep, I'll admit, but I believe I'm doing my job properly.'

'Yes, of course. I think we're working well together and everything is just about getting covered. I believe Jack has provided sterling support as well.'

Emma nodded her agreement.

'So, you're happy with the hours you're allocated? You don't want to reduce them at all?'

'No. Definitely not. Mike is part-time at the university, so between us we're providing full-time care for Genevieve. When she's old enough to go to a nursery, assuming we can find one, things may change, but that's a long way off.'

Would they be asking Mike this? she asked herself. *Probably not.*

'Good. That's good. Anyway, I have some news. We've been authorised to recruit another detective inspector to work part time, effectively job-sharing your position, so we will have the equivalent of a full-time DI on the team again. Adverts are going out and interviews will be held at the beginning of next month.'

So there is a problem. Why doesn't he just say so? Do I really look as exhausted as I feel? Perhaps he's right, though. We do need a full-time DI. Maybe it doesn't make sense to have a part-time DI doing a full-time job with support from over-worked colleagues. So why do I feel threatened?

'Oh. Er... that's good. It should lighten the load considerably. But what if I want to increase my hours in the future?'

'We'll worry about that when we come to it. Obviously, I would like to have more than one DI on the team but, as you know, it all comes down to funding. And that's beyond our control.'

'Right. Well, thanks for letting me know,' she said, her tone neutral. 'I'll look forward to working with a new colleague.'

'Excellent. I'll let you get on.'

Emma left Farlowe's office in turmoil. On the one hand, it

would be good to share the work with a colleague. She was feeling the strain, and was really missing her daughter, it was true, but she was sure it hadn't affected her work. The DCI had reassured her that there were no complaints. On the other, she liked to be in charge and wondered how she would feel sharing the responsibility for the team with someone else. *I suppose it all depends on personalities*, she thought, *whether the new person was easy to get on with or a difficult bugger. Fingers crossed that we get an angel and not an arsehole.*

Chapter Sixty-One

Day 27

ONE O'CLOCK and the street was deserted, the good citizens of that part of High Wycombe all tucked up in bed. No one had approached the dog waste bin since an elderly man, towed by a Labrador, deposited a donation three hours ago. That meant one of two things, he thought. Either the Blythe woman didn't have the photo, or she had it and thought she could hang on to it for whatever purpose. Blackmail perhaps? But the pool of potential victims had largely evaporated, so that didn't make sense, and she didn't seem the blackmailing sort. No. She was obviously terrified, so the former seemed most likely. He fingered the replica Glock 17 in his coat pocket and considered challenging her again, but decided it would be a waste of time and an unnecessary risk. Resignedly, he plugged in his seatbelt, switched on the radio and headed back to London. He had one more chance – and he wasn't planning to blow it.

Pandora had left High Wycombe long before 'Polaroid Man's' deadline. Lorna's address was unsafe and she knew Doug wouldn't want her there. Her presence was clearly a threat to him and her cousin. After a few hours fitful sleep, she had packed a few essential items, taken a taxi to the station and bought a ticket to Birmingham Moor Street. Her nerves were screaming and every stranger that looked at her seemed to be a threat. She had checked behind her constantly, and scrutinised the other passengers on the busy train, to make sure she wasn't followed, but still she was scared. In Birmingham she hired a car and drove south again, driving around randomly and eventually taking a room in a chain hotel just outside the M25. She had offered to pay for Lorna and Doug to stay in a hotel for a few days, but they had preferred to stay with friends in Derbyshire.

Still scared, Pandora had reviewed her situation. If 'Polaroid Man' wasn't the person who had tried to kill her at Carter Hall, and that seemed to be the case, then she was facing two separate threats. She couldn't go back to her flat or impose on her friends or relations. She would have to lie low, moving from hotel to hotel, like a criminal on the run. But how long could she keep it up before her nerves snapped or she was found?

She had to do something. With no more episodes of the Wellness Roadshow to film for several months, she could turn her attention to her true crime podcast. And what better crimes to focus on than the murders of those individuals who had been at the party of Marnie's she'd attended?

She knew about the deaths of the four people in Mexton. She could picture their faces, and other bits of their anatomies, as if she had just seen them yesterday. Memories were coming back to her. But what were the names of the others? Flipping through a copy of the *Daily Telegraph*, discarded in the hotel restaurant, she started as a face jumped out at her. That was one of them. Hugh Ventham, a backbench MP now being tipped for high office. He had come with a friend, someone else in finance. Justin someone. She Googled the words *Justin* and *Finance* and was shocked to read that Justin Kite had plummeted from the top of an office block and the police were treating his death as suspicious.

Oh fuck! There's only two of us left. But wasn't there also another man. Roger Gardner or something? His face, at least, had been unexceptional and he seemed quite reserved and unsmiling, until things got going, that is. He didn't drink much, took only a little blow, and left before any of the others did. But why can't I remember anything else about him? Is he Polaroid Man? If not, could he be the killer? She shook her head. *This is all too bloody complicated. Should I warn Hugh Ventham?* she wondered. *Is his life in danger? Or is he the killer? Can I discuss the party without admitting I was there? And would it really matter if people knew?* She grabbed a new A4 notepad and started to scribble.

Mel's phone chirruped while she was feeding and playing with the parrots before going to work. She had been inclined to ignore it until she saw the caller's name. She answered, and promised Bruce and Sheila she would be back.

'What is it, Pandora? Has something else happened?'

'No, no, nothing,' Pandora lied. 'It's just I'm interested in those names you mentioned when we spoke in the hospital. I looked them up and you don't seem to have made much progress in catching the killer or killers. As you know, I produce a highly successful true crime podcast, if I say so myself. I'm thinking of featuring these murders in a forthcoming episode and I wondered if I could talk to you, or someone else, about them.'

'Hold on, Pandora. You've been doing your podcast long enough to know that we cannot discuss the details of current cases with the media. And that includes you. Any officer doing so could be charged with misconduct in public office and would certainly lose their job. You can contact the press office, and they will help you as much as they can, but you cannot interfere in our investigations.'

'But I *am* involved, aren't I? You think the killer is the same person who attacked me twice. Aren't I entitled to a bit more information? I'm sure it would be therapeutic for me.'

Pandora playing the wellness card irritated Mel, but she tried to remain professional.

'Look. I can keep you abreast of certain developments pertaining to your attacks as they occur, but that information would be brief and not for public consumption. If there is a danger of it leaking out, I would be unable to tell you anything.' Her tone softened. 'I do sympathise, Pandora, I really do. I've been attacked more times than I care to remember. But you absolutely must not approach anyone on the force for unauthorised information. Do you understand?'

'I suppose so. But if there is anything you can tell me, anything at all, will you get in touch? I'd be so grateful. I'm staying in a hotel at the moment – I'll email you the address.'

'OK. If anything comes up that might help you, I'll clear it with my boss and let you know. But I'm not about to break the law or risk disciplinary action.'

'Thank you, Mel. Thank you.'

When the call was over and the parrots duly fed, Mel turned her thoughts to Pandora's podcast. She'd heard a few episodes and, she admitted to herself, they were well done. The research was sound and the tone not too sensational. They were certainly much better than the rubbish turned out in the *Mexton Messenger* by Jenny Pike when she was the paper's crime correspondent. But, still, she couldn't give Pandora confidential information, even though she recognised what the woman had gone through. She knew that senior officers did sometimes brief journalists off the record, to provide background and such like, but that was not the job of a mere detective constable. And she couldn't see DCI Farlowe agreeing to it either.

Chapter Sixty-Two

'THERE IS another link between some of the victims,' said Mel, knocking on Emma's open door. 'Pandora's flat was burgled and so was Justin's, according to DC Plover. Mark Sutton's place was also broken into and Mr Raven's house was burned down, as was Dale Moncrieff's boat. It might be worth talking to Avon and Somerset to see if there was an attack on Madeleine Hollis' Bristol flat. I'll ask DC Plover if anything happened at Moncrieff's London place.'

'So, what are you thinking?' asked Emma.

'I don't really know. Could it be that the killer was looking for something? Something valuable which they all knew about, and one of them could have possessed, perhaps?'

'It's worth thinking about. If you believe the maxim that once is happenstance, twice is coincidence and three times is enemy action, we're well into stage three. If, that is, there is a real link between them. OK. Make a couple of calls and let me know what you find.'

When Mel left her office, Emma switched on her personal laptop and connected to the camera monitoring baby

Genevieve. She was sleeping peacefully in her cot, and Mike was in a chair beside her, dozing. God, how she missed her! Gazing at the innocent child, oblivious to the horrors which her mother dealt with in her job, Emma consoled herself that she was trying her best to make the world a safer place for her daughter. But the separation was still painful.

The *Mexton Messenger* lunchtime edition

Is Mexton becoming the murder capital of the south?
From Jenny Pike, Deputy Editor

In the past ten days there have been four murders in or around Mexton and the police are clueless.

First, a brave detective superintendent from the Metropolitan Police, Mr Paul Raven, had his throat cut in a clinic outside town where he was recuperating from a vicious hit-and-run attack in London.

Then Dale Moncrieff, the much-admired head of the charity Welcome Relief UK, was killed in an explosion on his narrow-boat, a few miles upriver from Mexton, where he was taking a well-earned break from helping vulnerable people.

Then Mexton's 'Mr Green', Mark Sutton, was slaughtered at the recycling plant which he ran to help protect our precious environment from toxic waste.

Finally, the body of glamorous barrister, Madeleine Hollis, was

*fished out of Mexton canal by the Scouts after she had been
brutally strangled and dumped there.*

*Is it the same killer or are there four murderers roaming the
streets of our town? When will it end? Is anyone safe? What are
the police doing about it?* The Messenger *wants to know.*

*(For details of the individual murders, and who to call if you
have information, see pages 4, 5, 6 and 7)*

'I see Jenny Pike's up to her old tricks,' said Mel, waving a copy
of the *Messenger* at Jack as he looked gloomily at an over-
cooked lasagne on his plate in the canteen.

'Stupid bitch,' Jack replied. 'We saved her life and she still
wants to have a go at us. Sometimes I wonder why we bother.
The place would be better off without her.'

'You don't mean that, do you?'

'No, not really. But she'd be more useful complaining
about our lack of resources. It might help us get quicker results.
I suppose it's about time we held a press conference and got
some verbal shit thrown at us. Mr Farlowe has one planned for
later today. Here, do you want my lunch? I haven't touched it.'

Mel looked at Jack's leather sandwich that was oozing
pellets of reddish, dry meat onto the plate, and the limp lettuce
which garnished it.

'No, you're all right. I'll stick to my salad.'

Jack grunted and wandered over to a vending machine in
search of something edible, while Mel examined his discarded
dish with an almost forensic interest. *The police station may be
fresh and welcoming,* she thought, *but it's a pity the same can't
be said of the canteen food.*

Chapter Sixty-Three

'Good afternoon, ladies and gentlemen,' began DCI Farlowe, sitting behind a forest of microphones and addressing a room packed with journalists from national and local media. 'We are holding this press conference to seek the public's help with our investigations into a series of murders in and around Mexton, namely the deaths of Superintendent James Raven, Dale Moncrieff, Mark Sutton and Madeleine Hollis. We would ask motorists, dog walkers and other people who may have been out and about at the relevant times if they saw a black SUV, possibly a VW, parked or driven in the areas of the Mexton Recuperative Clinic, Babbacott Marina, Mexton Solvent Services, The Magnum and Flute wine bar and Mexton canal. Dashcam footage would be particularly useful. Full details are in your press packs. Any information we receive will be treated in strict...'

'Why haven't you made any progress?' interrupted a reporter from the *Daily Mail*. 'When do you expect to make an arrest?'

'We are following a number of promising leads but, for obvious operational reasons, I cannot provide any details.'

'What evidence do you have that these killings are linked?' asked a stringer for the *Mirror*.

'There is some evidence,' replied Farlowe, 'but I'm afraid I cannot say anything more at this stage. Next?'

'Is an organised crime group involved?' asked the *Guardian*. 'Is the Albanian gang back?'

'No. There is no suggestion that these murders are related to gang violence.'

'Is there any link between these killings and the attack on TV presenter Pandora Blythe?' asked the *Sun*.

'That is something we are looking at,' replied Farlowe, 'but there are significant differences. We will let you know if we find a firm connection. Right, if there is nothing more, I will close this session. Please feel free to contact the Press Office if you need additional information. Thank you.'

Once the press conference concluded, Jenny Pike approached Farlowe and Emma as they were leaving. 'I understand,' she said, 'that DI Thorpe is only working part-time and has the responsibility of a new baby to occupy her mind. Can she give her full attention to the job?'

Emma flushed and started to speak, but the DCI interrupted her.

'I have no intention of commenting on the internal workings of my team or the performance of individual officers, Ms Pike. As an experienced journalist, you should know this. I hope we can count on your support in our efforts to solve these dreadful crimes. Good day to you.'

Farlowe just managed to conceal his fury, but Emma looked at Jenny Pike as if she would like to murder her.

'So much for fucking female solidarity,' raged Emma, back in the incident room. 'Just what is Jenny Pike's agenda? Why does she hate us so much. Sometimes I could bloody well strangle her.'

'Perhaps she wants to work on one of the red tops,' suggested Jack. 'Throw enough shit around down here and she'll be qualified to hack celebrities' phones and make up stuff for a tabloid. Don't worry, Emma. We all know you're doing a great job and we've got your back.'

'Thanks, Jack. But I wish people like Jenny Pike would just let us get on with our jobs. Christ knows, it's hard enough dealing with criminals and budget cuts without getting shit from her. Sometimes I wonder if it's all worth it.'

'No you don't, not really. You're dedicated and we all recognise it. Now, come on, I'll get you a coffee.'

Chapter Sixty-Four

Hello, true crime fans. This is Pandora Blythe with a very special podcast for you. This time, I'm not looking at a crime from the distant past, on which the dust has long settled, but at crimes which are all too contemporary. The murders of five people, all within the past few weeks, murders which have left two police forces baffled. I can tell you now, listeners, that these murders are all linked. And I know how.

So, let's start with the death of a banker in London. Justin Kite was a high-flying financier, working for a company which funds oil exploration. Sadly, his last flight proved fatal as, just over two weeks ago, he fell 30 storeys from the office block in which worked. Police originally thought it was suicide, or some drug-induced accident, but he had no reason to kill himself and the postmortem found only small traces of cocaine in his pulverised body. My sources told me that police suspicions were aroused by accounts of a mystery visitor, apparently from Yorkshire, who entered the building before Justin's death and left shortly after. He claimed to have had an appointment with someone, but nobody in the building had arranged to meet anyone from Bradford, or anywhere else for that matter, at the time in question. Police have been unable to trace this 'Mr Bradford.'

Another of these murders had a connection with London. Detective Superintendent James Raven, an experienced Met police officer, was run down in a Mayfair side street nearly two weeks previously. His injuries were not fatal, although serious, and his attacker fled the scene when an ambulance appeared, quite by chance. But Mr Raven's reprieve was only temporary. He was brutally killed in a physiotherapy clinic in the country, near the town of Mexton, a week later. What is the link between these murders? Did the two victims know each other in London? We shall find out.

Mr Raven's murder is not the only one of these killings to occur in Mexton. Regular listeners will have heard of the town before. Podcast 125 described the activities of a serial poisoner who terrorised the town and number 137 covered revenge attacks on Mexton police by Albanian gangsters. These crimes were solved, but the next ones I describe are very much open.

Dale Moncrieff was the well-respected CEO of Welcome Relief UK, a charity which supports asylum seekers. His favourite way of relaxing, at the end of his extremely busy week helping others, was to spend time on his narrowboat, at a marina just upriver from Mexton. But eighteen days ago, his boat exploded, killing Dale outright. It looked like an accident but police are treating it as suspicious. Who could have killed a man who was clearly one of the good guys? No one saw anything and the police appear to have got nowhere.

Another watery fate beckoned, this time for Madeleine Hollis, a star barrister from Bristol defending a killer at Mexton Crown Court. She was strangled and dumped in a canal in Mexton. Again, no motive and no evidence.

Shortly before, a local businessman, Mark Sutton, was killed when his chemical recycling plant caught fire. Experts soon realised that this was not an accident and Mark was probably already dead when the fire started. Who would want to kill someone who was doing his best for the environment, retrieving something useful from wastes which would otherwise have caused pollution? For the fifth time, the police are getting nowhere.

So, what is it about Mexton which attracts so much death? Four of these murders, which I believe are connected, took place in or near the town. The answer, dear listeners, is nothing. The link between them is nothing to do with the place of death but goes back a long time to somewhere else. The fact that these people died there is pure coincidence.

I can now reveal that all five of these victims once, briefly, knew each other in highly salacious circumstances. My investigations have revealed that they all attended a particular sex party organised, for a substantial entry fee, by the notorious madam and blackmailer, Marnie Draycott, who, coincidentally, was murdered in Mexton a couple of years ago.

So who else was at the party? Is anyone else at risk from the killer, who seems like a character from an Agatha Christie novel – And Then There Were None. Well, my sources tell me that at least two other people were there, one of whom is now a rising politician tipped for high office. Is his life in danger? The identity of another man – a mysterious Mr X – is unknown. Could

Mr X be the killer or is he, also, at risk? Do get in touch if you know anything about these perplexing murders.

Tune in to my next podcast when I'll have new revelations. For now, this is Pandora Blythe and Crimes are Us, wishing you happy investigating. And stay safe out there.

Chapter Sixty-Five

Day 28

'WHAT THE BLOODY hell is this woman thinking of? And where did she get her information?'

DCI Farlowe's irritation rolled around the room, like an angry bear looking for someone to bite.

'Not from us, I'm sure,' replied Mel, defensively. 'She tried to pump me for details but I referred her to the press office. I also warned her not to interfere with our investigations.'

'What about this sex party?' asked Jack. 'It hasn't come up before.'

'I don't know. When I spoke to her, she seemed to be hiding something, so perhaps she was there, too, and didn't want to admit it.'

'Well, if she was,' said Farlowe, 'and everyone there is being killed, she's just put herself at enormous risk. I think you'd better go and talk to her, Mel. Warn her to keep quiet and also to take extra precautions to ensure her safety. She's been attacked twice and it's likely the killer will redouble his efforts now.'

'Will do, guv.'

'Do we know who the politician is?' asked Kamal. 'Someone had better warn him in case he's next.'

'We don't, but perhaps Blythe will tell Mel. This must be a priority.'

'We still don't have a motive, do we?' said Jack. 'Why are the attendees at a sex party being targeted?'

'All I can think of,' replied Mel, 'is that someone who was there doesn't want the world to know. Or perhaps they're scared of being blackmailed.'

'That could apply to three of the people killed – Hollis, Raven and Moncrieff. Surely it would have made little difference to Sutton or Kite.' Jack chucked a biro onto his desk.

'Yes, but perhaps someone else at the party has more to lose. Someone who hasn't been killed. Yet. I'll try and find out more about this mystery man from Pandora. He could be the key.'

'Do that,' said the DCI. 'And talk to your contact in the Met. See if he can tell us anything about these parties of Marnie Draycott's.'

'Who's Marnie Draycott, anyway?' asked Kamal.

'A woman who was trafficked and forced to work in a Scottish brothel,' replied Mel. 'She moved down to London and ran an escort agency which provided the usual extra benefits, and hosted some very, shall we say, uninhibited, parties. These activities enabled her to accumulate stacks of material which she used to blackmail her clients. She was part of the Maldobourne drugs gang, here in Mexton, and fled abroad after a shoot-out. Later, she moved back down here, after changing her appearance, and was killed in an alley by one of her victims.'

'I see. Charming lady.'

'Hang on, guv,' said Trevor, 'we may have some information ourselves. Marnie Draycott left us a USB stick with details of her criminal activities when she disappeared. Perhaps there's something there?'

'Good man. Have a rummage, see what you can find. Everyone else, keep chasing up the other avenues. We'll reconvene when Mel's spoken to Pandora Blythe.'

Chapter Sixty-Six

A GUILTY-LOOKING Pandora opened the door of her hotel room, glancing along the corridor to check that Mel hadn't been followed.

'I thought you'd want to see me. You'd better come in. Are you going to interview me under caution?'

'No Pandora,' said Mel, sternly. 'But you do have some questions to answer.'

With coffee and biscuits dispensed, the two women sat in the hotel room and Mel took out her notebook.

'You do realise,' she began, 'that you've put yourself in even greater danger by making that podcast?'

Pandora started to answer, but Mel interrupted.

'Now the killer knows you've worked out a connection between the deaths, getting rid of you must be his number one priority.'

'I don't agree.' Pandora looked defiant. 'Now it's all out there, he has no reason to go after me, surely.'

'Also,' Mel cut in, 'you could have compromised the investigation. Once you realised that this party had something to do with the murders you should have come straight to us. You've been doing your podcasts long enough to know that withholding relevant information is an offence. So, I need some answers from you. Clear and complete answers. OK?'

'Yes. I'm sorry. I thought my podcast might flush out the murderer. I realise I should have come to you, but I wanted to see what happened, first. I thought I'd be safe here, as very few people know where I'm hiding.'

'Well, the killer managed to track down his other victims without too much trouble. You'd be stupid to underestimate him. So, tell me what happened.'

Pandora paled, cleared her throat and started to speak.

'Back in 2007 I was working in London at the BBC. Someone knew about these naughty parties which went on and, as a joke, a few colleagues got me an invitation for my birthday. Out of curiosity, and with a few drinks inside me, I went along. It was all very secretive. I was picked up in a car, blindfolded and driven around for a while before being led into this building. My phone was taken from me and no names of the organisers were given, but I did overhear the name Marnie. I made the connection when I read that she'd been killed in Mexton the other year. I keep on top of crime reports for my podcast.

'Anyway, I won't describe what went on, as I'm too embarrassed. It was all consensual, though, and I wasn't too drunk or drugged to give consent. We exchanged first names, although some of them may have been false, and only one gave a surname. When you gave me those full names, I looked them up online. I recognised the murdered men, and Madeleine Hollis.'

'So who else was there?'

'Hugh Ventham – your local MP – and another man, who I referred to as Mr X. He called himself Roger Gardner, which was obviously an alias, and he had the sort of face you forget easily. He was reserved and didn't say much, although he participated enthusiastically. Four other women, who seemed to work there, joined in, to make up the gender balance as it were, but I never heard their names.'

'Just a minute, Pandora,' interrupted Mel. She pulled out her phone and dialled.

'Jack – Hugh Ventham, the MP, was at the party and may be in danger. I'm near London so I could go and see him if he's up here. Yes... OK... I'll wait to hear from you.'

She finished the call and turned back to Pandora.

'Where did you get the information about Justin Kite?'

Pandora looked guilty.

'From DC Plover. I spoke to him after my flat was broken into and got the measure of him. I asked to see him again and said I thought putting Justin's murder on my podcast might flush out someone who knew of a possible motive. I arranged to meet him for a drink the day before I produced the podcast, put on a short skirt and flashed a bit of cleavage. He was very co-operative.' She grinned.

Christ, thought Mel. *What a fucking throwback. Not only is he trying to get into my knickers, he risked his job over a glimpse of a pair of tits.* But she said nothing.

'There's something else I haven't told you,' continued Pandora. 'A man followed us to Lorna and Doug's place and threatened me with a gun. He was after a photo taken at the party and thought I had it. That's why my flat was trashed. He said if I didn't give it to him, he'd shoot me and Lorna. I had to put it in the dogshit bin at the end of the road by a certain time. I knew nothing about a photo, and certainly don't remember anyone taking one, so I couldn't give it to him. That's why I'm living in hotels at the moment.'

'Bloody hell, Pandora. Why didn't you contact us at once?

You don't piss around when you're threatened with a firearm.'
Mel looked incredulous. 'We could have taken you to a place
of safety.'

'He said not to talk to the police and I thought I'd be better
off on the move.'

'But it was important information relevant to the case.
Have you any idea how stupid that was?'

'Yes. I'm sorry. I admit it wasn't sensible, but I wasn't
thinking straight.'

'Why did he think you had the photo, anyway?'

'I suppose he'd established that the others didn't, somehow.
I don't think he's the killer. I think the person who tried to kill
me is someone else. If the burglar believed I had the photo,
why kill me before retrieving it?'

'I'm inclined to agree with you,' said Mel. 'Have you got a
description of the man who threatened you?'

'Not really. He wore a hat and mask, so I didn't see his
face. He was fairly tall, not thin or fat and his coat looked
expensive. I mean, I was scared shitless so I wasn't making
notes.'

'No, it's OK. I understand. But I wish you'd come to us
sooner.'

'So, what happens now?'

'Firstly, you have to stop podcasting about the case. If
you've had any responses to the last one from listeners, you
must tell us. In fact, you should take it down. It goes without
saying that you need to take extra care over your personal security. Get a rape alarm and if you see anything suspicious dial
999. Warn your cousin and her husband to be alert as well.
And keep away from DC Plover. I'll not say anything, but if his
boss gets wind of how he helped you, I advise you to answer
any questions fully and truthfully. Is that clear?'

'Yes, DC Cotton,' said Pandora, meekly.

'Right. I'll leave you now. You know how to contact me if anything else occurs to you. And, again, be ultra-careful.'

As Mel walked back to her car her phone rang.

'I was right, Jack. The attacks on premises are linked. Birdy sent me a text saying that someone tried, unsuccessfully, to break into Dale Moncrieff's place. I haven't heard from the Bristol guys yet. But that's not the main thing. Pandora's just told me that she was menaced by a male with a firearm who demanded a photograph taken at this party. The idiot didn't contact us immediately, and I've read her the riot act. Presumably the photo's compromising, so if he couldn't break in and search for it, he would set fire to its likely location, hoping to destroy it.'

'Sorry,' she said, realising that she hadn't given Jack a chance to speak. 'What did you want me for?'

'Just to tell you that Avon and Somerset did get back to us. Madeleine Hollis' flat was trashed the day after she was killed. Get back here as soon as you can. Hugh Ventham is at home in his constituency and officers are on the way to interview him. Well done, Mel.'

Chapter Sixty-Seven

MEL SPENT much of the time in the M25 mobile traffic jam wondering what it was about the orgy, for that's what it seemed like to her, that made it imperative for someone to kill the participants – or to search for a compromising photo. All those killed could have suffered embarrassment, and possible derailment of their careers or relationships, if their involvement had come to light, but was that really a sufficient motive for multiple murders? Certainly, the police officer and the MP would suffer, and probably Madeleine Hollis, too. But would it really matter that a waste recycler and a charity worker got up to something risqué in their past? Anyway, they were all, unequivocally, dead. Unless, of course, Dale Moncrieff or Mark Sutton was still alive, having substituted another body in their place. No, that was nonsense. That was thriller territory and Dr Durbridge would have made sure he knew who was on his table.

What about Pandora? Could she have faked the attacks and be killing off the others? No, there was nothing phoney about that shotgun. Anyway, her career might not have suffered that much. She didn't exactly present *Blue Peter*. Celebrities and failed politicians put themselves into all sorts of embarrassing positions, on reality TV shows, to boost their profiles and it doesn't seem to do them any harm. *Before I get stuck down the rabbit hole of popular culture,* she admonished herself, *I must make a phone call.*

'What the hell were you thinking of, Birdy?' she almost shouted, when her phone was answered. 'You gave Pandora confidential information about your investigation which could only have come from one of your team. And they know you've been in touch with her.'

'All, right, all right. Untwist your knickers. She asked me for some background, which was OK, and then pressed me for more details. She promised me she would use it responsibly.'

'And was she pressing her chest against you at the same time?'

She could almost hear him blush.

'Well, er, she is good looking, even though she's a bit older than me. Nothing happened, honestly. She led me on a bit, a flash here, a smile there, but she cleared off as soon as she got what she wanted.'

Birdy sounded annoyed and Mel wondered whether some of his conquests felt the same way about him.

'You could be in deep shit over this, you know. A disciplinary and even a charge of misconduct in public office. All because your dick overruled your brain.'

'Yeah. Sorry. I know I shouldn't have. Are you going to grass me up?'

'No, I'm not. It's just as well you didn't reveal anything confidential about our cases down here. But I advised Pandora to tell the truth if Professional Standards come knocking at her door. So watch your back. And for fuck's sake keep away from bloggers, podcasters and journalists.'

She cut the call before he had a chance to answer and hoped he got the message.

Ungrateful bitch, raged Birdy to himself. *Who does she think she is, coming up here and telling me how to do my job? She wouldn't last ten minutes in the Met. I offered her a night on the town, with a bit of fun to follow, and all she wanted to do was go and feed some fucking parrots. Frigid cow. I'd better buy the sarge a pint and get my story straight, in case she grasses. It's the last time I put myself out for some twat from the country. Waste of fucking time.*

Chapter Sixty-Eight

Day 29

'TREVOR,' called Jack, when Mel recounted her conversation with Pandora. 'Did you get anything from that stuff we got from Marnie Draycott? We now know that the sex party was on or around Pandora Blythe's birthday in 2007. Our victims were all present and it could be that our killer was there. Pandora said there were four women whose names she didn't know who worked there. Can you try and identify them?'

Trevor nodded and, an hour and a half later, he handed Jack a printout.

'Looks like the real names of the punters weren't recorded, just pseudonyms. We've got Lanky, Bouncy, Smiley, Ginger, Serge, Snowy, Saintly and Squaddie. Nothing on the other women.'

'What? No Sneezy or Grumpy?' asked Mel, prompting chuckles from her colleagues.

'So, who do we think these refer to?' she continued. 'Pandora's got auburn hair, so she could be Ginger and Madeleine was quite curvy, so she could be bouncy.'

'Mark Sutton was tall and thin,' said Trevor. 'He could be Lanky. Ventham did a short service commission in the Army so he could be Squaddie, although he was an officer, not a private or an NCO.'

'I bet Snowy was Justin,' said Sally. 'Financiers were notorious users of cocaine back in the day. But what about Serge? None of them was French.'

'The old police uniform,' said Kamal. 'That must have been Mr Raven.'

'If Moncrieff was involved in charity work back then,' said Jack, 'he could have been Saintly. That just leaves Smiley.'

'Pandora said there was another bloke there as well. He gave his name as Roger Gardner but didn't say much else. Maybe the nickname was sarcasm.'

'Sounds feasible, Mel,' said Jack. 'I think it's time we had a chat with our esteemed MP. I'll clear it with Mr Farlowe. I'll go myself, with you, Kamal. Oh, Sally, can you find out more about Roger Gardner?'

'Will do, sarge.'

'What's that dreadful smell?' asked Kamal as he and Jack walked up Hugh Ventham's gravel drive towards the MP's imposing Victorian house.

'Looks like a delivery of manure for the garden, but there doesn't seem to be much growing here apart from the lawn. Seems a bit odd.'

Jack tugged an old-fashioned brass bell-pull and the door was opened by a muscular, bearded man with short hair, who eyed them suspiciously.

'Police,' said Jack, as the two officers displayed their warrant cards. 'We have an appointment with Mr Ventham.'

Jack and Kamal were shown into Ventham's study, an imposing room lined with books and pictures. Pride of place was given to Margaret Thatcher's portrait, on the wall above an ornate marble fireplace. The MP, sitting at an antique mahogany desk, made a show of reading a document before setting it aside and glaring at them. He didn't invite them to sit.

'DS Vaughan and DC Chabra, sir,' began Jack. 'We would appreciate a few words about the contents of Ms Pandora Blythe's podcast.'

'First of all,' began Ventham, 'I categorically deny that I had any involvement with this Draycott woman or her sordid sex parties. I have always conducted myself with complete propriety, in both my professional and personal lives, and am in consultation with my solicitors with a view to suing this wretched Blythe woman for defamation. Furthermore, I was travelling for much of 2007, on business, so it's unlikely I would have been in London at the time.'

'But I understand, sir,' said Jack, 'that you weren't named in her podcast, although she informed one of my colleagues that you were there.'

'I repeat, I wasn't there. I've never met the ghastly creature in my life. Somehow, someone has misidentified me as the rising MP she mentioned. God knows, there are plenty of others, on both sides of the House, who are more likely candidates. Presumably it's because of the Mexton connection. Since then, I've been besieged by the press for comments. I had a friend, who runs a racing stables, drop me round a tonne of horse manure to keep them from hanging around the gates, and Kevin Dayton, from Mexton Security Services, is acting as my bodyguard while I'm down here. He was the one who let you in.'

'I'm sorry you've been pestered,' said Jack, diplomatically. 'But I'd be grateful if you can tell me whether you knew any of the other people named in the podcast.'

Ventham put on a thoughtful air.

'I met Dale Moncrieff a couple of times at charity functions. I wasn't a fan of his work but, as an MP, you have to show willing. I may have met Justin Kite when I worked in the City but I don't recall him, or the policeman for that matter. I've never met that green fellow or the lawyer, at least as far as I know. When you work as hard as I do for the constituency, you can't possibly remember everyone you meet.'

Ventham's smug remark irritated Jack, who knew he spent as little time in Mexton as possible. He remained polite.

'But, nevertheless, you still find it necessary to take extra security precautions. Are you worried that you could be targeted by the person who killed the others?'

'Of course not. How many times must I tell you, I wasn't involved. But I'm fed up with being pestered by muck-raking journalists and people who think I've done something wrong. And Kevin is here to dissuade them. Now, I want to know what you and your fellow officers are going to do about the situation in which I find myself.'

'If a specific individual is harassing you, sir, we can certainly look into it and take action. But, as to the defamation issue, I'm afraid that's a civil matter and not for us, as I'm sure your solicitors have informed you.

'I would advise you to take extra care over your personal safety, however, and please dial 999 immediately if you believe you're in danger. Obviously, I cannot give you any details about our investigations into the murders, but we are working tirelessly to bring the killer, or killers, to justice. If anything should occur to you which might help us, please give me a call. Here's my card.'

'I hardly think it will. So, if there is nothing else, I have to prepare a speech to a group of local businessmen. Kevin will see you out.'

The MP resumed his study of the papers on his desk and didn't look up as the detectives were escorted to the door.

'Charming bloke,' said Kamal as they returned to the car. 'But he did seem worried, though, what with the bodyguard.'

'Yes. He made out that Kevin was there to fend off journalists and the like but perhaps it's more than that. Mind you, our killer seems pretty determined and he could always attack Ventham when he's in London. One thing, though. Kevin looks a bit familiar. Perhaps he's ex-Job. Can you have a chat with Mexton Security Services and get some background? Just to be on the safe side.'

Chapter Sixty-Nine

Day 30

'GOOD MORNING, EVERYONE,' began Emma, calling the team to order. 'I'm afraid there is little to report. It's been nearly four days since Blythe's broadcast, and she's given us nothing helpful. Apparently, she's had dozens of cranks messaging her, claiming that the CIA, MI5, aliens and Jeremy Corbyn are all, variously, responsible. There was also a message claiming that someone had tried to engage a hitman to kill Dale Moncrieff. Utter rubbish, the lot of it. No one has contributed anything useful. Meanwhile, Hugh Ventham has been pestered online and aggrieved journalists have posted material on the lines of "Mexton MP in the shit", after they were driven away by his manure heap.'

Several officers laughed.

'At least,' continued Emma, 'he hasn't been attacked physically, and no one's tried to break into his premises, either down here or in London.'

'Maybe he's next on the list,' suggested Sally. 'Hence the bodyguard. Nothing to do with the paparazzi.'

'Do we believe him when he says he wasn't at the party?' asked Kamal. 'Pandora claims he was.'

'I'm not sure,' replied Mel, thoughtfully. 'Politicians are professional liars but Pandora could have been so pissed or stoned that she misremembered things, although she claimed that she wasn't. But it is a bit odd that he's remained unscathed, so far, if he was there. I suppose Kevin could have scared the killer off, but no one tried to get at him before Pandora's podcast.'

'I think Pandora may be right,' said Jack. 'When we spoke to him, he said he wouldn't have been in London very often in 2007, as he was travelling a lot, but Pandora didn't mention the year or the location of the party in her podcast.'

'Then he is a liar,' said Mel. 'So what else has he been up to?'

'Are you suggesting he's the killer?' Jack looked incredulous.

Mel looked affronted.

'Bear with me. Ventham would have a lot to lose if it came out that he was there. Promising MP, tipped for high office and all that. And he was in the Army for a while. Trained to kill if necessary. D'you mind if I make a few enquiries, guv?'

Emma frowned.

'OK, Mel. But don't spend too much time on it, and for God's sake don't go interviewing him without checking with me or Mr Farlowe. Ventham's pissed off enough as it is.'

'Righto, guv.'

'Oh, before you go, Mr Farlowe wants to see you in his office.'

'Any idea why?

'No, but I'm afraid he didn't look very happy.'

Chapter Seventy

Mel KNOCKED on DCI Farlowe's office door with trepidation. Surely, she hadn't done anything wrong? OK, her expenses for the London trip were more than expected, but he could have just sent her an email if he needed to query them. Her nervousness was compounded when he called her in, looked up grimly from his laptop and didn't invite her to sit.

'Mel,' he began. 'I'm afraid there's been a complaint against you. I thought I would raise it with you first, informally, before it became official, to give you a chance to explain yourself.'

'W... what's it all about, boss?'

'According to the Metropolitan Police, you supplied confidential information about an ongoing investigation, namely the inquiry into the death of Justin Kite, to Pandora Blythe. You then threatened her with arrest if she didn't claim that the information came from one of their detectives, a DC Plover, who had previously warned you not to say anything to the press. What do you have to say?'

Mel flushed with fury and snapped back.

'It's a fu... total lie, sir. I explained to Pandora that I couldn't give her any inside information on any of the investigations and that she would have to contact the press office. When I spoke to her after the podcast, she admitted that she had dressed provocatively when she went to see DC Plover and that he gave her the details. He's something of a lecher. I later had a heated conversation with DC Plover in which I told him exactly how unprofessional he had been. I said I wouldn't tell his bosses, as I felt it was up to the Met to sort it. Given what he's evidently done, I'm happy to make a full statement concerning my conversation with Pandora, in which I advised her to answer any questions about the leak fully and truthfully.'

Farlowe looked stern.

'I understand your reluctance to inform on a fellow officer, but you really should have mentioned this to me or to DI Thorpe. So why do you think the Met is accusing you?'

'Two possibilities, I think. Firstly, DC Plover's in the sh... in trouble and is trying to shift the blame. Secondly, he made advances to me when I was in London and I rebuffed him. I suspect it bruised his ego. Of course, it could be both. I wouldn't be surprised if he put pressure on Pandora to back him up, as well. I'll give you her number and you can check.'

'All right, Mel,' said the DCI, after a pause during which her stomach knotted up. 'I'm inclined to believe you. I still have contacts in the Met. I'll phone someone and put your side of the argument. I'll also find out a bit more about DC Plover. Let me have a written statement within the hour, please. I hope that will be the end of the matter.'

'Yes, boss. Thank you.'

Mel left Farlowe's office, fuming. *What the hell was the bastard playing at? She'd told him she wouldn't grass him up. It must be his dick*, she thought. *Some men just can't bear being turned down.* She had her statement on the DCI's desk half an hour later, with the language considerably moderated from her first attempt.

Chapter Seventy-One

A MISERABLE-LOOKING Mel joined Emma in the coffee queue.

'What's the matter, Mel?' asked the DI.

'That bastard Plover has alleged that I leaked the information on the investigation to Pandora. Malicious bloody nonsense. I think Mr Farlowe believes I'm innocent, but there's still a cloud over me until he's finished checking.'

'You have my sympathy, and I'm sure you wouldn't leak. Don't let it get to you. Anyway, what did you find out about our hard-working MP.'

'He's a high flyer, tipped for a ministerial post. His record seems to be reasonably unblemished, which was why his party put him up for the Mexton seat in the by-election following Maxwell Arden's death. They wanted someone squeaky clean following the scandal over Arden's activities.

'He got a decent degree at Oxford, did a short commission in the Army and then went into finance, working for a London-based firm. He stood for Parliament, unsuccessfully, in a couple of by-elections and was then offered the Mexton seat, which was deemed a safe one. They hoped someone with a clean sheet would repair the damage to the party's reputation.

'As to his personal life, he's divorced and has no children, but recently got engaged to Rosie Westmorland, the daughter of Sir Henry Westmorland. Sir H made a fortune selling PPE to the NHS during the pandemic. Unfortunately, it didn't work, but no action was taken against him. Ventham's hobbies are listed as model-making, sailing and clay pigeon shooting. He owns a flat in Pimlico and a substantial house down here.'

'So, you found nothing dodgy about Ventham himself?'

'Not really. But I did a bit of checking on his movements. He was in London when Mr Raven was attacked and also when Justin Kite was killed. His voting record proves it. He was back in Mexton at the time of the attacks on Moncrieff, Hollis, Sutton and Blythe.'

'Coincidence, surely?' Emma frowned and sipped her coffee.

'Possibly, although he's not usually in the constituency much. He prefers to stay in London, only coming to Mexton when absolutely necessary.'

'All right. Can you, discreetly, see if he has alibis for the times of the murders? Start by looking at ANPR and any public CCTV data on his vehicle. What does he drive?'

'A silver BMW. Top of the range.'

'Not a dark SUV, then.'

'No. I'll get on to that. I'll check the local news media, too, in case he was at any public engagements during the relevant periods.'

'What about that bodyguard? Jack said he looked familiar.'

'Kamal left a message on the security firm's voicemail, but they haven't got back to us yet.'

'OK. Chase it up, would you? Kamal's on leave at a family wedding in Leicester. Sally, did you find anything about Roger Gardner?', Emma asked, as the DC joined them.

'Nothing, guv. He seems to be a ghost. I've found no one who fits the age and demographic for the mystery man and I tried three different spellings of the surname. The people I found were either too old or too young at the time of the party, and another was a Benedictine monk. Gardner was obviously using a false name.'

'Brilliant. OK, thanks for trying.'

'Excuse me,' said the slim young man with an Eastern European accent, standing at the police station reception desk. 'I think I have some information for you.'

'Yes, sir. And what is it concerning?'

'That woman who was murdered. Ms Hollis. I saw someone with her in the wine bar where I work, but I've been off with Covid so I couldn't come in earlier. It's all right,' he said, as the receptionist backed away. 'I've tested negative. You won't catch anything.'

Still looking nervous, the woman behind the counter picked up her phone.

'If you'd like to take a seat, sir, I'll get someone to come and see you.'

Five minutes later, Trevor ushered the visitor into an interview room.

'I gather you have something to tell us?' he began. 'Can I take your name, please?'

'I'm Pavel Nowak and I work in the Magnum and Flute wine bar. I was serving on the night Ms Hollis was kidnapped, according to the papers, and I remember her ordering several glasses of wine. She stood out a bit from our other customers as she was smartly dressed and carrying an expensive briefcase. Anyway, I saw someone join her and I served him with two glasses of red.'

'And would you recognise this man? Could you work with an e-fit operator to help us produce an image?'

Trevor could barely hide his excitement.

'Better than that,' Pavel replied. 'I know who he is. I saw him on social media. He's that MP with the horse sh... manure in his garden. Mr Ventham.'

'That's extremely helpful, Mr Nowak. But can you be sure it's him? You seem to have a very good memory for something that happened two weeks ago.'

'I have an excellent memory for faces. I paint portraits in my spare time and I'm always studying people. Also, it was quiet in the bar and I remember the man paying cash. Nearly all our sales are contactless these days, so this kind of stood out.'

'Well thank you very much, Mr Nowak. I'll write down what you've told me on this form and ask you to sign it, then you can go.' Pavel nodded his head and waited for Trevor to complete the statement form, sipping at some dreadful tea supplied from the vending machine.

'One thing, though,' said Trevor, steering Pavel back into reception. 'Please don't mention this on social media. It could be that Mr Ventham's contact with Ms Hollis was perfectly innocent and it could cause serious problems for him if that's the case. It could also compromise our investigation if, indeed, there is a cause for concern.'

Pavel nodded his agreement.

As soon as Pavel had been signed out, Trevor rushed into Emma's office, interrupting her video call with Mike and Genevieve.

'Ventham, guv. We've got him! He was seen in the wine bar with Madeleine Hollis the night she was killed. I've a signed statement from a reliable witness.'

'OK, lad. Calm down. Get everyone into the incident room and we'll review what we've got.'

Chapter Seventy-Two

THE ROOM WAS FIZZING as excited detectives and support staff took their seats.

'First of all,' said Emma, 'I must remind you that we need to tread carefully with Hugh Ventham. No one's above the law, and he's not entitled to special treatment because he's an MP. But we need to make sure we're absolutely certain of our ground before we approach him. He plays golf with the Police and Crime Commissioner and could make trouble for us if we balls things up. So, what have we got? Trevor, you start.'

'Thanks, guv. This afternoon, a bartender from the wine bar where Madeleine Hollis was last seen came into the station and gave a statement. He's positive he saw Ventham with Madeleine on the night she died and I believe him. Previously, Ventham denied knowing her, so he was obviously lying.'

'Mel, how about you?'

Mel straightened up in her chair. 'As I told you before, boss, Ventham was in London when Justin died and Mr Raven was attacked. He was in Mexton when the other attacks occurred. However, I've looked in to the movements of his

BMW, on ANPR and CCTV, and it wasn't picked up anywhere near the Mexton crime scenes at the relevant times. More to the point, it wasn't picked up anywhere at all, so it's clear he wasn't using it. I've asked my contact in the Met to run a similar check but I've not heard back from him. I probably won't. I've also not heard back from Mexton Security Services about the bodyguard, despite my and Kamal's voicemails.'

'Thanks Mel. Anyone else got something?'

'I've checked with DVLA,' replied Sally, 'and Ventham has never owned a dark SUV. I also contacted local rental companies, and he hasn't hired anything from them.'

Emma thought for a moment before she spoke.

'OK. I don't think we've got enough to arrest him, just on the strength of his lie about Madeleine. A slick brief would dismiss it as a memory lapse or a marital indiscretion he wanted to keep secret, not that he's married yet. The location matches would be thrown out as coincidence. But I do think we've grounds to interview him again, this time under caution. Let's play it softly, though. Mel, take Sally and invite him to come in to clear up a few points. Be vague and try not to alarm him. Tell him we're looking into his online harassment, which we would do if we had the time. In the meantime, I think we've enough to request phone records. Thanks, everyone. I'll look forward to watching the interview with our MP. I think he'll find it a little more penetrating than Question Time.'

Emma knocked on DCI Farlowe's door and entered when summoned.

'I thought you should know,' she began, 'that Hugh Ventham MP is now a credible suspect. We have a witness placing him with Madeleine Hollis just before she died but he denied knowing her. Also, he lied about the party when we spoke to him. We're inviting him to come in for an interview under caution. Could you arrange a request for his phone records?'

'Of course. Are you planning to arrest him if he doesn't come in voluntarily?'

'If necessary, but if he's innocent he'll probably want to avoid the adverse publicity. Someone is bound to leak that we've nicked him.'

'All right, but tread carefully. And please keep me informed. Now I must let Mel know that the Met have suspended DC Plover and that she's in the clear. Apparently, he's known to have sexually harassed female officers in the past and has been less than truthful on occasions. One of the bad apples, I'm afraid.'

'I didn't believe it of her,' replied Emma. 'She may be a bit impetuous, but she's not stupid.'

'I didn't believe it either but we had to take it seriously.'

Emma left her boss's office with a spring in her step. Things were looking up. They had a suspect and Mel was off the hook. What could possibly go wrong?

Chapter Seventy-Three

'GOD THAT STUFF STINKS,' said Mel, as Sally drove the unmarked car through Ventham's open gates and past the simmering manure heap.

'I've smelt worse. I once had to help retrieve a packet of heroin from a septic tank. And there was that dead body in a south-facing flat during the really hot summer a few years ago. It had been there a week and the neighbours were too stoned to notice. Oh, and there was this woman who had seventeen cats, never let them out and hadn't heard of litter trays. There was shit here, there and everywhere.'

'All right, all right. I've just had a late lunch.'

She gazed at the building's imposing frontage.

'Hello, Ventham's front door is open. Shouldn't someone be on sentry duty?'

'I'd've thought so,' replied Sally. 'Ventham's car's here, and I presume the other one is the bodyguard's. Odd that the gates were open, too. I thought we'd have to use the intercom.'

'Something seems a bit off. Take it cautiously, OK?'

The two detectives approached the door slowly, scanning

the surroundings and checking the windows for any signs of movement. Sally pulled the doorbell and Mel called into the hall.

'Mr Ventham. It's the police. May we come in?'

No reply.

She called again. 'Are you alright Mr Ventham?'

Still no reply.

Mel mouthed the words protection of life, Sally nodded, and they entered the house, alert for any possible threat.

'Fuck!' shouted Mel, running towards the prone form of Hugh Ventham, crumpled on the Persian rug which decorated the polished wooden floor of the hall.

'He's hurt. Call it in.'

Sally pulled out her phone, but before she could dial, she heard a movement behind her. Something hard and heavy smashed into her upper arm and the phone flew from her hand. She half-turned and found herself looking down the barrel of a pistol, held unwaveringly by a man whose stance and demeanour suggested he knew exactly how to use it.

'You. Over there.' He gestured towards a small door at the end of the hall.

'And you, Cotton. Get away from Ventham and join your colleague. Put your phone on the floor. Do you have handcuffs? Tasers? Anything you could use as a weapon?'

The two women shook their heads.

'Take your jackets off and empty your trouser pockets. I need to be sure.'

Mel and Sally complied, piling clothing, keys and odds and ends on the floor in front of them.

'Turn around slowly, with your hands on your heads. Three hundred and sixty degrees.'

Evidently satisfied that the detectives had nothing concealed, the man pointed to the door.

'Open it.'

'Who the fuck are you? And what happened to Ventham's bodyguard?' spat Mel.

A small smile crossed the gunman's face.

'I am the bodyguard,' he pointed to a lanyard bearing the name Kevin Dayton. 'Ventham thought I was from Mexton Security Services. But I'm from somewhere much more distant than their shitty little office.'

Cogs whirred in Mel's brain.

'You're Roger Gardner. The other man at the party. You've been breaking into the victims' houses. You're looking for the photo.'

'Well spotted. Now get through that door before I shoot you.'

Sally pulled open the door, her arm still aching from the blow, and the detectives cautiously descended a narrow stone staircase that led to an enormous cellar. Racks of wine stretched along one wall but, on the opposite side, a small desk, with a swivel chair in front of it, held a couple of laptops and piles of paper. A heap of neatly-folded, dark clothing and a several ski masks sat on a table, a selection of knives arranged next to the garments. They had just enough time to take in the scene before the door slammed behind them, a lock turned and the light was switched off from outside. They were in complete darkness.

Chapter Seventy-Four

VENTHAM LAY STILL, watching with half-open eyes as Dayton turned casually towards him, the pistol hanging loosely by his side. He saw an opportunity. Hauling himself up, he swung a punch with his right hand which caught Dayton squarely in the groin. Dayton doubled over in agony. Barely believing his luck, Ventham fired his elbow into his assailant's jaw. Dayton slumped in a heap, out cold.

Ventham's head was still muzzy, and the fingers on his left hand, broken by Dayton, were sending currents of agony up his arm. But he had to escape. If he could get out through the back of the house, he could use the gardener's quad bike to take him out of pistol range before Dayton came to his senses. He dashed through the door leading to the servants' quarters, at the back of the hall, and locked it behind him. He headed to the rear of the house, grabbing his shotgun from the unlocked gun cupboard on the way. 'Fuck, there's no time to get cartridges from the safe,' he cursed. The weapon could still be useful, so he took it anyway. Jerking open the back door he ran towards the quad bike, leapt onto the saddle and roared off, his shotgun held precariously under his injured arm.

———

Dayton sat down heavily, his balls aching, and evaluated his options. Ventham was in the wind, despite a heavy blow to his head, and he had no means of finding him. But did that matter? He could hardly go to the police, given that there was almost certainly evidence of his crimes in the cellar, which Dayton had searched exhaustively for the Polaroid. The impromptu torture session, involving a hammer and Ventham's fingers, yielded an admission to the murders, but not a location for the photo. He didn't completely believe Ventham knew nothing of it, and would go through his London flat, using the keys retrieved when he searched him. He gazed around the old building, realising that there could be many hiding places that he had missed during several days of surreptitious exploration. He would have to burn it down, just to be sure.

And what about the police officers? He had made a mistake when he addressed Cotton by name. Could she have recognised him? They had met twice, although he had been clean-shaven and not so muscular on those occasions. She was a trained police officer, after all, so she may well have seen beneath the beard. So they would, regrettably, have to go. He collected a can of petrol from his car, poured it over the hall floor and ensured some ran under the cellar door. Then he lit a petrol soaked-rag, tossed it into the pool of fuel, and ran for his car.

Chapter Seventy-Five

'Jack,' called Kamal, 'I've just heard back from Mexton Security Services. They've been away on a team building exercise for a couple of days and someone forgot to put an emergency number on the answering machine. Only their clients had it.'

'And?'

'Well, they said Hugh Ventham cancelled the bodyguard. And they've never heard of Kevin Dayton. The guy supposed to be protecting Ventham was Lewis Shaw. He's never even met Ventham.'

'So, who the bloody hell did I see at Ventham's place?'

'I don't know,' replied Trevor. 'But I doubt he was there to protect him.'

'Shit. Mel and Sally are there at the moment. Give them a ring and tell them to get out until backup arrives.'

Trevor dialled first Mel's and then Sally's mobile.

'No reply, Jack.'

'Right. With me, Trev. We'll blue light it. But tell Control to send the nearest patrol car to Ventham's. Top priority, officers in danger.'

The two detectives rushed to the exit, pushing aside startled officers standing in their way, and grabbed the keys for a marked car from an astonished traffic PC who was just about to go on shift. Jack hammered impatiently on the dashboard as they waited for the new electric security gate to open, cursing at its slowness. The stench of burning rubber hung in the air as Jack shot out of the car park, a sick feeling in his stomach. Was Ventham alive? Had Dayton harmed his colleagues? And were they too late?

***

Ventham hurtled across the field behind his house on the quad bike, every bump aggravating the pain in his hand and the throbbing in his head. He jumped off, opened a gate, and shot onto the minor road behind his property, narrowly missing a slow-moving tractor. He was running almost on autopilot but knew he had to find somewhere to hide, at least for the night. Taking minor roads, he found his way to Mexton woods, dumped the bike in a picnic area and weaved his way through the trees until he found a suitable spot to build a shelter. Shifting branches and twigs one-handed was slow and painful, but he eventually managed to construct a bivouac which would keep him relatively dry if it rained. An uncomfortable night lay ahead, but he had endured worse in the Army. But would he be able to sleep with this headache and the pain flooding his arm?

Chapter Seventy-Six

'So what the fuck do we do now, Mel? And what's he planning to do with us?'

The answer to Sally's second question soon became apparent. The reek of petrol permeated the cellar and they could hear a liquid dripping down the stairs.

'The bastard's going to torch the place,' said Mel, grimly. 'Just like he did with Mr Raven's. And us with it. Fuck.'

'Then how the bloody hell do we get out of here? We can't see a fucking thing.'

Sally tried to quell the rising note of panic in her voice but failed.

'I don't fucking know,' Mel yelled back. 'We need a source of light. Did you see a torch or anything?'

'No, no. Nothing. Oh, shit, Mel, Helen will kill me.'

'Wait. I've an idea,' Mel said, after a few panicked moments.

A few seconds of stumbling and cursing later, the sound of a laptop whirring was followed by a dim glow from the computer's screen. A second joined it and the combined light enabled the detectives to navigate their surroundings, albeit cautiously. There was no obvious way out: no second door, no skylight, no window. And as they looked around, tendrils of smoke oozed around the cellar door. A small cascade of petrol flashed into flame on the steps.

Mel racked her brains. Something she'd seen, almost subconsciously, on the ground as they approached the door.

Then it came to her.

'The coal hole!' she shouted. 'I saw the lid. This must have been a coal cellar once. If I can find it, we can probably squeeze through.'

The flickering light from the burning petrol cast malevolent shadows across the walls, enabling Mel to spot the slope at the far end of the room, down which the coal used to be poured. But there was no hole visible. The ceiling had obviously been plastered during its conversion into a wine cellar.

'Do something about that petrol,' shouted Mel, grabbing a vicious-looking combat knife from the collection on the table. 'Use the wine, a cloth or something. I'll look for the hole.'

Sally grabbed a couple of bottles of wine from the racks and threw them into the expanding pool of fire. The flames abated slightly but the wine only spread the burning petrol. She tried again, with champagne, smashing the necks of the bottles against the steps so jets of foam shot out. This proved slightly more successful, the champagne temporarily blanketing the blaze, but only temporarily.

By now, no more petrol was flowing under the door, but a layer of thick black smoke was forming on the ceiling and the detectives were finding it hard to breathe as the fire ripped oxygen from the room. In desperation, Sally pulled off her trousers, soaked them in wine and beat at the flames, her bare legs stung by the heat.

Meanwhile, Mel, perched precariously on the office chair and, leaning up the slope, hacked furiously at the plaster ceiling with the knife. Flakes of paint and dust fell into her eyes. Finally, the blade jerked inwards, leaving a hole in the plasterboard which Mel could get her fingers through. She pulled and twisted, slowly widening the hole until she could pull chunks of ceiling away. Eventually, she could make out the underside of an iron disc. She hammered on it with the palms of her hands. But it wouldn't move.

'I've found it,' she called. 'But it's stuck. Fuck.'

With the flames now doused, and the smell of burnt trousers joining the smoke from the petrol, Sally eased her way through the cellar and joined Mel.

'Can I help?'

'It's rusted in. And we can't both get at it at the same time.'

'I've an idea,' said Sally. 'The chair.'

'We can't both stand on it, you idiot.'

'No. But look.'

She nudged Mel off the seat and reached down, yanking and twisting at the levers which adjusted the height of the seat and its back.

'Here.' Sally brandished the seat which she'd pulled from the chair's base. The steel pole which supported it gleamed faintly in the light from the laptops.

'Bash the metal with this, see if that will shift it.'

Mel grabbed the seat, upended it and slammed the support into the manhole cover. It clanged from the impact, and a few flakes of rust fell into her face, but it wouldn't move. Twenty, thirty times Mel hit the coal hole cover, with no discernible effect. Sally took over with the same result. By now, breathing had become more difficult and both women's strength was fading.

BRIAN PRICE

'We've got to keep going,' gasped Mel. 'If we're shifting rust, it must open eventually. Give it back, I'll try again.'

But repeated impacts from the steel pole failed to move the iron and Mel's strength deserted her. She managed a few more feeble blows before succumbing to a fit of coughing and slumped, half-unconscious, on the slope beneath the hatch.

Chapter Seventy-Seven

Five minutes earlier

THE POLICE CAR shot through Ventham's gate and pulled up sharply, in a spray of gravel, in front of the door.

'That's Mel and Sally's car!' said Jack, grimly, 'and the place is on fire. Call the fire service! I'm going in.'

'Don't be stupid, mate. Wait till the experts arrive,' said Trevor, who had been trapped in a burning building while on surveillance duty and knew how dangerous fire could be.

'I'm not bloody leaving them in there,' snarled Jack, leaping out of the car and rushing to the open door. Trevor dragged him back but he pulled away, almost knocking the DC over. But the flames in the hall blocked him from entering and he staggered back, coughing. He turned away from Trevor and began to sob.

'Look, Jack, there's nothing they can do. The fire engines will be here in ten minutes, they said. And an ambulance. All we can do is... hang on, what's that noise?'

Jack looked up. 'What noise?'

'It sounded like metal hitting metal. It came from over there.'

Trevor walked slowly towards the sound. 'Now it's stopped. Look – there's a metal plate in the ground.'

'It's a coal hole! A bloody coal hole. Someone's trapped in the cellar. Get it open. Quick!' Jack screamed.

'There's nothing to get hold of and it's covered in rust.'

'Well fucking find something!'

The two detectives scoured the area until Trevor spotted a spade beside the manure heap. He grabbed it and rushed back to the metal plate. He scraped the dirt and rust away while Jack frantically scrabbled with his fingers. Finally, there was a crack visible and Trevor managed to slip the corner of the spade into it. He leant on the shaft. The rusty corner of the spade bent, then broke away, leaving Trevor off balance. He tried again with the opposite corner of the spade and this time the metal plate began to move, millimetre by millimetre. When there was enough space for Jack to get his fingers in, he joined Trevor's efforts and the plate slowly rose, like a tooth being pulled from a dinosaur. A cloud of smoke poured from the hole and Trevor could just make out the figures of Mel and Sally, collapsed and barely breathing.

Kevin Dayton sat in his car, parked in a layby on the hill overlooking Ventham's house.

'Fuck,' he cursed aloud, as his binoculars picked up the arrival of fire engines and an ambulance. The place was supposed to burn and take those meddling coppers and the photograph, wherever it was, with it. He was relying on the blaze to destroy his fingerprints and DNA as well. He would have to go back to finish the job and hope that the detectives, if they had survived, wouldn't be able to provide a useful description of him, or his name for that matter.

When it got darker, he would take another can of petrol and make sure it worked this time. He would have to kill the PC they'd left on guard, though. Regrettable, but necessary.

He had never intended to commit murder. He hadn't planned to kill Ventham originally, but when the MP recognised him from the old days, he had no choice. Bashing him over the head and leaving him to burn seemed the only logical course of action. Things really got out of hand when the coppers arrived, and he felt everything unravelling. He was now faced with the prospect of killing another police officer which, he knew, meant the search for him would be unrelenting.

Breathing deeply and calmly, he convinced himself that the situation could be salvaged. Then he sat back in his car, ate an energy bar, and waited for the sun to set.

The cold air flowing through the coal hole drifted across Mel's face, and she stirred. Instinctively, she took a deep breath and broke into a coughing fit, spitting black phlegm over her chest. She looked up to see Trevor's terrified face.

'Are you all right?'

'Of course I'm not fucking all right. I've been threatened with a pistol, nearly been incinerated and my lungs are full of shit. Ventham was in the hall. Is he dead? It looked like the bodyguard killed him.' She managed a grin. 'Took your time, didn't you?'

'I'll explain later. Good job I heard you banging. Let's get you out of there.'

Mel coughed again and heard Sally stirring behind her.

'Sally first. I could squeeze through that hole, no problem, but she's got a bigger arse. I'll push and you pull.'

Mel dragged Sally to her feet and helped her scramble up the slope. With Trevor and Jack pulling her arms, and Mel shoving her backside, Sally emerged from the cellar, coughing and retching. She sat down on the ground, ignoring the puncturing gravel, and took deep breaths of the beautifully clean air. With a hand up from Trevor, Mel joined her and hugged her tightly. A minute later, their lungs slightly clearer, they both began to laugh, manically, at their reprieve.

'Stop looking at my knickers, DC Blake or I'll tell your missus,' said Sally to Trevor, sternly.

'I... I'm not,' he began to say, then realised she was teasing. He took off his jacket and Sally fastened it round her waist, grinning.

'What's wrong with you two?' asked Jack, perplexed. 'You could have died. Where's the joke?'

Mel gulped. 'It's just a reaction, mate. Better than breaking down. You either laugh or cry, don't you? I just told the thin bloke who speaks in capitals to fuck off, that's all.'

Sally turned away and began to sob quietly.

Two minutes later, an ambulance arrived, followed by two fire engines.

'Come on,' said the paramedic, after carrying out a brief examination of the two women. 'Into the wagon with both of you.'

'But I'm OK,' protested Mel, still coughing intermittently.

'No, you're not. You've been exposed to smoke, which contains all sorts of toxic materials, and you've been deprived of oxygen because the fire used a lot of it up. You need a checkup. No arguments.'

Mel and Sally allowed themselves to be taken to hospital, while Jack and Trevor watched the fire crews extinguish the blaze.

'The fire wasn't as bad as it looked,' said the senior fire officer. 'There was a sprinkler system which helped to contain it. Most of the damage was in the hall, where it appears the fuel was spread. There's extensive smoke damage, though. I'll let you know when it's safe to enter.'

'Thanks, guys,' said Jack. 'We'll cordon off the place and post some uniform to guard it until we can get a forensic team in tomorrow. My colleague thought she saw a body in the hall – did you find it?'

'No. We found nobody on the premises, living or dead.'

Jack watched as the fire engines drove away and, with Trevor's help, strung blue and white tape across the drive and around the side of the house. He told an officer in the patrol car that had arrived after the fire engines to stay on guard until someone could relieve him. PC Tamblyn grudgingly complied, and his mate drove away, a grin on his face.

'Oh shit!' said Trevor, as Jack pulled out of the drive. 'My wallet's in my jacket. Sally's still got it. Can we call at the hospital on the way to the nick?'

'All right. I suppose so. See where gallantry gets you!'

Chapter Seventy-Eight

SALLY SMILED as Jack followed Trevor into her hospital room, where Helen sat holding her hand.

'You can have your jacket back,' she said. 'Helen's brought me some clean clothes. The others stank of smoke.'

'How are you doing? You're looking a bit better,' Trevor replied.

'Not so bad. They're keeping me in overnight for observation. Apparently, the level of carbon monoxide in my blood was a little worrying, so they're monitoring that. Have you seen Mel yet? She's in the room next door.'

'No, we'll look in when we leave you.'

'Did you find our warrant cards and wallets? He made us drop them on the floor.'

'It's a right mess in there but I'll get the SOCOs to check. Ventham escaped, by the way. We're looking for him but there are no leads so far.'

'Did he? We thought he was dead. Before you go, that cellar where we were locked in. There was a couple of laptops, a load of documents and some gear which someone could have worn for sneaking around in. I thought of using it to put out the fire but I realised it was evidence, so I used my trousers. There were knives, as well.'

'That's really useful, Sally. Thanks. We'll take a look in the morning,' said Jack, thoughtfully. 'We'll leave you in Helen's capable hands – and don't come back to work before you're ready.'

'Thanks, Jack – and you Trev.'

Mel was fast asleep, with Tom at her bedside, when Jack and Trevor peered round the door of her room. They nodded to Tom and decided to leave her sleeping. On the way out of the hospital Jack came to a decision.

'I think we'll go back to Ventham's place and take a look at those things in the cellar. I'd rather not leave it until morning. Are you OK with that?'

Trevor sighed.

'All right Jack. I'll give Susie a ring and let her know I'll be late and won't be there for dinner. Let's get it over with.'

PC Tamblyn hated the countryside. Although Ventham's house wasn't exactly in the middle of nowhere, it was far enough away from the lights of the town for him to dislike it. It also had the countryside noises that unnerved him. The rustling trees, the barking of foxes and random bird calls which he couldn't identify. He should have had someone with him, but they were short-staffed so he was stuck here on his own, which made it worse. He put in a set of earbuds and listened to Pandora Blythe's latest podcast. Always good for a laugh.

BRIAN PRICE

It was unsurprising that he didn't notice the figure who
crept up behind him. He did notice the blow on the head
which poleaxed him and dropped him to the ground. Disorien-
tated as he was, he was keenly aware of his attacker's hands
round his throat and the weight on his chest. He flapped ineffectually at his assailant's face but couldn't do anything to
release his hands. PC Tamblyn's residual consciousness faded
into blackness as his brain was progressively deprived of
oxygen, his last conscious thought being, *fuck the country*.

Chapter Seventy-Nine

'LOOK, JACK,' shouted Trevor as the DS swung the car into Ventham's drive. 'By those trees.'

Jack turned the car so that the headlights illuminated the area in question. A figure was clearly visible, sitting on a uniformed PC with its hands around his throat. Jack stamped on the accelerator and the car sprayed gravel behind it as it surged forward, flattening a display of ornamental shrubs and carving tracks into the lawn. He pulled up just in front of the supine officer as the assailant sprang into the trees.

'Ambulance, Trevor. And check on the PC. I'm going after that bastard.'

'But Mel said he was armed. You should wait for an ARU.'

'Fuck that. I'm not having anyone trying to kill my colleagues. I'll get him if it kills me.'

'Be careful, please.'

Trevor's words were lost as Jack crashed through the undergrowth in pursuit of the attacker.

As Trevor checked the fallen officer's pulse, he stirred and moaned. 'Fuck off,' he shouted, striking out with a fist and hitting Trevor in the face.

'It's alright, mate,' reassured Trevor, spitting blood from a split lip. 'It's DC Blake. You're safe.'

'Uh? Yeah. Sorry. I thought it was him. He hit me from behind and was strangling me. Must have passed out.'

'An ambulance is on its way. I don't suppose you got a look at him?'

'No. Too dark. He might have had a beard, but I couldn't really see.'

'Never mind. I think we know who he is, or at least what he's calling himself.'

Jack's return, breathless and with anger and frustration radiating off him, coincided with the arrival of an ambulance. PC Tamblyn brightened up when Jack told him he wouldn't have to stand around in the menacing countryside for the rest of the night, but he was less cheerful when told that he needed to be kept under observation in hospital in case his throat swelled up and stopped him from breathing, following the strangulation.

'I missed the bastard, of course,' said Jack as the ambulance pulled away. 'I'll see if we can get a tracker dog out here in the morning, and we'll look at ANPR, but I reckon he'll be long gone by then. There's a can of petrol here, so it looks like he was planning a second arson attempt. I'll phone for a couple of uniforms to come out, but we'll take a look at this cellar in the meantime, just in case anything else happens tonight. I know it hasn't been cleared by the Fire Service, but we'll tread carefully. OK?'

Trevor nodded his assent and collected some equipment from the car.

Clutching torches and a selection of evidence bags, Jack and Trevor cautiously entered the house. Water squelched underfoot as they inched along the hall, stepping clear of the obviously badly burned areas and the charred remains of the rug. Despite the accelerant poured on them, the oak floorboards were in surprisingly good condition and the two detectives managed to get to the cellar door without falling through the floor. The door was locked, without a key in evidence, but a couple of sharp kicks knocked it off the charred frame. Slowly, they inched down the slippery, glass-strewn stone steps, swinging the torch beams in front of them.

'I don't suppose Sally will be wanting these back,' said Trevor, holding up a pair of singed and sodden trousers. 'I'll put them in a bag and...'

'Bloody hell,' interrupted Jack, gazing at the knives and piles of dark clothing. 'This looks like a serial killer's campaign headquarters. I suppose we'd better get SOCO's to do their bit, but we'll take those laptops now and get them to Digital Forensics in the morning. There's a couple of phones we'll have, too.'

Jack pulled on a pair of nitrile gloves and slipped the items into separate evidence bags, sealing, dating and initialling them as he did so.

'Right,' he said. 'I can hear a car pulling up, so it seems we can knock off at last. Sorry about your dinner.'

Trevor shrugged.

'It's all part of the job, isn't it? Anyway, I was never that fond of Susie's cottage pie, although I'd never say so. I'll get a takeaway on the way home.'

Mel was just dropping off to sleep again, after the latest round of tests and measurements, when she jerked upright, nearly pulling the monitoring leads off her chest.

'The spook!' she shouted.

'What?' said Tom, snatched from his own uncertain slumbers in the uncomfortable hospital chair. 'Are you seeing ghosts now?'

'No. The bloke who attacked us. I recognise him. He works for MI5.'

'Are you serious?'

'Deadly. Look, he knew my name when he was holding us up, so he must have met me before. It was Jack and Kamal who saw him the other day. I think Jack said he looked vaguely familiar.'

'Couldn't he have seen your picture in the papers?'

'Possibly, but I've only been mentioned in the local rag. But that's not my main point. I mentally stripped him of his beard as I was dozing off and I knew him. Do you remember the bomb in the shopping centre?'

'Of course.'

'Well, after I defused it, I was briefly interviewed by an MI5 officer who called himself David Cornwallis. I remember his piercing gaze, and I saw the same eyes earlier today. I'm sure it was him. And there's something else, a bit weird, though. Security Service personnel rarely give their real names to anyone. I think he bases his aliases on the names of spy novelists. John Le Carre's real name is David Cornwell, hence Cornwallis, and Len Deighton wrote *The Ipcress File* and a whole load of other espionage books. He just changed the spelling of the surname to Dayton.'

'Mel, you are brilliant,' said Tom, proudly. 'But tracking down a rogue MI5 officer is going to be bloody difficult. It's not like he's a known face on the Eastside Estate.'

'I know, but it's a start. Now, I want you to go home and pay some attention to the parrots. I'm fine here and you need to get some proper rest. It's sweet of you to stay, but all I want to do is sleep. Go on, off you go!'

Tom smiled, kissed his wife, and wandered off down the corridor, quietly whistling the James Bond theme, completely unaware that Mel started shaking with terror as soon as he left.

What a bloody shambles, he thought to himself. *Now the police would be going over it with a fine-tooth comb and the photo could turn up. But would they realise its significance? The Blythe woman might have told them he was looking for a Polaroid, despite his threats, so they would probably look at it with particular care. Should he try to burn the house down again, or simply cut his losses?* There were two coppers on guard now, and it would be even more difficult to gain access.

Then there was the question of the two DCs. He had to assume Cotton knew who he was. The other one he had never met before, and would be less of a problem, but it would be a good idea to eliminate them both. Of course, they might not have recognised him, but he didn't want to take the chance. Oh shit. Killing them would attract even more attention, when all he wanted to do was slip back into the woodwork. He would weigh up the options and make a decision. Very soon.

Chapter Eighty

Day 31

'SHOULD you two really be back at work?' asked Emma, as Sally and Mel stood beside the coffee machine at ten o'clock the following morning.

'Yes, boss,' they answered together.

'We're fine,' continued Mel. 'There's no permanent damage, our lungs are OK and we both decided to be useful here rather than bored at home. I can't get the smell of smoke out of my hair, though.'

'Well, if you're sure. I'm holding a briefing at eleven. Can you complete your formal statements beforehand? I'd like verbal reports as well.'

'No problem,' replied Mel. Sally nodded.

'Like your perfume,' said Trevor, passing them and grinning. 'Eau de combustion, is it?'

Mel threw a screwed-up paper towel at him and missed.

Mel had just sat down at her desk, with coffee and a biscuit cadged from Trevor, when she became aware of people looking at her. A few of the men sniggered and a couple of women looked outraged. Trevor blushed and Jack looked furious.

'What's up guys?' asked Mel, puzzled. 'Why are you looking at me like that?'

'Check your emails,' replied Kamal. 'You won't like it.'

Mel switched on her laptop and logged in to the email account. She clicked on the latest arrival and nearly spat her coffee out.

'What the fuck?'

The email, which had been sent to the whole team, included an attachment. A photo of her, stark naked, straddling a floppy-haired former prime minister.

'Delete it, all of you,' she shouted and stormed into Emma's office.

'Have you seen this, guv? It's gone to the whole fucking team and God knows where else. It's another bloody photoshop job. That woman clearly isn't me. Her arse is too big and,' she coloured slightly, 'some other bits are a different colour, not that I have any intention of proving it. I know who's behind it, too. It's that Plover arsehole in the Met. It's fucking revenge porn. And as to the other person in the photo I would rather screw a warthog. He's utterly...'

'Let me stop you there, Mel,' said Emma, holding up her hand. 'How could DC Plover manage this?'

'He took a selfie with me before I left. That must be how he got an image of my face. Then either he, or a sleazy mate of his, stuck it on this woman's body. People do it all the time. I want the bastard sacked and prosecuted.'

'OK, OK. I'm sure you're right. But we need proof before we can formally accuse Plover. I'll ask Amira to look into it. In the meantime, I'll have a word with the team. I've no doubt that DSup Gorman will send a message around ordering everyone to delete the email and the attachment, and emphasising that anyone downloading and keeping the image will be subject to disciplinary action. OK?'

'I suppose so. For the time being.'

'Good. Now, I've got a briefing to run.'

'Listen up, folks,' called Emma as she started the briefing. 'First of all, the image purporting to be of Mel and a prominent former politician is completely fake. It's an extremely nasty attempt to embarrass her and will be investigated thoroughly. Now, before we proceed, you are all to delete the email and delete it from your bins, if you haven't already done so. That's an order.'

There was a flurry of keyboard clicks.

'Now, some of you already know this, but Hugh Ventham's house was set on fire last night, with Sally and Mel locked in a cellar. As you can see,' she gestured to the women, 'they are unharmed. The house was damaged, though not seriously. Ventham escaped. Can you take us through what happened, please, Mel?'

'Yes, guv. We went to Ventham's place because we had a witness statement strongly suggesting that he lied about not knowing Madeleine Hollis, and also because he lied to Jack and Kamal. He was seen with her on the night she was killed. We intended to invite him to come into the station for interview and would have arrested him if necessary. When we arrived, we saw him flat out on the floor and the bodyguard, who was not from Mexton Security Services as we originally believed, threatened us. He pointed what looked like a Glock at us.'

'How do you know it was a Glock?' asked Trevor.

'It's pretty distinctive. Anyway, he forced us into the wine cellar and locked us in. He then poured petrol on the floor and down the steps into the cellar and ignited it. Sally put the fire out while I located the metal hatch to the cellar which was originally used to deliver coal. We banged on the metal to try to open it, but it was rusted shut. Trevor and Jack heard us and pulled us out before we died. Just a normal day at the office, really.'

Several officers chuckled and there was a short round of applause for Trevor and Jack. They both stood up and made mock bows.

'Anyway,' she continued, 'I recognised the phoney bodyguard. He's an MI5 officer and came down here following the murder of Duncan Bennett and, again, after the bomb in the shopping mall. He talked to me briefly. He was using the name David Cornwallis and now calls himself Kevin Dayton.'

Someone whistled in surprise and Sally took up the narrative.

'The wine cellar seems to have been where murders were planned, presumably by Ventham. There was kit there, documents, knives and a couple of laptops. We spotted some phones, presumably burners, as well.'

'I gather you retrieved the tech, Jack,' said Emma.

'Yes. Trevor and I went back that evening and collected it. When we arrived we saw a figure, presumably Dayton, strangling PC Tamblyn. I chased him but he got away. Tamblyn's OK, by the way. IT support are looking at the laptops and phones at the moment, but Amira couldn't say how long it would take.'

'Thanks, Jack. So, ladies and gentlemen, we have three key problems. Firstly, how many of the murders we are looking at were committed by Hugh Ventham? secondly, where the hell is Ventham and, thirdly, how do we track down an MI5 officer who's skilled at evasion, subterfuge and deceit? We can pick up his DNA and fingermarks from the scene, but they won't be on any database we can get access to, I'm sure. We've got SOCOs going over the cellar, which should help with the Ventham murders, but that won't tell us anything about Dayton, or whatever he changes his name to. Basically, he's a sodding ghost.'

'There's a vehicle, guv,' said Mel. 'A silver Ford Zetec. I saw it at Ventham's place. I've got a partial plate so we could look at ANPR.'

'Probably pointless,' said Jack. 'A silver Ford was burned out on Mexton Common in the early hours. I saw it on the overnights. I'd be surprised if it wasn't the one you saw.'

'Can we trace him through CCTV, leaving the common?' asked Trevor.

'There's only one camera in that area and it's focused on a car park, to deter doggers. He could have gone anywhere after torching the car. For all we know, he camped in the woods overnight and got an early train to God knows where.'

'All right,' said Emma. 'I'll ask the Super to approach MI5 and request their help. Perhaps they'll let us have a recent photo. If they won't, you'll have to do a photofit, Mel.'

'I wouldn't do that, Emma. I think we should avoid them.'

'What are you suggesting, Jack?' Emma looked surprised.

'We should hold off notifying Five for the time being. They might panic and pull him in. He'll know his cover's blown and he could fuck off to anywhere. I think we should go with an e-fit from Mel rather than an official photo. Treat it like any other case.'

'Can you manage that, Mel?

'Yes, boss. He had a beard yesterday, but he'll have shaved it off by now, I'm sure. I'll do an e-fit, with Sally's help, looking as we saw him, and a techie can remove the beard. There's one more thing, though. I had a message to phone Pandora Blythe and I called her back before the briefing. She's had a whole bunch of loony calls in response to her podcast but one was definitely of interest. A woman who was present at the party came forward. She was there to provide refreshments, she said.'

'Presumably the horizontal kind,' someone said, to grins from the team.

'Yes, probably,' continued Mel. 'But, anyway, she positively identified Hugh Ventham as one of the participants. She remembered Roger Gardner but found it hard to describe him, apart from a piercing gaze. Apparently, he participated fully in the entertainment but said hardly anything. Also, she confirmed that someone had taken a Polaroid but she couldn't remember who.'

'That's useful Mel. Did Pandora give you any contact details for this woman?'

'No. She refused to give her name. But it's better than nothing. And, by the way, his alias could be a reference to John Gardner, another spy writer who started in the sixties.'

'Yes!' said Trevor, almost leaping from his chair. 'Smiley was Marnie Draycott's nickname for him. It refers to John Le Carré's character George Smiley. She must have known what he did for a living.'

'I think Marnie made it her business to know a lot about her guests,' said Mel.

'There's another problem,' said Jack.

'What, only one?' interrupted Mel.

'I mean, suppose we catch him and charge him. Will it ever get to court or will MI5 shut everything down in the interests of national security? I don't know about anyone else, but I don't trust the spooks. Look at the murder of that Chinese bloke in London. Massively interfered with, and no proper result.'

There were murmurs of agreement from the assembled detectives.

'Any road,' said Emma, 'we'll deal with that if and when it comes to it. For now, our job is to catch the bugger and that's what we'll do. When we get useable images, we'll take them round car rental places and those garages we know do cash sales with no questions asked. See if he's obtained a vehicle. Check vehicle thefts around the relevant times. Someone needs to look at CCTV at the railway and bus stations, and on any local buses running near the common. Put out an appeal for dashcam footage from anyone driving near the common last night or this morning. I think we can assume he's behind the burglaries, so we need similar checks around those premises, if there's anything left of the recordings. Liaise with the Met, Mel, please. He's canny so he would probably have covered his face and avoided cameras, but anyone can make a mistake.'

'What about the stuff we found at Ventham's?' asked Sally.

'When we get the forensics back, we can begin to tie him to specific murders, with a bit of luck. I'm hoping the electronics won't take too long but any analysis of fibres from the clothing could take quite a while. We haven't got the funds to fast-track the work, and we can forget about doing a mitochondrial DNA match with the hair in Pandora's parcel. We can't justify the expense.'

'Any news on Ventham's whereabouts, guv?' asked Kamal.

'I was coming to that. We've had a report from a tractor driver who was cut up by someone on a quad bike, on the minor road behind Ventham's place. He said the rider was carrying a shotgun. A bike was found abandoned at a picnic spot in Mexton woods. There was no sign of the rider, but the vehicle was registered to a gardener who works on Ventham's premises. Apparently, he leaves it there when he's not using it. Ventham's phone is not in use so we can't track him. So, we need to put out a press release asking the public to look out for Ventham. On no account should they approach him. I'll contact the Press Office. His photo is being circulated to patrols and on social media, so we hope someone will spot him. We have an ARU on standby to arrest him, and teams with dogs are already searching the woods.

'OK. You've all got things to do. I think a session in the Cat and Cushion one evening would be handy, if anyone's free in the next couple of days.'

The grins from the team gave her the answer.

Jack called Mel and Sally into an empty office and told them to sit down.

'Just what the hell are you two doing back at work?' he asked, his voice kindly rather than angry. 'You're not bloody Wonder Women. You should be taking it easy for a while. What about delayed effects from the smoke?'

Sally started to speak but Mel interrupted.

'The docs gave us the all clear and sent us out at eight this morning. There's no physical damage as far as they could see. We had a chat over a coffee before we went home to change and agreed it was best to get back on the horse. At home we would just go over and over what happened and end up crazy.'

Sally nodded her head and spoke quietly. 'It's not easy, but I figured that the longer I left it, the harder it would be to go back. Mel agreed with me. This was the closest I've come to dying on the job, and I'm determined to get over it.'

Jack frowned.

'I understand, but it's not that simple. You may know that I nearly died when I was stabbed by a knife-wielding priest. I had flashbacks for years. You really must take advantage of the counselling service.'

'I've told Sally about my PTSD and how useful the counselling was,' said Mel. 'But there's something else. We both want to get the bastard who did this to us, and sitting around at home isn't going to help.'

Jack nodded. 'OK. But if you think things are going to shit, come and talk to me. At least I've been there.'

'Thanks, Jack,' said Mel.

Sally nodded her agreement, a slightly distant look in her eyes, and the detectives got back to work.

Chapter Eighty-One

Earlier

HUGH VENTHAM CRAWLED out of his makeshift shelter and brushed leaves and twigs from his clothes one handed, the pain from his broken fingers swamping his dull headache. After relieving himself, he sat on a tree stump to consider his priorities. He could do without food for a while, although he would need water soon, preferably to wash down some pain killers. In normal circumstances he would call into A&E to get his head checked out but he could hardly do that now. He would just have to wait for the headache to go away.

His ultimate goal was to get out of the country, which meant making his way to Southampton where his yacht was kept. It wasn't registered in his name, and it was a fair bet that the police wouldn't know of its existence. On the way, he would call into an A&E department to get his hand looked at, preferably a long way from Mexton. But first he had to retrieve his emergency cash, the documents he'd hidden and his spare car. He needed a vehicle to get him back to civilisation and the shotgun would help him acquire one, but there wasn't much traffic on the roads through the woods at six-thirty in the morning. Then he heard footsteps.

A young man carrying binoculars and a camera was walking along the path, his eyes scanning the treetops. A bird-watcher, presumably. Even Ventham, whose principal interest in wildlife was in shooting at it, had heard of the red kites which had recently spread to Mexton.

'Stop!' shouted Ventham, stepping into the birdwatcher's path and swinging the shotgun to bear on his chest. 'Where's your car?'

'B... back there, a couple of hundred metres. In a layby.'

'I need it. Give me your keys. The terrified ornithologist fumbled in his pocket and handed them over.'

'Have you got a phone with you?'

'N... n... no.'

'Give me those binoculars.'

The young man complied, shaking. Ventham ripped the strap from the glasses and ordered the young man to put his hands behind his back. He tied his thumbs together, using his good hand and the two undamaged fingers of the other, and marched him into the woods. When they were invisible from the path, he steered his captive towards a young sapling and made him sit on the ground with his back to the trunk.

'What are you going to do to me?'

'Nothing, if you behave yourself.' Ventham waved the shotgun menacingly. 'I have things to attend to, but I'll let someone know where you are when I've finished. You could be here sometime.'

He searched through the birdwatcher's rucksack and found a bottle of water, which he drank greedily, and a protein bar. He then ran the young man's belt around his neck and the tree trunk, securing it so his victim couldn't escape but could still breathe. Hiding the shotgun under his jacket, in case there were any other bird spotters about, he made his way back to the path and followed it to the road where he found a Nissan Leaf parked. He wouldn't normally be seen dead in such a vehicle, but it would do until he could retrieve his own transport. Dropping the shotgun on the floor behind the front seats, he switched on the car and drove smoothly back towards Mexton.

Chapter Eighty-Two

'WOULD YOU LIKE A CUP OF TEA?' Martin Rowse asked his new client, as the receptionist at Mexton Investigations showed Mrs Collier, an elderly but sprightly woman, into his office.

'No. No thank you. You're a detective and I want you to do some detecting.'

Martin smiled and invited her to sit down.

'So how can I help you?'

'It's my dog, Norman.'

'Can I interrupt you there, Mrs Collier? I'm afraid we don't look for missing pets.'

'I don't want you to find him. I know where he is. But someone tried to run him down the other day and I want to give the driver a piece of my mind.'

'Oh dear. Is Norman all right?'

'Well, he was quite upset at the time. He wouldn't eat his dinner. I took him to the vet, who said he was just shocked.'

'So, er... Norman wasn't exactly hit by a car.'

'No. That's why the police wouldn't help me. They said

that if he'd been hit the driver would have been obliged to stop, by law, but, as he wasn't, there was no offence committed.'

'I see. So can you tell me exactly what happened?'

'Certainly. I was walking Norman down by the allotments four nights ago when this big black car came rushing down the lane. The horn made a terrible noise and I had to jump out of the way. I jerked on poor Norman's lead so hard he yelped pitifully and the noise upset him so much he hid under a bush. It took me ages to get him out.'

'But surely, the car could have gone anywhere after that? Unless you got its number, no one would be able to track it down.'

'Ah. That's where you're wrong.'

Mrs Collier looked pleased with herself.

'The lane is a dead end and we get very few cars along it. That's why I take Norman for walks there. I live at the top of the lane and I'm sure the car hasn't returned. So, it must be in one of the lock-up garages at the end of the lane.'

'I see. So, what exactly do you want me to do?'

'Well, as you're a detective, you must have lock picks and things. I want you to look in the garages and find the car. Then I'll keep watch from my bedroom window until the driver comes back. And then I'll tell him what I think of his driving.'

'I'm afraid there are two problems there, Mrs Collier. Firstly, it would be illegal for me to break into the garages. If I was still a police officer, I would need a warrant to do so and I wouldn't get one without a very good reason. Secondly, if you go accosting this man – I presume it was a man driving – you could put yourself at risk. I suspect he wouldn't just apologise politely and promise not to do it again.'

'Well I'm not afraid of that, I assure you. Look, even if you're not allowed pick the locks, can you at least look for

BRIAN PRICE

evidence? Tyre tracks or something? I suppose it would be safer to put a note under the door. I could do that, couldn't I?'

'I suppose so.'

Martin was on the point of declining the job but decided a stroll in the fresh air would be quite pleasant.

'OK. I'll come and take a look at the garages. But I won't break in.'

'Splendid! How much do you charge?'

'Well, we usually ask for a fee in advance, but let's just see if I find anything. Then we can come to an arrangement. All right?'

Mrs Collier beamed and stood up.

'I'll give you my address and you can park outside my cottage. You must have some tea before you investigate. Is three o'clock suitable.'

'Yes, Mrs Collier. I'll see you there.'

Martin showed her out and forbore from mentioning that the last time he'd looked into a lock-up garage he'd found three skeletons there.

This isn't working, thought Ventham. Driving the electric car one-handed was relatively easy but he knew that it would be much more difficult to handle his own vehicle, especially on a long drive. There was no alternative but to seek treatment. He couldn't go to Mexton General. He was too well-known there, having recently opened a new scanner suite, partly paid for by the private health company in which he held shares, the deal being that they would have priority access to it for their patients. He decided to take his chances at the minor injuries unit in Highchester so he turned the car around and headed away from Mexton, hoping that there was enough charge in the car's battery to get him there.

'Guv, we've got a lead on Ventham!' Trevor called through Emma's open door. 'The search team found a birdwatcher tied to a tree in the woods. He said that a man threatened him with a shotgun and took the keys to his car, early this morning. The man fitted Ventham's description and appeared to have a head injury and something wrong with his hand.'

'Excellent. See if you can find the car on ANPR and give the number to the control room so they can alert patrols. If he's still in the Mexton area, we'll get him!'

Chapter Eighty-Three

MARTIN SAT on Mrs Collier's chintz-covered sofa which smelt slightly of dog. He gazed at the walls, covered with pictures of Norman, and the mantelpiece which bore a single photo, presumably of the late Mr Collier. After drinking two cups of tea, consuming a large slice of Dundee cake and listening to a substantial fraction of Mrs Collier's life story, he suggested it was about time they looked at the garages. Norman trotted happily alongside, having clearly got over the trauma previously experienced in the lane.

The garages were formed of slabs of concrete, with up-and-over doors exhibiting varying degrees of corrosion. Two of the five had clearly been unused for some time, judging by the weeds flourishing in front of them, but the other three showed signs of recent occupancy. Two of these were padlocked shut but the third had recently been forced open. Wearing a latex glove, Martin cautiously lifted the door a few centimetres, crouched down and shone a torch inside.

'That's interesting, Mrs Collier. I think we may have found your black car. But there's something odd about this garage.

There's a collection of number plates on the floor, all with different numbers, and it looks as though someone has searched it. Boxes have been emptied on the floor and a cupboard door is hanging open. I think I'd better call a friend of mine in CID.'

'Oh. Should I leave that note, then?'

'No, I wouldn't. If something's happened here, the police wouldn't want anyone adding to the scene. I'll walk you back to your cottage and make my phone call.'

'Oh, that's kind of you. And how much do I owe you?'

'Nothing, Mrs Collier. Consider the tea and cake sufficient payment.'

Back in the cottage, Mrs Collier offered more cake, which Martin politely declined.

'I'd better make a move,' he said. 'It's not often we solve a case this quickly.'

'Thank you so much, Mr Rowse. I'll be sure to recommend your agency to my friends if they ever need a private detective.'

'Please do, Mrs Collier. But, remember, we don't look for missing pets.'

———

'Hi, Martin. In another sticky situation, are you?' asked Mel, when she answered her phone.

Martin laughed.

'No Mel. And I'm not in a jam, either. I've found something that might be of interest to you guys. There's a row of garages at the end of the lane running alongside the allotments. One's been broken into and searched, from the look of it, and there's a load of reg plates on the floor. The car inside is a black VW SUV. Are you still looking for one of those? I heard something on the grapevine.'

'You're well informed, but yes. How did you find it?'

'I was working on a case involving psychological cruelty to a domestic animal,' he replied, his tongue firmly in his cheek. 'Don't worry, I didn't do anything illegal or contaminate the scene.'

'Well if that vehicle is the one we're looking for, we owe you several pints. I'll tell the boss and be in touch. Thanks ever so!'

'My pleasure. Happy to be of service. And I'll take you up on that beer.'

Chapter Eighty-Four

MEL AND SALLY eased open the garage door, which screeched in protest and dropped a shower of rust over their hair.

'Looks promising,' said Mel. 'There's a dent on the offside wing, perhaps where it hit Mr Raven. What do you think?'

'I reckon you're right. And look, here, scratches on the door. From the bushes on the road from Carter Hall perhaps?'

'OK. I don't reckon we should open the car doors. I'll phone the guv and ask for a recovery vehicle. The SOCOs can have a crack at it in the police garage. I'm sure this place has been searched – by Dayton, perhaps?'

Sally nodded.

'Martin was right about the number plates,' continued Mel. 'I recognise at least one of these numbers from ANPR footage. I'll make a list and we'll try to match them with each of the murders. Well done Martin!'

'Do you know him well?' Sally asked. 'I remember him from when I joined CID.'

'Yes, he's a mate. We worked together for some time. He was stabbed badly on one occasion, and other attempts were made on his life. After the bombing he left the Job and joined Mexton Investigations, hoping it would be safer. He still got banged on the head during the honey job, though. He hasn't said anything, but I think he has a hankering to come back, though his wife wouldn't be too pleased if he did.'

At that point a recovery vehicle clanked and rattled as it reversed slowly down the lane, followed by a woman leading an excited small dog. The dog sniffed at Mel's trouser legs, presumably picking up the strange scent of the parrots.

Its owner asked, excitedly, 'Have you found him? The man who frightened my Norman? That nice Mr Rowse said what he did wasn't illegal but here you are.'

'Sorry, madam, who are you?' asked Sally, slightly confused.

'I'm Mrs Collier. Mr Rowse was helping me find the car which nearly ran Norman over and frightened him so much.'

Cogs whirred in Sally's brain.

'Norman is your dog, right?'

'Yes, he is.' Mrs Collier peered over Sally's shoulder. 'And that's the car that nearly hit him. It came down the lane so fast. I'll leave a note for the owner, telling him to drive more slowly.'

'I'm afraid you can't do that, Mrs Collier. This is a crime scene. Tell me, when did this happen?'

'Oooh. It was four days ago at around six forty-five. I remember because The Archers was just starting when I got back. I live at the top of the lane.'

'Did you see the driver, by any chance?'

'I only got a glimpse. I'm sure it was a man, but he had one of those American hats pulled down over his face.'

'You mean a baseball cap?'

'Yes. And it happened so quickly.'

'Well, that's very useful, Mrs Collier. I'll make a note of

what you've said, but we may need to take an official statement from you later.'

'How exciting. And all because Norman was so desperately frightened.'

'I'm afraid it's not about Norman. I can't give you any details, but you may have helped us with a major inquiry. Thank you.'

'Oooh! I feel just like Miss Marple. Would you like me to bring you some Dundee cake?'

'No, thank you. That's very kind of you, but we must get on. I think this truck will be ready to leave soon, so you'll need to get clear of the lane. There's not much room. Thank you again for your help.'

The two detectives smiled as Mrs Collier trotted back up the lane, pulled by an eager Norman.

'OK,' said Mel. 'We'll have a look in the garage when the car's gone, but it looks as though someone's been through it already. It's a total mess and, as Martin said, the door's been forced open. Worth a look, though. I've asked for someone to bring a new padlock to secure it when we've gone. We also need to find out who rented the place. The guys in our garage will give us the car's VIN so we'll be able to get the genuine reg and trace the vehicle's history.'

'I'll get onto it when they get back to us. Pity you turned down that offer of cake. I'm quite peckish.'

'You're sounding like Trevor, always after a biscuit. Go on, there's some chocolate in the car. Help yourself.'

Chapter Eighty-Five

VENTHAM, using the name George Arkwright, managed to convince a sceptical doctor that the damage to his fingers had been caused by him shutting the door of his touring caravan on his hand. An X-ray revealed that the injury wasn't as bad as it felt, and the doctor had straightened his fingers, binding them together, after giving him a local anaesthetic. His hand was now heavily bandaged and slightly more comfortable.

When he mentioned the blow on the head, the doctor had taken it more seriously, checking him for concussion and urging him to go to the main hospital for a CT scan without delay. Waiting until 'Mr Arkwright' returned home to York-shire would be extremely inadvisable, he cautioned. He also advised Ventham not to drive. Ventham thanked the doctor, promised to take a taxi, and headed for the hospital car park.

To his horror, he saw a police car parked behind the Leaf. Two officers were peering into the vehicle and he saw one speaking urgently into his radio. 'So how the fuck am I going to get back now?' he muttered. If he stole another vehicle it was bound to be reported and, anyway, he didn't know how to break into a car and hotwire it. He would have to take his chance on the bus, which he saw pulling into a layby a few metres ahead. The hooded outdoor jacket he had taken from the Leaf should help to conceal his face from any CCTV, and he had enough cash in his wallet to cover the fare.

The journey back to Mexton was nightmarish, every bump and pothole sending daggers through Ventham's head and reawakening the pain in his hand. He got off the bus several stops before the terminus, in case anyone was watching the bus station, and made his way towards his hidden vehicle. In an hour he would be on the road to freedom, with plenty of cash, a vehicle no-one knew about and a yacht waiting to take him well clear of the UK.

His optimism melted like chocolate in a heatwave when he approached the allotments. *Fuck! Police!* He had been certain that no-one knew about his secret garage. The sight of police towing away his escape vehicle made him feel physically sick and he watched with dread as SOCOs entered the garage. There was no reason why they should move the old engine block, which covered the hole he'd hacked in the concrete floor to hide his cash and documents, but, if they did, he would be royally screwed. He might even have to give himself up, a thought which horrified him.

He walked onto the untended allotments, looking as though he had every right to be there, and was gratified to see that no one on the search team seemed to notice him. A gardener's shed, around a hundred metres from the garages, opened easily when he yanked on the padlock which gave up its tenuous hold on the rotten door frame. Slipping inside, he could see, from the spider webs covering the garden tools, that it had been unused for some time. He pulled the door to and watched, through a crack, the officers searching his secret

BRIAN PRICE

domain, the thumping of his overdriven heart intensifying the pain in his head.

By dusk, the scene was deserted with only a strand of crime scene tape, stretched across the garage door, indicating that the premises had been visited by the police. His head still aching, and his fingers throbbing, Ventham made his way to the side of the garages and lifted the brick under which he had hidden the spare padlock key. Trembling, he slid the key into the lock and twisted. *Shit!* It wouldn't turn. Must be rusty. He looked closer and, despairing, realised that the padlock had been changed. He was fucked.

Chapter Eighty-Six

TREVOR RUSHED into the DI's office; his face flushed with excitement.

'Guv! We've got a sighting of Ventham!'

'Where?' asked Emma, cutting off a call on her personal phone.

'A bus driver recognised him from the photo on social media. He picked him up from the hospital, where the patrol found the Leaf and the shotgun this afternoon and dropped him off at Pennyfields Close.'

'So, he's back in town. Any CCTV there?'

'No, but look. It's only a fifteen-minute walk to the allotments and Ventham's garage.'

'Excellent! Who's watching the garage?'

'No one, I'm afraid. Jack asked, but Uniform couldn't spare anyone to stand there all night. The PC on duty left about an hour ago. There's some kind of demo going on in town, apparently. Mobile units have been told to keep an eye on the place but, as it's a dead end, I doubt they'll be driving down the lane to check.'

'But that's bloody ridiculous! It's obvious he could go there. He'd want his car for a start. What the fuck are Uniform playing at?'

'I know guv. The cuts, isn't it? And it's mayhem in town.'

Emma swore again, under her breath.

'OK. Get down there yourself and I'll give the duty inspector some earache. Wait until someone relieves you. And check Ventham hasn't tried to get into the garage.'

'Will do.'

Ventham rushed back to the shed on the allotment, seized a spade from its dusty recesses and shoved the end under the garage door. He strained with all his might, his left hand pulsating with agony, and the door moved upwards a few millimetres. He tried again, desperation lending him strength. He could feel the padlock's fixings giving way so he redoubled his efforts, throwing all his weight on the haft of the tool. The metal creaked, moved a little more and, with a bang and a screech, the door jerked upwards. He was in – and, to his relief, the engine block was where he had left it.

'Oh, what's all that fuss about, Norman,' grumbled Mrs Collier as her pet scratched at her back door. 'You've already had your walk.' She paused. 'Well, alright, just a quick one. It's a nice evening and the moon looks lovely.'

With the lead clipped onto the little dog's collar, she put on her coat and shoes, and stepped outside, inhaling the fragrance of the evening blossoms with pleasure. Norman strained at the leash as they walked down the lane so Mrs

Collier released him and he bounded off, his tail wagging, coming to a halt in front of the half-open garage and growling.

'What is it, Norman? Is there someone there?'

Leaning forwards, curiosity mixed with trepidation, she peered in. Something stirred in the shadows. A hand grabbed her coat and jerked her inside. Her heart pounded and she started to scream. Losing her balance, she fell face-down on the unforgiving concrete floor. With blood pooling on the floor from her broken nose, Mrs Collier passed out.

Chapter Eighty-Seven

'SHIT,' cursed Ventham, kicking at the barking dog snapping at his ankles. Ignoring the woman on the floor, he pushed Norman out of the garage with a broom and pulled the door down. The dog continued barking furiously, which did nothing for his throbbing headache. 'I should have throttled that bloody animal,' he swore. Switching on a torch, lifted from a hook beside the door, he slumped wearily into a rickety chair and contemplated his options.

Trevor drove the unmarked police car slowly down the lane, dodging the ruts left by the transporter that had carried away Ventham's SUV. Half way down, he stopped as his headlights picked out a small dog barking at a garage door.

'Guv,' he said, when Emma answered her phone. 'I think Ventham is here. There's a dog barking outside the taped-off unit.'

'That would be Norman, Mrs Collier's dog. Which means she's probably inside. OK. Hold back and don't approach. We could have a hostage situation. I'll call for armed response and ask for a negotiator to stand by. Keep me informed.'

'Will do.'

Trevor switched off his engine and stepped out of the car, watching carefully for any signs of Ventham. *At least he doesn't have his shotgun*, he thought, *but does he have another weapon?* Pushing aside his fear of being shot or stabbed, he crept slowly down the lane, took up position behind a large Buddleia bush from which he could watch the garage, and settled down to wait for backup. Then he saw movement.

He had to get away, no question. But first he had to retrieve his cash. Using a crowbar, he moved the engine block along the floor, in agonisingly small increments which jarred his wounded hand. He had just managed to uncover the hidden recess when he heard a car outside. He froze. Grabbing the bag of cash and documents from the hole, he stumbled over Mrs Collier's inert form, yanked up the garage door and dashed towards the allotments, his eyes partly dazzled by Trevor's headlights.

The moon cast treacherous shadows over the flower beds and vegetable patches that made up the site and, more than once, he tripped over a hose or section of netting. His throbbing head and burning hand were almost forgotten in his desperate urge to escape, but he knew his strength was fading. So, this was it. Failure. Total failure. But he would take someone else with him, whoever they were. Reaching in to his pocket for the clasp knife he'd retrieved from the garage, he turned to see the solitary form of Trevor lumbering towards him. *On his own?* thought Ventham. *Perhaps there's a chance after all.* Waiting for Trevor to get closer, he opened the knife and prepared to kill his pursuer.

Chapter Eighty-Eight

TREVOR LURCHED to a halt when he saw the moonlight glinting off Ventham's blade. *Oh fuck,* he thought, his bowels beginning to tremble. *What will happen to Susie and little Luke?* He had no baton or PAVA spray, nor even a stab vest.

Ventham moved towards him, holding the knife low for a gut thrust. Trevor stumbled, the swinging blade missing his stomach by a centimetre. Ventham overbalanced slightly and swept the blade towards Trevor's face as he regained his stance. Trevor jumped backwards, entangling himself in a thin netting fence enclosing a crop of cabbages. Ventham advanced, a wild gleam in his eyes. He slashed again, this time slicing Trevor's sleeve. Trevor pulled himself free of the net, brushing his hand against a metal supporting stake. Before Ventham could strike again, Trevor jerked the stake from the ground and blindly swung it at his attacker. Ventham howled as the iron struck his injured hand and Trevor followed the blow up with a kick to Ventham's stomach. Winded, Ventham doubled over, grasped his head with a groan, and fell to the ground, unconscious.

'What about Mrs Collier?' asked Trevor, as he watched paramedics loading Ventham into an ambulance, his hands cuffed to a stretcher.

'Who?' queried PC Halligan.

'The woman with the dog. In the garage. Did no one check?'

'Dunno, Trev. We were kind of busy with you and Ventham.'

'For fuck's sake! Come with me, now. And shift.'

The two officers raced across the allotments and stopped at the entrance to the garage, horrified at the sight of the elderly woman lying with her head in a pool of blood, Norman whimpering by her side.

'Paramedics!' screamed Trevor, just as the ambulance driver opened the vehicle's door. 'Over here!'

The driver paused, shook her head and began to climb into the rig. Trevor screamed again, joined by Halligan, and, this time, the driver started to walk towards them.

'Get a fucking move on!' yelled Trevor, feeling a faint pulse in Mrs Collier's neck. 'She's dying.'

'No need to be rude,' protested the driver, an aggrieved expression on her face as she arrived. 'Oh. I see what you mean.'

She knelt beside Mrs Collier, checked her pulse and called to her colleague. Within minutes the casualty was stretchered to the ambulance, with an oxygen mask on her face and a collar supporting her neck. An anxious-looking Norman whined as the vehicle doors closed.

'What about the mutt?' asked PC Halligan. 'Should I give him to the dog unit to look after?'

'No. You're all right. I'll take him home. Susie'll look after him until Mrs Collier gets out of hospital, and Luke will love to meet him. Now, let's get this area sealed off. I've got a statement to write and then I need to get home, for a long bath and a beer.'

Chapter Eighty-Nine

MEL CLOSED her front door and walked disconsolately down the hall, wondering how Tom would react to the revenge porn. Her mood lifted immediately when she saw an old friend sitting at the kitchen table.

'Robbie! Great to see you. What brings you here?'

Tom kissed her, took her jacket and pressed a glass of wine in her hand.

'I heard what happened,' he explained. 'A really shitty thing to do. I thought Robbie could help track who's behind it.'

'That's lovely, but Amira's looking into it.'

'I know, but she's snowed under. She's bloody good, but Robbie's quicker. And he can do this officially, which is great.'

Mel remembered occasions when Robbie had used his prodigious computer skills to help out, risking his liberty in the process.

Mel took a large swig of her wine.

'I don't know how much Tom's told you, Robbie, but I met this DC from the Met in London in connection with a couple of cases. He came on to me and I rejected him. Then he divulged confidential information to a podcaster and blamed me, which, fortunately, neither the Met nor my boss believed. He was then suspended and blamed me for it. I reckon he's behind the photo.'

'Arsehole!' said Robbie, and the others nodded in agreement.

'OK,' he continued. 'I can probably trace the IP address but if it leads to a machine operated by the Met, there's no way of my proving who sent it. You would have to get on to them and find out who was logged into it at the time the email was sent. If it was a private machine, it would be more conclusive. I'll have a go tomorrow and let you know what I find.'

'Thanks so much, Robbie. You're a star. When this is all sorted, we'll buy you a curry.'

'My pleasure Mel. Right. I'd better be off. Dinner's waiting.'

'Thanks for calling him, love,' said Mel as Tom gathered up the empty glasses. 'If anyone can track the bugger quickly, it's Robbie.'

'Exactly. By the way, that new parrot food arrived by courier.'

'What new food?'

'The stuff you ordered.'

'I didn't order anything. Show me.'

'Well it's addressed to you,' said Tom, reaching for a cardboard box on the worktop.

The box was labelled 'Parrot food. Please keep dry' and bore no return address or company name.

'That's bloody odd,' said Mel, 'and deeply suspicious. Should we call the bomb squad?'

'I think it's a bit late for that. I shook it when it arrived and it definitely sounded like seeds and grains. If there was a bomb inside it would have gone off then, or when they chucked it around in the courier's depot, for that matter.'

'I suppose so.'

Tom fetched a pair of scissors, put on a pair of latex gloves, and cautiously cut through the parcel tape, opening the box with his face averted.

'Phew,' he said. 'Tension over. It is bird food.'

Mel looked closely at the contents of the box and then tipped some onto a plate.

'I recognise some of this. Sunflower seeds and so on. But there's a couple of oddities. These look like apple pips, and there's some chopped leaves I can't identify.'

'Apple pips? But you should never feed apple pips to parrots. They're poisonous to them.'

'Shit. Someone's trying to poison Bruce and Sheila. I'll bet those leaves are toxic. Rhubarb or something. And I've got a bloody good idea who. I mentioned to Plover that I had to get back to feed the parrots and he must have remembered. He's added these things to ordinary parrot food, hoping we wouldn't notice. The bastard!'

'So what are we going to do about it?'

'I've got an evidence bag in the car. We'll put the stuff and its packaging in there and see if we can get it tested.'

'In your dreams,' said Tom, ruefully. 'No force is going to spend money looking for DNA on a box of dodgy parrot food. They can't do him for administering a noxious thing. The Offences Against the Person Act doesn't apply to parrots.'

'Well, it bloody well should. And if I see that arsehole again, I'll kick his pathetic little bollocks to pulp.'

Chapter Ninety

Day 32

'A BRILLIANT RESULT,' beamed Farlowe at the start of the briefing. Kudos to Trevor for taking down Ventham last night.'

There was a ripple of applause and a few cheers.

'There's a uniformed officer with him at Mexton General. They've operated and Ventham is recovering from his head injury. They said there was unlikely to be any permanent brain damage, so he should be fit to be tried, but he's not going anywhere for a while. He was lucky.'

'There's a nice warm cell waiting for him when he gets out,' said Jack. 'Great news.'

'How about Mrs Collier?' asked Kamal. 'She was injured, wasn't she?'

'I popped in to see her this morning,' replied Trevor. 'She's got a broken nose and a lot of bruising. They're a bit worried about her heart, so they're keeping her in for observation. Her first thought was Norman, and I reassured her he was in good hands. Luke loves him.'

'Now we've got to build a solid case against Ventham,' continued Farlowe. 'What have we got on the SUV and the garage?'

'We've managed to trace the vehicle's owner,' replied Trevor. 'It's a Mrs Emily Player who's in a care home and hasn't driven for twelve years, although her driving licence has been renewed regularly. The car was bought on her behalf from a dealer in Petersfield. The salesman couldn't be sure, but he thought he recognised Hugh Ventham. I did some digging and Mrs Player is Ventham's aunt. She's in a care home and he has power of attorney over her affairs. The garage was rented by a Dominic Durham, who happens to be Ventham's constituency party secretary. He admitted that Ventham had asked him to rent the place and pays him monthly. Apparently, Ventham told Durham that it would be useful for storing campaign materials – placards, leaflets and such.'

'How about forensics? You were liaising, Jack.'

'Yes. The paint from the bushes near Carter Hall matches the vehicle and the scratches correspond to the damaged bushes in the lay-by. Tyre tracks also matched. The dent on the wing is consistent with it hitting Mr Raven. Fingermarks throughout the vehicle match Ventham, and there were some from Madeleine Hollis on the passenger door. There were hairs on the passenger headrest, which we could send off for DNA, hopefully to confirm Madeleine's presence in the vehicle, if we can afford it. The fingerprint evidence may have to do.'

'Anything to link the vehicle to the sites of the Sutton or Moncrieff murders?'

'Possibly. The lab's got the clothing from Ventham's cellar and are looking for a match with the fibres found on the marina's fence. There are fibres in the car, too. They're looking at soil and dirt in the wheel arches and think they could match some pollen with the plants growing near the marina, but it could be expensive to consult an expert.'

'I'll ask Mr Gorman to authorise it.'

'Also, there was some kind of sticky residue on the wheel rims and tyre walls. The lab is sending someone out to look at the solvent recycling plant in case it came from there – waste from the process, they wondered. If Ventham parked away from the areas affected by the fire, there could be something still there that matches. It'll take a couple of days. The guys are also looking at the vehicle electronics which should contain a record of journeys made, unless he managed to disable them.'

'Cameras? You were looking at those, Trevor,' said Farlowe.

'Yes, boss. I've been running the different numbers through the systems and, so far, I've been able to place the car on roads leading to the marina, the solvent plant and the canal where Madeleine was dumped. It was also in the centre of town when she was taken and in the general area of the physiotherapy clinic when Mr Raven was killed, although not very close because of the broken cameras. The overall pattern is a bit patchy, as he probably used back roads and avoided cameras where he could, but it's all suggestive. The Met are doing the same to see if they can place him in Mayfair when Mr Raven was attacked and in Docklands when Justin Kite was killed.'

'Thanks, Trevor. Jumping the gun on the forensics a bit, I think we've got enough evidence, albeit circumstantial, to link Ventham to the murders of DSup Raven, Dale Moncrieff, Mark Sutton and Madeleine Hollis, as well as the attacks on Pandora Blythe here in Mexton. If the Met come up with anything on Justin Kite, we'll have the full set.'

'So, we believe that Ventham committed the murders.

What about the burglaries and arson on the victims' premises?' asked Kamal.

'Almost certainly Dayton, looking for that bloody photo. No proof, though – he didn't leave traces apart from at Ventham's place. It must have been him who threatened Pandora Blythe. I take it the photo hasn't turned up?'

'No,' replied Jack. 'A PolSA team went through the house and found nothing of interest apart from some dodgy sex DVDs and a small stash of coke.'

The briefing was interrupted by Amira Khan, the IT technician, bursting into the room.

'DCI Farlowe, you'll be very interested in what we found on those laptops,' she said, overflowing with excitement. 'Ventham used project management software to plan all the murders down to the last detail. He collected information on the victim's workplaces, habits and leisure activities and identified every step to be taken in each murder. It's a murderer's manual. Also, we tracked the burner phones found in the cellar. They weren't on permanently, but each one of them pinged towers in the general area of a murder, at relevant times, before being switched off.'

'Well done, Amira. I think we can consider Ventham's murders solved, pending a few loose ends and a mountain of paperwork. So that just leaves us the job of catching Dayton.'

'Piece of cake,' muttered Jack, sarcastically.

'Dundee cake?' said Mel to Sally, who grinned.

Farlowe frowned at them.

'OK,' he said. 'We've got Dayton's e-fits printed off and uniforms are eager to help distribute them, given that he tried to kill Mel and Sally. They're on social media as well. Hopefully, he won't be able to move without being spotted, assuming, that is that he's still in Mexton. We'll get him. That's all for now. Thank you everyone.'

As Mel wandered over to the coffee machine she reflected on Jack's words. It will be bloody difficult to find a spook on the run. He will know all their moves and methods, and what to expect. It was part of his training and he had proved himself clever and ruthless. The thought of what he might do next was chilling. Was there a different approach they could take? She would have a chat with Tom when she got home, preferably with a bottle of wine to lubricate the brain cells. But not too much wine.

As expected, Mel's employers declined to run DNA tests on the box of adulterated parrot food. She brooded on this as she walked up the path to her front door, wondering whether it would be worth paying a lab to do it privately. There would be problems of admissibility, of course, but it would satisfy her own mind.

She reached into her shoulder bag for her keys. A noise behind her made her jump out of her skin. Her heart rate shot through the roof. She turned to find a man standing behind her, his face contorted with rage, an open plastic vessel of some kind in his hand.

Birdy.

'This is for you, bitch,' he yelled, jerking the container forwards.

Instinctively she ducked and held her bag in front of her face. A jet of liquid struck the bag, smaller splashes hitting her clothes and hands. A few drops landed in her hair although she didn't notice at the time. She threw the bag at her assailant, hitting him in the face, and followed it up with a kick to his groin which he dodged. Her foot slipped in the pool of liquid on the path and she started to tumble backwards, her hands flailing.

Before she could overbalance completely, firm hands gripped her shoulders and moved her aside. Tom stepped past her and kicked Birdy in the stomach. He wrested the container from him with his prosthetic hand and hit him in the throat with his other fist. Birdy collapsed, gasping for breath, and Tom secured his hands with a length of garden twine. Then he turned to Mel.

'What was that he threw at you? Acid?'

'I don't know. My hands feel all soapy and they've started to sting.'

'Right. Shower. Now. I'll deal with this piece of shit. Go on before things get worse. And leave your shoes and bag outside, or you'll ruin the carpet.' He smiled grimly at her.

Mel needed no encouragement and dashed to the bathroom where she soaked herself in a cool shower for fifteen minutes, emerging with sore pink patches on her hands and clumps of hair missing where the liquid had eaten it away.

———————

Tom turned to his captive.

'What was it? What did you throw at her? Acid? Tell me or I'll fucking throttle you.'

Birdy started to whimper.

'Please help me. My face is burning. It was caustic soda not acid. Wash it off, please.'

Tom looked at him with utter contempt then turned away. He found a bucket full of rainwater in the corner of the front garden and picked it up. A layer of rotten leaves in the bottom had turned the water brown and imparted a particularly unpleasant odour. Good, he thought, and threw it over Birdy's face.

'One more thing,' he said. 'Mel wanted to do this but she's indisposed. If anyone asks, this happened in the fight.'

He kicked Birdy savagely in the balls and left him writhing while he went into the house to phone for the emergency services. He retrieved a pair of handcuffs from the drawer of the hall table, and replaced the garden twine which bound Birdy's hands. After quickly checking on Mel, Tom returned to the front of the house and kept watch on the disgraced detective until an ambulance arrived, closely followed by a police car.

Half an hour later, Birdy had been transported to Mexton General for treatment of his alkali burns in A&E, accompanied by a uniformed officer. A paramedic had dressed the lesions on Mel's hands, urging her to seek medical attention if they became any worse. She sat with Tom in the kitchen, both of them nursing large brandies, her head on his shoulder.

'Good job you turned up, wasn't it?' she murmured.

'Pure luck. I happened to glance at the laptop which was running the feed from the door camera. I saw something going on and dashed out. I felt a complete idiot, running into bother in my slippers. Still, Tae Kwan Do has hardened my feet.'

'Ah. My nit in shining armour.'

Both collapsed with laughter at Mel's dreadful joke, the tension draining away.

'So what's the damage?' she asked.

'Your hair looks like it's been savaged by a drunken barber, you'll need new shoes and I'll need some slippers. The stuff was all over the path. You'll also need a new bag, and clothes to replace those with burn holes. My prosthesis has changed colour slightly in places but otherwise seems none the worse for wear. A real hand would have suffered more damage.'

'Better than a new face, I suppose. How about Birdshit?'

'When the hospital discharges him, he'll spend the night in the cells. The paramedic didn't think the burns were particularly bad. She said that caustic soda turns the fat in your skin to soap and then destroys the tissue underneath. You were both lucky it didn't get in your eyes.'

Mel shuddered.

'He'll go down, won't he? For the caustic soda attack, if nothing else.'

'Oh yes. Administering a noxious thing with attempt to cause harm or whatever. I've heard from Robbie. He's traced the email to an IP located in Bermondsey. Birdy has a flat there. Now he's been arrested, they can search his premises and examine his laptop. The Met are being very co-operative. The top brass don't want people like him in their ranks. He's not going to have a very nice time inside.'

'Serves the fucker right.'

Tom sat silently for a few seconds.

'Look, Mel. Are you all right? You've had a tonne of shit fall on you lately and you've tried to laugh it off. But what's really going on?'

Mel's eyes moistened and her shoulders drooped.

'Sometimes I feel as though I can't go on. I never thought I'd admit it. But I don't want to end up like Mum, killed on duty by some random arsehole.'

'Do you want to leave the Job?'

Tom poured himself another large brandy and drank it in two gulps.

'No. If I did, I'd be letting Mum down, Dad too. After all, he carried on after Mum died and made DCI. Fuck, at least I haven't been blown up, unlike you. Apart from an occasional ache in my shoulder from that sword cut, I'm reasonably intact.'

'You don't have to remind me.'

A shutter fell in Tom's eyes.

'No, sorry. I didn't mean it like that. It's just that I shouldn't really be grumbling. Danger is part of the job. And I think being a detective is in my blood. I just don't want my blood spilled all over the floor.'

'OK,' said Tom, slurring slightly. 'You are a bloody good detective. You shouldn't give up. But for fuck's sake be more careful. After all,' he said, forcing a grin, 'how could I look after Bruce and Sheila on my own?'

'You twit,' said Mel, smiling again. 'It's late and I think we should go to bed.'

Tom needed no encouragement.

Chapter Ninety-One

Day 33

'WHAT'S WITH THE HAIR, MEL?' asked Trevor, as she entered the Major Crimes suite. 'Been at the thallium again?'

'If it was anyone but, you, Trev, they'd have been looking at a knuckle sandwich.' Mel smiled. 'Last night DC Plover attacked me with caustic soda. I'm OK but it's rotted some of my hair. I'm thinking of going punk, but Tom's not so keen. What do you reckon?'

'I'd let it grow out. Safety pins in your nose would set off the metal detectors in any secure buildings. You're still our mate, whatever you look like.'

'Hmm. Loved with faint praise. For that, you can get me a coffee. And I'll have one of those custard creams you're trying to hide from us.'

As Trevor headed for the coffee machine, Jack came over, a smile on his face but worry lines on his forehead.

'Go on. Tell me what happened. And please convince me you're OK.'

Mel recounted the night's events and Jack whistled when she had finished.

'You were bloody lucky. I got some of that caustic soda on my hands when I was trying to clear a blocked toilet. It's wicked stuff.

'Changing the subject, I wondered whether you'd be prepared to act as a mentor to Kamal? He's an experienced officer but he needs to find his way around Mexton and learn how we do things here. He's had a brief induction, but perhaps you could spend some time over the next few days, helping him with things missed because of the current mayhem?'

'Jack, I'd be delighted.'

'Excellent. Oh, I think there's a think tank planned for the Cat and Cushion tonight. Hope to see you there.'

***

There was nothing for it. He would have to find out what the police knew and whether or not they had the photo. If it had been part of an official operation, he would have had access to Holmes2 and would have been able to track at least some of the investigation's progress. But he was officially on sick leave and had no legitimate access to MI5's systems. Given time, he might have been able to befriend, threaten or blackmail someone working on the case locally, preferable a civilian support officer, and persuade them to provide the necessary information. But he didn't have that time, so he would have to be more direct. And brutal.

Perhaps he'd start with the younger one. Cotton had a reputation, but this one seemed less confident, from what he'd seen when they found him at Ventham's. She would probably be easier to take – and to persuade.

'OK, OK, that's enough war stories,' said Emma, as Sally finished a complicated tale about the hunt for a prolific garden gnome thief. 'What are we going to do about this Dayton bugger. We can't go to MI5 for help; we have to be clever.'

She sipped her Theakston's Old Peculier and waited for suggestions.

Nobody spoke.

'Come on. Someone must have an idea?'

'Well, guv,' said Kamal, tentatively. 'We could set a trap.'

'Go on.'

'He's obviously obsessed with this photo. Suppose we let it be known that we had it, or knew where it was. He would try to get hold of it and we would nick him when he did.'

'A good idea in principle,' said Emma, 'but I can't see it working in practice. He's not going to charge into a police station demanding it, is he? And how could he find out unless he has someone on the inside? I'm bloody sure he hasn't.'

Kamal looked deflated.

'Pandora!' said Mel. 'We could use her.'

The others turned to her looking incredulous.

'You're not suggesting we should involve a civilian are you?' said Jack. 'And a rather flaky one at that. We can't put her at risk. Dayton's armed and ruthless. It's much too dangerous.'

'I'm not suggesting we use her as bait, Jack, but she could claim to have received it, on her podcast. We could stake out her place, with her well away from it, and arrest him when he breaks in. Job done!'

'OK. But her flat is in London and she's staying in a hotel outside London, so we'd have to involve either the Met or, probably, Thames Valley. They wouldn't be happy with us running an operation on their turf.'

Emma sounded doubtful.

'Can we do something down here?' asked Sally. 'We believe he's still in the area.'

'Yes, but Pandora has no local connections.'

'She has one, though, doesn't she?' said Trevor. 'Carter Hall. She was nearly killed there, twice.'

'Suppose,' said Mel, excitement building in her voice, 'she let it be known that someone down here was going to hand over the photo to her at Carter Hall. Ventham's ex-cleaner or someone. She would have a reason for being here, and our own AFOs could take Dayton down.'

'It might work,' said Emma, slowly. 'We would need to make bloody sure that Pandora wasn't put at risk and there was a credible reason for her choosing Carter Hall. OK. Work up a proposal, with Pandora's help. We'll need to clear it with Mr Farlowe and the DSup. And the risk assessments must be bloody watertight.' She smiled broadly. 'I'm feeling good about this. Thanks, guys. I must get back to Genevieve, but here's a twenty to get another round in. G'night.'

Chapter Ninety-Two

I<small>T HADN'T BEEN</small> hard to work out that the detectives drank in the Cat and Cushion. The shooting there, by the Albanian gang, had been all over the internet. So, it was just a question of keeping an eye on the pub and waiting for a chance to grab his prey. Whether she would leave on foot or in her car didn't matter, as long as she was on her own at some point. The elderly Land Rover he had stolen was sturdy enough to stop most cars, should he need to block her vehicle, and there was plenty of room to throw her in the back. She would probably walk home or get a bus if she'd been drinking, anyway. Piece of piss!

'Shit!' muttered Sally, as she saw the number nine bus pulling away just as she reached the, now deserted, stop. The LED display informed her that the next one would be along in twelve minutes and she debated with herself whether to wait or start walking. Perhaps the exercise would do her good. She turned up her collar against the cool evening breeze and started to walk.

Maybe this isn't such a good idea, she shivered, as well-lit pavements gave way to unlit verges. Within a few minutes she was jumping at shadows and flinching at every rustle in the bushes. Should she phone for a taxi or hope she would get to the next bus stop in time?

The decision was made for her when she felt something hard grinding into her lower back and a voice in her ear whispered.

'Don't turn around. Keep walking normally. You see that Land Rover over there, thirty metres down the road? You're going to get in the back. But first, put your hands behind you. Fuck about and I'll blow your spine to pieces.'

Sally nearly threw up and she started to fall. Her attacker grabbed her hair and pulled her upright again. She winced as she felt a cable tie cutting into her wrists, and her legs started to tremble.

'What do you want?'

Panic rose in her voice.

'I want the photo and I want to know what you know. But we'll get into that when we're somewhere private. With tools.'

Sally held back the urge to vomit. She didn't dare run. He would shoot her, she was sure. And wouldn't he kill her anyway, once he'd got what he wanted? She was damned if she would make it easy for him so, when they reached the back of his vehicle, she feigned a faint and dropped to the floor. The impact of her cheek with the kerb sent waves of pain across her face, but she remained inert.

'Get up, you stupid bitch.' Dayton kicked her viciously in the ribs.

Another flare of pain.

'Get in the fucking car.'

Sally moaned but didn't respond. Dayton drew back his foot to kick again but froze as the headlights of a car approached. He crouched down, pretending to fiddle with a tyre, and shielded Sally from the view of the oncoming vehicle's occupants.

'All right,' he snarled, when the vehicle had passed. 'Have it your way.'

Sally heard the weapon clatter to the ground as he grabbed her by her hair and the back of her jacket. He shoved her face-first into the back of the Land Rover. She drew back her knees and kicked backwards with all her strength. Dayton doubled over as her feet connected with his solar plexus. She rolled over to her back, still half in the car, and tried to kick him again, this time in the face. He was too quick and, as she slid out of the vehicle, he punched her in the head. Everything went black.

A few minutes earlier

As Tom and Mel were getting up to leave the pub, Mel spotted something on the floor.

'It's Sally's wallet,' she called. 'We'd better get it back to her. Her keys are in it.'

'Do you know where she lives?' asked Tom.

'Yes, and I know which bus she'll get. Come on. You're driving. I've had three pints, remember?'

She tossed the car keys to Tom who caught them with his prosthetic hand, proud of his newly developed dexterity.

'Humph. I don't really like orange juice that much, you know.'

'It's good for you. And I'll be the designated driver next time.'

'So which bus does she get?'

'Number nine. The stop's just along there.' Mel pointed as Tom started the car engine.

'Shit,' she said, as they passed a deserted bus stop. 'It's gone and she must be on it. Get a wriggle on and we'll intercept the bus along the route. She'll panic when she finds her wallet's missing. Hang on, what's going on there? That Land Rover...'

Tom's gaze flickered briefly from the road ahead.

'Looks like someone's got a flat tyre.'

'It didn't look flat to me. Turn around and we'll take a look. We can always catch up with the bus further on. I've got an uneasy feeling.'

'Sure that's not the three pints of ale?'

Tom joked as he swung the car around in an impromptu U-turn, seriously annoying a boy racer, in a noise-enhanced Corsa, who had been planning to overtake.

'Oh fuck,' shouted Mel, as they pulled up in front of the Land Rover. 'It's Dayton.'

The man purporting to fix the flat looked up as Mel leapt out of the car and ran round towards him.

'Kevin Dayton, I'm arresting you on suspicion of attempted murder and arson,' she began.

'The fuck you are.'

He picked something up from the ground and held it in both hands, pointing it towards Mel.

'Back off and get back in your car or I'll shoot you. And your stupid friend on the floor here.'

Mel heard Sally groan as she regained consciousness. Dayton stepped into the road aiming his weapon at Mel's head. She heard a crunch as Tom engaged first gear and she leapt aside as he drove straight for Dayton, the engine screaming.

Dayton anticipated and ducked behind the Land Rover as Tom shot past. He hesitated briefly then, cursing prolifically, jumped over the fence beside the road and disappeared into the clump of trees that came up to the verge. By the time Tom had turned and shone his headlights on the scene, Dayton had disappeared completely.

Chapter Ninety-Three

UNDERGROWTH TORE at his clothes as he hurtled through the trees. He stumbled down a slope and found himself on the bank of a small stream that glistened in the moonlight. Good. A chance to lose the dogs they'd inevitably send after him. He waded downstream for several minutes, with water coming half way up to his knees, until he came to a single-track railway line, separated from the water by a simple wire fence that he climbed over with ease. Cautiously, he walked along the track, his boots squelching, and eventually arrived at a small station. Just before the moon went behind a cloud, he could make out a porter's trolley laden with ancient trunks, a cluster of milk churns and enamel advertising panels for products which no longer existed. *Christ*, he thought. *It's one of those restored steam railways. It looks like I'm back in the 1930s.*

Using the light from his phone he studied the timetable on the wall of the building. Trains only ran at weekends and, occasionally, during the week. It would be several days before anyone came here, unless some eager volunteers turned up to grease the engines or something. That shouldn't matter. He would spend the night here and review his options in the morning.

It only took a few moments to break into the building and scope the place out. There was a small shop selling railway memorabilia and ancient VHS tapes of trains. More importantly, there was a counter that sold sweets and snacks. Helping himself to a miscellaneous selection of food, and a couple of cans of drink, he continued his search. A cupboard provided him with some ancient uniforms which would serve as blankets, and a bench in the waiting room would do as a bed. He used the adjacent gents, washed his face and sat down to eat, desperately trying to work out a way of retrieving that photo. Under no circumstances could it fall into the hands of his superiors, and he would do anything necessary to prevent that.

Chapter Ninety-Four

'Fuck, fuck, fuck,' shouted Mel as she ran towards Sally. 'I nearly had the bastard.'

'Whoa, hold on,' said Tom. 'I love you just the way you are, without a bullet hole in your forehead. It's body piercing you really don't need.'

Tom's attempt at levity defused Mel's anger somewhat, but she nearly wept when she crouched over Sally.

'What's he done to you?' she asked, taking in the blood running down the side of Sally's head and the blooming contusion on her cheek.

'Face, head, ribs,' Sally replied. 'He knocked me out for a bit but I'm OK. What are you doing here? Not... not that I'm not grateful. Tried to... Rand Loaver. Kicked him... gut.'

Sally's speech became unsteady.

'You left your wallet in the pub, you twat,' replied Mel, affectionately. 'We were trying to catch up with the bus when we gate-crashed this little party. Now, you're going to listen to me talking bollocks for a while until the ambulance arrives. You are not, repeat, not, going to sleep.'

For the next ten minutes Mel prattled on about the DIY attempts she and Tom were making on their house, their parrots, and the life story of Ernie the tortoise, much of which she made up. Sally remained conscious but, when the blue lights of the ambulance flickered over the scene, she became drowsy again.

'We'll take it from here,' said the paramedic, as she and her colleague manipulated Sally onto a stretcher. 'Looks like a serious head injury. We'll alert the A&E registrar on the way.'

As the ambulance left, sirens howling, two police patrol cars and an ARV pulled up. DCI Farlowe climbed out of the first car and ran over to Mel and Tom.

'What's happening? The call to control said there was an armed suspect and DC Erskine was injured.'

'We nearly had him, boss,' said Mel, omitting her previous industrial language.

'He scarpered into those trees and he's well in the wind by now. You can stand the AFOs down. Sally's gone off to hospital with a head injury and some other damage. This,' she indicated the Land Rover, 'is the vehicle he was using. Sally didn't say much, but I got the impression he was trying to get her into the back of it.'

The DCI nodded.

'Right. We'll cordon this off and get a team in. I'll see if a dog unit's available. We may be able to track him, although I think there's a stream down there. I take it you're unharmed?'

'Yes, guv. Just a bit pissed off, I mean annoyed. He pointed his pistol at me but he didn't fire.'

'OK. Please call into the station and write your statement before you go home. You too, DC Ferris.'

He looked at Tom.

'We'll have a briefing in the morning. You needn't stay here any longer. I'll see you tomorrow.'

'Shit,' said Tom as they headed off for the police station. 'I was hoping we could curl up with a film and a takeaway when we got home.'

'Well, *Mission Impossible* and the veg biryani will just have to wait, won't they?'

They both laughed.

Chapter Ninety-Five

Day 34

'You'll all be pleased to know,' said Farlowe at the start of the briefing, 'that Sally is recovering and has been discharged from the hospital. She's had a scan and the blow on the head doesn't appear to have caused any permanent damage. However, she is on indefinite sick leave and we don't know when she will be able to come back.'

Murmurs of concern followed the DCI's announcement.

'Do we know why she was attacked?' asked a civilian investigator.

'I visited her in the hospital last night. She was conscious and reasonably clear but she hasn't made an official statement yet. She did say that Dayton wanted to find out what we knew and the whereabouts of that photo. He hinted at torture. It's a damn good job Mel and Tom came along when they did.'

'But why is the photo still so important to him?' asked Kamal. 'Surely it's irrelevant now his cover's blown and he's wanted for attempted murder.'

'That's what I wondered,' said Mel. 'Presumably, he originally thought he could be blackmailed over a picture of him shagging someone he shouldn't. But none of that matters now.'

'Perhaps,' said Jack, thoughtfully, 'it depends on who he was shagging.'

He declined to elaborate on his suggestion.

'Anyway,' said Farlowe. 'Down to business. The Land Rover Dayton used was stolen earlier that day. We've traced the owner and he's pleased it's been found. Tracker dogs followed Dayton to the stream that parallels the road at that point and then lost him. We've got uniforms searching both upstream and down, with strict instructions to call for armed back up if they spot anything promising. I'm not hopeful.

'The good news is that we've got the go-ahead to use Pandora Blythe's podcast to set a trap. She will say that someone has contacted her, saying they have the photo, and that they are prepared to do a deal with her as long as they remain anonymous. One of us will take Pandora's place at the meet and armed officers will be put in position several hours beforehand. When he turns up, we'll take him. So, we need a volunteer to impersonate Pandora – not you, Trevor. The beard's a bit of a giveaway.'

The team laughed and Trevor feigned disappointment.

'It'd better be me, guv,' said Mel. 'I'm about Pandora's height and I can wear a wig, bright lipstick and some of her clothes. The guys here are the wrong shape.'

'But he knows who you are,' protested Jack. 'He could shoot you on sight. You don't have many of your nine lives left, you know.'

'I'll wear a vest under her coat. She's more buxom than me so there should be room. It won't notice. As long as the light isn't too bright, we should get away with it.'

Jack drummed his fingers on the table and looked sceptical.

'How are we going to get him to the meet?' asked Mel. 'Pandora's not going to tell everyone she'll be at Carter Hall at midnight, is she? She'll have to leave a clue he'll pick up on.'

'She could make some reference to a dangerous place or something and make it clear it's in Mexton.' suggested Trevor.

'Not a bad idea,' the DCI replied. 'OK. Mel, you talk to Pandora and see what she says. If she's agreeable, we'll work on a script and run it by her. As soon as she's happy, we'll get going. Dayton may leave the country if he can't get what he wants, so let's not waste any more time. Oh, I'd like a word with you, please, Mel.'

'What's the matter, guv?' asked Mel as she followed Farlowe into his office.

'Nothing to worry about, I promise. Firstly, I wanted to check on how you were coping. I know Jack's had a word with you but I wanted to reassure you that you have my support. You had a narrow escape last night, the latest of many, and you would be superhuman if it didn't affect you. I speak from experience.'

He fingered the scar on his face.

'I'm OK, sir. At least, I hope so. I've got brilliant support, at home and at work. I'll handle things, don't worry.'

'Well, don't let things get to the stage where you collapse, mentally and emotionally. It can be insidious, so be careful.'

'Yes, of course. I will.'

'There's one other thing,' said Farlowe, as Mel got up to leave.

'Yes, guv?'

'How do you feel about taking your sergeant's exams?'

Mel thought for a moment.

'Tom and I discussed it, briefly. I'm not sure I'm ready to step up a rank. Anyway, there isn't a vacancy. Jack doesn't want to retire, I know.'

'No, he doesn't. But there's nothing wrong with being prepared for when one arises, and it will take you quite a while to do the studying. What do you think?'

'I'll give it some thought. Thank you, boss. I appreciate your confidence.'

'Not a problem. You're an intelligent officer and you get on well with people. You'd make a good DS. Now, you'd better go and talk to Ms Blythe.'

'What me? Help catch the killer,' squeaked Pandora when Mel phoned her. 'That is so fucking cool. What do you want me to do?'

Mel explained what they had in mind and she readily agreed to come down to Mexton to work on the podcast.

'I'm not keen on going back to Carter Hall, though,' she said.

'Don't worry. You won't have to. But please bring down a coat I can wear over my bullet-proof vest. I'll try not to get any bullet holes in it.'

Pandora laughed a little uncertainly and promised to be in Mexton by the afternoon.

Chapter Ninety-Six

Hello again true crime fans. Pandora Blythe here. And boy do I have news for you! Your very own podcaster, yes, me, is going to help catch a killer! But before I get to that, I have news about the murders I told you about last time. The police are now satisfied that Detective Superintendent Raven, Dale Moncrieff, Justin Kite, Mark Sutton and Madeleine Hollis were all killed by one man, who was also behind the attacks on yours truly while I was working on my Wellness Roadshow TV programme. They have arrested a suspect! Hugh Ventham, the MP for the death-haunted town of Mexton, is currently helping the police with their enquiries. His solicitor has, of course, insisted that this client is innocent.

Why someone would want to murder the other participants at the party is anyone's guess. But perhaps the killer was doing something not-very-respectable which could damage his career? Maybe the answer lies in a mystery photograph taken at the scene! Now dear listeners, this is where I come in. An avid fan has contacted me. He used to work for one of the people at the *party as a handyman. He has the photo and is prepared to hand it over to me, for a consideration. Imagine! Of course, I'll give it to the police, but not before I've had a good look at it. I'm sworn to secrecy about where, although I can say that it's somewhere significant to me and not even the police know where it is. It's happening tomorrow night at ten o'clock and there will be a special edition of the podcast at noon the day after. So, keep listening, crime fans, and wish me luck. Stay safe out there!*

The podcast ended with a snatch of the William Tell Overture by Rossini.

Chapter Ninety-Seven

Day 35

HOW MUCH LONGER COULD HE wait for a reply? Dayton agonised. Help should have been on the way by now, in response to the email, and he should have been well on his way to safety. The railway station was a convenient place to hide, and he had taken pains not to advertise his presence there, keeping the door shut and avoiding lights after dark. There was plenty of food and the building was warm and dry. But he couldn't stay there much longer; trains were due to start running shortly. Meanwhile, he needed to find out as much as he could about the hunt for him.

He switched on his burner phone and scanned a few local websites, looking for anything which would indicate what the police were doing. Nothing turned up, but a Google search led him to Pandora's podcast. *Now that is interesting*, he mused. *Very interesting indeed*. He thought for a few moments and began to formulate a plan.

'I'm really worried about you, love,' said Tom. 'What if he shoots you? It's a completely hare-brained plan. He'll be expecting police there to protect Pandora, so he may not even turn up. He's not a moron. Even if he doesn't suspect a trap, he won't think he's the only one who can work out the location.'

'Yes, but he's desperate to get the photo so he may take a chance. I know it's a risk, but there will be more firearms there than in a Texan's garage, so I'm not too worried. My guess is he'll wait until the handover's taken place and try to take the photo from me afterwards. Then we'll have him. We may even get him beforehand – we've got all the approaches covered. A man from the ARU, posing as Ventham's handyman, will meet me outside Carter Hall and pass me an envelope. He'll be wearing a vest and will be armed, discreetly. He'll clear off immediately afterwards and I'll walk back along the drive to my car. I'm not sure it will work, but I'm not too worried about my safety.'

'Well, I bloody am!' He enfolded her in a hug. 'For fuck's sake, be careful.'

Chapter Ninety-Eight

Day 36

A LIGHT WIND made the leaves on the trees bordering the drive leading to Carter Hall rustle softly. Weak light from a single lamp glinted off the open gates. The Authorised Firearms Officers were invisible, lurking in the bushes and the long grass of the wildflower meadow. The man who walked slowly up the drive towards the woman standing in front of the building was oblivious to their presence, but Mel was more than grateful that they were there.

The walker was illuminated by the pale moonlight that served to keep Mel's face in shadow. The hairs on the back of her neck stood up as the man came closer. There's something wrong, thought Mel. This doesn't seem right. He doesn't look like the AFO and he's early. Then the man reached into his coat pocket.

Lights flared and shouts shattered the silence.

'Armed police! Armed police! Get on your knees with your hands on your head. Do not move.'

The man froze. He started to whimper and a moist patch appeared on the front of his trousers.

'What? What have I done? I don't know what's going on. Don't shoot me, please!'

He sank to his knees as instructed and burst into tears.

Two AFOs rushed over, handcuffed him and searched him for weapons. Finding none, they allowed him to stand up.

'Why are you here?' asked Mel, gently, 'and what's your name?'

'Grove. Matthew Grove. A bloke met me outside the Jobcentre. He offered me a hundred quid to deliver a message to a woman outside Carter Hall at ten o'clock tonight. He didn't say nothing about no guns.'

'What's the message?'

'It's in my pocket. An envelope.'

Mel pulled a thin white envelope from the man's pocket and opened it cautiously. She unfolded the single sheet of paper it contained and read the message it bore. In bold capitals were the words 'You must think I'm bloody stupid.'

Aaargh, screamed Mel inside, but she remained outwardly calm. She radioed the Tactical Firearms Commander and told him that the AFOs could stand down.

'OK, Mr Grove. It looks like someone played a trick on you. We were expecting a dangerous criminal tonight and I'm really sorry you were terrified by the firearms. We'll need a statement from you, I'm afraid, so I'll get a car to take you back to the police station. We won't keep you there long.'

Still nervous, Grove muttered something about them owing him a new pair of trousers, but Mel didn't hear. She undid Pandora's coat and loosened the Kevlar vest, wondering which unfortunate soul would have to clean the urine-stained seats in the police car.

Chapter Ninety-Nine

Day 37

'How DID DAYTON TWIG,' asked Mel, when the detectives assembled for the morning briefing.

'Because he's a highly-trained MI5 officer with a strong sense of self-preservation, I suppose,' replied Emma. 'Perhaps the trap was a bit obvious, but it was worth a shot. So what the hell is he going to do next? He's still after that bloody photo, presumably.'

'Obvious? A complete balls-up,' said Jack. 'Why on earth did we think it could work?'

'Because we were running out of ideas,' Emma replied, tartly, 'And no-one had a better one. This is probably the most elusive, and dangerous, individual I've come across in my whole career and I'm at my wits end. Any suggestion, however daft, has to be considered. We are bloody desperate. Now let's get on.'

Jack scowled but didn't reply.

'Could we get Pandora to pretend she's got the photo anyway and set another trap?' asked Trevor.

Emma frowned.

'I don't think so. It would put her at greater risk and we couldn't control things enough to ensure her safety. The Super would never allow it and Dayton wouldn't rise to the bait, anyway.'

'I'd better warn her not to do anything stupid, then,' said Mel. 'But, surely, the photo's irrelevant now he's wanted for attempted murder. There can't be anything on it more incriminating than that.'

'So do you think he'll just lie low for a while and then try to leave the country?' asked Sally. 'It's what I would do.'

'You could be right, lass,' replied Emma.

'Is there any other way we can draw him out?' asked Kamal?

'I think we blew it with the podcast trap. He'll be deeply suspicious of anything that could expose him.'

'How about getting MI5 to bring him in? They must have some way of contacting him, surely?' said Trevor.

'We've already discussed that,' said Emma. 'But we could consider it as a last resort. I think we'll have to rely on traditional policing from now on. Have another chat with Mr Grove and find out as much as you can about Dayton's current appearance. See if they were picked up by CCTV outside the Jobcentre. It's on a bus route, so find out if a bus passed at the relevant time and check any onboard recordings. Once we know what he was wearing, we may be able to follow him using shop and Council CCTV. We might, at least, get an idea of the direction he was heading. Can you divvy up the jobs, Jack? Thanks.'

'So, what have we got on Dayton's movements?' asked Emma, as the team reconvened, late in the afternoon.

'The Jobcentre camera did pick him up, along with Matthew Grove,' replied Trevor. 'He was wearing a dark jacket and trousers, and pale, probably white, trainers. This confirms Mr Grove's observations. He had a baseball cap pulled down low, but it was clearly him. He's now clean shaven, so we'll use Mel's e-fit with the beard removed when we're canvassing for witnesses.'

'Have we any ideas where he went after that?'

'Some. CCTV at a jewellers near the Jobcentre picked him up a few moments later, and a Council camera caught him at the end of the High Street. I've contacted the bus operator and they said there was nothing running past at the relevant time.'

'Anything else?'

'Possibly. There's some blurred footage from a camera on Abbey Street, showing a cyclist nearly knocking over a teenager on an electric scooter. They were both riding on the pavement. The cyclist looks like Dayton. I checked, and we had a report of a bicycle being stolen from a rack where the High Street joins Abbey Street so it's a reasonable bet that it's Dayton. Sally's contacting the owner for details of the bike.'

'Where does Abbey Street lead?'

'It connects with the main road out to Highchester,' replied Jack. 'There's a cycle path about three hundred metres further on. Once he's on that, we've got no cameras.'

'Bloody great,' said Emma, exasperated. 'The bugger's mobile, but we can't trace him on ANPR. Put out an appeal for dashcam footage for that stretch of road and get notices on the cycle path asking for witnesses. Probably a waste of time, as there must be plenty of dark-clad cyclists using the path every day. But we need to try everything.'

'Can we get a drone up to look for possible hiding places?' suggested Kamal.

'Maybe,' replied Emma, 'if it's available. But he might have doubled back or changed direction completely. I'll look into it, though.'

'I don't suppose there's an electronic trail,' said Mel, resignedly.

'No. There's no bank account or credit card that matches this Kevin Dayton, and we don't have a phone number to track him with. If he is using cashpoints, he's got another alias. We looked under David Cornwallis, Roger Gardner and variations on Fleming, too. Nothing. And there's no vehicle registered to any of those names. He's still a bloody phantom.'

'Bloody spooks,' said Trevor.

'Before we disperse,' said Emma, 'I've heard from Sally. She won't be coming back until Occupational Health have cleared her, which could take some time. She would be pleased to receive visitors at home, but please phone or text her before-hand to avoid surprises.'

'I'll go and see her tonight,' said Mel, 'and we'll set up some kind of rota. My guess is that the best therapy she could receive is news of Dayton's capture.'

The others voiced their agreement and returned to their desks to continue the hunt for a would-be cop killer.

Chapter One Hundred

Day 38

TRAINEE FIREMAN DESMOND BARROW whistled to himself as he unlocked the gate leading to the restored station on the Mexton and Highchester Steam Railway. He was looking forward to giving his favourite engine a polish before services started the following day. It gave him an immense sense of pride to see its brasswork gleaming, and the Great Western green paint almost glowing in the sunshine, as eager children of all ages climbed aboard the chocolate and cream carriages behind.

That's odd, he thought, staring at a section of damaged woodwork around the door. *Someone's broken into the waiting room.* He phoned the General Manager of the railway, a volunteer like himself.

'Steve, it's Des. I'm at the station. Someone's broken in. Do you want me to call the police?'

'Wait for me, Des. I'll be there in half an hour. Is there much damage?'

'The door's been forced and the woodwork...'

A sharp blow on the side of his head curtailed Desmond's response. He sank to his knees then toppled forward, falling off the platform and landing across the tracks, like the imperilled heroine in an old black-and-white film, but without the oncoming express.

Dayton stamped on Desmond's phone and kicked the debris under a bench. He grabbed his meagre belongings, shoved them in his rucksack, retrieved his bicycle from the waiting room and cycled off without a glance behind him.

'Des? Des? What's happened?'

Getting no reply, Steve Webster pressed cancel and redialled Des's phone. Unavailable. He tried again and got the same response. Could Des have disturbed an intruder? he asked himself. Fearing the youngster was in danger, he dialled 999 and asked for the police.

'Hello, police. What is your emergency?'

'Um. I think a colleague might be in danger. He's a volunteer on the Mexton Steam Railway. He was just telling me about a break-in at the station when he was cut off in the middle of a sentence. I tried calling back, but his phone's switched off. I'm worried he may have disturbed someone.'

'OK, sir. Can you give me your details, the name of your colleague and the location of the incident?'

Steve complied and the call handler assured him that help was on its way.

'There's nobody here,' sarge, reported PC Pepper as he walked along the deserted station platform. 'There are signs of a break-in – the door's been forced – but it doesn't look as though there's anyone inside. I'll take a look.'

As the constable was removing his PAVA spray from his belt, he heard a faint moaning noise and a scuffling sound. He rushed to the platform edge, peered over and saw a young man in blue overalls almost hidden by the overhang. He seemed to be attempting to climb back up to the platform, but the effort was obviously too much for him. Blood was streaming down his neck and his fair hair was matted with it. His face and over-alls were smudged with soot and dust from the track, and one wrist was pointing in an unnatural direction.

'Hang on mate. Are you hurt?'

The stupidity of the question struck PC Pepper as soon as he uttered it, and he changed his tack.

'Don't move. I'll call an ambulance and they'll get you up on a stretcher. Is there a train due?'

'N... no. Tomorrow. Hit on head.' Desmond managed to say, before collapsing back on the track bed and groaning.

———————————

Forty minutes later, Desmond was on his way to hospital and PC Pepper was searching the station building. Someone had clearly been at the snack counter. Crisp packets and energy bar wrappers were piled in a corner, along with a stack of empty fruit juice bottles and soft drink cans. A discarded copy of the *Mexton Messenger,* folded over at the page which described the police's lack of success in apprehending the local arsonist and would-be murderer, lay crumpled on the floor. He radioed in his findings.

'Looks like someone's been living here, sarge, and recently

too. The bloke who thumped the railway lad, I expect. Probably some tramp who didn't like being disturbed. He's buggered off now, anyway. Do you want me to wait until another trainspotter comes along?'

'Yes, son, I do,' replied the sergeant, somewhat testily. 'CID have been looking for someone in hiding. The arsehole who tried to kill three coppers. This could be him. So, treat it as a crime scene, don't let anyone in and don't touch anything else. And you'd better keep your eyes open in case the bloke comes back. I'll let the SIO know.'

Nervously, PC Pepper walked back and forth along the platform, one hand holding his spray and the other gripping his baton. *If the killer comes back and I catch him,* he thought, *it will look great on my record. But if I'm killed, it won't look so great on my obituary.*

Chapter One Hundred One

'SHIT! MISSED THE BUGGER AGAIN,' swore Emma, when details of the incident at the station were relayed to her.

'We don't know it was him,' said Jack. 'It could have been a tramp.'

'Don't be daft, lad. It's got to be. SOCOs are out there and dusting for prints. I'll lay good odds that some of them match those from Ventham's place. We knew from CCTV he'd gone off in that general direction, so it's not exactly a surprise. Can you get over there when the scene's released and see if there's anything suggesting where he's gone? It's easier to catch a greased pig than this bastard.'

'Will do. Oh, there's an email from forensics. Fibres from the clothing found in Ventham's cellar match those at the scene of the Carter Hall shooting and a tear in a jumper corresponds to those picked up at the marina after the Moncrieff murder. More indications of Ventham's guilt, as if they were needed.'

'Aye. Well, I've not got the time to write it all up. We need to catch Dayton first. And that's like trying to catch a fart in a butterfly net.'

_____

Fuck! I reckoned I was OK there for another few hours. I should have guessed someone would turn up before they started running their toy trains. Bloody schoolboys.

Dayton pedalled briskly along the cycle path, heading away from Mexton, avoiding eye contact with dog walkers, joggers and other cyclists. The sound of a drone flying over-head made him duck under some overhanging branches a few metres from the path, attracting a puzzled glance from a middle-aged man walking a labradoodle. He needed to stay low for another couple of days until arrangements could be made for his escape. He'd sent the email and then made the phone call he'd always dreaded having to make, left a message and was awaiting a reply. The photo was now irrelevant. He had to get out.

His immediate problem was finding a new hiding place. The countryside might provide an old barn or some other disused farm building, but he felt too conspicuous on the new racing bike he'd stolen. Perhaps he should double back into town, ditch the bike and find a derelict building? He realised the police would have CCTV from the job centre but, if he swapped the baseball cap for a beanie, turned his reversible jacket the other way out and put on some glasses, there was a good chance he wouldn't be recognised. The town would also be more convenient if he had to steal another car in which to make his escape.

Dayton swung the bike round and headed swiftly back along the path, cursing at the labradoodle that leapt at him and forced him to swerve. When he felt he was close enough to the town, he pulled into some bushes, unzipped his bag and made the adjustments to his appearance. He walked casually back into Mexton, avoiding being caught by cameras where possible, and began his reconnaissance.

———————

By the end of the afternoon, pictures of the clean-shaven Dayton had been circulated and put up in shop windows, the library and anywhere else which would take them. The *Mexton Messenger* put his face on the front page of its evening edition and, without explicitly naming him as a murderous arsonist, made it quite clear why the police wanted him to help them with their enquiries. His image was also posted on the force's social media pages, with exhortations to readers to repost it where possible. Staff at the bus and railway stations were briefed on what to do if they thought they saw him and motorists were urged to check their dashcam footage in case he was on it. The examination of CCTV footage around the town continued and many hours of overtime were authorised.

'Will it do any good, do you think?' asked Kamal as Emma passed him on her way to the car park.

'Frankly, lad, I haven't a bloody clue. But, at the moment, relying on the good old British public is all we can do.'

———————

As Dayton queued for fish and chips, watching a TV screen with his image displayed on the local news, he chuckled. The e-fit wasn't too bad, he conceded, but it bore only an approximate resemblance to his current appearance. He would have bet a grand to a cold chip that the woman behind him wouldn't recognise him. He would have won.

Chapter One Hundred Two

'WE'VE GOT A POSSIBLE SIGHTING, GUV,' called Kamal. 'A member of the public walking his dog said a cyclist resembling Dayton passed him twice on the cycle path this afternoon. The first time, the cyclist suddenly left the path and hid under some trees, which he thought was odd. The second time he frightened the man's labradoodle.'

'Which way was he going?' asked Emma.

'Heading away from town at first, then heading back. So it looks like he could be back in central Mexton.'

'Excellent! What would we do without dog walkers? And crime writers would be completely at a loss. Is he sure about the ID?'

'Pretty sure. He used to work for the Border Force and he has a good memory for faces.'

'OK. Find out exactly what time these sightings occurred and see if there's any CCTV between the end of the cycle path and town. The bike's quite distinctive so it should be easy to spot.'

'OK, guv. On it.'

Jakey couldn't believe his luck. A racing bike, just left in the bushes. He'd used the cycle path as a short cut to his girl-friend's place for months, but all he'd seen dumped before was the odd supermarket trolley, beer cans and the occasional mattress. But this was awesome. He pulled the bike from the bushes, checked the tyres were inflated and cycled back towards town. Could he keep it? A bit risky. He knew that bikes like this could cost a couple of thousand quid, and someone like him riding it would be bound to attract suspicion. But perhaps he could sell it. He knew a bloke who might give him a good few hundred, no questions asked. *How many computer games, and how much weed, could I get from that?* he wondered.

Lost in his reflections, he didn't notice the police car which suddenly pulled up at the end of the path. Frantically, he jammed on the brakes but the bike skidded on a patch of mud and shot from under him, landing with its front wheel under the car. He fell heavily, cracking his elbow on the ground, and cursed his inattention.

'Are you all right, son?' asked PC Halligan, helping him to his feet.

'Yeah, yeah, thanks. I'm OK. No damage. I'll be off.'

'That's a nice bike. Where did you get it?'

'A birthday present. From my dad.'

'Looks a bit expensive for a birthday present. Do you have a phone number for your dad so I can check?'

Jakey licked his lips, nervously. He realised he'd never get away with it so he decided to cut his losses.

'I found it in the bushes back there. I was going to hand it in, honestly.'

Before the PC could react, he dodged around the car and ran towards the town centre, weaving his way through moving traffic and provoking a barrage of hoots and curses from furious drivers.

Halligan sighed. He'd got the lad's face on his bodycam, if they needed to find him. But, right now, the bike was more important. It looked like the one reported as stolen by the murder suspect, and his priority was to call it in.

After three hours tramping around the darkening streets of Mexton, avoiding CCTV cameras where he could, Dayton was beginning to think he'd be better off back in the country-side. *And why wouldn't those bastards reply to his communications?* There were plenty of disused shops around, where he could hide undisturbed, but they were all securely locked and claimed to be monitored by CCTV or a security firm. A derelict church was similarly boarded up, presumably to prevent the homeless from seeking salvation or, at least, shelter from the elements.

Now, that would do, he thought, looking at a five-storey building which seemed to have been a department store at one time. A roller shutter sealing off one of the entrances didn't quite reach the ground and there was no sign of a lock. Checking that he was unobserved, he managed to get his fingers under the shutter. He heaved upwards but there was no movement. *Fuck! It's rusted shut or there's a bolt inside,* he cursed to himself. *Maybe there's another entrance.*

On one side of the building a short passageway led to the

back of some kind of office building. There was a side door, protected by a keypad, but he rejected that as it was over-looked. On the other side an alleyway decorated with flamboyant street art led to the road behind. What could have once been a fire exit was blocked by a steel plate. That left the back, which he approached with rapidly diminishing optimism. Then he laughed.

The whole ground floor of the building was a building site. The floor was covered with piles of panelling, wood and other materials which, presumably, had once divided up the shop floor. A battered sign warning of the dangers of asbestos had been propped up against a wall and a pile of hi-vis jackets and safety helmets was visible in a corner. All this could be seen by the light of a street lamp and the judicious use of his phone torch. He couldn't see what lay in the depths of the building, but that he could explore later. Getting in would be childishly easy. The wall had been replaced by steel fencing, held in place only by metal ties bolted to concrete pillars. He pulled on the sections of fencing until he found one that was looser than the others. He managed to tilt it slightly so it left a gap between its base and the ground. A gap just big enough for him to squeeze through.

Once he had rolled clear of the fencing he stood up, brushed the dust from his clothes and explored. Dodging piles of rubble, and the occasional steel rod that threatened his ankles, he found a staircase. *Good*, he thought. *The higher the better*. By the time he reached the fifth floor he was slightly out of breath. There was less debris up here and the windows had escaped the attentions of local youths with stones and air rifles. It was pleasantly warm and dry, this part of the roof, at least, having remained intact. Provided that no builders came up here, and there was no sign of them having done so, he should be safe for a couple of days.

As Dayton settled down for the night, he was completely unaware of the red light flashing on the alarm console in Mexton Security Services' office a mile away. A light which would prompt a request for an inspection from a patrol, as soon as the operator allegedly monitoring it woke up.

Chapter One Hundred Three

'WHAT'S THE BLOODY POINT?' grumbled Stuart Best. 'No one's gonna nick anything from there, are they? It's probably an alarm fault. Can't it wait 'til morning?'

'The bloody point, Stu,' replied his exasperated supervisor, 'is that you're paid to provide night cover and respond to alarms that go off. And we're paid to make sure you do. So get your lazy arse over there and see what's happening.'

'All right, all right. I'm on my way.'

By the time Stuart had dragged on his uniform and grabbed a quick breakfast it was nearly six o'clock. Mexton Security Services' promise to respond within half an hour to any alarm was looking increasingly hollow, not least because it had been flashing on the board all night. They'd had false alarms from the site before, the last one because a herring gull had decided to investigate one of the sensors as a possible food source. Complaints from local residents had led to the security firm agreeing with the owners that the alarms should be silent, rather than emitting the original ear-splitting howls, but the frequency of errors hadn't diminished. Crying wolf syndrome had long since set in.

Dawn light was illuminating the top of the building when Stuart arrived on site. He took a torch and a ring of keys from his van and undid the padlock which held two sections of fencing together.

'Is there anyone there?' he called, feeling a complete idiot.

No reply.

He swept the beam of his torch across the floor, not expecting to find anyone there, and suddenly stopped. There were shoeprints in the cement dust leading from a disturbed area beside the fencing towards a staircase. *Odd*, he thought. *Work's been suspended for weeks because of asbestos but these marks look fresh.* He followed them to the staircase. *Shit. I'm going to have to search every bloody floor and I forgot the face mask I'm supposed to wear on the upper levels. Still, I shouldn't be here long.*

An hour later he had made a cursory inspection of the first three floors. No footwear marks were visible on the concrete staircase which once served as a fire escape, apart from a few on the bottom half-dozen steps, so he had no idea where the intruder, if there was one, had gone. He climbed laboriously upwards, debating whether to call in what he had seen and deciding against it. *Waste of bloody time. There's no-one here.* But he didn't hear Kevin Dayton, creeping up behind him on rubber-soled shoes, as he pushed open the door to the fourth floor.

Stuart felt his legs kicked from under him and he fell backwards, crashing to the floor. He banged his head and elbows on the concrete. A stabbing pain shot through his head. When his dizziness cleared, a face he vaguely recognised loomed over him in the early morning light. He felt something cold and hard shoved against his throat.

'Behave yourself or I'll blow your fucking head off.'

Chapter One Hundred Four

Day 39

WHERE'S *that lazy sod got to?* wondered Kyle Forbes, nursing a cup of coffee in the Mexton Security Services' main office. *He should have called in by now. It doesn't take four hours to check a bloody alarm. And I bet he forgot to charge his phone, because the twat's not answering. I suppose he could have fallen over or something. I'll give it another half hour and send someone to look for him if he doesn't surface.*

Stuart had come within a fart's breadth of soiling himself when he felt the muzzle of Dayton's pistol against his throat. He relaxed a little and preserved his trousers when his attacker assured him that he wouldn't be harmed if he co-operated. Of course, that depended on your definition of harm. Being tied up, gagged and bound to an uncomfortable office chair, with a raging headache and what felt like a cracked elbow, hardly counted as no harm. But at least he was alive.

He had no compunction about giving Dayton, who he finally recognised from the posters the police had distributed, all the information he needed. How he'd been called out because a sensor at the bottom of the staircase had triggered an alarm and that, eventually, someone would come looking for him, although not for a while. He explained that the CCTV only worked on the ground floor and that work was not expected to restart there for several weeks. He also pointed out that the alarm system was not linked directly to the police and there had been so many false alarms that no one took them particularly seriously. Dayton had seemed satisfied and locked him in an office without further comment.

Dayton mused over what the security guard had said. He couldn't afford to move again, especially not in daylight. Even with his changed appearance there was a chance he could be recognised by some keen-eyed copper. That was how they caught Christie, the Rillington Place killer, wasn't it? He would have to hide when the guard's colleague or colleagues came looking for him. Exploring the building further, he found an unsecured door leading to the roof.

Various structures were dotted around the roof – the heads of two disused lift shafts, heating and ventilating equipment and something that looked like a window cleaner's cradle. *Perfect!* Unless they brought dogs in, no one would find him up here. He could force the door to one of the lift shafts and hide inside if he needed to. But, first, he had to make sure no one found the guard.

Half an hour later, he had piled debris and old panelling

against the door of the office that contained Stuart. To the casual eye, it looked as though no one had been in there for ages, and he had taken the precaution of checking that Stuart's gag was still in place.

'Don't worry,' he had told him. 'I'll let someone know you're there when I go. You're not there forever.'

Stuart hadn't seemed reassured.

Before settling down to a late breakfast, consisting of a tin of cold baked beans and a chocolate bar, previously purchased from a late-night convenience store, Dayton once more left a message on an answering machine and followed it up with a text. *If I get no response this time, I'm screwed. I'll have to go it alone and that would be a fucking nightmare.* Then he settled down to wait.

———

Detective Superintendent Gorman was about to enter a budget strategy meeting when his phone rang. *Any excuse to put off this boredom marathon,* he thought, as he answered it.

'Good morning, Detective Superintendent,' a smooth voice said. 'We've not met, but my name is Paul Tabernacle. I work for the Security Service. It seems you're looking for one of our chaps. He appears to have gone rogue.'

'You mean Kevin Dayton?'

'That's so. I believe you once knew him as David Cornwallis. You see, the thing is, we'd rather like to get our hands on him ourselves. With your assistance, that is. It could be rather awkward if he was tried and identified as an MI5 officer.'

'Well, it was rather awkward for my officers. Being nearly burned to death or strangled, that is,' replied the DSup.

'Quite so. But there are national security implications. I'm sending a couple of people down to Mexton to assist you. Please don't let your officers do anything impetuous.'

'Well, we're hardly likely to charge in on a whim. He has a firearm. Anyway, we don't know where he is.'

'He didn't get a weapon from us, I assure you. We're not an armed service, as you know. I think I can help you with his location, though. GCHQ picked up some calls and texts, to a number we're interested in, which we believe may have come from him. The phone in question was used in central Mexton a short while ago. I'll send you details of the approximate location.'

'Thank you,' said Gorman, making no promises about the force's intentions.

Chapter One Hundred Five

DAYTON'S STRATEGY had been successful. From his vantage point on the roof, he saw a Mexton Security Services van arrive and two men get out. He listened at the top of the stair-case and heard the men grumbling about a waste of time, casting aspersions on Stuart Best's parentage and competence, and discussing last night's football. An hour later he saw the van pull away again, without the captured guard on board. They didn't even venture onto the roof, so he had no need to hide in the lift shaft. What he didn't see, or hear because a recycling lorry was grinding along the street below at the time, was the police drone flying over the building.

Emma called the team together for an emergency briefing. A buzz of excitement filled the room and the team waited expectantly for her to speak.

'We've had a couple of leads,' she said. 'Firstly, we've had a call from MI5. They must have seen our publicity somehow, because they know we're looking for Dayton. They want us to hold off on arresting him until their guys arrive, and DSup Gorman said he had the impression they wanted to take him off our hands and avoid a scandal.'

'Fuck that,' said Mel. 'He's tried to kill me, Sally and PC Tamblyn, set fire to a house and injured the train man. He has to go to trial, surely?'

There were shouts of agreement from other detectives.

'I'm inclined to agree,' replied Emma. 'I'm not sure what actual authority they have over us. It may be down to the Home Secretary. For now, we'll proceed as if he's a normal suspect in a murder inquiry. One thing of use which did come from the spooks is an approximate location.'

She projected a map of central Mexton on the screen.

'Five picked up his phone, very briefly, somewhere within the circle in the middle of this map. As you can see, there are several hundred buildings within this radius, but we need to narrow them down. So, look for disused premises, derelict buildings, empty properties for sale – anywhere he could be hiding undisturbed.'

'What if he's in someone's house, holding them hostage?' asked Kamal.

'Then we're buggered,' she replied, 'so let's hope not. OK. Alert patrols to look for possible premises in that area and also get onto estate agents for details of empty houses. Check with the guys operating the drone in case they've seen anything odd. Talk to the planning department at the Council. See if they know of any places under redevelopment he could use. So let's get out there and catch this bastard!'

'Just before we go, guv,' said Trevor, 'there was something I heard on the way in. Mexton Security Services seem to have lost one of their guards.'

'Great. I'll not have them as babysitters, then. So?'

'It's just... I wondered whether he came across Dayton on his patrols or whatever. If he did, Dayton could have killed him.'

'Worth checking. Good thinking, Trev. Get on to the firm and find out where he was last heard from. All right, everybody. Carry on. I'll be in my office.'

An hour later, Kamal and Mel knocked on Emma's door.

'I've got something, guv,' said Kamal, excitedly. 'The Mexton Security guy, Stuart Best, was sent to check on the old Co-op department store in Matthews Street, early this morning. It's been derelict for years and they're monitoring it while it's being redeveloped. Anyway, an alarm went off and he should have reported back within an hour or so. They thought it was a false alarm, as they've had so many in the past, so they didn't expect there to be a problem. Mr Best hadn't reported in by mid-morning so they sent a couple of blokes round to look at the site later on, but they found nothing. The manager conceded that they'd only spent an hour searching, and someone could have been hiding there.'

'Excellent, Kamal. Well done. What've you got, Mel?'

'I've been talking to the droneys.'

'Droneys?'

'It's what I call the guys operating the drones.'

Emma raised her eyebrows but said nothing.

'I asked them to review the footage of flights over the building. They picked up a brief clip of someone on the roof, peering over the parapet. They couldn't identify who it was, but the fact that the person was on the roof at all is suspicious. I think we've got grounds for a warrant.'

'Bloody right we have! I'll talk to Mr Farlowe and DSup Gorman. With a bit of luck, we'll strike this evening before it gets dark.'

'What about waiting for MI5?' asked Mel.

'Sod 'em!'

Chapter One Hundred Six

THERE'S SOMETHING WRONG. *Why has it all gone quiet?* He would have expected a steady flow of traffic at the front and back of the building at this time of the evening. Instead, the streets were empty of pedestrians and vehicles. At both ends of James Street, reflected in shop windows, he could just make out strobing blue lights. He looked up and saw the drone hovering above him, well out of pistol range. *Fuck!*

He knew, from experience, what the police's strategy would be. Evacuate the buildings, close off the streets and send in an armed response unit. Then they would try to negotiate. Persuade him that they were trying to help him, that he would be unharmed if he came out unarmed and with his hands on his head. That may be true, but he couldn't be confident that his colleagues in MI5 would be so accommodating. Given what he had done, any milk of human kindness which the Director General may have possessed would have turned into an extremely smelly cheese some time ago. He had to find a way out. If only he had wings.

Wings? He recalled an old programme about escapers from

Colditz Castle during World War Two and that gave him an idea. But would he have time? He rushed down to the ground floor, hoping that snipers weren't in position and covering the open back of the building. He grabbed a selection of building materials, rubbish and tools and dragged them back up to the roof.

For half an hour, he frantically cut, hammered, tied and nailed his materials, ever conscious of the impending arrival of armed officers. Eventually he was finished and he gazed, with a mixture of pride and trepidation at his creation. A giant kite, formed from lengths of plastic pipe, bits of rope and thick polythene sheeting. Would it take his weight? Could he steer it? He didn't know, but if he crashed it would still be better than getting shot, or spending the rest of his life in Belmarsh.

Just as Dayton was testing the rudimentary harness he'd rigged up, his phone buzzed with an incoming text. Could this be the help he needed? Perhaps it wasn't too late and he could be spirited away somehow. He fumbled for the device and read the text with dismay.

One word.

'Nyet.'

He felt sick. After all the work he had done for them, they'd hung him out to dry. They could have picked him up at any time during the last few days but had obviously decided that he wasn't worth it. So fuck 'em. Should he turn himself in, confess and give the authorities what little he knew about the Russian network, in return for a lighter sentence? No. He couldn't bear the thought of his parents, both proudly patriotic, finding out that their son was a traitor. Much better, in their eyes, for him to be branded a would-be murderer. He would try to escape on his own, with his gimcrack flying machine and, he hoped, a decent wind. Perhaps the weekends at the gliding club would come in handy.

Strapping on the harness, Dayton stepped back from the building's edge as far as possible and ran as fast as he could into the wind. He felt a small amount of lift developing and, when he reached the low parapet, it was easy to leap over it. He launched himself into space and was delighted that he didn't immediately plummet to the ground. He could even steer the device a little.

He managed to glide the length of the street without losing too much height and cleared the police cars blocking it off, with dozens of metres to spare. Then he heard a tearing and flapping sound. He realised that some of the polythene was breaking away. The kite became increasingly unstable and he just managed to turn it and head for a clump of trees in a small park. The instability increased and he lost all steering. There was a rending crash and Dayton found himself suspended in a tree, two metres from the ground.

He could see police cars approaching. He slashed frantically at the harness with his knife. Eventually it gave way and he crashed onto the grass, twisting his ankle. He limped through the park until he came to a riverside path which he followed for a few dozen metres until it reached a bridge over the River Mex. *If he could just get to the other side*, he thought, *he might be able to lose his pursuers in the alleys and snickets which formed part of the old town. If he could just cross.*

Chapter One Hundred Seven

APPROACHING the scene from the other side of the bridge, Mel stared in amazement as Dayton launched himself off the Co-op building, gliding like a giant flying squirrel. She watched him coming closer and, as soon as she saw him crash into the tree, she switched on the blue lights of the unmarked police car, slewed it across the road to block the traffic and ran across the bridge towards him.

They met in the middle and he greeted her with a punch to the gut which she dodged. Slightly overbalanced, Dayton ran into Mel's elbow as she whipped it round towards his face. Blood sprayed from his nose and he staggered slightly but recovered enough to kick viciously at Mel's knee. Her leg gave way and she fell to the ground. Stumbling to her feet, she found herself staring down the barrel of Dayton's Glock.

'Up!' he commanded. 'Put your hands on the parapet where I can see them.'

'Don't be fucking stupid, Dayton. There's armed officers coming towards you. And if they think I'm at the slightest risk of being shot, they'll fire. They know you've tried to kill me before.'

'Nothing personal, DC Cotton. You were just in the way.'

'Like that makes me feel better?' She just managed to keep her voice steady.

Dayton shrugged and positioned himself so that Mel was between him and the oncoming AFOs.

'What's it all about, Dayton? Why try to kill Ventham? And why are you so obsessed with this bloody photo? What went on at that party that was so fucking damaging to you?'

'What are you expecting, detective constable? A deathbed confession before I make them shoot me? No chance. I'm getting out of here but I'll humour you. Ventham was killing off people who had been at the party because they could have blabbed and derailed his political career. I'm sure you knew that. The fact that I'd been there wouldn't have done me any great harm as an MI5 officer, so I had no reason to kill them. We're all anonymous, after all. It was who I met that was the problem.'

'What do you mean? They're all dead, apart from Pandora Blythe and she doesn't know who you really are.'

'The photo shows me screwing an agent from the Russian Foreign Intelligence Service, the SVR, although I didn't know it at the time. She was working there and we met up afterwards. I fell in love with her, she turned me and then became my handler. I've been working for the Russians ever since. I still don't know who took the Polaroid but, when I heard about the first death, I had to take action. It was vital it didn't fall into the hands of my bosses at MI5, so I searched or destroyed the premises of those attacked.'

'And Ventham?'

'He recognised me from the party. I was coming out of

Thames House one evening, when he was a junior MP. I didn't acknowledge him but he waylaid me on another occasion. He threatened to tell my bosses about the party, although he didn't know about Irina. He wanted information about some of his colleagues which would help advance his career, their security clearances, for instance. I gave him a few titbits, just to keep him off my back – nothing that the PM didn't already know about – and, eventually, he stopped contacting me. He didn't recognise me when I turned up pretending to be from Mexton Security Services, as I'd changed my appearance. I had to rough him up a bit just before I hit him over the head, and he denied having the photo. I set the fire, in case it was on the premises. I was gutted when they put it out. I don't suppose you found the Polaroid?'

'No,' said Mel. 'It never turned up.'

'It doesn't matter now. My Russian so-called friends have deserted me so I must make my way on my own. That's all you're going to get from me. Oh, that guard is behind some rubbish on the fourth floor. He's OK. Now it's time to say good bye.'

He tapped Mel on the shoulder with the barrel of his pistol and her legs turned to jelly.

Chapter One Hundred Eight

PC Adeyemo crept slowly forward, holding his carbine firmly but not too tightly. He was sweating, but not from any heat. This was the crunch, the point at which he might have to take a human life. But could he do it? All the training he had been through – the target practice, the blank-firing exercises and the psychological counselling – was supposed to have prepared him for this moment. But that wasn't real. This was.

He'd received a briefing from the Tactical Firearms Commander on the situation. A male, apparently armed with a Glock pistol, who presented a threat to life. Taking him down would be justified if he refused to surrender his weapon. But Addy knew that the decision to fire was his and his alone. When he saw Dayton, five metres away, holding a pistol to Mel's back, any lingering doubts he had evaporated. He would fire if he had to and he wouldn't miss.

'Armed police,' he yelled, raising his weapon.

BRIAN PRICE

'What the devil do you think you're doing?' yelled an enraged MI5 officer. 'You were told to wait until we got here.'

DSup Gorman turned round and glared at the newcomer.

'Firstly, we do not answer to MI5. Secondly, we are always happy to co-operate with the Security Service, but only as long as operational requirements permit and, thirdly, there is an armed man out there on the bridge and I'm not going to put people, including my officers, at risk any longer than necessary, just for your convenience.'

'So who's running this show then? I need to speak to him.'

'Chief Inspector Callaghan is the Tactical Firearms Commander. He's just over there. But, as you can see, he's busy.'

The MI5 officer strode over to Callaghan, shoved his ID under the officer's nose and demanded his attention.

'Is that him? Dayton? He's armed isn't he? Then shoot him.'

The TFC looked at him in amazement.

'Are you suggesting we execute him?'

The spook backed down slightly.

'No, no. Of course not. But it would be very convenient for His Majesty's Government if Dayton failed to survive this encounter.'

'I don't give a flying fuck about the convenience of the Government. My priority for this operation is to preserve life. Including the life of the suspect. It is the decision of the officer on the ground whether to fire, not mine, and he will only do so if it is necessary. Now, with all due respect, kindly fuck off and let me do my job.'

At Addy's shout, Dayton turned towards him, the pistol moving away from Mel. As he turned, Mel elbowed him hard in a kidney and he doubled over in pain, dropping the weapon on the ground. She brought her knee up and caught him under his jaw. He staggered, but Mel, unbalanced by the impact, fell back against the parapet. Dayton straightened up and launched a punch at Mel's face which only just missed, as she jerked backwards. She pivoted on one leg and managed to kick Dayton hard in the solar plexus. Winded, he sank to his knees, the fight having left him.

'All right. All right. You win,' he gasped. He pulled himself to his feet using the parapet for support and held out his wrists. Before Mel could cuff him, he called out to Addy.

'It's all right, mate. It's just a replica. Here.'

He kicked the weapon along the ground towards the armed officer and used the distraction to kick off his shoes and climb onto the bridge parapet.

'No, you don't, you bastard,' yelled Mel, grabbing hold of both his legs.

Dayton's intended swallow dive was aborted, and he tumbled forwards, dangling inelegantly from the bridge with Mel gripping his legs. He struggled and kicked, managing to catch Mel on the side of the face. Still, she held on and Addy rushed forward to help. There was a brief pause in Dayton's movements, a clink of a belt being undone and Mel was left holding an empty pair of trousers. Less than a second later, she heard the crunch of Dayton's head slamming onto a submerged bridge support, hidden by just a few centimetres of water.

As the two officers peered over the bridge they caught a brief glimpse of Dayton's body, face down in the river, his white boxers standing out against the dark water. Then it disappeared completely.

Two days later, in a small office in the Russian Embassy, a so-called cultural attaché tossed a faded Polaroid photo on to his colleague's desk.

'We might as well destroy this, now. We didn't need it after all.'

His colleague shrugged.

'Irina did a good job, making him fall for her. Still, it was good insurance in case she failed. I gather our man spent a lot of time and energy looking for it. Did he really think we would miss the opportunity to seize such a useful item?'

'What happened to the photographer? Do you know?'

Another shrug.

'Under a car park somewhere, I suspect. Vladimir took care of that sort of thing. Now, there's a general election coming up and Moscow wants us to make our preparations. Who can we blackmail over some indiscretion or other?'

'There are so many to choose from, my friend. So many to choose from.'

Chapter One Hundred Nine

Day 42

IT TOOK the intruder less than twenty seconds to pick the door lock and work a hand through to remove the safety chain. They were confident that these efforts would not be heard but they waited for a few minutes to be sure. They had followed the target from the wine bar, where she had knocked back several large glasses of wine, and her unsteady gait declared that she would sleep soundly tonight. Stepping into the hall, wearing a forensic suit, booties, gloves and a mask, the intruder padded almost silently through the flat.

Quiet snoring identified the bedroom where a woman lay on her back, on the bed, still half dressed. *Easy!* They approached without disturbing her and slipped a large plastic bag out of a pocket. It only took a few moments to slide a pillow into it and press the whole thing over the woman's face, legs straddling her torso.

Nothing happened for a few seconds, then the woman bucked and heaved as her body realised that her breathing was cut off. She pounded at her attacker's chest and tried to scratch and jab at the face looming over her, but her fingernails simply slid off the plastic eye protection. After twenty seconds her strength began to fail. After thirty, she lost consciousness. Five minutes later, sure that she was dead, the attacker lifted the pillow away, took off its plastic covering, and replaced it on the bed.

Before leaving, there were a few more things to do. The killer removed what was left of the woman's outer clothing and added it to the pile on the floor. They propped her up on the bed, inserted a pornographic DVD into her laptop, switched the power on and arranged it on her thighs, pulling her knickers down to her knees. Then they placed a plastic bag over her head, fastening it tightly around her neck with a velvet ribbon, making sure that the bow was tied too firmly to be opened easily. Lifting the victim's inert fingers, they rubbed and scraped them along the velvet, to give the impression that she had tried to remove it, then also used them to add finger-marks to the plastic. Satisfied that the results would be regarded by the coroner as death by misadventure, they slid off the bed, collected the materials and left the flat, checking that no-one was watching. They bundled the protective clothing into the large plastic bag and dropped it into a dustbin, put out for collection the following day, three miles from the scene.

That'll teach her, they thought. *That'll fucking teach her.*

***

'Guv! Guv!' Trevor's voice shattered the early morning quiet of the Major Crimes suite as he ran towards DCI Farlowe's office.

'Jenny Pike's been found dead.'

Epilogue

HUGH VENTHAM PLEADED guilty when charged and received a whole-life tariff for the murders of Detective Superintendent James Raven, Dale Moncrieff, Mark Sutton, Madeleine Hollis and Justin Kite.

In a statement approved by MI5 and the Home Office, Mexton Police said that civil servant Kevin Dayton had jumped into the River Mex, as he was about to be arrested for attempted murder and arson, and is presumed drowned. No indication of his motive was given but rumours of mental illness were fed to the press. No mention was made of Dayton's connection with the Security Service and attempts by MI5 to trace his handler proved fruitless. His body was never found.

Social media was rife with speculation about Marnie Draycott's party, but Pandora Blythe maintained a dignified silence in public. Her career flourished and she became a regular narrator of true crime TV programmes. She co-operated with a major TV streaming company in the production of a documentary which exposed Hugh Ventham's crimes and sordid behaviour. The tabloids had a field day, publishing, and embellishing, the details of his sexual habits. Any reputation he previously had was completely destroyed.

A Green Party MP took Ventham's former seat in the by-election which followed his arrest.

DC Plover was sacked by the Metropolitan Police and charged with misconduct in public office and with the attack on Mel, as well as computer offences. He was sentenced to five years in jail.

Nigel Willstone was jailed for three years for a variety of offences, including the possession of a firearm without the appropriate certificate.

Martin Rowse rejoined the police as a civilian investigator.

Sally Erskine returned to work once Dayton had been declared dead and Ventham had been committed for trial. She required considerable support.

Glossary of Police Terms

AFO: Authorised Firearms Officer
ANPR: Automatic Number Plate Recognition (camera)
APT: Anatomical Pathology Technologist
ARU: Armed Response Unit
ARV: Armed Response Vehicle
Carbine: Short-barrelled rifle used by AFOs
CEOP: Child Exploitation and Online Protection Centre
CHIS: Covert Human Intelligence Source
CPS: Crown Prosecution Service
DBS: Disclosure and Barring Service
Directed surveillance: Planned, covert observation of somebody (*see* RIPA)
DSO: Distinguished Service Order, a medal awarded to officers
DVLA: Driver and Vehicle Licensing Agency
DWP: Department for Work and Pensions
EA: Environment Agency
ESDA: Electrostatic Detection Apparatus
GDPR: General Data Protection Regulations

GCHQ: Government Communications Headquarters – electronic intelligence gathering establishment in Cheltenham

HMRC: His Majesty's Revenue and Customs

HOLMES2: Home Office Large Major Enquiry System – national police IT system for investigating major crimes

IED: Improvised Explosive Device

IOPC: Independent Office for Police Conduct

Met (the): Metropolitan Police Service

MUFC: Manchester United Football Club

NABIS: National Ballistics Intelligence Service

NCA: National Crime Agency

OCG: Organised Crime Group

Periodic Table: A list of the known chemical elements arranged in groups according to their common properties

PolSA: Police Search Advisor

PNC: Police National Computer

PSNI: Police Service of Northern Ireland

QGM: Queen's Gallantry Medal

RIPA: Regulation of Investigatory Powers Act

RTC: road traffic collision

SOCO: Scene Of Crime Officer (aka CSI)

TIE: Trace, Interview, Eliminate (possible suspects)

VIN: Vehicle Identification Number, stamped on the chassis of every motor vehicle

Acknowledgments

First of all, my thanks are due to my wife, Jen, for her unfailing support and awesome ability to improve my draft manuscripts. Without her I would not be a writer! Thanks, also, to Vaseem Khan for his advice concerning DC Chabra and to Captain Tim Gooding for military information. Graham Bartlett, as always, provided invaluable corrections to some of my police procedures – I do recommend his novels!

The technique used by Rachel Willstone to stop her husband's bleed is a recognised emergency measure. It was used to save the life of a stab victim in Weston-super-Mare, in 2023, by Mark Bradshaw who responded to someone rushing into his local pub, the Black Cat, calling for help. Assisted by the landlord, Nick Sith, he kept the victim alive until paramedics arrived. Nick is campaigning for all local pubs to have emergency bleed kits. Thanks to Mark and Nick for their account of this incident. (The use of a plastic clip was my own invention and may or may not work.)

Thanks, again, to Rebecca and Adrian at Hobeck for continuing to publish my books and also to Jayne Mapp for another great cover.

I'm especially grateful to the reviewers and bloggers who say nice things about my books. Your support is tremendous!

Finally, thank you to you, as a reader, for buying (or borrowing) this book. You are the reason I write.

BRIAN PRICE

About the Author

Brian Price is a writer living in the South West of England. A scientist by training, he worked for the Environment Agency for twelve years and has also worked as an environmental consultant, a pharmacy technician and, for twenty-six years, as an Open University tutor.

Fatal Trade was his first full-length novel and has quickly been followed by more novels featuring DC Mel Cotton. He has also contributed to a number of short stories to a local writing group's anthology, called *Cuckoo*. He is the author of *Crime Writing: How To Write the Science*, a guide for authors on the scientific aspects of crime. He has a website on the topic **www.crimewriterscience.co.uk** and advises crime writers on how to avoid scientific mistakes in their books. He was once credited with keeping author M.W. Craven out of jail, as a result of advice given.

Brian reads a wide range of crime fiction and also enjoys Terry Pratchett, Genevieve Cogman and Philip Pullman. He may sometimes be found listening to rock, folk and 1960s psychedelic music. He is married and has four grown-up children.

To find out more about Brian and his crime fiction writing please visit his website: **www.brianpriceauthor.co.uk**.

The Mel Cotton Crime Series

Fatal Trade

Fatal Hate

Fatal Dose

Fatal Blow

Fatal Image

Available from book retailers.

Fatal Beginnings – a free prequel novella available if you subscribe to Hobeck Books www.hobeck.net.

Hobeck Books - the home of great stories

We hope you've enjoyed reading this novel by Brian Price. To keep up to date on Brian's fiction writing please subscribe to his website: **www.brianpriceauthor.co.uk**.

Hobeck Books offers a number of short stories and novellas, including *Fatal Beginnings* by Brian Price, free for subscribers in the compilation *Crime Bites*.

Also please visit the Hobeck Books website for details of our other superb authors and their books, and if you would like to get in touch, we would love to hear from you.

Hobeck Books also presents a weekly podcast, the Hobcast, where founders Adrian Hobart and Rebecca Collins discuss all things book related, key issues from each week, including the ups and downs of running a creative business. Each episode includes an interview with one of the people who make Hobeck possible: the editors, the authors, the cover designers. These are the people who help Hobeck bring great stories to life. Without them, Hobeck wouldn't exist. The Hobcast can be listened to from all the usual platforms but it can also be found on the Hobeck website: **www.hobeck.net/hobcast**.

Printed in the USA
CPSIA information can be obtained
at www.ICGtesting.com
LVHW031533161124
796659LV00014B/237

* 9 7 8 1 9 1 5 8 1 7 6 6 2 *